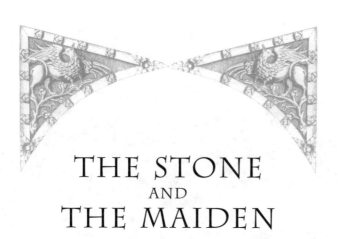

THE STONE
AND
THE MAIDEN

THE STONE
AND
THE MAIDEN

BOOK ONE OF THE HOUSE OF THE PANDRAGORE

Dennis Jones

This is a work of fiction. Names, characters, places, and incidents either are the
product of the author's imagination or are used fictitiously. Any resemblance
to actual events, locales, organizations, or persons, living or dead,
is entirely coincidental and beyond the intent of either the author or the publisher.

AVON BOOKS, INC.
1350 Avenue of the Americas
New York, New York 10019

Copyright © 1999 by Dennis Jones
Published by arrangement with
HarperCollins Publishers Ltd., Canada
Interior design by Kellan Peck
ISBN: 0-380-97801-6

Library of Congress Cataloging in Publication Data:
Jones, Dennis, 1945–
The stone and the maiden / Dennis Jones.
p. cm.—(The House of the Pandragore ; bk. 1)
I. Title. II. Series: Jones, Dennis, 1945–. House of the Pandragore; bk. 1.
PR9199.3.J6276S76   1999   99-20948
813'.54—dc21   CIP

First Avon Eos Printing: August 1999

AVON EOS TRADEMARK REG. U.S. PAT. OFF. AND IN OTHER COUNTRIES, MARCA REGISTRADA,
HECHO EN U.S.A.

Printed in the U.S.A.

FIRST EDITION

QPM   10 9 8 7 6 5 4 3 2 1

www.avonbooks.com/eos

※   ※

To my parents, who never lost faith.

My deepest thanks go to the Wise Readers of the manuscript: Logan Murray, Tamara Jones, Eric Lawlor, Marie Hamilton, and Peter Leliveld. The book is a far better story because of their advice; however, all flaws of characterization, plot, setting, and applications of sorcery remain the responsibility of the author alone.

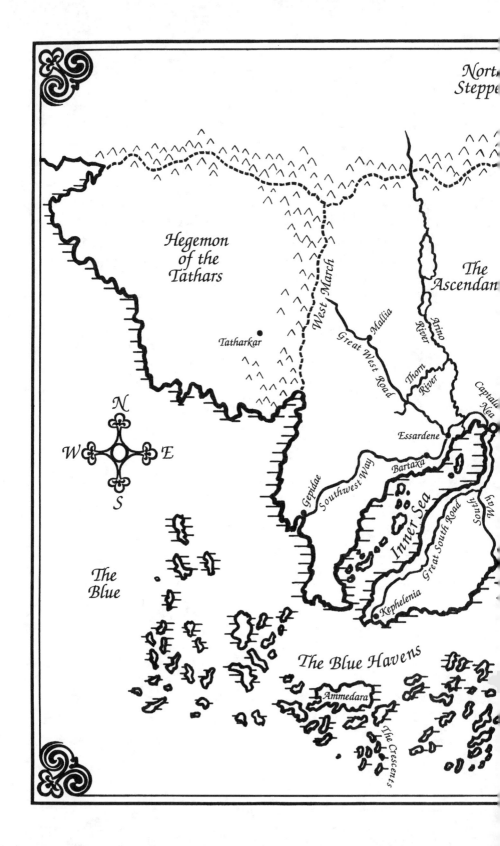

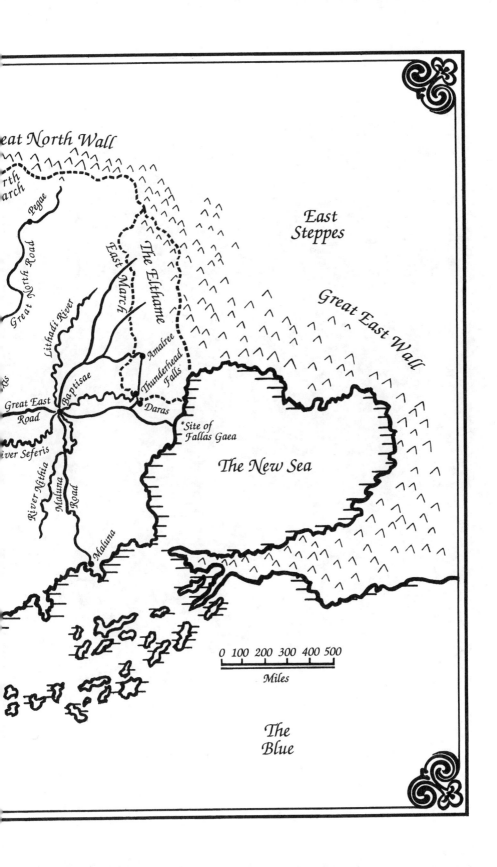

eat North Wall

rth
arch

Pegae

Great North Road

Lithadi River

East March

The Elthame

East Steppes

Great East Wall

Amalree

Thunderhead Falls

Baptisae

Daras

ss

Great East Road

iver Seferis

River Nithia

Maluna Road

Maluna

*Site of
Fallas Gaea

The New Sea

0 100 200 300 400 500

Miles

The
Blue

I

THE SCOURGE
FROM THE WEST

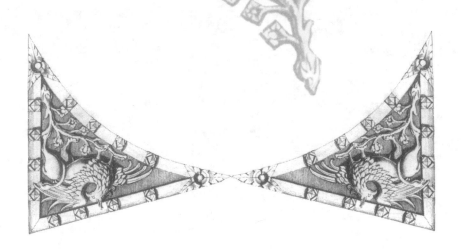

✳ 1

MANDINE CROUCHED IN THE DIM UNDERGROWTH AT the forest's edge, and peered nervously at the thatched cottage in the clearing. The dwelling had plainly been looted; its door hung askew from one leather hinge, and broken pottery and the splintered remains of an ark-chest littered the yard. The plunderers had trampled down all the young crops in the vegetable patch, and from the ruins of a burned stable rose a tendril of pale smoke. To Mandine it looked unpleasantly like a resentful ghost.

Hunger suddenly squeezed at her midriff, and she winced. Evening was drawing on, and she desperately needed to eat. Her knees had been weak all day, and since midafternoon she had been suffering from fits of dizziness. A woodsman's daughter would know how to live from the forest, she imagined, but she was no woodsman's daughter. And if she had been, she likely wouldn't have gotten herself so hopelessly lost.

Mandine scrutinized the cottage again and bit her lip in indecision. The raiders seemed to be gone, and they might have left a few scraps of food she could scavenge. Still, if they were not too far away, they might decide to return and take shelter for the night at the pillaged farm.

She held her breath and listened intently. A bellbird sang its resonant *doum, doum* from a hilltop, and the feather-pines whispered over her head. But she heard no hoofbeats, no jingle of harness or clank of weapons, no shrill voices calling in the harsh tongue of the Tathars.

Hunger clutched again at her belly, and she made up her mind. Brushing her long black hair away from her face, she straightened her slender shoulders; then, keeping low, she eased back through the undergrowth. When she could no longer see the cottage or the stable's smoking remains, she stood up and set off through the gloom toward the shallow ravine where she had left her gelding. It was there she had first smelled the stink of burning; unwilling to risk the noise the horse might make, she had dismounted to reconnoiter on foot.

The gray lifted his head at her approach and whickered softly. "Hush, Siro," Mandine whispered, and touched his soft nose. She took his bridle, and led him through the deepening shadows beneath the feather-pines and ancient sagbark oaks. The waning of day was unnerving, and she watched her surroundings carefully. In the dusky aisles of the forest this afternoon, she'd seen a flash of movement that might have been a person in green and brown, but when she looked again there was nothing. Had it been a trick of light, or could it have been a hemander?

She wasn't sure. Raised in the city, she'd never seen one of the Near Folk. The hemandri were denizens of the deep woods, and elusive; they were found only when they wanted to be found. Even so, there was some small trade between the two races, the hemandri exchanging rare herbs and aromatic gums for metals and ceramics, and though they were a little eerie, she had never heard of them harming someone of her race. There were even stories that told of how they would sometimes help lost or disabled travelers. Mandine found herself wishing, with suddenly stinging eyes, that one might materialize to help her.

She rasped the back of her free hand across her moist eyelids. Enough of such self-pity, she told herself harshly. She might be lost and half-starved, but she was Mandine Dascaris of the House of the Dascarids, and if she could survive the viper pit of the court, she could survive this. She was a grown woman of twenty-two, and she had her wits and a horse. If she kept the rising sun on her right, and the setting sun on her left, she must strike the Great West Road eventually. It couldn't be much farther, and with luck there might be enough scraps of food left at the ransacked farmhouse to sustain her for a day or two.

When she could see the building through the trees, she paused and studied it warily. Nothing appeared to have changed. Mandine pondered, then took the cavalry helmet from her saddlebag, put it on, and tucked her hair into hiding. She tried closing the visor, but the mesh restricted her vision, so she pushed it up. Then she drew a deep breath and moved into the open. Siro followed placidly, flicking his tail.

In the wreckage strewn about the dooryard there were many footprints of men and horses. An earthenware pot, miraculously intact, lay by the threshold, and a hitching post stood a few yards from the door. Mandine looped Siro's reins through the post's iron ring and walked slowly toward the cottage's dark entrance. Her heart thumped against her ribs, and her breath came short. Would there be bodies, or had everyone escaped into the forest before the Tathars could butcher them?

She stood on the threshold and peered inside. The cottage had only one room, and there were no bodies in it. A table with three broken legs slumped against a wall, and an iron kettle was upside-down in the fireplace. Near the fireplace lay a wooden bread trough that someone had hacked almost in two. There was also an overturned keg by the hearth, and spilling from it a small drift of dirty brownish powder. Hardly daring to hope, Mandine hurried to the keg and found some four double handfuls of roughly ground barley flour.

She let her breath out in a long sigh of relief. Suppressing her urge to stuff the flour into her mouth, she searched the cottage for anything else edible, but found nothing. The flour would sustain her for a day or two, though. She could mix it with stream water in the intact pot she'd noticed outside, and if she had a fire, she could make flat bread on a hot stone. She knew that the poorer sort of common people baked that way, though she had never seen it done. But she had no way to make a fire.

Then she remembered the burned stable. There had been smoke, and smoke meant embers. She could take one away with her, find a hiding place in the forest, and try her hand at baking. Her stomach growled at the prospect. She hurried out to the yard, brought the earthenware pot inside, and scooped the flour into it.

As she finished, it occurred to her that she was taking things that belonged to someone else. She ought to leave money, but how much? It was a mystery; she had no idea of the worth of a pot or a few measures of flour.

But just now, she thought, *they're worth a great deal, at least to me.* She searched in the sabretache at her belt, found a copper dandyprat, and put it on the hearth. After a moment's consideration, she took the coin back, and replaced it with a silver minim. Outside, her gray stamped and whickered.

"Coming, Siro," Mandine called softly. She settled the helmet more firmly over her tucked-up hair and walked through the doorway.

There was a blur of motion over her left shoulder. Mandine dropped the pot and opened her mouth to scream, but a thick arm clamped around her neck and cut the sound off before it reached her throat. She smelled sweat, heard harsh grunts behind her, and the arm tightened. She struggled, her fingernails scrabbling at hard muscles, but the arm simply yanked her off her feet. And then, to her horror, she saw a grimy fist and a long knife in it, and the blade swinging up and back for a deathblow to her heart.

"*Quill, no, Quill, she's us'n!*"

The woman's shout came from Mandine's right. "What?" said a rough male voice at her ear. The knife paused, wavered.

"She's not a silverhair! Look at her!"

The clamp around her neck let go. Mandine fell to her

knees, gasping for air, and dragged the helmet off. She saw a woman in ragged green at the corner of the cottage. In the woman's hand was a heavy cudgel.

"Up," said the man. He hauled Mandine to her feet and turned her roughly around. He wore a stained gray tunic and tan leggings of coarse hemp cloth. He wasn't old, but weather had browned and furrowed his skin, and his chin and cheeks were darkly stubbled. "What're you, then?" he demanded, and shook her. "What're you wanting here?"

Mandine swayed. She could not believe what had just happened. No one had ever laid violent hands on her. He could be flogged for this.

"I'm a traveler," she croaked. "I'm trying to get to Essardene."

The woman approached, holding the cudgel warily at her side. She looked older than Mandine, though not by many years, with large features crowded into a small face. "Why are you thieving us?" she asked angrily. "We been thieved enough. The silverhairs burned our barn, took our cattle."

"I wasn't stealing," Mandine said. "I *wasn't*. I was hungry. I didn't know you were still here. I left money on your hearth. Go and look, if you don't believe me."

"She's quality, Ardis," said the man abruptly. "Look there, at her horse."

Ardis did. A frightened look came over her golden brown face, and her eyes went to Mandine. "Oh, my lady," she said in a suddenly tremulous voice, "my Quill didn't mean hurting you. My lady, please believe me. He didn't see your hair being black, for the helmet, or your color. We thought you was one of the White Death, come back alone, and Quill wanted the horse and gear."

Uneasily, Mandine looked around. "Might they come back?"

"They might," Quill said. "We have to see if they left us aught, and go. We're safer in the wood." He picked up the pot. It hadn't broken, and only a little of the flour was spilt.

He went into the cottage, and Mandine heard him muttering curses.

"Will you come along with us, my lady?" his wife said. "We can give you hearth-bread at least, and good water. Better not to bide out of doors, after the sun goes down. My name's Ardis, by the by. That there's my husband, Quill."

Human company. She would not have to face a third night alone in the deep woods. "I would be in your debt," she said, and looked around at the wreckage in the dooryard. "When did they come?"

Ardis's voice trembled. "This morning. They near took us, but we got into the trees ahead of 'em, and they got busy with our stock. Good thing we were at our weeding, and not inside, or they'd have had us."

Quill reappeared, grinning shamefacedly. "She left silver on the hearth, Ardis." He turned to Mandine. "My lady, you're free-handed. We can give you a roof and bread, if you'll take 'em, soon's we find whatever the Tathars didn't thieve."

Mandine felt light-headed with hunger and relief. "Use my horse to carry for you," she said.

Their hiding place lay a half mile from the farm. To the casual glance it seemed only a cleft in a steep, thickly wooded hillside, but it opened out within and bent sharply left, to end at a low cavern with a sandy floor. The entrance passage was just large enough to admit Siro. In the cavern lingered an earthy smell of animals and dung, and an odor of smoke. A faint light glimmered from above, where a natural chimney slanted up through the rock.

"Mind out for cow flops," Ardis warned. "We keep the herd here, off and on. There's hay in the corner there, for your horse."

Quill and Mandine unloaded Siro, while Ardis lit a small cooking fire in a circle of stones. They had little enough to unload: the iron kettle, the remnants of the flour, the earthenware pot, and a sack of dried medlars a Tathar had dropped or discarded behind the stable. Quill took the kettle outside for stream water, and Mandine unsaddled the gray.

"You use this for your cattle?" she asked as she laid the gear on the cave floor. She was wondering why.

"Sometimes," Ardis said, "when we've had a bad year, and the Dynast's taxmen come." She looked up at Mandine in sudden alarm, and her hand flew to her mouth. "My lady, oh, please. You won't be telling the collectors, will you?"

"No, no. I won't."

"Don't tell Quill I said aught. Please."

"Of course not, Ardis. I promise."

Ardis nodded, a small, uncertain smile on her mouth. "Isn't it dangerous to have a fire?" Mandine asked, to draw the woman's thoughts elsewhere. "Someone might see it, or see the smoke."

"Bend in the tunnel hides the light, my lady. You use good dry wood, and it don't smoke."

"Oh," Mandine said. Why hadn't she worked this out for herself instead of asking such a stupid question? *Until a few days ago,* she thought, *I believed I knew all the important things: history, governance, our literature, our traditions. But there's so much I'm ignorant about, and until the last few days I didn't even realize it.*

She finished unbridling Siro and turned him loose on the hay just as Quill returned with the water. She was walking to the fire when a fit of dizziness struck at her, and she put her hand to her forehead and wobbled. Quill seized her arm and helped her sit down on her saddle.

"Quick with the food, Ardis. She's near perished of hunger."

"It's coming, my lady," Ardis said. "You rest now, you're safe here."

While Mandine watched in a dull stupor, Ardis briskly made bread on a flat stone heated in the fire, and boiled half the medlars in the kettle. The tart smell of the cooking fruit made Mandine's mouth water. When the medlars were piled steaming on the flat round sheets of bread, they ate with their fingers, too hungry to talk. Then, as energy trickled back into her blood, Mandine realized what Quill had done.

"Quill," she said, "you've given me half yours. Please, take it back."

Quill shook his head. "No, my lady, you've a long trod ahead of you, if you're going to Essardene, as you said you were. As for Ardis and me, I can always snare game."

He was looking sidelong at her with suppressed but obvious curiosity. *My manners*, Mandine thought. *What have I been thinking of? They don't know what to call me. But I don't want them to know who I really am.*

"I'm sorry," she said. "My head's been full of wool. I am"—she hesitated, and plucked a name from the air—"Palla. My family has property in Essardene." That much was true, anyway.

"We're Quill and Ardis," Quill said, bowing awkwardly as he sat. He paused, and added hesitantly, "You're a tad lost, my lady Palla, aren't you?"

Mandine's shoulders slumped. In her relief at warmth and safety, she had for a while put aside her dread of tomorrow. "Quill," she said, "I'm more than a tad lost. I have to go to Essardene, and I'm not sure of the way."

"I've been there," said Quill. "It's where the Dynasts have that great palace of theirs, that they go to in the hot months. I know a peddlers' track that will bring you citywards fair prompt. I'll show it to you come daylight. Essardene would be a day's ride on a beast like yours, maybe a whit more, I'm not sure. The Tathars may have found the trail by now, though, so you'd best go careful."

"Thank you," said Mandine. "Thank you very much."

"At least you'll have good weather, my lady," Ardis said. "The rain crows have been quiet of late, and they always know when there's a wet coming."

They had not asked why she was wandering the hills. They wouldn't, of course; no hill-farmer or hill-farmer's wife would dare ask a noblewoman to account for herself. For a moment she saw herself through their eyes: her smooth golden skin, not browned like theirs by the sun, her high cheekbones, fine straight nose, slender hands unroughened by toil. Her eyes were indigo-blue, like theirs, but she was almost as tall as Quill, and a full head taller than Ardis.

She glanced at Quill. If she told her father how the hill-farmer had offered her violence, even mistakenly, the man would be whipped, or worse, even if Mandine tried to intercede for him. It was better for his peace of mind if he did not know who she was. Once she was safe, she could have him rewarded, with a new herd of the best cattle, a new stable, and a better cottage. It was the least she could do.

"Will you yourselves stay here?" she asked. "The Tathars might come back."

"We were talking 'bout heading coastwards," Ardis said. "Maybe to Bartaxa. It's a big city, with militiamen. We'd stay there till the White Death are gone away."

"You shouldn't go to the coast," said Mandine. "I left Bartaxa three days ago. The silverhair horsemen are all over the lowlands now. A raiding party ambushed and killed my escort the evening of the day I left. Bartaxa itself may have fallen—its walls would hardly keep a child out. That's why I'm trying to reach Essardene."

Quill's eyebrows shot up. "The White Death's as far as Bartaxa? The Allfather and Lady help us, they've never raided so deep."

"Maybe they *won't* go away," Ardis said in a tremulous voice. "Ever."

Mandine shivered at the thought. The morning after she escaped the Tathar ambush, she had found a vantage point on a cliff overlooking the coastal plain. Below her, stretching to the distant glint of the sea, drifted a haze of smoke from burning farms and villages, and the dark hurrying smudges of Tathar cavalry squadrons. Even now, she could hardly believe the catastrophe. The Hegemon of the Tathars lay six hundred miles to the northwest, yet the silverhairs were in the plain between her and the Inner Sea, deeper into the lands of the Ascendancy than they had ever come. She had realized then that this was not raid, but invasion. So she had turned back into the hills, in what she thought was the direction of Essardene, and gotten lost for two days.

"Our army will run them out," Quill said, looking into the fire. "Soon's we get a proper battle."

"But there's *been* a battle!" Mandine said wretchedly. "You mean you didn't know about it? We heard in Bartaxa, three days ago. That was why I left."

They stared at her. "No," Ardis said. "Never a peep of a battle. Up here we don't see many folk, for news. All we knew was that the silverhairs were over the border. We heard they took Mallia, way northwest, but all on a sudden they were right here, right this morning."

"The battle," Quill said, looking anxiously at Mandine. "We won, to be sure?"

"We lost," Mandine answered in a shaking voice. "We lost. The army's destroyed. All of it. Eighty thousand soldiers, wiped out."

Ardis's hand went to her mouth, and Quill gave a harsh, startled grunt. "The Lord Allfather save us! My lady, you're sure it's true?"

"Yes, it's true. It happened at Thorn River, up between Mallia and Essardene. The rider who brought the news to Bartaxa was one of the few who got away." Mandine wrapped her arms around herself. "The army's gone. All our soldiers are scattered, or dead. Mostly dead. The Tathars don't take prisoners."

There was a long silence. Mandine stared into the fire, hardly seeing the embers. She had never really feared the Tathars until these last few days, though she had known all her life of the threat beyond the western mountains. It was not a new peril, for the Tathars had burst into the Ascendancy's awareness for the first time a hundred and fifty years ago: a vast horde of white-faced, silver-locked horsemen from the back of the west wind, their women and children with them, a nation on the move.

Until then the lands beyond Great West Wall, the mountain

range that marked the Ascendancy's western border, had been inhabited by the barbarian Scaths. These violent tribal warriors had bitterly troubled the Ascendancy more than once, but the Tathars burned them up like grass in an oven and swept onward and over the West Wall itself. They had been driven back over the Wall in three savage battles, but had then settled in the ancient lands of the Scaths, whose remnants they enslaved. There they prospered and grew to greater multitudes, but their hostility to the Ascendancy had never faded, and for the past two generations they had grown bolder and bolder in their raids across the Wall. For their ferocity and their pallid faces, the common folk, and not a few others, called them the White Death.

Quill at last broke the stillness. He looked down at Mandine's helmet, and said, "My lady, you've got a bit of armor. You weren't fighting Tathars your own self, were you?"

"No, I wasn't," Mandine said. "I was running." She gazed at the helmet's steel dome, remembering Erappis, the commander of her escort, who had made her wear it when they left Bartaxa. He feared for her even then, all too rightly. In the ambush she saw him fall with a Tathar lance in his side, and only the confusion and the poor light of dusk had saved her from a similar fate. Tathars had been everywhere. One, his saber high and his bone white face drawn into a demon's snarl, had ridden straight past her as she spurred Siro into the trees beside the road. The Tathar had slashed at her head, and the blow barely missed as she ducked. Others chased her, but Siro was too fast for their shaggy horses. Then darkness fell, and silence. She did not think that any of her escort had lived, and she dared not return to the road to find out. When dawn came, she had headed north.

Poor Erappis, she thought. *My poor guards.* She wondered, again, what it had been like for the men at Thorn River. So many, many dead. Her father had gotten away, though, with a fragment of the rear guard. She knew that much, from the survivors' news. Where her father might be now, she had no idea. She hoped it might be Essardene, and that the Tathars would not yet be there. If they were, she'd keep going some-how, and head for the capital.

"The army's gone?" Quill said, in a slow, pained voice. "But how? How did it fall out so bad?"

"There was a trap. Our men were marching west, to stop the Tathars this side of Mallia, before they could come any farther into our lands. Their whole army caught ours in the river valley, and our men were in march order and couldn't fight properly."

"Was the Dynast at the battle?" Quill asked. "Did the lord Archates get himself away?"

Mandine rubbed her eyes; the smoke was stinging a little. "It's said so."

"Ah," Quill said, as he and his wife exchanged glances. "That makes good hearing."

Mandine thought: *They're not sure it does. But they won't say anything against their ruler, not in front of me, a noblewoman. But they have no love for him, nor does anyone else.*

She suddenly wanted to change the subject. "I saw some-thing odd this afternoon, in the forest. Like a man or woman, in green and brown, but it vanished before I was sure. Are there hemandri in these parts?"

Ardis frowned. "I don't think so, my lady. But then, we'd not notice the Near Folk unless they wanted noticing. We do see wood sprites now and again, if the light's just so at sunup or sunset—there's a syliad haunts Kettle Pool, but we don't take fish or draw water there, so she don't trouble us. But hemandri, no."

Quill had been lost in thought. "Wife," he said, looking up, "I think we'd best go deeper in-country. I don't like the tidings of the silverhairs all over, as my lady Palla says they are." He turned to Mandine. "You can come alongside us, my lady, if you don't mind living rough."

Mandine shook her head. "I thank you, but I must risk Essardene."

Quill yawned and stretched. "Then forgive me, my lady, but first light'll be here before we know it, and we all have to be off." He hesitated. "The fire'll burn down, and the hill-cold's getting in. We keep a couple blankets here, for sleeping over with the herd. One'll be good enough for Ardis and me, if we keep close. You can have t'other. And we'll all have a bit of that hay, to lie more soft."

"I have a cloak in my saddlebag," Mandine said, touched at the man's offer. She got up to get it, and only then did she see that Siro had eaten nearly all the hay. She stood woebegone in the firelight, and said, "I'm sorry. My horse—"

"Ah, don't fret over it," Ardis said, when she saw what had happened. "It was old forage. We can go out and cut us dimfern. Smells better, anyway."

Mandine, still feeling dismal, helped them bring bundles of the sweet fern into the cave. Ardis showed her how to make a hollow in the sand for her hips, to rest more comfortably, and Mandine made up her bed. Then she wrapped herself in her cloak and lay down. Ardis and Quill stretched out on the other side of the fire, and she heard them murmur to each other a few times before silence fell. Their soft speech made her feel even more alone. But then, she'd always been alone, in that way. She wondered what it would be like, to drift off with someone lying close and warm beside her.

She was numb with weariness. She tried to imagine not being exhausted, not being alone, but couldn't, and with that, she went to sleep.

SHE WOKE LATER IN THE NIGHT. THE FIRE HAD
burned to dead ash, and at first she did not know where she
was. Then Siro shifted his hooves on the cave's sandy floor,
and Mandine saw the slender blade of moonlight that slipped
down through the rock chimney, and she remembered. She
was not at all drowsy, but she knew she needed more rest;
perhaps, if she stretched her legs, she would find sleep again.
Very quietly she stood up, drew her cloak around her, and
after a brief search in the darkness found the passage that led
out of the cave.

Outside, the moon shone at the half, its pale light dappled
by the foliage above her. There was no wind. Mandine walked
a few yards from the passage's mouth, and stopped to look
over her shoulder. The entrance was invisible; around her, the
moonlight glimmered like the unreal illumination of a dream.
Suddenly she wondered if she had left the cave at all. Was she
still there, asleep in her gray cloak, while her dream self stood
here in the silent wood?

I don't believe so, she thought, *because I feel very, very awake.
But I do feel strange. Perhaps I should go back.*

"Do not go back," murmured a woman's voice from behind her. Mandine spun around in alarm. Not twenty feet
away one of the Near Folk stood within a pillar of dim light.

The figure was slender, with a skin of dusky green, its slanted eyes golden in a delicate feminine face, the long curling hair the brown of turned earth. Its only clothing was a green kirtle. There were no visible breasts, but neither did Mandine see the arm tattoos of the Near Folk males.

It must be a hemandra, she thought with astonishment. She had never heard of a human encountering a woman of the Near Folk. Only the males, and only when they wished to do so, crossed the paths of humankind.

A shadow floated from the darkness behind the hemandra, and suddenly on the woman's naked shoulder stood a winged and footed serpent, with an eagle's head. Speechless, Mandine stared at it. Emerald scales armored its coiled length, its talons were silver, and its plumage and beak were gold. Its eyes were bright as diamonds in sunlight.

It's a pandragore, she thought in awe. *The old wonder tales are true, and the pandragore is real. Or am I dreaming this?*

"What do you want?" she asked. Curiously, she was not afraid.

The pandragore regarded her gravely with its eagle's eyes, slowly spread its wings, and slid into the air. A quick, silent wingbeat, and the creature vanished among the trees.

"Follow," the hemandra said. Her voice was the chime of water over stones. She turned and began to move away.

Mandine stood as if rooted. The hemandra looked over her shoulder, and gestured. "Come," she said.

Mandine took a step, then another and another. Now she was following the hemandra. The light around the green woman dimmed, though it did not disappear entirely. Mandine had the impression that she had made the light to show what she was, and could now allow it to fade. The light spoke of magic, the rumored Near Folk magic. Perhaps the plumed serpent was the hemandra's familiar. Such things could be, at least in the old tales.

"Where are we going?" Mandine asked softly.

The hemandra shook her head in a very human gesture,

as if to say: Do not ask questions. Mandine began to speak again, thought better of it, and closed her mouth.

For several minutes more they walked beneath the trees. Then the hemandra stopped, and Mandine saw beyond her a narrow glade, lit almost as day by the clear moonlight. In the glade's center lay a quicksilver pool of water, and all around the pool grew tall ripe wheat.

"Go in," murmured the hemandra.

"Why?" Mandine whispered, joining her at the glade's edge. "Please tell me what's happening."

A breath of air on her cheek. The pandragore settled again onto the hemandra's shoulder. "Go in," it said, in a voice like the rustle of summer leaves.

It speaks, Mandine thought. *It speaks. I should be frightened. Why am I not frightened?*

She squared her shoulders and stepped into the glade. Her vision was wonderfully clear, as if the moon revealed more than the light of day. Each blade of grass, every stalk of the wheat, shimmered distinct and vivid in the pale radiance. The air lay cool as silver on her skin, cool as the water the grain drank. Mandine looked around, but the hemandra and the pandragore were gone. She turned again to the glade.

And saw the couple waiting for her by the pool. She felt no disquiet, only a profound recognition.

"Come to us, Mandine Dascaris," the woman said.

In her voice Mandine heard the lilt of youth and hope, of dreams not yet cast off. She walked slowly toward the couple. Now she saw that they were young, no more than her own age.

She stopped before them. Her heart fluttered as the youth's mouth curved in a grave smile. His eyes were blue, blue as the Inner Sea, as blue as sky and water. His cloak was blue, and on it, almost hidden in its folds, was the wheel of the sun. The young woman wore green, and down her breasts flowed garlands of flowers like the torrents of spring.

Mandine bowed her head. She felt heavy, dusty, begrimed by the weight of her flesh, of her mortality.

"Look up," said the youth quietly. "Look at us."

Mandine raised her eyes to them. In their faces she saw time pass, the maid become wife, the wife become mother, the mother become grandmother and wisewoman, the circle closing. Before her, the youth fled down the years, transformed to bridegroom and husband, to father and grandfather and seer. Then they were young again.

"Who are you?" she whispered. But she knew. They were the Lady and the Allfather, he in his aspect of the Youth, and she as the Maiden of the First Flowering. They were the Two. Suddenly Mandine was shaking with terror, and with a joy so piercing she feared it might stop her heart.

"But you know us," said the Lady. "You have prayed to us all your life, Mandine."

Mandine fell to her knees and buried her face in her hands. Terror and joy streamed through her, and anguish. After this night there would be nothing. To encounter their beauty was to lose the world. All after this was dust and ashes.

"Why have you done this to me?" she asked, in a voice choked with tears. "Why could you not leave me as I was? Why?"

A touch on her hair, and her anguish was stilled. "Lady Mother," she whispered, "Lord Allfather, where am I?"

Cool hands raised her to her feet. Mandine found she could look at them now, for their light burned low, a dim glory. "You are not altogether in the world, Mandine," the Lady said. "Your earthly body still sleeps beside the fire, though you feel that you wear flesh. This is a place of spirit, and of symbol made manifest."

"But why am I here? Have I done a terrible wrong, without knowing it?"

"No," said the Youth. "You have done nothing wrong. But you have need of us."

"My Lord?" said Mandine. "My Lady? I don't know what you mean. What do I need of you?"

"Knowledge," said the Lady, "of what must be done for your world, if it is to be saved from the coming terror."

She did not understand. "The terror of the Tathars?"

"In part," said the Youth, with an aching sadness in his voice. "Though they were not always as they are. They have turned aside from us, to our great sorrow, and love the evil of the Adversary."

"And by that they have become a weapon of the Adversary, though they do not know it," said the Lady. "But that old enemy has found a better weapon than those you call the Tathars."

"What?" Mandine asked. "Who?"

"His name is Erkai," said the Youth. "He whom your people called Erkai the Chain."

Mandine blinked in confusion. "But how can that be? Erkai's dead. Dead before my father was born." She hesitated. "Though there were always rumors, stories, that he was still alive."

"The stories were true. He aids the Tathars, and wills the extinction of your race and your world. We would not have it so."

"But why can't you stop him?" Mandine cried out. "You are the Two, the God and the Goddess."

"Yet we are bound, like you, by Law and Necessity and Cause," said the Lady, and in her voice Mandine heard sorrow beyond measure. "Those in the mortal world must preserve it, or ruin it, win or lose, or your will is not your own. Were it not so, creation would be yet unborn. Even Erkai acts from his own will, though in doing so he serves the purposes of the Adversary, the old Power of ruin and evil."

"And you would have *me* stop him? Stop a sorcerer of the Adversary?"

"We would have you try," said the Youth.

"Erkai was of my blood. Is that why you put this to me?"

"No," the Lady said, "though such weavings may hold a design that even we cannot perceive. We call on you because you love us, Mandine, and because you have been tested and not found wanting. You have great courage in adversity, and that is part of it. But courage is not enough. Had you been imperious and harsh with Quill and Ardis, you would not be here."

Mandine pressed her palms together. "But how could I stop Erkai and the Tathars? What can I do against the Adversary? I know nothing of sorcery. I am no soldier. There are people stronger than me you could call."

"All are called," the Lady said, "but few listen. Will you accept the burden?"

"Accept?" Mandine blurted. "*Accept?* You are Our Lord Allfather and Our Lady Mother. I am only a mortal woman. How can I refuse what you ask?"

"Mandine," said the Youth, "you may freely refuse. And if you do, you will forget this meeting, and with it the knowledge that you turned aside. We would not make you bear that burden all your days."

She was trembling inwardly. "What will happen if I—if I refuse?"

The Youth held her eyes with his. Mandine saw fire eat the marble halls of palaces and the thatch of farms, heard the cries of men slaughtered in their dooryards, heard children's shrieks from the depths of wells, the howls of women violated by flesh and iron. Mill wheels crumbled, grass sprouted between the stones of the highways, saplings grew in the markets' ruined colonnades. Horsemen with silver hair and white faces watered their mounts in the sacred pools of the temples, and melted the temple bells for misshapen coins.

Despair clutched at her. "Must this be? If I fail?"

"We do not show you what *must* be," the Youth said quietly. "Even we do not know as much as that. It is what *may* be. But if the lights go out, Mandine Dascaris, you will not see them lit again, nor will the children of men and women not yet born."

"But if you have chosen me, can I still fail?"

The Lady bowed her head. "Yes."

"It's not fair," Mandine said in desperation. "I am to do what you cannot? How can you ask this of me? I trusted you, my Lord. My Lady, I have revered and served you all my life. Tell me how to decide. I beg you."

"We cannot," the Lady said. "The burden is yours to take, or put aside, and yours only. But you must decide, Mandine, and soon. You are not now in the world of humankind. Your body sleeps, and here, even with us, you are at risk."

Mandine looked at the pool, at the ripe wheat. *I have always prayed to serve you,* she thought, *and you listened. I asked for this, and now I must bear it.*

"All right," she said. "Yes. Yes, I will. What must I do, to fight Erkai?"

The Lady smiled. "You are my good and faithful daughter. Mandine, you will not be alone. There is a man whose path nears yours even now. With him you must seek the place that contains all places, and the moment that contains all moments. In that may lie the salvation of your world."

Mandine was stunned. "What? I don't understand."

"You will know him," the Lady said.

The night shivered. Mandine blinked, and in the blink the Two were gone. With them had vanished the pool and the stand of wheat. Only the moon-silvered grass remained.

"Come back," Mandine beseeched the forest and the empty glade. "It isn't enough. Please, oh please, come back."

There was no answer. Mandine's head drooped, and she saw on the grass before her an ear of wheat, full and ripe. In the moonlight it gleamed like worked silver. Without thinking, she stooped, picked it up, and slipped it into the inside pocket of her cloak.

The light dimmed suddenly. She looked at the sky, saw clouds roiling and gathering about the moon. A violent gust of wind lashed at her eyes, forced them shut, then seized her cloak. The heavy cloth billowed and swept over her head and face. Mandine struggled against the clinging folds, and with a tremendous effort threw them off. But the forest was gone. Everything was gone. Open-eyed she was blind, choked in blackness. Around her a gale howled and shrieked. She shouted, but the wind tore the shout from her lips and dragged it into the dark. The wind wanted her, it trawled for her, it was a tongue reeling her toward an open maw.

Riding the gale, shimmering gold and green in the black wind, came the pandragore. It settled on her shoulder, and she felt the bite of its claws, and she knew it sought to help her. But the air congealed in her throat, and then the gale was in her head, and she felt walls rise between her and the memory of the Two in the glade.

It's the Adversary, Mandine thought in horror. *It's making me forget.* Desperately she clung to the knowledge of what she was to do, but the walls rose despite her, and sealed it away. And then, as the memories dwindled and winked out, she realized she was forgetting who she was. She might never find her way to the cave and her sleeping self. She might wander, a lamenting and nameless ghost, forever.

The pandragore's eagle beak swept to her mouth, breathed into her. Its breath strove against the wind, and in its breath she heard the hemandra's voice, calling, calling. She found herself and remembered her name.

I am Mandine. I am Mandine. I am Mandine.

Suddenly, there was the scent of dimfern in her nostrils. She opened her eyes and sat up with a convulsive jerk and a shuddering gasp. Nearby, Ardis stirred, and rose to one elbow.

"My lady? Are you all right?"

Mandine rubbed gritty palms over her face. She'd been dreaming, and the dream had been intense enough to wake her. But *what* had she been dreaming? She could not quite reach the memory. There might have been a terrible wind, and a strange birdlike creature. . . . But the dream had been frightening, she knew that much. So frightening she didn't want to think about it, much less remember it fully.

"I'm fine," Mandine said, looking around. "A nightmare." She saw that the night was over, for a shaft of gray dawnlight was falling through the rock chimney. For an instant she had a notion that she must do something very important, but then the feeling faded away.

"Not much wonder, my lady, with what you've been

through," Ardis said. She threw off her blanket and sat up, yawning. "Well, it's morning time. We'd best be moving on, all of us. Quill! Quill, wake up, you nod."

They made a scant breakfast of the remaining medlars. Afterward, with Siro watered, Quill showed Mandine where the peddlers' track began at the north side of the clearing. Then he and Ardis set off westward, for whatever safety they could find. Mandine lingered a moment to watch them go. Ardis turned, just as she and Quill slipped under the trees, and waved. Mandine waved in return. Then they vanished.

After they disappeared, she felt very alone, and with the loneliness was a nagging sense that she'd forgotten something. Some bit of gear? No; she had almost none, anyway, except for Siro's tack, some grubby extra clothing in one saddlebag, the cavalry helmet in the other, and the dozen coins in her sabretache. And she had parted from Quill and Ardis gracefully, after giving Quill another minim (over his protests) for the hay Siro ate. Then she'd promised to find them again, and further repay their help. So it wasn't that.

It's my imagination, Mandine told herself. She reined Siro around toward the track and set out at an even trot into the forest, over the hills to Essardene.

❄ 3

THE FOURTH TATHAR RIDER HAD ALMOST REACHED
the trees when Key rose in his stirrups and hurled his javelin
at the man's back. The iron point caught the Tathar under the
left shoulder blade, and went in. He screamed once and toppled off his horse. The terrified animal pounded into the forest's black shadows, leaving the Tathar facedown on the
clearing's thick grass. The javelin shaft swayed gently above
him, like a sapling in a summer breeze.

Key's sword was already in his hand, but a glance over
his shoulder told him he would not need it. All the Ascendancy cavalry was in the clearing now, and the Tathar's three
companions lay in a small knot of death at its center, where
they had gathered for their hopeless last stand. The dawn's
violet light made their contorted faces even colder and whiter
than they had been in life.

Key sheathed his sword and rode to the Tathar he had
killed. He was leaning from his saddle to retrieve his javelin
when Lydis trotted up. The victurion's mail was speckled with
rust, and his eyes were bloodshot.

"A good cast," Lydis said, looking briefly down at the
body. "Lucky their light lancers haven't much back armor. If
he'd gotten away . . . never mind. You were in the lead. Did
you see any others?"

"No, victurion," Key said, "only these." He glanced at the corpses of the Tathar cavalry pickets who would ride guard to their army no more. They'd foolishly trusted the thick woodland to slow their pursuers' heavy mounts, and for their overconfidence had found themselves trapped in the clearing and as good as dead.

"No warning for their main force, then," said Lydis. "We've still got a chance."

"Yes, victurion," Key said, and thought: *What kind of chance, with so few of us left?*

He scanned the other riders for evidence of wounds, but saw none. Like him, the men were cataphracts, the heavily armored, elite troops of the Ascendancy, distinguished from the horse cavalry not only by their name but by the huge black hippaxas they rode. A cataphract's mount was a foot higher at the shoulder than the largest horse, with a body like that of an enormous, heavily muscled cat. The head resembled a bull's, with two vicious fighting horns, and in the chest were heavy protective plates of bone. Hippaxas would ride down a hedge of enemy pikes, a thing a horse would not do, and they ran faster than any horses but the specially bred mounts of the Dynast's stud.

But there had never been many cataphracts, for hippaxas were hard to breed, and harder to train. The Tathar raids and the civil strife of the past fifty years had devoured most of them, and they could not be replaced; Key's unit, the Fifth Tercia of Cataphracts, had been patched together from odds and ends of other formations. Its four thousand men had been the last of the Ascendancy's elite heavy cavalry, but now they were gone, too, except for this pitiful remnant. Trapped with the rest of the army in the Thorn River gorge, bombarded from above by boulders, arrows, and showers of catapult bolts, all but a few of the tercia's men had perished. The infantry and the horse-mounted cavalry had been annihilated in the river's bloody shallows, and only nightfall, and the speed and endurance of their hippaxas, had allowed the surviving cataphracts to escape.

Now, twelve days after the battle, they were two hundred exhausted riders with mauled armor and dented shields, armed with scavenged javelins instead of their accustomed heavy lances. The senior officers were all dead or missing, except Lydis. And Lydis had marched this ragtag remnant through the hills all night, planning to lead it over the ridge to the north, in a last mad charge into the jaws of the Tathar army. Though Key had survived the bloody catastrophe at Thorn River, he did not think he would survive this.

Beside him, Lydis looked at the sky. Around the clearing the trees still hunched over the gloom beneath their branches, but the light of the nearly risen sun had already touched their crowns. Key's stomach grumbled; they had eaten only quarter rations since reaching the rough country two days ago.

"Form rank by pelta," Lydis ordered.

Harness jingled as Key and the others walked their mounts into three perfectly straight lines. Key's hippaxa snorted, and he patted the mat of coarse black hair between her horns. He had named her Rush when he first rode her three years ago, and since then she had carried him faithfully on parade square, patrol, and battlefield. She deserved, he thought, a better end than this.

Lydis stood in his stirrups and pointed uphill into the trees, toward the ridge to the north. "Over there is Essardene," he said, his eyes sweeping along the meager ranks of his men, "where our lord the Dynast is trapped. Others may flee, and leave him to the Tathars, but we will not. He needs us, and we will ride to him."

"What then, victurion?" someone called from the ranks. *That's Melias,* Key thought, with surprise. *Is he questioning an order, or almost? None of us would have done that two weeks ago.* But two weeks ago was before Thorn River.

Lydis scowled at the speaker. "This morning we will get into the city. Tonight, or the next night, we will break out with the Dynast and escort him to Captala Nea. There we will join the new army he will raise. Does that satisfy you, peltarch?"

"Yes, sir," Melias said, and fell silent.

"We will charge in three ranks," Lydis said. "We ride straight for the south gate. The gate garrison will see us coming and open for us. Make full charge from my hand signal, which I'll give as soon as we're atop the ridge." Lydis raised his fist to the brightening sky. "Ride!"

The hippaxas padded into the gloom beneath the trees, with Key at the extreme right of his men, in the second rank. He kept his face impassive, but within he seethed with frustration and anger. Victurion Lydis was a good officer, and a brave one, but this was madness. They might break into Essardene, if they surprised the surrounding Tathars, but Key did not think they would get out again. He wished they hadn't met the fleeing glass merchant a day ago, with his tale of seeing Archates' crimson house standard carried through Essardene's west gate, with a torrent of Tathar cavalry in howling pursuit. Until then, unsure whether the Dynast had been butchered along with the rest of the army, Lydis had been making for the capital. To Key, it still made better military sense to go on to impregnable Captala Nea and join a relieving force that might reasonably expect to rescue Archates.

He grimaced at the fantasy. There would be no relieving force, not now, not a trained one large enough to stand against the Tathars. Barring the eight thousand men of Captala's garrison, almost every professional soldier the Ascendancy possessed had died at Thorn River. The army was gone, and very probably he was about to follow it.

Melias had ridden up beside him. Key glared at the junior officer. "What are you doing out of rank, peltarch?" he snapped. "Get back."

"The victurion is horn-mad," Melias said in a low voice. "We should be looking for reinforcements, not throwing ourselves away. Not till we have to."

"You tell him that." *Melias is right,* Key thought, *but I'm a securion and his senior, and I can't say so.*

"There won't be a new army," said Melias, his words sharp with bitterness. "No matter what Lydis wants to believe, there won't be. Nothing's left but the citizen militias, and strag-

glers like us, and the garrison at Captala, and that's outnumbered fifteen to one. This is the end."

"It'll be the end for you here and now, if you don't obey
orders," said Key. He softened his tone, and grinned. "Go on,
Melias, get in rank. We'll be eating breakfast in Essardene.
Maybe Archates will peel a grape for you."

Melias grunted, and fell back. He was not much younger
than Key's twenty-three years, but Key felt far older. What had
his father called that feeling? The burden of command. *I might
have been a demarch of the Elthame*, Key thought, *if I'd stayed at
home. I wonder who will rule after my father, with me gone?*

But home was a thousand miles to the east, and there was
no use thinking about it. He braced himself straighter in his
saddle, a tall young man with the aquiline nose and gray eyes
that betrayed his origin in the high plateau of the Elthame.
The soft stubble on his cheeks was not black, like that of the
native Ascendancy troops, but dark bronze, like his hair. A
dozen other Elthamers had served with the Fifth, but as far as
Key knew, his countrymen were all dead.

The hippaxas passed among the trees, the huge splayed
pads of their feet rustling and crackling through the undergrowth, their massive black shoulders brushing saplings aside.
Key saw light ahead; that would be the tree line and the crest
of the ridge. On the other side, he remembered from the march
west—how long ago *that* seemed now—was a long, lightly
wooded slope that ran down to the walls of the Dynast's summer capital.

Maybe the silverhairs won't see us till it's too late, he thought.
*We approached by night, and we got their pickets. Maybe some of
us will make the city. But then, as Melias said, what then?*

Suddenly, he saw a flicker of motion to his right, where
there should not be any. He whirled in his saddle and peered
into the dimness beneath the trees. Again the motion, barely
glimpsed. A gray shadow, a dull glint. A Tathar picket?

It vanished as suddenly as it had appeared. He couldn't
break ranks to investigate; they were too close to the ridge
crest. Key took a fresh grip on his javelin and shield. His palms

were sweating, but his mouth and throat were dry as blown chaff.

Just below the ridgetop the trees thinned to scattered clumps. Lydis glanced over his shoulder, to check the formation. Then he raised his arm and brought it down. Key thrust spurs into Rush's flanks. She shifted from trot to canter as the cataphracts poured over the crest of the ridge, and he saw below him the white towers of Essardene. Around the city's walls crept the black scars of Tathar siege lines, and above the south gate the battle standard of the Ascendancy billowed green and gold in the dawn wind.

Key spurred Rush into full gallop. In the valley the Tathar encampment boiled suddenly with men and horses. Small knots of cavalry churned about, gathering swiftly into larger clumps. A mile to go, a mile to the south gate of Essardene. Broken lines of fresh-turned earth ahead betrayed unfinished trenches, and some fifty Tathar dragoons were already racing to intercept the cataphracts before they reached the diggings. Now Key could see tiny figures pointing and gesturing on Essardene's walls. He hoped the garrison wouldn't suspect a ruse and hold the gates closed against them.

He glanced right to check their exposed flank, and saw motion over his shoulder. He cursed. Who was so far out of position?

But when he looked again, it wasn't a cataphract. It was a helmeted figure in a gray cloak, on a gray horse, riding at breakneck speed and angling to slide into the cataphracts' wake. Key grunted with surprise, for the horseman was somehow keeping up with the hippaxas. To run so fast his mount had to be from the Dynast's stables, and the man's dress wasn't Tathar. His helmet was visored, and the visor was down.

Key had no time to puzzle it out, for the enemy's heavy cavalry was racing headlong to meet the cataphracts. The fifty Tathar dragoons had become a hundred, two hundred. Beyond them, infantry scrambled from their trenches to form a thin hedge of spears. Other foot soldiers heaved frantically at the catapults, the arrow throwers, trying to turn the machines on their attackers. One crew was quick, and a bolt four feet long streaked over Key's head.

Shooting high. How long till they get it right?

He spared a second glance for the strange horseman. The gray was still with the charge, a hundred yards back and just on Key's right. *He's trying to break through by riding behind us,* Key realized suddenly. *He's using us to clear his way.*

A hippaxa ahead of Key bellowed and reared, its rider flying. Key saw the catapult bolt in its neck, as the animal fell in a thrashing heap. Another bolt shot past him, and then the vanguard smashed into the mass of enemy dragoons. The cataphract charge slowed, but kept going. Swords and lances rose and fell. A Tathar slashed at Key. He took the blow on his shield, and stabbed his javelin at the man's neck, but missed. Before he could strike again, the impetus of the charge swept them apart. Another Tathar blundered into him, and Rush tossed the man from his saddle with one sweep of her black horns.

Suddenly, the Tathars fell away, smashed aside and outrun by the cataphracts. Only a scatter of enemy cavalry stood between them and the trenches, and these were galloping furiously to get out of the way. But the Tathars had struck hard, and several hippaxas bore empty saddles. One had a white scar on her shoulder: Lydis's mount.

They raced at the trenches. The thin rank of Tathar infantry wavered uncertainly. If they were veterans, they'd know that hippaxas wouldn't hesitate to smash through a spear hedge. Closer now. Key picked his target, a Tathar in scale armor and a spiked helmet. The man had braced his spear butt in the earth, as if determined to stand.

At the last moment the Tathar infantry lost their nerve, and they broke. Key's target flung himself to the left, and threw his round shield up for protection. Key struck at him with the javelin. The blade hit the shield's center, stuck fast, and tore the shaft from Key's grip. He reached for his sword, then saw the trenches ahead. Leaving the blade in its scabbard, he rose in his stirrups as Rush sailed over the raw cut in the earth. She

landed smoothly, and Key angled her toward the city gates. No
Tathars now stood between the cataphracts and safety. Key
left his sword alone, and bent over the hippaxa's neck to urge
her on.

Until that moment he had forgotten the horseman. Suddenly, there he was, not ten yards to Key's right, tucked in
behind the disordered lead rank. He'd caught up when the
fighting slowed the charge. The gray was lathered white, its
flaring nostrils rimmed with blood. Its rider, slim as a youth,
crouched low in his saddle, his cloak streaming behind him.

The gray screamed. A catapult bolt, shot from the flank,
suddenly stood black and stark in the animal's haunch. It
stumbled, throwing its rider across its neck, and screamed
again. Without thinking, Key yanked Rush around. She bellowed in protest, her claws scattering dirt and turf as she
wheeled. The gray's rider tried frantically to stay in his saddle,
but the horse was already toppling. At the last instant the man
flung himself clear, to land with brutal force on the short grass.
Then, astonishingly, he staggered to his feet.

Key slowed, reached down, and shouted, "Take hold!" The
rider still had his wits, for he seized Key's mailed forearm
in a desperate grip. Key dragged him across the saddlebow,
facedown, and spurred Rush for the gate. It was still closed,
though most of the cataphracts were nearing the walls.

Open, open, can't you see who we are?

A fine dark line appeared between the gate's wooden
leaves. Men on the barbican towers shouted and waved. The
dark line thickened, lightened, showed inner walls beyond.
The gates were opening at last.

"We're going to make it!" Key shouted to the prone figure
before him. "Hang on!"

No answer. Key glanced over his shoulder and saw how
much ground he had lost in his impulsive rescue. He was a
straggler, with even the rear guard flying before him, and in
frenzied pursuit galloped a pack of Tathar dragoons. They
were trying to rush the gate, to break in with the cataphracts.
If they had to, the gatekeepers would shut him out, and leave

him to die under the Tathar blades. He shouted encouragement at Rush, and felt her strain under him.

He was going to be the last in. Already most of the cataphracts were through, and the gates slowly began to close. Another glance over his shoulder. The Tathars lagged behind, but not far, and the gates might yet shut against him. *Stay open, stay open,* Key pleaded silently. *It's only a few more yards. Stay open, in the Allfather's name.*

The gap narrowed to the width of a wagon, a cart. Key dug in his spurs, and Rush gathered herself and leaped. Wood brushed Key's legs as they shot through the opening, and the gates crashed shut behind him with a thunderous *boom.*

Cursing, cheering cataphracts and rumbling hippaxas jammed the gate's inner courtyard. Key dragged Rush to a shuddering halt; she lowered her head and panted, foam flying from her jaws. He could smell her sweat, and his own. But he was alive, and the morning sunlight and the air were sweet.

The limp bundle in front of him stirred. The visored helmet was awry, and Key, looking down, saw that the strap had broken. A dirty hand reached up and pulled the helmet off. From beneath the steel tumbled a flood of jet-black hair. Key blinked. The bundle squirmed, and a face looked up at him: a woman's frightened face, a woman no older than himself, with the pale golden skin and indigo eyes of the high Ascendancy blood.

Key gaped at her. "Who are you?" he blurted.

"I am Archates' daughter," the woman said in a shaken voice. "I'm the Luminessa Mandine. Who are you?"

✳ 4

THE LUMINESSA MANDINE.

Aghast, Key yanked his hand from her shoulder. To touch a member of the Dynast's family without permission was the highest insolence, an offense against the dignity of the throne. And he had been carrying the woman like a sack of barley at his saddlebow. His palm might even have been on her rump; horrified, he remembered a warm, firm curve against his skin. She was Archates' eldest daughter, and she could have him flogged.

Wait, he thought. *I saved her from the Tathars. No one's going to flog me.*

She was already sliding from the hippaxa's back and dropping lightly to the ground. Key stared down at her. Under the dust and grime her face was lovely. He wanted to speak, but his tongue would not obey him.

The left corner of her mouth lifted in an uncertain smile. "Well?" she said. "Who are you, my tall savior?"

Key knew how terrified she must have been when her horse fell, and how much that smile must have cost her. He wrenched his gaze away, and said, with a dry throat, "Kienan Mec Brander, my lady, securion in the Fifth Cataphracts."

"A securion?" Her voice quavered only slightly.

"Yes, my lady." Key's palms were sweatier than they'd

been when he charged the Tathars. He had never even seen the Dynast's two daughters, much less spoken to one. Around them in the gate courtyard the surviving cavalry still shouted and jostled, but curious faces began to turn toward Key and the luminessa.

"That rank will soon be higher," she said, and managed another smile, this time with her whole mouth, and Key's heart jumped.

"You're an easterner, aren't you?" Mandine said, when he remained tongue-tied. "From the high plateaus?"

Shaken though she must be, she had noticed his accent. Key nodded, and dared look at her again. "Yes, Luminessa. My father is ruler in Oak Haeme of the Elthame."

"Ah," she said. "So you are a king's son."

"In a way, my lady," Key said, unwilling to contradict her directly. "In the Elthame we have demarchs, not kings. My father is Oak's demarch."

"I remember now," she said. "It is an elected rule. I spoke without thinking."

Key stared past her at the cobbled pavement. What kind of woman was this? Moments ago she fled Tathar sabers, and now she was calmly—almost calmly—asking him about his background and ancestry. He stole another glance at her. Her eyes were on the closed gates.

"My poor horse," she said softly. "Poor Siro. He carried me so far."

"My lady," Key blurted, "how did you come to be on a battlefield? Why aren't you safe in Captala Nea?"

Mandine grimaced. "I wish I were. But I—"

She broke off as shouting erupted on the farside of the courtyard. Key, looking up, saw an ironbound door standing open at the base of the gate barbican. Someone there yelled, *"Make way, damn you! Make way for the auctator!"*

A hard-faced senior officer, wearing the blue cloak of the Dynast's military staff, was forcing his way through the crush of hippaxas and dismounted cataphracts. Behind the auctator marched six elite Paladine Guards in their silvered helmets;

someone in the barbican towers must have recognized the luminessa. Key watched the officer approach, feeling an unreasonable disappointment. She would be gone in moments, and he probably would never speak to her again. But what had he expected? That she would give more than a few words to a junior cavalry officer, no matter if he'd just saved her life? That wasn't the way of the high nobility. He might be a demarch's son, but to the Luminessa Mandine he must seem no more than half-civilized. He tried to imagine her in the Winter Hall of Oaken House, with wind and snow beating at the casements, and failed.

The auctator reached them. He was Key's father's age, with cheeks flat as slabs of wood and a cleft chin. He knelt before Mandine, then rose and gave Key a cold, measuring look from beneath thin black eyebrows. Key saluted hastily, then dismounted. The courtyard had fallen silent, except for the jingle of harness and the scrape of hippaxa claws on stone.

The auctator turned to Mandine. "Has this man harmed you, Luminessa?"

Key heard a faint mutter from the cataphracts. Mandine's eyebrows rose. "Not as much as the Tathars would have," she said in a sharp voice. "Of course he has not harmed me, Bardas. What do you take him for, an enemy?"

The auctator flushed. "No, my lady. It's only that these young field officers—he might have given you offense—"

"He didn't," said Mandine. "Never mind it, Bardas. Where is my father?"

The flush faded from the officer's cheeks. "The Dynast is in the Summer Palace, Luminessa. I've sent a messenger to tell him you're safe. These Guardsmen will escort you there."

"Good," she said, and Key thought: *Already she's forgotten I exist.* The auctator gestured to the Paladines, and they moved to surround her.

"Just wait one moment, Bardas," Mandine said. "I'm not finished here."

"My lady?" Bardas was clearly anxious to be on his way.

"What is to be done with these cavalrymen? They are here to help my father, but they need food and drink."

The auctator's gaze swept indifferently over the haggard, exhausted cataphracts. "It will be arranged."

"When?" Mandine demanded.

"Soon, my lady. As soon as the victuallers are told about them. No more than an hour or two."

Mandine stared at him. Then she said, in a low voice that only Key and the auctator could hear, "Bardas, these are my father's cataphracts. The *Dynast's* cataphracts. They are not here to wait on the pleasure of the victuallers. Do I make myself plain?"

Bardas's mouth tightened. "Yes, Luminessa. I understand. They will be tended to immediately."

"Good. See that it is done, because I will ask. As for this man, he is Kienan Mec Brander, a securion in my father's service. His father is a ruler in the Elthame. I would be on a Tathar spear or worse, but for him. Treat him accordingly."

"Yes, Luminessa." Bardas's expression was carefully blank.

Mandine turned to Key. "I owe you my life," she said. "I will not forget."

"My lady," he managed, and bowed. Mandine smiled again, and Bardas snapped an order to the six Paladines. Key watched them escort her away, her slender, gray-cloaked figure gliding silently amid the heavy tramp of armored men. He hoped she would give him one more smile over her shoulder, but she did not look back. Then she was through the inner gate, and gone.

A mile to the southwest, two horsemen watched the towers of Essardene and the just-closed gate. They wore the black-and-silver sashes of ducal rank, and their faces were the blue-tinged white of the Tathar nobility. Their mouths were full-lipped, the lips pigmented so dark a red they were almost black.

"Those were cataphracts," said Duke Ragula. He was holding a polished brass tube to his right eye. "I didn't think the goldskins had any left. Must have been stragglers from Thorn

River. Eh, Nollai?" He lowered the spyglass and glanced at his younger companion.

Duke Nollai's face was twisted with fury. "They must have surprised our pickets. By Scyl's teeth, I'll have the picket commander's balls for this."

"If the goldskins haven't already got them," Ragula said. He looked around in the brightening morning sunlight. The two Tathar dukes were on the crest of a knoll that swelled from the valley's side; nearby, the Great West Road ran down into the valley, on its way to Essardene. Before the road reached the walls of the summer capital, it vanished among the tents and diggings of the siege lines. In the lines, tendrils of gray smoke rose from watch fires that were now breakfast fires. Pennons fluttered, horses neighed, dogs barked, soldiers yelled. Squads of engineers were assembling siege machines just back of the trenches.

"Not that it matters, Nollai," Ragula added. "A few cataphracts on the walls won't make any difference."

"They never should have gotten into the city at all," Nollai said, chewing his dark lower lip.

"The lines were thin over there," Ragula pointed out. "The palisade will be up by tomorrow morning. Not even cataphracts will get through a palisade."

Nollai shaded his eyes. "I want a closer look at the gate," he said. "Lend me that toy of yours, Ragula."

Ragula reluctantly handed over the precious spyglass. It was Ascendancy manufacture, of a rare precision. Nollai raised the glass and fiddled with it. "The south tower looks weak," he muttered. "Flaking masonry. Two days to put the Dynast's skin on a drumhead."

"Too bad we didn't catch him at Thorn River," Ragula said. "If he'd been with the main body when we sprang the trap, he wouldn't have gotten the chance to run away."

"Archates is a coward," said Nollai. "The garrison here might remember that and open the gates. I doubt they want to be another Mallia."

Ragula nodded. A month ago the Tathar army had taken

Mallia by storm; the forty thousand men, women, and children who survived the city's fall were then put to death in the public gardens. King Hetlik spared twenty of the defenders and released them to spread the news of Mallia's fate. The maneuver had worked, for not one city on the army's line of march had resisted until now; when the citizen-militias saw the impaling stakes and the skinning frames going up before their walls, the gates opened. For the moment, the captured cities were garrisoned and left intact. Later, when King Hetlik sat on the Dynast's throne in Captala Nea, their populations would be killed and replaced by Tathar settlers. But the full cleansing of the newly taken lands, city and countryside both, would take a long time. Ragula sometimes wondered if it were actually possible to slaughter all the goldskins, for the Ascendancy was vast. As he had heard it, a man would need three months to walk from its western border to its eastern, and nearly that to go from the northern mountains to the shores of the great southern ocean that the Ascendancers called the Blue. But for all its vastness, the Ascendancy was weak and its people soft. Essardene was holding out only because Archates and a few survivors of Thorn River were inside.

"Essardene next," Nollai said, and handed the glass back to Ragula. "Then, when we get Captala, the war's over."

Ragula scowled. "I wonder what Erkai's got up his sleeve for that trick? Nobody's ever taken Captala, by siege or by storm. And he was useless at Mallia, damn his eyes. Didn't do a thing."

"That was King Hetlik's decision."

"We *think* it was," Ragula said, the displeasure deepening in his white face. The king's plan had been to tempt the goldskins to march deep into the west, toward the invading Tathar army. Hetlik had said he didn't want rumors of sorcery making Archates cautious, so Erkai had sat back while good Tathar soldiers died in the storming of Mallia.

"Do you think it *wasn't* the king's decision?" Nollai asked.

"Maybe not. Maybe it was Erkai's. He's crept into the king's ear, like a worm into a nut."

"Careful," Nollai warned. "I don't bear tales, but there are some who do."

"He comes out of nowhere," Ragula said angrily, as if Nollai had not spoken, "spends a year in the king's service, and now he thinks he can tell Hetlik how to rule the world."

"Well, if the king manages that, even if it's with Erkai's help, we can get rid of Erkai afterward, can't we?"

Ragula grunted. He would never have admitted it to the other duke, but he was afraid of Erkai, and he knew without being told that Nollai and the other officers felt the same way. As for the rank and file, they cringed when Erkai passed, and had done so since the night after the big battle at the river, when the goldskin army was crushed. That night, with Hetlik's permission, Erkai had taken the two hundred or so goldskin prisoners over the back of a hill, ordered the guards to tie them to stakes, and then sent the guards away. Soon after, there'd been strange lights hanging over the hill's farside, and noises from it that Ragula did not want to remember, though he was well accustomed to screams. Some of the harder troops went up to look, and had come back down shaking and staring. Things coming out of the air, they said, when they regained their power of speech the next day. Since then, everyone had trod very softly in Erkai's presence. Even the king.

Ragula was still not sure why Erkai was helping Hetlik attack the Ascendancy. He did not really believe the sorcerer's tale of avenging an ancestor, an ancestor whom some dynast had killed about seventy years back. Anyone could understand blood-vengeance, so the tale might be true, but anything Erkai said was of immediate suspicion to the duke.

Nollai was glowering at the road. "Speak of a demon, look what comes. Erkai."

Already close by, approaching them from the camp, trotted a small black mare. Its rider wore a smoke blue robe whose hood covered most of his face. Ragula could not decide how Erkai had approached so near without attracting his attention.

It was disquieting; the man had an art of appearing unexpectedly at one's elbow.

Erkai halted his mare and pushed back his hood. "Good morning, my lords," he said in his soft, clear voice.

Ragula gave a brusque nod and stared at Erkai as rudely as he dared. The sorcerer's complexion was the hue of gold alloyed with copper, and his thick, curling hair was blue-black, like his eyes. The long nose with its flaring nostrils made Ragula think of some exotic predatory beast, sniffing where a scent lay hot. Yet when Erkai smiled for the king—he did so for no one else—his face could be warm as sunlight. For this, Ragula trusted him even less.

"What brings you out here, Erkai?" he asked.

"The vantage point. You have an eye for observation posts, my lords."

"It's our trade," said the duke roughly. "We'd prefer to practice it by ourselves."

Erkai stared at him. "You do not like me, my lord Duke," he said, "do you?"

The stare and question were a challenge. Ragula's distrust and anger growled in him. "I neither like nor dislike you," he said.

"Your manner tells me otherwise."

"Does it?"

Erkai shrugged, with insolent indifference. "Ah, well. Whatever your opinion of me, remember that I have my uses to the king, just as you do. We are all instruments, my lord Duke, some of great merit. And some, my lord Duke, of less."

The insult was plain. Ragula's anger heated. "If you want to be of great merit," he said harshly, "why don't you just knock the gates down now, and let us in? And deal with the garrison, while you're at it?"

Erkai's blue-black eyes narrowed. "You think it is that simple, do you? My lord Duke, forgive me, but you do not know very much of my profession." He paused, then added deliberately, "Your ignorance of it is deeper than you can imagine."

"You—" Ragula said in a hot voice. He kicked his stallion

forward until the huge animal's shoulder pressed roughly on the shoulder of Erkai's little black mare. Erkai's hood slipped forward, hiding his face. The stallion, driven by Ragula's spurred heels, thrust hard to jostle the mare back onto her haunches. *Teach him manners*, Ragula thought, so angry he was heedless of consequences.

Erkai spoke a guttural word, and spat on the stallion's neck. Ragula thought he saw the spittle quiver, then change to something hard to see, a suggestion of red with many legs. The stallion whinnied in alarm, and danced away from the mare, which stood as if rooted in the earth. The ghostly red thing scuttled onto Ragula's mailed thigh; the duke's skin crawled, and his blood chilled and stung in his veins. He lashed at the shape with his reins, and it vanished. Cursing under his breath, he stilled his horse. The animal stood with its head drooping, and its flanks shivered.

"Leave me," Erkai said, looking at neither of them. "Now."

"Never mind him, Ragula," Nollai said urgently, as he yanked his bay around. "Let's go. We have work to do."

Ragula, utterly humiliated, followed him. Erkai, however, did not stay to watch them canter off. Instead, he directed his mare into the hollow behind the knoll, where a rowan tree stood in early summer leaf. He dismounted, and sat cross-legged on the grass, with his back against the rowan's trunk. There, away from the racket of the Tathar camp, he had privacy for thought and meditation.

He closed his eyes. "It's going well," he said quietly to the darkness behind his eyelids. He had labored forty-five years to come as far as this, but his ends were at last in sight.

He opened his eyes, and drew back the sleeve of his overmantle. Wrapped around his left forearm was a silver chain of a hundred flattened links. Erkai touched it, and in slow fluid motion the chain uncoiled to hang from his fingers. He stroked it reverently. Even his grandmother, from whom he received it, had not known what the chain was. She had believed, like her ancestors who had handed it down from time out of mind, that it was merely an amulet against danger. But Erkai had found other things in the chain. His earliest discovery, when he was thirteen, was that it strengthened his innate ability to control the Black Craft.

That innate ability was great. It came through his mother's blood; she was a daughter of a witchwoman of the Gandara nomads, a copper-skinned, black-haired people who inhabited the steppes beyond the Ascendancy's northern borders. Seventy-six years ago, fleeing drought, the entire Gandara nation came down through the mountains of the Great North Wall into the Ascendancy, but was promptly attacked and driven out by an army led by Sedir, son of the reigning Dynast. Erkai's mother was captured. She was young and fertile; Sedir held her in his camp for three days, and in raping her got her with child. When the army marched, she managed to escape and reach her people. But she died in bearing Erkai, and her mother swore revenge on Sedir.

In adolescence, Erkai showed great talent for the Craft, far greater than that of his grandmother. But she knew the Craft's blackest spells, though she had never dared use them, and she taught him all she knew. When he was sixteen, the two of them left the steppes and made their way into the Ascendancy. After three years, during which Erkai learned its language and ways—he was a quick study—she contrived to put him in the way of Sedir, now Dynast. By that time Erkai, who had inherited his father's indigo eyes and golden complexion, could pass for an Ascendancer, and Sedir had long forgotten the violated steppe woman.

And from that encounter, Erkai thought, *there has flowed a river of vengeance that is not yet at its flood. Though it soon will be.*

His grandmother gave him the chain for his own when he went to the Fountain Palace to become Sedir's favorite. She had taught Erkai hatred, but also patience. He never used the Black Craft in Captala, for it was a hanging offense in the Ascendancy, and within the priesthood of the Two there were minds trained to detect its traces. Nor did he consider murdering Sedir, for his purpose was larger: to take the throne for himself, and only then use sorcery to sustain his power. He was able, silver-tongued, and open-handed, and his influence waxed with Sedir's dissoluteness. The Dynast did not know, until it was too late, that Erkai was his son. When Erkai was thirty, he declared himself and raised a rebellion.

It failed.

A rowan leaf fluttered onto Erkai's lap, and he brushed it away. His mare grazed placidly nearby. *Yet it was my good fortune to fail,* he thought. *If I'd won, I would still rule in Captala, but I might never have reached out to break the Ban of Athanais, and grasp the Deep Magic. Even I might not have dared as much as that.*

The rebellion failed because of his one great miscalculation: To fight the Dynast, he resorted to the Black Craft, and for the first time in many years used the chain to enhance his power over its arts. But he had not fully realized how deeply Ascendancers loathed the Craft and despised and dreaded those who practiced it. Fear of his sorcery kept his forces together for a time even so, while his rebel armies and the Dynast's loyalists fought their way through the Ascendancy's south and southwest. His grandmother joined him there, and rode with the army, for like all the Gandara nomads she was a flawless horsewoman. But her presence undermined his cause still more; the rebel lords who were supposed to be his allies despised her as a savage, and they guessed that she, like her grandson, knew far too much of the Black Craft for comfort. So in the end they deserted him, and on the last battlefield he met the Dynast's legitimate son Maniakes, sword to sword in the cold, rain-drenched dusk, and he lost. Only his name remained, bad luck to hear, and misfortune to speak: Erkai the Chain.

They had been right to believe him dead, in fact. He'd taken a sword blade though the lung, a sucking wound that let him live for an hour, long enough to escape the battlefield in the fog and the fall of night. Riding friendless and alone, he'd fallen into an icy mountain stream, and there died. He remembered the stream and his tumble into it, though nothing else until he awoke in the rock cleft above the rushing water.

His grandmother was with him, but she was dead, her body so black and charred that he knew her only by the gold torques about her neck and wrists. After weeping over her for a time, he discovered what she had done, for she had scratched a message to him on the rock wall, in the jagged runes the nomads used.

She had used the blackest spell of the Black Craft to bring him back from the dead. It could work only if the body had been chilled almost to ice, as his had been in the stream, but that was not the true key to the spell. Its essence was that the person casting the spell must die a death of appalling torment as the corpse returned to life.

If the spell had ever been used, Erkai didn't know of an example. Only someone steeped for a lifetime in the Black Craft would have the knowledge and the strength of will to call on it, and no such person was likely to sacrifice her own life to save another's. But his grandmother had done so. She gave him his second birth.

The scratched runes called on him to avenge her and her daughter on House Dascaris, or be cursed. He did not need the threat; he would have sworn a terrible revenge without it. His grandmother had given him nurture and knowledge from the time of his mother's death, and he had loved her. House Dascaris would pay for her death, and pay in a coin out of its worst nightmares.

And now, years later, he knew that she had bequeathed him much more than a second life. More, in fact, than she had ever realized. She had given him the chain, not knowing, for all her craft, what it truly was. Neither had he known it, even during his rebellion; only his long researches after that failure had revealed to him the treasure he possessed.

Erkai slid the chain's links slowly between his fingertips. It was far older than the Ascendancy, as ancient perhaps as the drowned Old Dominion in the east, from which the Ascendancy had sprung. It was a spell chain, an ancient tool forged to control the Deep Magic. If other such chains existed, Erkai did not know of them; indeed, outside a few old tales it had been forgotten that they had ever been forged at all. But they *had* existed, and Erkai knew who had made this one. After years of research and very, very cautious experiment he had discovered the meaning of the glyphs on the single marked link, and the glyphs said: *Spardas the Thanaturge made this.*

Two years later, Erkai still felt the cold delight of that revelation. He possessed the spell chain of a thanaturge.

Thanaturge: deathmaker, in the common tongue.

The thanaturges had been deadly evil, or considered so in the ancient world. To Erkai's mind, they simply knew how to draw on the Deep Magic and did as they pleased with it, regarding no law. For that, the White Diviners had fought and destroyed them twenty centuries ago, but now there were no White Diviners. Athanais had been the last, and it was she who set the Ban, the ancient interdict on the calling of the Deep Magic. And for good reason; that power made even Erkai's Black Craft seem a child's conjuring trick, for it reached beyond the world, into the raw energies of creation and chaos. It could crack mountains, and it had. Seventeen centuries earlier it had escaped the control of even the White Diviners, and the sea had covered the lands of the Old Dominion in a single night. And so Athanais had locked its terrible strength away from the meddling ambitions of humankind, as she thought, forever. Her sepulchre still stood in Captala Nea on the Hill of Remembrance, where she had tested her greatest strength against the Ban she had made, and in the testing died.

The chain's links drifted through Erkai's fingers. *But,* he thought, *you didn't foresee me, did you, Athanais? All else, perhaps, but not me. A thousand and seven hundred years your Ban's endured, the most powerful spell ever cast. It stood against even you. But there was a flaw in your spell, and I know what it is. And when I break your Ban, and become a thanaturge, neither you nor anyone else will rise from the dead to contest me. The White Diviners are long gone, and you with them.*

Until recently the chain had had the one marked link of

Spardas's signature, and ninety-nine blank ones. Now the blanks had been reduced to ninety-two. He found the seven newly marked links and inspected the fine lines of the glyphs. They were the beginning of the spell that would reverse Athanais's interdict. When there were forty-nine of them, it would be ready. He needed many more deaths to bespell the energy of the symbols into the chain, but that was what the Tathars were for. All went as it should; he was satisfied.

Erkai let the chain fall, flexed his shoulders, and sat up straight. Though he was well over seventy, his body seemed half that. Among its other delights, the chain diminished aging; that had been a slow discovery, but gratifying once he was sure of it. A youthful body made long meditative sitting much easier.

He reached into his robe for a bundle of folded vellum and opened it flat on his crossed legs. Tiny intricate designs, drawn with reddish black ink, covered the sheet. This was his finest work, and creating it had taken him forty years of secret, relentless labor, a labor driven both by his ferocious will and by his craving for knowledge and revenge.

It was a symbol table of the forgotten hieroglyphic language of the White Diviners. They had used the secret tongue for many purposes, one being to call on the Deep Magic, but most knowledge of the language had vanished in the Flood, when mountains fell and the sea burst in to drown the splendor of the Old Dominion. Now Erkai had brought it back from the dead, as he himself had been brought back from the dead. It was his only and most precious child.

He fingered the smooth edge of the vellum. It had been a long time in the making, this sheet of ink and cured skin. He had wandered endlessly, sometimes out of the Ascendancy but more often within it, his researches hampered always by his need for concealment and secrecy. He did not dare disguise himself by his arts, for his enemies had never found his body, and were suspicious; because of that, they kept a vigilant watch for any notable manifestations of the Black Craft. Accordingly, he found other ways to conceal himself, usually as a middle-aged man of no memorable appearance.

It was in the face of such difficulties that he compiled the symbol table, working from scattered manuscript fragments preserved in the libraries of the Ascendancy's oldest cities, and from shards of worn carvings he discovered in the Ascendancy's earliest temples, and in obscure ruins. From these he had reconstructed the table and the usage of the symbols, a labor of forty years. And never once did he dare call on the Craft or the chain to aid him.

He was hampered further by the rumors that he was still alive, and that he might come back someday to exact a terrible revenge on the House of the Dascarids. These rumors swirled through the Ascendancy for decades, never truly dying away, and made his life precarious; he never dared stay long in one place. Only seven years ago, he was living obscurely near a logging town in the Ascendancy's far east, eking out a living as a woodturner; by night he worked diligently on the table, using an enigmatic inscription he had discovered in a local temple of uncertain age. Then a neighbor's entire flock of game hens suddenly died. The neighbor owed Erkai a few minims, and Erkai was an outsider; the man raised questions of sorcery in the death of his hens. Erkai knew fowl blight when he saw it, but despite this he immediately went on the road. Much later and very far away, he heard a rumor that he had been detected in the east, and that in his fury at his discovery he had inflicted terrible sorceries on a whole village of lumbermen.

Yet he stubbornly persevered, and at last succeeded in completing the symbol table of the ancient language. His first cautious test of it was to investigate the chain, and that very first trial had revealed, to his enormous delight, that Spardas the Thanaturge had made the artifact. But how to use the chain escaped him, until, seeing no other choice, he gambled his very being. He used one of his grandmother's most dangerous spells and attempted to call Spardas from the dead.

But what answered his call was not Spardas. In a dimensionless place of blackness and glacial cold he met the Adversary Itself, the ancient Enemy that had sprung into existence at the Beginning, when Creation and Nothingness arose entwined.

It did not show hostility, rather seemed oddly pleased with him, and It offered him perfect knowledge in exchange for perfect obedience. Erkai, gathering his wits from his first shock and protected by his spell-wards, declined; the Adversary was also, and for excellent reasons, called the Father of Lies. Strangely, It showed no anger at his refusal, only a cold amusement; then, to Erkai's astonishment, It offered up the wisp of Spardas that It contained. There was only a wisp, for It had absorbed the ancient thanaturge almost utterly, but in that wisp was the knowledge Erkai needed. He discovered the flaw in Athanais's Ban, and how with his Black Craft he could embed into the chain's links a Deep Magic spell of reversal, and turn that spell against the Diviner's interdict. But the preparation would be difficult. The Black Craft required the taking of life to empower its spells, and Erkai would need many agonizing deaths to force the needed energies into the chain. Then, to ensure the spell's potency as he released those energies in one cataclysmic burst, he must stand where Athanais stood when she invoked her Ban. He must stand on the Hill of Remembrance in Captala Nea.

Erkai took a deep breath of the summer air and slowly let it out. He alone in the world could do this and succeed; anyone else who attempted it would be instantly struck down by the Ban. He was unique. Even the Adversary had recognized this, in giving him Spardas's knowledge; either that, or It considered his ends akin to Its own. Hoping for more such help, Erkai had from time to time probed It again, though he knew this was a dangerous business. Nothing useful had so far come of his attempts. The Adversary was capricious, and in Its very nature perverse. It answered him with gibberish, or not at all, or offered him grotesque temptations in exchange for his allegiance. Even if these had tempted him, he would never have accepted; the Adversary was falsehood itself, and even Its claims to certain powers were, to Erkai, suspect. If he had not perceived Its cold, unfathomable cunning in his first encounter, and if he had not been so uncertain of how far Its powers did run, he would have disregarded the thing entirely.

Erkai folded the symbol table and slid it into his robe. *In any case,* he thought, *I do not need the Adversary. And I am not Spardas, to be devoured. I am the twice-born, whom my grandmother raised from the dead by her own death. I am the power Athanais did not foresee.*

He rose to his feet. His time would come, but for the moment he had another task at hand. King Hetlik did not want Archates to escape from Essardene, and Erkai's part in this was to prepare lurking-spells on the roads out of the city. The work would take time, energy, and concentration, and the sun had already climbed well into the sky. He flicked bits of dried grass from his robe, mounted his mare, and rode out of the hollow.

❋ 5

"DOES ANYONE KNOW EXACTLY WHAT HAPPENED TO Lydis?" Key asked.

The surviving cataphracts were encamped in the grassy parade square next to the Summer Palace's south wall. On its east, the square was bounded by the city wall and the fortifications of Dynasts' Gate; on its west were the stables, where the hippaxas rumbled and bellowed.

Melias looked glum. "Somebody saw the victurion take a catapult bolt through the chest. Knocked him clean off his mount, and that was that. At least the silverhairs didn't take him alive."

Key nodded, and sat down crossways on his saddle. "How many did we lose?"

"Twelve outside the walls, sir." The peltarch consulted a wax tablet and read off the names. An hour earlier Key had made Melias the unit's executive officer, for Lydis's death had left Key in command of the Fifth Cataphracts, or what remained of them.

"And we have eighteen wounded," Melias finished. "Eleven badly. Can't ride."

Key struck his knee with his clenched fist. "Eleven?" He had hoped for none.

"Yes, sir. They're all in the barracks, other side of the stables. There's a civilian surgeon tending them."

Key nodded again and looked around the parade square. Most of his men were asleep in the midmorning sun, motionless bundles under their stained green weather cloaks, heads pillowed on saddles, armor and weapons stacked beside them. A few remained awake, gnawing heels of the rough bread the victuallers had supplied.

"Sir," Melias said. "Permission to ask a question?"

"Go ahead."

"What're they going to do with us? We're not infantry. Are they going to make us fight on the walls? Or is it true what the victurion said this morning, that we're going to break out, with the Dynast?"

"I don't know," Key said. "I suppose we'll have orders soon." He studied the young man's face; it was gray with weariness. "That's enough for now. Get some rest, Melias. I'm going to do the same. Wake me if you need to."

"Yes, sir."

Melias tramped away. Key wrapped himself in his cloak and stretched out on the grass. But the sun lay bright on his eyelids, and he could not sleep. He thought of home, far to the east, far beyond the Inner Sea, the high plateau country with its dark forests, its rivers plunging through dim green gorges, its lakes hung with mist. He remembered the summer's heat drawing sweat from him as he swung the heavy practice sword in the training yard of Oaken House, and the salt taste of the tiny silver fish the countryfolk called miller's-thumb. He rode again with his father among the barley sheaves of autumn, stubble crackling under their horses' hooves like frost, and saw again the hard low skies of winter, heavy with snow.

Enough, he told himself, turning restlessly under the cloak. *Enough. I am here, and can be nowhere else. I am here because I decided five years ago to be here, when my father would have had me stay. That was the only time I ever went truly against his wishes. But he relented in the end. It is an itch young men must scratch, he told me the day I left, but be careful you don't scratch it too deep, on an enemy blade. I shouldn't have laughed.*

He tried to think of something that was not home, not the

Tathars, not tomorrow. He saw her face. Her skin the color of sunlight. Her eyes the hue of the deep sea.

I am a fool.

The sun on his cheek was warm as a girl's fingertips. He slept.

Mandine trudged wearily down the long Gallery of Hermodia. Two hundred years ago, that faultless painter had left her frescoes of Spring Triumphant on the Gallery's walls, and still the colors glowed as if fresh from the brush. But Mandine hardly saw them. The notion that she had forgotten to do something important was with her again.

She remembered feeling it when she rode away from Ardis and Quill at dawn yesterday. But her fear of encountering Tathar raiders had driven it to the back of her mind as she followed the peddlers' track, and she'd traveled well into the night, directing Siro by the light of the moon. When the gelding began to stumble with fatigue, she dismounted and dozed for a few hours. Birdsong roused her well before sunup, and she went on through the forest, hoping she was near Essardene.

Then from her left she'd heard hoofbeats, and a sudden din of metal on metal, and the shrill shouts of Tathars, followed by abrupt silence. Heart pounding, she had stolen away uphill, over a crest, and down into a tongue of woodland on the crest's farside. Not until the trees thinned did she see Essardene in the valley below and the banners of the Tathars flying above the siege lines. She had almost despaired then, until she saw the cataphracts pouring over the ridge crest on her left. If she had known how few they were, she might not have joined them, but they had seemed then like the vanguard of a relieving army. As it was, she'd almost failed in her mad dash for the city. If it had not been for Kienan Mec Brander, she would be . . .

The possibilities were sickening, and she refused to imagine them. Now, walking the length of the Gallery, she was for the moment safe. Still, this disquiet. *What* had she forgotten?

Something . . . it hovered at the edge of memory. Joy followed by terror, suffocation, falling.

It's something I dreamed and can't remember, she thought. *I've been having nightmares, and no wonder, as Ardis said.*

Mandine reached the end of the Gallery and turned into the corridor that led to the Summer Kellion, the suite of offices from which the Dynasts ruled while residing in Essardene. Bardas had said her father would be there. At least she was presentable. Most of the palace staff had fled back to Captala at the news of Thorn River, but a few of the braver ones had remained, enough to provide her with food, a bath, and a clean tunic and overmantle.

Suddenly she was at the doorway of the Kellion. A violent argument raged within. Mandine waited, listening as her father's voice suddenly rose above the others.

"—but how? How are we to get out of here? There's no one—"

"There're those cataphracts who came in this morning, my lord." Mandine recognized Tracien Bardas's harsh voice. "A hundred and seventy-odd of them are fit to ride."

"A hundred and seventy! We had a full tercia of cataphracts at Thorn River. What good did they do me then?"

There was a silence. Mandine felt sick. Her father should be telling his officers what to do. Ask them for counsel, certainly, but then *tell* them. *He's the Dynast,* she thought. *Why doesn't he decide? He'll lose their confidence. Or has he already lost it?*

"If we broke out tonight, to the east," said another voice, "we could reach the Inner Sea by tomorrow afternoon. There must be naval units in the area. A dromon could sail or row us to Captala in under two days. Faster than we can ride."

"Unless the Tathars have reached the coast before us," said Bardas.

"Do you think they have?" said her father. "Damn them to the Waste, how many of these vermin are there?"

No one answered him. Then Bardas said, "Well, we've got their main army outside the walls now, my lord Dynast. I saw Duke Ragula's colors this morning, beside King Hetlik's standard."

"The trouble is," said the other voice, "we're locked up here and don't know how far past us their other columns may have penetrated. My lord, those cataphracts may have information that would help us. Your daughter, the luminessa, has been riding with them. Could we ask her?"

"Yes. Damn you, Bardas, bring her here. Why isn't she here?"

"My lord, you said to wait. I took her to the women's quarters. Also, my lord, the luminessa was not actually riding with the cataphracts. She said she happened on them by chance, this morning."

"She's been up-country, hasn't she? Get her here. After she gives us what she knows, question whoever's commanding those cataphracts."

"Yes, sir," Bardas said. "I will request the luminessa's attendance on you immediately."

Mandine took a deep breath. She stepped into the doorway, and said, "I'm here, my lord."

Archates Dascaris, Dynast of the Ascendancy, gazed at her almost without recognition. With a chill creeping over her, Mandine stared back at him. Her father was half-shaven, his graying hair dirty and unkempt, his eyes sunk deep in their sockets. Mandine had never seen him so. To her he had always been aloof, distant, armored in brocaded robes of state, face impassive, bending stiffly to touch her cheek with a dry kiss. For the past nine years, since the Tathar attacks worsened, Mandine had hardly laid eyes on him.

"Mandine?" he said.

"Yes, Father. I'm safe." *I am your daughter,* she thought, *and I almost died. Why didn't you bring me to you, when you heard? Why didn't you hold me, weep for joy?*

She knew the answer, of course. He cared for no one but himself, and for his throne. To Archates Dascaris, his daughters were instruments of policy; counters to be moved on a game board of alliances. Now that they were grown, she and Theatana had no purpose other than to serve his political needs. How they might feel was of no consequence; Mandine was not sure if he even recognized that she and Theatana had feelings.

"How long have you been listening?" he demanded.

Mandine's throat ached. "Not long, my lord. I listened only to find out if I should interrupt your—your council."

"A council without counselors," said Archates. He glowered at the table, which was spread with maps. Next to him stood Bardas, and across the table was a heavyset man she remembered as Cardutos, the army's chief engineer.

The two officers shuffled their feet. Mandine felt suffocated by the tension in the room. The chill deepened on her skin, and she closed her eyes. She heard fires roaring, screams, savage laughter.

"Luminessa?" Cardutos's voice, alarm in it.

Mandine opened her eyes. They were all looking at her. "Are you ill, Luminessa?" asked Bardas.

"Bring her something to sit on," said her father, not moving to do it himself.

Cardutos put a carved chair behind her. He almost took her arm to help her into it, but stopped himself just in time. Mandine, who would have been glad of a human touch, smiled at him as she sank onto the cushion. After days in the saddle the upholstery felt oversoft.

"How did you get here?" her father asked. He was breathing heavily, and a flush had risen in his sunken cheeks.

"I was at Bartaxa, my lord. You gave me leave to visit the Maiden Shrine there, before you took the army south." *So short a time ago that seems*, she thought. *When everyone still believed the Tathars were only raiding. Who could have imagined this?*

"Are you nine kinds of fool, Mandine?" Archates said, in a low, cold voice. "Did you not stop to think, girl, before you left Bartaxa? Suppose you'd been taken? Do you know what Hetlik could have demanded of me?" His voice rose to a shout. *"Do you?"*

Mandine flinched, then bowed her head. "I am greatly at fault, my lord," she whispered.

Her father said nothing. Mandine thought: *And if the Tathars had taken me, Father, would you have submitted, or would you have let them put me on a stake under the walls of Essardene?*

A foolish question. You would have let me die. You could do nothing else.

"Go on," Archates said at last. "What did you see?"

Mandine told them of the death of her escort and her flight through the hills. She spoke only briefly of meeting Quill and Ardis; she knew these men would be indifferent to the couple's fate and to what they had done for her. Bardas studied the maps as she spoke. When she finished, he asked, "Did you see Tathars south of here?"

Mandine shook her head. "The only signs of them were at the hill-farm I told you about. But they're on the coast down around Bartaxa."

"What of the north?" her father said. "Have they cut the road to Captala? Or is the way to the east open? To the sea?"

"I don't know, my lord. I did not come by either way. I came from the southwest, as I told you."

"What about those cataphracts? Do they know?"

"I have no idea, my lord."

Archates muttered a curse. *I can't give my father what he wants,* Mandine thought, *and he thinks the worse of me for it, as though I have failed in my duty to him.*

"My lord Dynast," Bardas said, "we must break out tonight. The Tathar ring can only get stronger. By tomorrow evening it will be too late. They are already palisading their siege lines."

"Damn you, someone will come from Captala Nea to raise the siege. The whole Paladine Guard's there, except for my bodyguard detachment. That's eight thousand trained men, and the citizen levies can make up the rest."

Bardas and Cardutos exchanged glances. "My lord Dynast," Cardutos said, "there are sixty thousand Tathar infantry, almost as much cavalry, and Essardene's walls are weak. I agree with Bardas. We must escape tonight, or not at all."

"We have the cataphracts—we have the city militia, and my bodyguard—" Archates's voice shook. *My father is afraid,* Mandine realized suddenly. *He is terrified, and he will infect the others with his fear and his indecision. This is what we of House*

Dascaris have finally become. A shame to the Ascendancy, and to the dynasties that came before us. What would the Dynasts of the House Tessaris think of my father? What would Galion Tessaris think, who threw the Tathars back over the West Wall three hundred years ago, and saved the Ascendancy? My father must do the same, and he does not even know how to begin.

"Even with the Paladines, the cataphracts and the militia are not enough," Bardas said, adding, "my lord."

Archates turned to the engineer. "Cardutos, how long can we hold?"

"Three days at most, before the south gate towers go. After that . . ." Cardutos shrugged. "The Summer Palace is indefensible."

Bardas's right hand stabbed angrily at the air. "We won't last three days, Cardutos. Perhaps not till tomorrow's dawn."

"What?" Archates stiffened. "What do you mean, not till dawn?"

"I cannot answer for the city militia, my lord Dynast. They're not regulars. I've put what regulars we have at the gates, but there aren't enough of them, and the militia may surrender the city as soon as they see a chance. Everyone here knows what happened at Mallia."

"A curse on Mallia. I was not at Mallia. I am the Dynast. They must protect me. Am I surrounded by traitors?"

Bardas turned red. "No, my lord, you are not. But we can't hold long enough for relief. We must try for Captala Nea, and we must try tonight."

Mandine waited, while silence hung thick in the air. Then her father said, "Whatever you like, Bardas. Let it be done." He looked at Mandine, as if suddenly remembering her. "My daughter will ride with us. And I want those cataphracts for escort, not horse cavalry."

Relief crossed Bardas's hard face. "Of course, my lord Dynast. I will find out what the cataphract leader knows about the roads and plan from there." He paused, and looked at Cardutos. Cardutos remained expressionless, except for the twitch of an eyebrow. Mandine watched them. They were edging toward something they disliked.

Bardas said, "There is something else, my lord."

"Yes?" Archates muttered, bending over the maps as though he could somehow leap to safety in the colored vellum. "Get on with it."

"I sent out a patrol last night. They caught a Tathar sapper scouting the south gate and brought him in. During interrogation, he said King Hetlik has an advisor who isn't Tathar."

Archates straightened. "What of it?"

"This—advisor appears to know something of the Black Craft. According to the Tathar we caught, he used our men taken alive at Thorn River, used them for some foul purpose. Our prisoner didn't know what it was."

"Sorcery," Archates said uneasily. "But there was no word of it from Mallia. And the Tathars didn't use magic at Thorn River."

"No, my lord," Bardas agreed. "But the Black Craft's clumsy in war, so it's not surprising. The odd thing is—"

"What?"

Bardas looked down at the maps. "My lord, before he died, the prisoner said that this advisor's name was Erkai. He has a chain he always wears."

A cold finger touched the nape of Mandine's neck, and dizziness swept through her. For an instant she felt a fierce pressure inside her head, as though an invisible noose strangled her thoughts. She pressed her fingertips to her temples, and the sensation vanished.

The others hadn't noticed her movement, and she returned her hands to her lap. "That's not possible," Archates said. His voice was frightened. "Some barbarian conjurer's using the name to frighten us. There are always these rumors. We investigate them, and it always turns up nothing."

"I know, my lord," Bardas admitted. His face had a stubborn set. "Yet his body was never found after that last battle, back in the rebellion, and the search was thorough."

"What do you think, Cardutos?" In her father's voice Mandine heard the plea: *Say you don't believe it, Cardutos. Say it can't be so.*

"My lord, the dead don't come back, not in these days. So if he's out there, it means he didn't die after your father fought him back then, and that's why no one ever found the body. But if he's alive, then where's he been, these past forty-odd years? Surely we'd have heard something from him by now."

"Unless," Archates said, "unless he was waiting. Waiting for something, like the Tathars, to be ready to help him. He can't defeat armies with the Craft alone. He knows he needs men with swords. Bardas, is that possible? That he was simply *waiting*?"

Bardas nodded slowly. "It's possible, my lord. I never believed the Tathars would come against us in this much force, until they did." His words lay cold on the air, like drifting snowflakes. "They have always raided before. It is as though they have had encouragement. And it's odd that the prisoner knew so precisely about both Erkai and the chain. I would not have expected it from a common Tathar soldier. They are very ignorant of the Ascendancy and its former . . . troubles."

Archates glared at him, then at the engineer. "So it may very well be true, even if he's so old he's dancing on the edge of his grave. Damn you both, why didn't you tell me this before? If he's out there, we have to reach Captala as soon as we can. With the gates closed and the seal-beams drawn, his Craft can't touch us there. Get to your planning and be quick about it."

The officers saluted in silence and left the Summer Kellion. Mandine watched them go, without really seeing them. *The cataphracts are escorting us,* she thought. *Kienan Mec Brander and I will be riding together. I never expected to see him again. It warms me, and oh, sweet Lady, how I ache for warmth.*

"Mandine."

She and her father were alone. Mandine turned to him, still hoping in the face of all her knowledge of him. "My lord?" she asked softly.

"Get out," her father said.

✳ 6

KEY STOOD ON THE BATTLEMENTS OF ESSARDENE'S
east wall. On his right rose the towers of Dynasts' Gate,
crowned by a watch beacon in a huge iron cresset. The moon
had not yet risen, and the light of the beacon's wind-whipped
flames flickered red across the parapet's white stone.

An hour ago he had ordered his men to stand to arms
with their mounts, and since then he had been up here on the
ramparts, studying the pattern of the enemy watch fires that
burned in a diadem around Essardene. The smaller sparks of
torches and lanterns moved among the siege works where the
Tathar engineers toiled relentlessly at their trenches and palisades. By morning the city would be locked in a cage of wood
and iron. Key chewed his lower lip and looked over his shoulder. Behind and below him, in the parade ground beside the
Summer Palace, gleamed the fires of his own men. They were
pitifully few beside the firmament of the Tathar army, for Hetlik's main force was now massed at Essardene. That afternoon
Key had seen the king's red standard outside the city's west
gate, and near it Duke Ragula's insignia, a white clawed hand
on a black ground.

He had just returned to his scrutiny of the siege lines when
a movement to his left caught his attention. He turned, and
saw a shadow grow solid as it approached him along the wall-

walk. The shadow became a slender figure in a gray cloak, the hood drawn close about the face.

Key's heart beat faster. He knew the cloak, or hoped he did.

The figure stopped a yard from him, and a slender hand drew back the hood, revealing the face to the beacon's light. Key dropped to one knee, head bowed. "My lady Luminessa," he said. He heard the wind's hiss in the stones of the battlements, and the low mutter of the flames above.

"My lord Brander," Mandine said, "please get up. It's not necessary to do that every time you see me."

"My lady is gracious." Key rose, looking past her to the round tower where the palace fortifications met the city wall. She must have come from there, he thought. "How may I be of service?"

"By being less formal," she said. "This is hardly an occasion of state."

"If the Luminessa Mandine will forgive me," Key said, "I am not of a rank to be informal in her presence, no matter what the occasion."

A smile touched the corner of her mouth. "You were extremely informal when we first met."

Key's cheeks warmed, and he thanked the flickering light for hiding his discomfiture. "I had no choice," he said, "and I didn't know who you were."

"Would it have made a difference if you had?"

"No, Luminessa. There was no time."

"I thought as much. Anyway, you're nobility in your homeland. Even my father could not fault me for speaking with you as I do." She studied him. "You're dark-haired for an easterner."

Key nodded. "I know. But we don't all have bronze thatches in the Elthame, my lady. We've lived next to the Ascendancy for a long time, and intermarriage isn't uncommon. Many of us are darker than our ancestors were, when we came from the plains to the high plateaus. But I'm very much an Elthamer."

"Yet you fight for a people not yours."

"It's one of our traditions, Luminessa. Seven years' service with the Ascendancy is a good education in the arts of leadership and war, not to mention the arts of civilization. Men like me have been enlisting in the Dynasts' service for six hundred years. We go home knowing another world, and the knowledge helps us manage our own."

Her face became somber. "But you, my lord, fight for us even now, even knowing we may lose? Even knowing that you may die in our service?"

"Civilization is better than anarchy and barbarism," Key said, hoping he did not sound pompous. "And if the Ascendancy fell to the Tathars, I don't see how we in the Elthame could beat them back. My people and yours are together in this, I think."

"I see." Mandine smiled, a little sadly. "And does this Elthamer wonder why I wander the battlements in the dark, without a suitable retinue of guards and attendants?"

"My lady's reasons are her own," Key said. Before he could stop himself, he added, "As for the dark, the Luminessa banishes it with her presence." As the words left his mouth, his ears burned and he thought: *Now she thinks I'm a flatterer, and very likely a fool.*

Yet she smiled again, as if not displeased. "Very elegantly spoken, my lord, though I don't consider myself a substitute for a good lantern. In truth, I'm here because I'm restless, and the palace stifles me." She paused. "Does it still puzzle you that I appeared so abruptly on a battlefield this morning? You asked, and I never answered."

"Yes, Luminessa." He sensed that she wanted to talk about it, so he said, "What happened?"

"It was an accident. The Dascaris ancestral estates are near Bartaxa, and every year the eldest son or daughter of the house goes to sacrifice at the Maiden Shrine there. It's supposed to bring us luck, though in these days it doesn't seem to. Anyway, when we heard about Thorn River, my escort commander thought we'd better hurry for Captala." She gazed into the night beyond the walls, where the Tathars labored. "We left it too late . . . am I keeping you from your duties?"

"No, Luminessa. Please go on."

"Very well." She told him of her flight through the forest, about the farm couple who helped her, and about falling in with the cataphract charge. As she spoke, a new respect for her wakened in Key, a respect that was more than regard for her exalted birth. Her slender frame hid a tenacity and hardiness he had not expected, not in a woman so cloistered by rank and by the luxuries of the Fountain Palace.

When she finished, he said, "You're lucky to be alive, my lady."

"I know." She looked up at him. "And you are one of the reasons I am."

"Please don't speak of it, Luminessa," Key said uncomfortably. "Anyone would have done the same."

"Would they? Well, there will be more on the matter, but for now . . . why are *you* out on the walls, my lord Brander?"

"I'm trying to see any weakness in the Tathar lines," Key said. "We ride out at the twelfth hour, from Dynasts' Gate here. Auctator Bardas gave me my orders this afternoon."

"He gave me mine, as well. Will your hippaxas really carry two people, and still be fast enough to outrun Tathar cavalry?"

"Yes, my lady. Anyway, we have no choice but to double up. A hippaxa doesn't always behave well, not right away, with a strange rider. And they don't respond exactly like horses."

Mandine glanced through the embrasure of the parapet, between the stone tongues of the merlons. "So then, have you found a weak place for us?"

"I think so. At sunset there was still a gap in the palisade down there, and as far as I can tell they haven't filled it in yet. Luminessa—"

"Yes?"

He spoke reluctantly. "My lady, with respect, you've been here for some time. You should go back to the palace. It's not seemly for you to be here alone with me. Your father would be out of countenance if he knew."

"I don't want to go back to the palace till I have to," Mandine said, "and my father cares little about where I am. Has he thanked you for saving my life?"

"No, my lady, but I didn't expect an audience with the Dynast, under these circumstances."

"But don't you think a father should be grateful to the man who saved his daughter's life? Grateful enough to spare a personal word, no matter what the circumstances, as you call them?"

Key had indeed thought this. But Archates' behavior was of a piece with the rest of him, and for the rest of him, Key had little but contempt. The man had sent the Ascendancy's last army into the Thorn River ambush, and when the fighting was at its bloodiest he fled with the remnants of the rear guard. Key still believed they might have fought clear of the gorge if Archates had stood firm, but his desertion had shattered the infantry's resolve, and they broke.

He said, "It's not for a junior cavalry officer to judge the actions of the Dynast."

"I judge him, then," Mandine said, her voice sharp with bitterness. "I went to him this morning. He was not pleased to see me. He did not even embrace me, Kienan Mec Brander. He only wanted to know if I'd seen Tathars, and where. And when he'd finished with me, he told me to get out."

"I'm sorry," Key mumbled. He wished she would change the subject.

"Is that all you can say?"

"It's all I should say, Luminessa."

"You're very careful. But I suppose you're right. We mustn't forget who we're talking about, after all." Her tone softened. "Did you see much of your father and mother while you were growing up? I'm not sure how these things are arranged in the Elthame."

"Yes, my lady, I did. Of my father, at least. My mother

died when I was three. I hardly remember her. My father never remarried."

"I'm sorry. I never knew my mother, either. But I suppose you were aware of that. It's no secret that the Dynast has been unlucky in his wives." She paused. "Have you a son in the Elthame? A daughter, perhaps? Or sibs?"

"No. I've never broken the marriage glass. As for sibs, I have only a sister. Her name's Riata, after our mother, but everyone calls her Ria. She's two years younger than I am."

"Are you close to her?"

"Yes, my lady. When we were children, we were always getting into trouble together."

A pause, while the wind gusted around them. "I also have a younger sister," Mandine said. Key heard no expression in her voice. "Theatana, who spins her webs back home in the Fountain Palace. My half sister, who hates me."

Out in the Tathar lines, an orange light flared. In silence it soared from the ground and arched toward the walls. Key leaned into the gap between the merlons to watch the fall of the shot. The ball of flame struck low on the tower from which Mandine had come and spattered in streaks and splashes of smoky light. The burning oil dribbled down the masonry, slowly guttering out.

"Ranging shot," Key said. "They don't even wait for daylight."

Mandine had leaned past him to look, and a scent of hyacinths was in Key's nostrils. He imagined he could feel her warmth on his skin, and he stepped hastily back.

"What's the matter?" she asked, straightening.

"Nothing," Key said. His next words were out before he could stop them. "Why does your sister hate you, Luminessa?"

He expected a reprimand for his presumption, but to his surprise she answered. "Because I'm the elder, and my father has no sons. He's had two wives, my own mother and Theatana's, and they both died. If he never remarries, if he never gets a male heir, I will take the throne on his death. Theatana is careful how she steps, but I have eyes and ears, and I use them. The truth is that my half sister wants to be Dynastessa, and that's the first reason she hates me."

To discuss the succession was to walk on dangerous ground, but Key could not resist his curiosity. "And the second?"

"The second is that my father intends Theatana to be married next year, to a decent young man from an old family. But Theatana despises him, perhaps because he *is* decent. My sister's appetites are . . . peculiar. Anyway, she believes I had a hand in the arrangements, which I did not." Mandine gave a humorless laugh. "Or perhaps she is simply angry that she must submit, as she sees it, to the bonds of marriage, while I escape. I will not have a husband anytime soon. My father wouldn't risk it. Do you know why, my lord Brander?"

Key, wishing now that he hadn't pursued the subject, muttered, "No, Luminessa."

"It's very simple. The man I marry will be Dynast on my father's death. My father is afraid that my husband would be unwilling to wait."

This had gone too far. Key said, "Politics is beyond my competence, my lady."

"Ah. You're a simple soldier, is that right?"

"Here in the Ascendancy I am, my lady."

"I see." Mandine gazed between the merlons, into the hostile night and the wind's rush. Key waited.

"We're losing, aren't we?" she said at last, in a soft, grieving voice. "They're out there, the White Death, and they're destroying us. They are putting out the lights forever."

Her pain and sadness were a quick, cold blade under his ribs, and suddenly he had an overwhelming desire to throw his arms around her. Alarmed at himself, Key put his hands behind his back and clenched them tightly. "My lady," he said, "it's not over, and we haven't lost yet."

"Don't give me false assurances," she said. "You and I may die before the sun is up."

"Luminessa, you mustn't think of that. It saps the will."

"I know." She sighed and drew her cloak closer about her.

"You're right, of course. But you're a soldier. You've learned not to fear."

Key shook his head. "No fighting man ever learns that, my lady. But it's not good to talk of one's fear, especially before a battle. Everyone's afraid then. But no one wants to hear about it. It only makes the fear worse."

"I don't understand that. I don't understand how men can keep such terrors inside. Wouldn't it relieve your mind to talk of them?"

"No," Key said. "No, it wouldn't."

She studied him, with a puzzled frown. "You trouble me, Kienan Mec Brander," she said slowly. "To my knowledge I have never seen you, nor heard your name, until today. So why do I feel I should know of you? Were you in Captala long enough that your name might have reached my ears?"

Her question startled him. "I don't think so, Luminessa. I was there only for my training to ride a hippaxa. All my active service has been in the northwest." Despite her presence, he remembered, for a moment, his first awe at the Ascendancy's ancient and lovely capital, the white city that rose where the broad estuary of the River Seferis flowed into the azure cup of Chalice Bay. Nothing in his experience had prepared him for Captala Nea: her six hills embraced by three colossal walls, her citizens beyond count in the bustling streets, her spice-scented markets, the boom of her forges, her manufactories redolent of leather, sawdust, and hot iron. And at her center, on the crown of Dynasts' Hill, the great fortress of the Numera, looming above the gardens and colonnades of the Fountain Palace.

"But I'm sure I must have heard someone speak of you," Mandine said. "What else do they call you?"

The memories vanished, and he shook his head in perplexity. "Just Key, usually, for short."

"Key," Mandine said. She sounded distracted.

"Yes, my lady. Is something wrong?"

"I don't know." Mandine closed her eyes, opened them. "I don't know, I don't know. Something strange has happened to me. I keep feeling as though I *must* remember something important, and I can't think what it is."

For no good reason, Key's skin prickled. He hesitated, reluctant to be too bold, but then asked, "How long has this been troubling you?"

"Since dawn yesterday. It's been coming and going. Just now it's very strong." She shook her head in frustration. "There. Now it's slipping away again. I've never felt anything like this in my life."

"Did anything odd happen to you, before it started?" He was thinking of her wanderings in the forest, and nature sprites, and of the lingering uneasiness a meeting with them could cause. But this sounded different.

"No. I thought I might have glimpsed one of the Near Folk, but the farm woman I spoke of said there were none in the area. Apart from that, nothing strange has happened. Not that I can remember. But that's the problem, isn't it? I can't remember, so if something odd *had* happened to me, I wouldn't know." Her mouth tightened with exasperation. "It's maddening. My memory's very good. I don't forget things, not like this."

"My lady, you'd better see a priestess when we reach Captala. This doesn't sound right."

"No, it doesn't. Now that I've spoken of it, it doesn't sound right at all." She shivered. "And this morning, Bardas said something . . . it made me feel even worse, when I heard it. A Tathar prisoner told Bardas that King Hetlik has help from a sorcerer, and the sorcerer's said to be Erkai the Chain."

"What?" Key exclaimed. "I thought Erkai was dead long ago."

"He's supposed to be. How much do you know of him?"

Key rummaged in his memory. "He raised a revolt against the Dynast Sedir, and he knew something of the Black Craft. A few men from the Elthame fought in that war, on the Dynast's side, and they brought back stories. But now that I think of it, I've never heard Erkai's name spoken in the Ascendancy."

"People here don't talk of him," Mandine said. "It's supposed to bring bad luck. He was very evil." She paused. "He was also my great-grandfather Sedir's bastard son."

"The stories had it so. I never knew if I should believe it."

Mandine sighed. "It's almost certainly true. I've read the accounts of the rebellion, and they say that Erkai looked very much like my great-grandfather. Sedir fathered him on a woman of the Gandara steppe nomads, or at least Erkai said so when he started the revolt. There were enough rebellious nobles to give him a following, for a while. In the end, Sedir's legitimate son defeated and killed him, and just after that, Sedir died suddenly and the son took the throne. The son was my grandfather Maniakes."

"How did Erkai get into Sedir's good graces in the first place?" Key asked.

"My great-grandfather found him, or perhaps it was the other way around, when Erkai was eighteen. Sedir was hunting, and he flushed a grimarr. Something went wrong, and the creature was at his throat, and Erkai came out of nowhere and put a javelin in the grimarr's eye. That in itself commanded a great reward, but something about Erkai caught Sedir's fancy. Perhaps it was blood calling to blood. Whatever the reason, Erkai came to the palace and turned into Sedir's favorite." Mandine's voice became harsh. "It would have been better for the Ascendancy if Sedir had died in the beast's mouth."

This was dangerous speech, even from a luminessa. Key said, "Erkai was killed, as you say. He can't have come back."

"But no one actually saw him die, or found his body. The last battle ended after dark. Maniakes put a sword into him, but then the fighting swept them apart. No one ever saw Erkai again."

"That's a very good reason to think him dead, my lady."

"So I hope. I'm not at all sure of it, now. Neither is my father, or his staff." Mandine stiffened, and turned to the parapet. "Look! They're shooting again!"

Key looked, and saw a flaming projectile rise from the siege lines. It appeared to travel straight up. As it ascended, its size and brilliance grew. Key blinked, then understood.

"My lady, quick! It's coming straight at us!"

Mandine stumbled as she turned. Key grabbed her arm, dragged her at a run along the battlements. He heard a whistle and rush behind, then a heavy thud, and underfoot the granite wall shuddered. A glance backward told him that the projectile had hit the merlons, smashing their stone blocks across the wall-walk exactly where he and Mandine had stood. Oil smoked and blazed sullenly in the wreckage.

"Did they see us?" Mandine exclaimed, as they stopped, and Key released her arm. "Were they aiming at us?"

He heard shouts from the gate barbican, calling for sand to put out the fire. "Maybe. My lady, I'd better see you back to the palace before—"

He broke off. From the direction of the west gate, across Essardene's rooftops, rolled a dull, hollow thunder.

"What's that?" Mandine said urgently.

Key listened. "Storming drums. The Tathars beat them for hours before an attack. It works on the defenders' nerves." He squinted. Far off across the city, lit from below by cressets, the battle standard of the Ascendancy flew above the west gate's barbican. From this distance it was only a tiny bright rectangle of green and gold, blazing defiantly against the encroaching dark.

The standard moved. Or did it? Key stood transfixed, watching.

It moved again, downward, slowly. It hesitated, halted, then suddenly descended in a rush, and vanished. The drums boomed louder, then stopped. Cutting through the silence came faint shouts and screams. Above the west barbican rose a long yellow banner.

"It's the flag of surrender!" Mandine's voice was sharp with shock. "The garrison's opening the gates!"

Key seized her arms, spun her to face him. "Luminessa, run to the palace. Tell Bardas and your father the city's lost. Tell them to get to the east barbican here, as fast as they can. My men are already standing to arms, and we'll be waiting for you. Do you understand?"

Her face was ashen in the trembling firelight. "Yes. Here at the gate."

"Go, my lady, please, *hurry!*"

Mandine turned and ran for the palace tower, hearing as she ran the Tathar drums reawaken in a roar of triumph. She reached the tower door, banged through it, rushed down a stone staircase, and through another door into the gardens. The heavy sweet fragrance of coriyas blossoms hung in the air, and lights glimmered orange in the palace ahead. In the faint illumination she saw a guard at the main doorway, his spear at the ready.

"Halt! Identify!"

"Mandine Dascaris," she cried out. "Open!"

He obeyed, and she raced past him into the great building. Up the Grand Staircase she ran, and along the Gallery of Hermodia. Her lungs burned, and spots of blackness swam in her vision. At last, panting, she stumbled into the lamplit Kellion, and saw Bardas and her father raise startled eyes.

"What—"

"The city's lost," she gasped, as she sagged against a document cabinet. "The garrison's surrendered. Kienan Mec Brander says his men will wait for us at Dynasts' Gate. Father, we've got to go."

"Betrayed?" Archates' voice was a trembling thread. *"Betrayed?"*

"Yes. Oh, please, Father, come quickly. Can't you hear the drums?"

Bardas said, "How do you know about the gates?"

"The standard's been lowered. Someone's raised the yellow flag on the west barbican."

Bardas swore, and snatched up his sword from a map chest. "If she's right, my lord," he said urgently, "we have to leave, and leave now."

"But where's Cardutos?" Mandine said, remembering the engineering officer's concern for her.

"Damn Cardutos," said her father. His voice still shook, but he had pulled himself together and, like Bardas, was buckling on his sword. "He's on the walls somewhere. It doesn't matter."

"My lord," Bardas said, "the luminessa's armor isn't here yet—"

"On your head be it, fool. You should have seen to it earlier." Archates was already out the door, and did not see what Mandine saw: Bardas's face contorting with outrage and insult, as they followed the fleeing Dynast at a run.

Key hurried down from the parapet, from where he had been watching the Tathars, and took Rush's reins from Melias. Behind the peltarch, the cataphract column waited at the east barbican's gate passage. Within the passage itself, four dismounted cataphracts stood ready to raise the gate bars. The barbican's militia garrison had already melted away.

"A hundred and seventy-seven of us present for duty," Melias reported, "including yourself, sir. How does it look out there?"

"They've given us an opening," Key said. "I saw a lot of lanterns on the move—Tathar infantry heading for the west gate. It'll make it easier for us to get out."

"Yes, sir," Melias said, without much conviction. He peered toward the Summer Palace. "Where in the name of the Allfather *are* they?"

"There," Key said, as he saw the three figures hurrying from the small gate in the palace wall. It was none too soon. Fifteen minutes had passed since she left him, and they were running out of time.

The trio, Mandine in her gray cloak and two men in black ones, reached him. Key, uncertain in the darkness about who was Archates, saluted. The shorter man said, "I am the Dynast. Who's got the fastest mount?"

"Trooper Melias does, my lord Dynast."

"I'll ride with him," said Archates. "Bardas, find yourself an animal. You, securion. See to my daughter."

"Yes, my lord," Key muttered. He barely managed to keep his contempt from his voice. Not only was the man unfit to rule, he would not even attend, as a father should, to his daughter's safety before his own.

"My lord Brander?" Mandine stood before him. "With whom shall I ride?"

"With me, my lady. My Rush here is almost as fast as Melias's hippaxa." Key mounted, reached down, and swung Mandine onto Rush's back. Melias was already in the saddle and helping Archates up behind him. Bardas had gone farther down the column.

"I have no armor or helmet," she murmured over his shoulder. "There wasn't time."

"You won't need them," Key said. They had to run, not fight; if fighting slowed them, they were as good as dead, armored or not. "Hold on to me, as tight as you can."

Her arms encircled his waist and clamped around him, and he was sure he could feel her warmth, even through his mail. In the west the Tathar storming drums boomed and thundered, and under the heavy beat he heard screams and wails, the people of Essardene crying out in terror. For them there was no escape, as there was no escape for the eleven wounded cataphracts left behind in the barracks. They'd known what it meant, when he told them earlier this evening, and they'd asked for their daggers. The Tathars would find none of them alive.

Key started the cavalry column into the gate passage. The four dismounted cataphracts heaved the bars loose, then ran for their mounts as the massive wooden leaves swung open. The instant the gap allowed two hippaxas abreast, Key shouted, "*Ride*," and spurred Rush into a charge.

✳ 7

THE THOUSANDS-CAPTAIN OF DRAGOONS KICKED THE prisoner into the pool of lanternlight before Duke Ragula's tent. Ragula looked the captive up and down, and the man fell to his knees as if his sinews had given way. He wore good armor, but had lost his helmet. A dark bruise stained his left cheek. His eyes were terrified.

"Report," Ragula said to the dragoon officer.

"This goldskin came out as soon as the gates opened, great Duke. My men wanted to put it on a stake, but it looks to be an officer, so I thought it might know where the Dynast is."

"You did well." Ragula's gaze flicked to Essardene's torchlit east gate. For the past ten minutes, a torrent of infantry and horsemen had been pouring into the city. The garrison no doubt hoped their surrender might save Essardene from the horrors of storm, sack, and massacre, but in that they were wrong. The city had sheltered the Dynast, and its people were forfeit. Many would suffer worse deaths than flaying and impalement, for the king had promised Erkai a free hand with the captives.

Ragula looked down at the prisoner. "Who are you?" he demanded. He had a rough command of the Logomenon, the common tongue of the Ascendancy and beyond, and in spite of his accent the man understood him.

"I'm the city militia commander. My lord, I—"

"Be quiet. Militia commander, eh? Did you order the gates opened?"

"Yes. My lord, I beg you—"

The duke gestured. The thousands-captain hit the man across the face. The Ascendancer moaned and fell silent. Ragula said, "Where's the Dynast?"

"My lord, the . . . the Dynast is still in the Summer Palace."

Ragula narrowed his eyes. "How do you know this?"

"Everyone in the city knows it, my lord."

"You die on a stake if you're wrong," Ragula began, and stopped abruptly as two men walked into the puddle of lanternlight. One was Erkai, and the other—

"Dread King," Ragula said, and prostrated himself on the muddy, trampled grass. The thousands-captain followed, after striking the prisoner facedown in the dirt.

"Get up, Ragula," said Hetlik. "You also, thousands-captain. What have we here? A goldskin officer?"

"Yes, Dread King, the militia commander." Ragula scrambled to his feet. Though the duke was a large man, Hetlik, King of the Hegemon of the Tathars, outstripped him by far in height and bulk. The king's one eye stared down at Ragula; a silver plate gleamed over the socket of the other. Many years ago, Hetlik had fought his three brothers for the throne, and the third and last brother had gouged the eye out before dying.

Hetlik prodded the prone captive with a booted toe. "An officer, is it? What's it doing here?"

"It says it gave the order to surrender. Also, it says the Dynast's still in the Summer Palace."

Erkai glided forward. "Then we must be quick," he said, without waiting for the king to speak. "The Summer Palace is on the farside of the city, my lord Ragula. If Archates decides to break out with those cataphracts, can your men stop them?" He paused, and added deliberately, "They couldn't keep them from getting in, this morning."

Ragula glowered at him. "The palisades weren't up, this morning. They're almost finished now. Perhaps, Erkai, if you think my men's steel isn't enough, you might try your own profession. We've seen little enough of it, when it comes to fighting."

"Ragula," warned the king, "take care. Erkai has already made preparations."

"Yes, Dread Lord," the duke said quickly. "I spoke only out of concern for our victory."

Hetlik turned to Erkai. "Are you sure your craft will prevent Archates' escape?"

Erkai did not quite shrug. "Majesty, nothing is sure. But this morning I set lurking-spells on the four roads that lead out of Essardene. If I waken them, they will mislead anyone using those roads, and such persons will believe they are going where they are not. Nevertheless, illusions are best backed by armed men. If the Dynast is in the Summer Palace, he'll likely try to slip off by the east road. Send Duke Ragula that way with horsemen, and the Dynast may fall into his hands like a ripe bellberry. All the duke needs to do is keep to the pursuit, and ignore signs that he is going the wrong way."

Hetlik's grin was savage. "Good. Waken your spells, Erkai. Ragula, get men, and go."

Ragula turned on his heel and stalked off. Hetlik watched expectantly as Erkai looked down at the prisoner. "Well?" the king asked.

"This is poor stuff," Erkai said, "but it must do. Bring it into the tent."

The militia commander had understood nothing of the Tathar conversation that had just decided his fate, and he remained docile as the thousands-captain pulled him to his feet and shoved him through the tent door. There, in the smoky orange light of the oil lamps, Erkai put a hand on the man's throat, gazed into his eyes, and began to murmur softly. The captive's eyes glazed. Slowly, his body stiffened and became rigid. The king and the thousands-captain looked on in uneasy fascination.

The chain slithered from Erkai's sleeve, crept over his hand, and glided onto the prisoner's face, where it paused at the frozen lips. Erkai's eyes, the pupils now contracted to black points, remained fixed on the captive's. Then the chain's head slid into the man's left nostril. The rest followed, squirming slowly into the skull like a worm into a wormhole. The man quivered, as though straining against unseen bonds. His paralyzed face remained expressionless, but agony and horror now stared from his eyes. Hetlik gave a soft grunt and his fingers twitched. The dragoon captain shifted nervously on the balls of his feet, edging very slightly toward the tent doorway.

Suddenly the lamps flickered and almost went out. The man gave a strangled gasp, then shrieked. Erkai sucked in the shriek and the gasp, swallowed them, and spat into the air. The spittle became a smoky, luminous orb that hung trembling in the gloom. Then it gathered itself, and with a hiss shot through the tent flap and vanished into the night. The tent leather drummed and cracked in a torrent of wind, then stilled.

The chain seeped from between the prisoner's bloodless lips and returned to Erkai's sleeve. Erkai released the man's throat. The corpse folded as though boneless and crumpled to the ground. The lamps suddenly burned bright, showing a glaze of sweat on Erkai's face.

"It is done," he said, as he allowed his concentration to break.

"Good," said Hetlik, and swallowed. The dragoon backed toward the tent door, and, without Hetlik's permission, fled.

The hippaxas were almost at the gap in the palisade when the Tathar sentries raised the alarm. Their shouts and horns sounded too late, for most of the silverhair infantry, with the fragrance of pillage in their nostrils, were already hurrying away to join in the rape of Essardene. Key aimed Rush at the breach between the sharpened stakes, and she shot through the opening. Tathar worklights showed the dark gash of a trench ahead; Rush soared over it, cleared a mound of earth, and left the diggings behind. Key glimpsed tents, high-wheeled wagons, and the skeleton of an unfinished siege tower. Ahead, spectral in the starlight, glimmered the pale band of the road to the Inner Sea.

Mandine's voice sounded in his ear. "Are we going to make it?"

"Yes," Key answered, for the first time allowing himself hope. He looked over his shoulder. As far as he could tell in the starlight, the cataphract column was intact, without stragglers. He and Mandine rode in the lead, with Melias and the Dynast ten yards behind. With luck, they might get clean away.

Mandine said, "I see lights moving back there. I think they're coming toward us."

Key looked, and saw that she was right. A dozen sparks had detached themselves from the Tathar campfires: torches, carried by horsemen. At this distance they seemed to move slowly, but their movement was full of purpose.

"It doesn't matter," he said. "We're on hippaxas, and they aren't."

He settled down to ride. Wind rushed in his ears. Mandine's arms were locked tight around his waist, and for a fleeting moment Key was almost happy. He wanted to ride into the night, with her behind him, forever.

Watch for Tathar pickets, he told himself sharply.

Ahead, the road descended in a curve to enter a wooded valley. Key glanced at the stars, to judge their direction of travel. To his surprise, the Crown's points of light were disarranged, and the other constellations were blurred.

And they were in the wrong place.

"Something's wrong," he called over his shoulder. "This isn't the right road. It's tending west, not east."

"What? It has to be. There's no other road from Dynast's Gate."

"It isn't. By the stars, we're going back to Essardene." He peered into the darkness. Ahead the valley opened out, the road still curving to the right. Lights appeared, like red sparks. He saw a distant pale blur beyond them, and suddenly a far-off tongue of flame speared into the sky above the blur.

"It's Essardene," Mandine cried. "It's *ahead* of us."

"Pull up," Key shouted. "Pull up. Column, halt."

He heard the order pass back along the formation. Curses and hippaxa bellows echoed from the valley sides as riders and animals collided in the darkness.

"What are you doing, you fools?" Archates shouted. "Why are we stopping? They're behind us!"

"Father, the road's wrong," Mandine called. "It's going back to the city. Look, up ahead!"

A second double-mounted hippaxa cantered up, and stopped. Bardas's voice came from the dark figure behind the rider. "It's true, my lord. But the Tathars are behind us, too."

Archates' voice became shrill. "Then where are we?"

"I don't know," Bardas said. Key saw the pale blur of the man's face turn upward. Suddenly the auctator burst out, "Look! Look at the sky!"

Key also looked up. The stars were too bright, bright as tiny moons, the constellations unrecognizable. He heard fear in his men's voices, as they muttered and exclaimed at the apparitions above them.

"Sorcery!" Archates quavered. "Sorcery! Lady and the All-father sustain us!"

"And look at the Crown!" cried Bardas. "This is no hedge-wizard's work! It's too powerful—"

Mandine suddenly called out over Key's shoulder, making him jump. "Father, it's in the accounts of the rebellion! They said Erkai could make roads go wrong! The Tathar prisoner was telling the truth. Erkai's alive after all! This is *him*!"

"But in those days he couldn't touch the stars!" Panic laced the Dynast's voice. "Great Allfather, he's *grown*."

So it's Erkai come again, Key thought, with a cold dread in the pit of his stomach. He had never fought with black sorcery in the air, and the Craft that had twisted the road and was brightening the stars was powerful, and full of malice. He could feel it now, coiling in the dark beneath the trees, gathering in the sky overhead.

From the distance behind, hooves drummed. "They're coming!" Archates wailed. "Erkai's bespelled us for them."

Mandine's arms tightened around Key. All our effort, he thought, come to this. "Fifth Cataphracts!" he shouted. "Prepare to meet charge, facing to column rear! Third pelta, reserve for countercharge!"

The men nearest Key shook into formation. What the others were doing, he could not tell in the gloom. He took up his shield, drew his sword, and turned Rush toward the oncoming Tathars. Perhaps they could drive the silverhairs back, gain enough time to find an escape from the trap.

"You've got to get me away!" Archates yelled, presumably at Melias. "Damn you, trooper, into the trees!"

"Melias, stand fast!" Key snapped. "My lord Dynast, riding blind into the forest is no good. If we've lost our direction through sorcery, you might meet Tathars no matter which way you went." He thought hurriedly; a panicky Dynast in the ranks would be a liability to his men. "Melias, fall back along the road a little, and try to keep our lord Archates out of the fighting. His life is too precious to risk."

"Yes, sir."

"Bardas!" Archates said. "Come with me. I need a bodyguard."

"Yes, my lord Dynast." The two hippaxas, bearing their four riders, moved off into the gloom. Key turned his attention to their pursuers. The Tathars' streaming torches were closing fast. Mandine said, "What are we going to do?"

"We'll have to fight our way out. If you fall off, run for the trees, no matter what I told your father." He hesitated. "There's a dagger in my belt. Take it. Use it if you can't get away."

He felt a tug at his waist. "I have it," she said. "I won't let them take me, Key."

From down the road, shrill Tathar war hoots cut the air as the enemy slammed into the cataphract rear guard. Steel clanged, cries of fury and pain rose to the distorted sky. Key listened, judging the Tathar strength. From the sound, they were more than two hundred, but not a thousand. Against a hundred and seventy-seven cataphracts that was uneven, but not desperately uneven. Rush quivered beneath him, and tossed her horned black head. He waited. He would have to judge by instinct when to throw his reserve at the Tathars.

Suddenly there were hoofbeats close by in the gloom. Key yelled, "Third pelta, enemy on the left flank! Countercharge, wheel left, *go!*"

He heard the thud of hippaxas' pads as the animals broke into a run. Hammer of metal on metal nearby, a wild shrill ululation, still nearer. He spun Rush around, raised his shield—

A rider came at him, spearpoint edged with the blazing starlight. Key took the blade on his shield, slashed as the rider hurtled past. Instinctively he glanced back to find the man, as Rush chose that moment to dance sideways. He slipped off-balance, with his sword lying across the saddlebow. Without warning a second Tathar was upon him, on his right and un-protected side. Key saw the saber's blade against the stars' glow, saw the white clawed hand on the black shield. It was Hetlik's war-leader, the great duke himself. He saw Ragula's face, and Ragula his, and Key knew he would never, never raise his sword in time.

Mandine moved violently behind him, and her arm banged across his shoulder as she threw the dagger. Its pommel struck Ragula over the left eye. The blow threw him off his stroke, and the saber glanced harmlessly from Key's mailed forearm. Key swung at the duke, aiming for the join of helmet and neckpiece, but a charging hippaxa appeared from nowhere and knocked the duke's horse away. Key caught a last glimpse of Ragula's eyes fixed on his face, and knew he would be remem-bered. Then the duke was gone, into the half-dark, and from the horse sounds, the Tathars seemed to be withdrawing.

The trooper on the hippaxa was yelling at him. "Sir! I missed that one, sorry. Any more back here?"

"I don't think so." The racket of the fighting down the road had died away, but he knew the Tathars would regroup and try again. Half-turning, he said to Mandine, "You saved us with that throw."

"I was trying to kill him," Mandine said fiercely. "I missed, I'm sorry."

"You still stopped him from cutting us down. Where's your father?"

Archates and Bardas were not far away, under the roadside trees. As Key rode up to them, Bardas snapped, "What are you playing at, securion? Can't you do better than this?"

"I'm not a sorcerer, lord auctator." Key looked west, west that should have been east. Essardene was still there in the distance, aglow with flames. He saw sparks move between the valley's end and the city. More Tathars, approaching fast. Were they illusion, or reality? Could the spell have been powerful enough actually to shift the road, and it really was Essardene up there?

He had no idea, but the Tathars behind them were too many to overcome. Surely, if they could ride long enough in a straight line, they'd escape the spell's influence. It had to be the trees, after all. He swung Rush around, and called, "Form rank by pelta. Ride into the woods, left of the march line."

He waited for a moment until he heard the order repeated, then spurred Rush for the trees. The hippaxas carrying Archates and Bardas were close behind him. As they passed under the first branches, Key heard the bray of a Tathar war horn. The silverhairs had taken up the pursuit again, and in dense woodland, in the dark, hippaxas were little faster than horses. Worse, he didn't know the terrain. The Tathars might trap them against a cliff, or a river gorge. He remembered Thorn River, and his heart sank. They had to get to clear ground, out of the woods, where they could run for it.

He gave Rush her head, trusting her night vision to keep them from hitting tree trunks. All around him, undergrowth thrashed and twigs cracked as his men cursed and fought their way through the darkness. The Tathars were ululating behind them, but he wasn't sure whether the cries were closing in or falling back.

After a few minutes he lost his sense of direction. He glimpsed stars through the leaves overhead, but they were as malevolently bright as before and told him nothing. At length the ground rose slowly, and the trees seemed to be thinning a little. It might be the edge of the woodland. Mandine held tight to him, but she hadn't spoken since they left the road.

"Are you all right?" he said over his shoulder.

"Yes. Don't worry about me."

The trees suddenly ended. He saw dark rising ground ahead, a ridge, but the spell was still upon them, for the stars were still too bright, the constellations still awry. Key jabbed his heels into Rush's flanks, and heard his men yell as they broke out of the forest. The yells were answered with Tathar baying, and again the hoot of war horns. Rush pelted upward, and as they neared the ridge's summit Key saw a dim glow at the skyline. He swore and reined her in, but she was running hard, and he couldn't stop her until she reached the top.

"Oh, no!" Mandine gasped.

He had lost his sense of direction indeed. In the valley below and ahead of them, Essardene stood in flames. He stared at the city for a long moment, then drew his sword. The heights would give them a place to stand, until they were overwhelmed. His mouth was dry as ash, the taste of his failure. From his right he heard his men's yells turn to cries of disbelief and despair as they saw the burning city.

"We're not going to get away, are we?" she asked softly.

"No," he said. He turned Rush around, to face the enemy. Bardas and Archates were close by. Bardas had his blade out, but Archates was only muttering a disjointed stream of oaths.

"Look!" Mandine exclaimed abruptly. "Over there!"

Key looked around. He saw a faint glimmer of light to their left, where the woodland crept up to the crest of the ridge. He squinted at it, and it took form. A figure stood there, limned in a pale glow. "I see it. I think it's a wood sprite."

Her shiver transmitted itself even through his mail. "It's not. Sweet Lady, it's one of the Near Folk! I think it's trying to help us!"

She might be right, but he didn't trust it. What would hemandri be doing here, so close to a city of men, so close to battle and war? "It could be a trap," he said, as he watched the unmoving pillar of spectral light.

"It's not. I know it isn't. Follow it, Key. It's our only hope. I know it. *Please.*"

Her passionate certainty convinced him. But he couldn't go without his men, and desert them as Archates had deserted the army. He didn't know if they all could see the ghostly beacon, and already he could hear the *uluu-uluu-uluu* as the Tathars worked themselves up for another charge. Yet not to ride away was to condemn Mandine to death.

He stared in desperate indecision at the glimmering figure. Another light appeared above it, something like a huge bird. It floated upward, lost itself in the trees, and as it did so the figure also faded out. The air about Key shuddered, then hissed and gusted as if two angry winds labored against each other. Puffs of dust rose from the ground, and suddenly, where the bird had vanished, a treetop silently burst into violet flame.

"It's for us, Key!" Mandine cried. "For us!"

He had no idea how she knew this, but it was the beacon he needed. "Cataphracts!" he shouted. "Ride to the burning tree! Repeat order, down the line!"

He spurred Rush, and she sprang toward the violet blaze. Only it was not truly fire; lavender flame streamed from the tree's branches, but did not consume them. Now Rush sped beneath the beacon, and in front of Key suddenly loomed a massive trunk. Before he could pull her aside, the black pillar of wood wavered, and to his shock they rode straight through it. Some at least of his men were coming; he could hear the soft drum of hippaxas running, and yells of bloodlust as the Tathars charged.

The wood turned ghostly. They plunged through another trunk, then through a boulder that should have shattered Rush's breastbone. Rush seemed not to notice them; she ran as if she were on an open flat. Key could see through the leaf canopy above, as though it were gossamer, and he realized that the harsh brilliance of the stars was fading.

"We're getting out!" he shouted. "The spell's breaking!"

As he said it, the spectral forest faded away, dissolved into thin air. The night shook itself, and Key's eyesight blurred almost to vanishing. He yelped with surprise, heard Mandine cry out, and then, as his vision cleared and Rush surged under him, he looked up.

The world was restored. In the sky hung the Archer and the Crown, bright as new silver, exactly where they should be. Ahead lay the road to the east, shining under the newly risen moon. Key found himself shaking with relief as Rush flew onward. He had thought himself dead, and her also. "They can't catch us now, Luminessa," he called. "Is your father back there?"

A pause. "Yes, I see him."

"But what happened? Why did the Near Folk help us?"

"I don't know," Mandine answered. "I have no idea."

"It doesn't matter now. We're away. Hang on, my lady."

They rode all night, and into the morning. Ragula's men fell far behind, and at last gave up the chase. A hundred and sixty-two cataphracts survived, more than Key had dared hope. They encountered a small Tathar patrol shortly after sunrise, but the enemy took to their heels at the sight of hippaxas and never reappeared. In the early afternoon they reached the coast, and the small fishing town of Aptera. Though the Tathars had not yet attacked the place, its people had already fled in their boats. But offshore, oars flashing in the sun, cruised two long black dromons, warships of the Ascendancy fleet. The cataphracts broke discipline and cheered until Archates silenced them, before Key could do so, with a furious shout.

But there were no transports for the hippaxas, and the dromons were not built for any cargoes but fighting men. Knowing the Tathars would kill the animals if they caught them, Key ordered them released. Rush didn't seem to know what to do with her freedom, and tried to follow him as he started back through the town gate. With an aching throat, he struck her across the rump, as hard as he could. She bellowed, tossed her vast horned head, and lumbered away into the afternoon sunlight.

He got his men onto the ships and boarded the dromon that carried Mandine. He was hoping she might be on deck when they sailed, so that he might at least exchange a word with her. But Melias told him she had gone to the shipmaster's cabin, on her father's orders.

Key made sure his men were settled and out of the way of the crew. Then he stood at the dromon's stern alone, watching the land fade to a distant blue-green haze, and vanish into the summer sea.

II

CAPTALA

8

AT THE FOURTH HOUR OF THE AFTERNOON, MAJOLIS Latias's concentration was broken by a clatter below his open office window. He raised his eyes from his papers, listened to the racket of shod hooves on granite paving, and frowned. A horse in the Grand Kellion's inner court was a breach of protocol, unless a very exalted person rode it.

The High Chamberlain rose from his desk and walked to the window to look down. There, three stories below him in the courtyard, Tracien Bardas was dismounting from his horse, while an aide held the animal's reins. Latias noted the triple golden band at the hem of Bardas's short blue military cloak. So the man had received his promotion after all, in spite of the debacle at Thorn River. He was now a treimarch: commander in chief, after the Dynast, of the Ascendancy's armed forces.

Or of what's left of them, Latias thought. Below, Bardas vanished into the building. The chamberlain half turned from the window, and called, "Phylact!"

Latias's secretary appeared in the doorway to the outer office. Phylact also had a window above the courtyard and certainly knew who had arrived, but his round bland face showed as little expression as ever.

"Yes, Eminence?"

"Tracien Bardas is here, unannounced as usual. I am unfortunately occupied for the moment. Give him my compliments, offer him refreshments, and require him to wait."

"Yes, Eminence. For how long?"

Latias glanced at the massive ring-clock that *tocked* softly across from his desk. Only three such clocks existed in all Captala Nea. The second stood in the Red Council Chamber of the Dynast's residence; the third, much larger, occupied the bell tower of the Pantechnion and sounded the hours for the entire city.

"About one turn of the sand-glass. I will ring for you. Close the door."

Phylact nodded, and silently vanished. Latias permitted himself a half smile. Bardas would be infuriated at the wait, but he would have to swallow his fury. Latias, as chamberlain of the Grand Kellion and therefore head of the Ascendancy's civil service and its treasury, had more power than Bardas did . . . especially now, with the army destroyed. It would do no harm to remind the man of his standing.

The chamberlain gazed out the open window. The Kellion offices occupied the upper floors of the Numera, the ancient fortress on the crown of Dynasts' Hill, and from there Latias could look across half the city, to Chalice Bay and the distant glint of the sea. If he leaned well over the sill to look left and downward, he would glimpse the green-tiled roofs of the Dynasteon, where Archates resided and held court. On the hill's slopes below the Dynasteon were the lesser buildings of the palace complex, set among fountain-fed pools and gardens luminous with flowers, the whole guarded by a towering bluestone wall. And beyond the palace's sprawl stretched the metropolis: Captala Nea, greatest and richest city of the known world, symbol and guardian of the Ascendancy for seventeen hundred years.

And now, Latias reflected morosely, a city in mourning. At the news of Thorn River, Captala had cried out with one voice, cried out for husbands, fathers, sons, for the multitude of the slain. As the word continued to spread through the

Ascendancy, so would that cry, and by month's end many a family would have hung a mourning wreath of dark green bittersweet at the house door. Latias himself wore a sprig of it, pinned to his tunic with a brooch of jet.

The chamberlain squinted against the light. In the far distance, Captala Nea's colossal triple walls rose into the golden heat haze of afternoon. Those walls had never been breached, though they had known bitter sieges; twice from the Sea Peoples long ago, once from the Scaths when the Ascendancy had been weakened by famine, twice from rebel armies during a succession war ten generations back. Their battlements ran twenty-five miles around, and an army would be hard-pressed to march a full circuit of them in a long midsummer's day. They were the strongest fortifications in the known world; even ancient, drowned Fallas Gaea had possessed nothing like them.

So, Latias thought, *Captala is as impregnable as it is possible for a city to be. The Tathars may be coming, but while we have the eight thousand men of the Paladine Guard, plus the city militia, and control of the sea, King Hetlik may save his breath to cool his porridge . . . unless it's true that Erkai has come back.*

A frown creased his high, smooth forehead. Was it really Erkai the Chain who bewitched the road from Essardene? Latias found the proposition almost too disturbing to accept. But to judge by Archates' account, the spell that misdirected his party outside Essardene had been a very powerful one, and precisely the kind of Craft work that Erkai had used in his rebellion two generations back. Then there was the information provided by the captured Tathar at Essardene, who was unlikely to have fabricated such a story out of whole cloth. Along with both these pieces of evidence was the novel determination of the Tathars; the scale of this attack was unprecedented since their defeat by Galion Tessaris, a century and a half ago. So it was very probably Erkai who faced the Ascendancy again, much as Latias was loath to believe it.

He summoned his optimism. Powerful though Erkai now seemed to be, the spell that had so terrified Archates was an illusion, and illusions could not pierce the defenses of Captala Nea. Nor could any power of the Black Craft; Athanais the White Diviner had seen to that, at Captala's founding. She had laid the walls' foundations with the aid of the Deep Magic, not long before she set the Ban, and in a deep recess at every gate she placed a stone beam, carved with the Deep Magic's now-indecipherable symbols. When those beams were drawn from their sockets (so Athanais had promised long ago) no Black Craft spell could affect the walls or gates, nor touch anyone within them.

Her ancient sorcery did not, however, secure the city against armed attack. For that, Latias reminded himself, there must be soldiers to man Captala's ramparts, and especially to protect the Water Fort's naval harbor, so that ships could get men and supplies into the city. Only if the Tathars somehow cut the sea road could they starve Captala into surrender. That was unlikely, for the invaders, fortunately, had little knowledge of ships. Archates had weakened the Ascendancy's navy by drafting sailors and marines into the land forces, but a hundred dromons still remained. The big galleys, beaked with iron-shod rams and armed with catapults, would protect the sea-lanes from the unlikely prospect of Tathar interference.

Still, it would take a well-led field army to defeat the White Death decisively, and the trained men slaughtered at Thorn River could not be easily or quickly replaced. The immediate future looked grim, for the Tathars were the most formidable enemy the Ascendancy had faced in its long history. They were still at Essardene, but that was only fourteen days' march away for their tireless foot soldiers, much less for their hordes of cavalry. Captala would soon be under siege, and nothing in Archates' power, or in the chamberlain's, could prevent it.

Latias sighed and returned to his desk. Faintly, through the thick kingwood door, he heard a deep, annoyed voice. That was Bardas, trying to browbeat Phylact into giving him entry. It would do the treimarch no good; when ordered to be obstinate, the secretary was as immovable as Temple Mount.

The chamberlain picked up the document he had been

working on before the interruption. It was a dictum increasing hearth taxes; the treasury was empty, and a new army, if the Tathars allowed time to raise it, would cost a great deal of money. Latias read the dictum through, made a small correction, and carefully dated it. All it needed now was Archates' signature and seal. A dozen more tax dicta waited in a pile at Latias's elbow.

Bardas's voice rose again. Perhaps it was a bad idea to keep the man waiting too long. Latias reached for the bellpull behind his desk, but his fingers had only brushed the tassel when the door flew open, crashed against the wall, and rebounded. Bardas stood in the doorway, eyebrows arched in fury.

"Your secretary is obstructive, Chamberlain," he snapped. "Do you permit him to delay everyone in this manner?"

Latias rose smoothly to his feet, and gave a precisely correct bow. "I am troubled at your displeasure, my lord. I plead duty as a reason."

Bardas gave a curt nod. "Duty, yes."

"Please sit down," Latias said. He gestured at the pearl-inlaid sideboard. "Will you have wine?"

"No." Bardas dropped into the carved chair opposite the desk. "I'll have money."

"Ah." Latias likewise seated himself. He nodded at the triple gold band on Bardas's cloak. "Congratulations on your promotion, by the way, Treimarch."

Bardas shrugged, but Latias noted a flash of gratified vanity in the man's eyes. "You're gracious, my lord Chamberlain," he said. "Back your words with coin and I'll be content."

Latias touched the stack of papers. "The tax dicta are here. This evening the Dynast will authorize them. Shortly the money will begin to flow."

"I need it now, not shortly. There is an army to raise and equip. The Tathars will not wait while your tax gatherers squeeze the population."

"The treasury is empty," Latias said. "And, unfortunately,

I cannot transmute the lead on the Numera's roofs into gold. I would do so if I could."

"Use the moneylenders."

Latias looked pained. "They do not want to lend money to the government. The treasury has been unable to meet payments on the vast debts already incurred. This has ruined a number of the lenders, and the rest plead impoverishment."

"Very well. In that case I want a dictum of military requisition, for both money and supplies. There's plenty of grain and iron in private hands, and if the moneylenders won't lend what they've got left, they can donate it. Even if they do so with their feet to a fire."

So you'll raise an army, Latias thought, *and you and Archates will throw it away, as you did the last one. I'm no soldier, and I could do better than this. If I were on the throne—*

But even if Archates and Archates' daughters vanished tomorrow, he never could be, despite his power and influence. The Latiae were of the lesser nobility, but that was not a real barrier, for Dynasts had come from that rank before. The barrier was a physical one.

Latias was a eunuch. Yet because he was already adult when gelded, he appeared completely a man, slender and lean-faced, his voice a masculine tenor. He had been thus since his twentieth year, when the marsh-boar and its ten inches of razor tusks came up a spear shaft to slice his manhood away. The accident, ironically, had been the making of him. Eunuchs were rare in the Ascendancy, and Dynasts who sat uneasily on the throne valued them for high positions. Barred from the supreme power because they could not produce a successor, they could not threaten the man who wore the diadem, and an exceptionally able eunuch could rise very far indeed. As had Latias.

"A dictum of requisition is possible," he said carefully. "Will you propose it to the Dynast?"

"Why don't you?"

"Your influence with the Dynast in military affairs is greater than mine," Latias said. This was not precisely true.

But if the dictum precipitated riots, he wanted the disturbances at Bardas's door. Also, flattery was never wasted.

The treimarch pulled at his chin. "All right. I'll go to the Dynasteon after I leave here. You'll put the paperwork through as fast as possible?"

Idiot, Latias thought. *No wonder you and Archates blundered into the Tathars. Can't see a potential ambush to save your life. And on top of that, to be incompetent enough to get trapped in Essardene, with Mandine there, too. If you hadn't all been very, very, fortunate, Theatana would now be ruling in her father's place. And we have enough disasters without that.*

"Certainly," he said. "By tomorrow."

"Good." Bardas sounded quite amiable now. There was a pause, during which the ring-clock *tocked* four times. Then Bardas said, "The Dynast *will* see you tonight? He's been keeping, ah . . . very private since he returned here."

This was an understatement. Only a day had passed since a dispatch boat sailed into Captala with news of Archates: apparently the Dynast and his party (including, to Latias's astonishment, the elder luminessa) had escaped from Essardene, reached the harbor of Aptera, and found a dromon squadron there. The dispatch boat's master said that Archates was aboard a warship, three hours behind. Latias hurriedly summoned a state carriage, and accompanied it and a Paladine Guard escort to meet Archates at the Water Fort. The city also turned out to greet its Dynast, but not with rejoicing at his deliverance. As the carriage rolled toward the palace, the crowds along Central Street did not cheer; they muttered. Latias, following on horseback, heard several shouts of *Where's the army?* Even with the Paladine Guard escort it was a very tense journey, and the chamberlain half expected stones or at least rotten vegetables to fly. None did, probably because Mandine's presence in the carriage restrained the crowd. Unlike Theatana, she had always been popular in the city.

That was yesterday evening. Since then, Archates had shut himself in the Dynasteon, seeing no one but Latias, Bardas, and a few military men Bardas had proposed to replace the senior officers killed at Thorn River. For the moment, Latias was running the government by himself.

"I'm sure the Dynast will see me tonight," he said. "Did you have a larger concern, Treimarch?"

"None in particular. I have thought that perhaps Archates should show himself to the people, to reassure them. But perhaps the Dynast is merely fatigued. Temporarily, of course."

"No doubt," Latias said. He did not believe that the sight of Archates would reassure the people very much, but he would not say so to Bardas.

Tock, said the ring-clock.

Tock.

Tock.

"Although he is not himself," Bardas added. "Do you agree?"

Latias leaned back in his chair. "He has much on his mind."

"Yes," said Bardas. "As do we all. This is a terrible time in our history. It needs leaders with strength of will and character."

By the Allfather, Latias thought, *is he sounding me out, to see if I might consider . . . changing allegiance?* With a smile, he said, "Then we're fortunate that we have such men as you, Treimarch. It's unfortunate that Cardutos didn't get out of Essardene. He was a good engineer."

"That's true," Bardas said, without much interest. "Cardutos was indeed a loss. The question is, do we have *enough* men of strength and will among us? Are there, perhaps, some who are adequate in peaceful times, but less suitable in war?"

"I'm not a soldier," admitted Latias, "but it seems to me that the new general staff is very satisfactory. Is that not your opinion?" *Yes*, he thought, *Bardas is indeed sounding my loyalty. How could my spies have overlooked this, unless it's just begun? Yet Bardas would not be this bold unless he already had someone of consequence on his side. So who else is there? The other senior commanders? Some, obviously. But there's something more here—*

A click in his memory. Three incidents, in routine informant reports. Not so routine, perhaps.

The reports mentioned Theatana. On two occasions, just before Archates marched west with the army, an observer saw Bardas speaking with her in the Alia Gardens. Yesterday evening, apparently by chance, the treimarch met the younger luminessa again in the gardens, where Theatana and her maidservants were taking the air. Theatana and Bardas had spent several minutes in private conversation. The informant did not know what they had discussed.

"You wish my opinion of the general staff?" Bardas said. "There's nothing wrong with it—the Dynast appointed the new officers himself. Certainly the *staff* is adequate."

The emphasis was subtle, but deliberate: The staff was good enough, but the Dynast was not. Yet Bardas had said nothing that Latias could use against him. He might be a fool, but he was not so much a fool as that.

"My mind is eased to hear it," Latias said. "These times do indeed require strength and competence." *Theatana and Bardas,* thought the chamberlain. *It's possible. I should not have disregarded those reports. But why Theatana? If Archates dies, Bardas's way to the throne is through Mandine, not through her half sister. Unless, that is, Theatana has encouraged him in such a direction. He might believe she'd marry him in exchange for helping her to the throne. But if he believes that, he's misjudged her badly. Dynastessas have ruled alone before now, and if Theatana ever got her hands on that power, she'd never share it with anyone.*

Bardas remained silent, idly stroking the chair arm with his right thumb. Latias said, "In my belief, our Dynast merely needs rest to restore his powers of decision and command."

"Exactly so," Bardas replied, perhaps a little too promptly, as though he feared he might have overstepped a mark. "This also is my position. I am glad you share it."

"Difficult times require unity of purpose at the highest levels," Latias observed blandly. He decided to try a shift of ground: the sisters. "I was horrified to hear how close the Luminessa Mandine came to being killed."

"It was very close," Bardas agreed.

"It would have been a tragedy. She is much loved by the people of the city. Also, her death would have caused significant political problems, given that Archates intends Theatana to marry the Pargenes boy next year."

The chamberlain's words produced no apparent reaction in Bardas. He merely said, "No doubt."

And it *would* have been a serious problem, Latias reflected, if Mandine had died. Archates would have canceled Theatana's marriage, for if it took place, only the Dynast's life would stand between the younger luminessa's husband and the diadem. Archates would never risk that, not that Aidar Pargenes was a likely usurper. He was a decent enough young man, if a little dull, and he was far from ambitious. Perhaps that was why Theatana despised him. But breaking the marriage contract would have added the wealthy Pargeni to the Dynast's enemies; a pity, since the family had always been loyal to the throne. Latias, who had proposed the match, had intended—still intended—the marriage to cement that loyalty.

A thought struck him. "By the way, what's become of that cataphract officer who rescued the luminessa outside Essardene? According to Phylact, the tale's all over Captala today, and growing in the telling."

Bardas half sneered. "Oh, him. He's an Elthamer, one of that petty nobility from the plateaus. Barbaric name, what was it? Kienan Mec Brander. While we were at sea the luminessa persuaded her father to reward him with the command of her personal escort. So now he's an officer in the Paladine Guard."

"That's a high appointment."

A scowl replaced the sneer. "She also got the Dynast to promote him to victurion. I was against it, but the luminessa has a whim of iron, like all the Dascarids. At least he can't do much damage commanding thirty Paladines."

Latias smiled. "A fortunate young man. Valor and skill rewarded. That's too rare in the world."

"Indeed."

"Anyway," Latias said, allowing indifference to seep into

his voice, "returning to our previous subject, Theatana's marriage will take place as planned."

"Good," Bardas said, with equal indifference. "It's an excellent match."

But is it, from your point of view? Latias wondered. *You've betrayed nothing. So why do I feel there's something here? Theatana in league with Bardas . . . I must watch this closely.*

Bardas rose, adjusting his cloak. "Until we meet, then. You'll make sure the money starts flowing?"

"I will."

The door shut silently behind the treimarch, leaving Latias to gaze unseeing at the richly polished grain of the kingwood panels. He considered reporting the almost-treasonous conversation to Archates, and instantly dismissed the idea. Nothing had been *said*. The true meaning concealed itself in tone and phrasing, in ambiguity, in too-long silences. The treimarch would plausibly deny any treasonous intent, and make Latias look a fool, or worse. It was too soon. He needed more information.

He stood and returned to the window. If he discovered a plot to depose Archates, what then? He was sure he would find it, if it existed; he had spent years constructing his net of spies and observers, and they missed little that happened in the capital. But he now believed he had erred, in paying too little attention to Archates' daughters.

Theatana and Bardas. What is she up to?

He detested the younger luminessa. Nineteen-year-old Theatana had the charm that all the Dascarids—including Archates, in his better moments—could exert, but she also had her father's vicious temper and a streak of outright sadism. Her servants were justly terrified of her, and her mother Eirema had been as bad, if not worse. Sixteen years ago, not long before Eirema's death, Latias's spies had reported that she had an unhealthy, though very discreet, interest in the Black Craft. How far the Dynastessa had gone with that interest he never found out, for Eirema was shipwrecked and drowned while returning by sea from the summer capital. To

Latias's profound relief, the possible scandal, a very serious one, died with her.

At least, Latias thought, *Mandine's fit for civilized company. She has the Dascarid charm, but not the cruelty, and her escape from Bartaxa to Essardene shows she's got the toughness her father so unfortunately lacks. Archates is a weak ruler, no matter what I said to Bardas, and his weakness makes him cruel and cowardly. Worse, it's a pattern. For a century the Dascarids have ruled our Ascendancy, and for half that they've ruled badly. Erkai's was the first rebellion against them, and it showed the way. Every few years some magnate raises a revolt, and off goes the army again to stamp it out. Blood and treasure spent, lands devastated, cities and citizens impoverished, all to no purpose. And the last nine years the worst of all. Two rebellions on the North March, another down in the south, and raid after raid by the Tathars. They've known for years we were weakening. Now we are at the end of our strength, and the barbarians are here. What a misfortune, that Archates' house ever got to the throne. No wonder people like telling stories of the old dynasty. The House Tessaris gave us a golden age, or so it seems to us now, a century later.*

He leaned out the window and craned until he could see Temple Mount. A thin trail of smoke rose from its summit, from the high altar by the House of the Sacred Marriage. They'd be praying over there, and burning incense by the cartload. He drummed his fingers on the windowsill, and his gaze shifted to the northwest and the distant Hill of Remembrance, three miles away. There, through the heat shimmer, rose the tremendous black shaft of the Obelisk, monument to the lost Old Dominion in the east, and to its capital Fallas Gaea, the city once called the Axle of the World.

Latias blinked. The Obelisk blurred suddenly in the quivering, heat-drenched air, and for a long moment appeared to totter and lean. Then, as he blinked again, the illusion vanished. *A bad omen,* the chamberlain thought glumly. *I wish I hadn't noticed it. Seventeen hundred years since the Flood. Are we now to be swept away in a new deluge, this one of barbarian hordes instead of water?*

The clock ticked. The chamberlain shook himself, sighed, and returned to his desk. He leaned back in his chair and looked around his office, at the radiant tapestries, the mechanical marvel of the ring-clock, the crystal decanters on the pearl-inlaid sideboard, the cups of white jade. Outside Captala lay his vineyards and his country house; within the walls stood his splendid city home, rich with art and comfort.

He wanted to keep what he had earned. If a conspiracy overthrew the Dynast, and he had not joined it, he would fare badly at the hands of Bardas and Theatana. Especially Theatana. The younger luminessa loathed him as much as he detested her.

What will I do if I find a conspiracy? And if Theatana is in it? Do I dare warn Archates, if she is? If I do, and she convinces him she's innocent, it will mean my death.

But his oath of office was to the Ascendancy, not to the person of Archates Dascaris. If the Dynast's removal would save the realm, his duty was plain. On the other hand, it was not clear to Latias that Archates' demise would be for the good, at least not at this moment of crisis.

It was too soon to decide. He lacked information. Latias reached behind his chair for the bellpull and tugged it.

A mile away, on a stone table deep within Temple Mount, Orissi the Perpetua, high priestess of the Lady, lay in trance. The scent of rose incense filled the dim room, rising from a small brazier on a bronze tripod. Hanging above the table was an array of a dozen bronze lanterns, of which only three were lit.

The Continuator, high priest of the Allfather and Orissi's husband, sat beside her with head bowed, his lips moving in silent prayer. His name was Taras. He was a man of middle age, gaunt of face and limb, with a short graying beard and bristle-cut hair. His hands, which rested open and palm up on his knees, were so slender as to be almost frail.

The lanterns flickered. The Perpetua's eyelids also flickered, and she opened her eyes. Their pupils were huge and dark. The Continuator ceased praying and sat still and silent, waiting for her complete return. She had been away for a long time.

A minute passed, then two. The Continuator became slightly alarmed. "Orissi?" he said.

His wife slowly turned her head toward him. "I dreamed the true dream, Taras," she said, in a soft, thick voice.

Taras stood up, went to a cabinet, and poured half a goblet of watered white wine. Though she was normally the most even-tempered of women, Orissi was sometimes irritable and snappish when she came out of a true dream, and the wine eased her mood.

He helped her sit up, and held the cup to her mouth. She drank it in a few gulps, and said, "Thank you."

"More?" She would tell him about the dream when she was ready to, or not. He loved her dearly, but he had learned long ago not to press her to talk at these moments; the true dreams were very rare, and she needed her strength and his silence to cope with them. A few times she did not tell him for days what she had seen. Twice she had never told him at all. Once he had wished he had the talent for such dreams himself, but they were sometimes so difficult for his wife that he had long since stopped yearning after the ability.

"No, thank you, my dear," Orissi said. She was sitting up now, on the edge of the table; her small bare feet did not reach the stone floor, for she was quite short, and she could never have been called slender. She had a round plump face, which in private moments could still display the merriment of the young woman she had been three decades ago, but her normal public expression was grave and austere. Her hair was graying prematurely, so that she appeared as old as her husband, though Taras was ten years her senior.

He waited patiently. At length Orissi set the cup on the table beside her, and said, "A man and a woman are coming to us. I don't know who they are. The woman troubles me."

"Why?"

"Something lies within her that should not be there."

"Light, or dark?"

"Dark. It stinks of the Adversary, though the woman is not herself evil. And the man—" She bit her lip, frowned.

"What of him?"

"He's a soldier, and not of our race, but he does not know what else he is."

Taras also frowned. "How so?"

"Something is hidden from him, and from me. It was a long time ago, and there was a death in it." Orissi coughed heavily, then again and again, and Taras thumped her on the back. When the fit passed, she said, "He doesn't know, but he must find out."

"Can we help him?"

She shook her head twice. "I know nothing more of him. The mirrors were clouded. I sensed an intervention against me. The Adversary has knowledge of the woman, I think, and wishes her ill, hence whatever infects her. About the man, I couldn't tell."

The Continuator sighed. "When will they come?"

Orissi closed her eyes in exhaustion. "Soon," she said.

* 9

KEY LED THE MOUNTED ESCORT ACROSS THE PALADINE
Barracks' parade square, toward Guards' Gate. Ahead of him,
the bluestone wall of the Fountain Palace reared sixty feet into
the blue afternoon sky. Above its ramparts the gate tower
soared higher yet, the gilding of its parapets shimmering in
the sun. Rain had fallen in the night, and the heat of the previous day had passed, leaving the air cool and fresh. The
weather change had made Key's bay mare frisky, and he had
to remind her occasionally that she, like her rider, was on duty.

He fingered the parchment tucked into his sword belt. On
it was written, in the flowing script of the Logomenon: *The
compliments of the Luminessa Mandine, and would Victurion Mec
Brander furnish an escort at the House Azure at the first hour after
midday.* The message's formality had not prevented his heart
from beating a little faster when he read it. He hadn't seen her
since the dromon docked at the Water Fort, the day before
yesterday.

He rode into the cool shadow of Guards' Gate, an arched
tunnel that connected the Paladine Barracks to the palace
grounds. The passage smelled of damp stone, ancient mortar,
and the scent of cut grass and flowers from the palace gardens
beyond. At its far end a marble avenue, shaded by linden trees,
curved away into the sun-dappled distance. The avenue led to

the House Azure, the minor palace where the Dynast's eldest son or daughter traditionally lived.

As Key emerged from the tunnel he glanced over his shoulder to make sure the escort was properly formed up. The thirty soldiers of Mandine's personal guard were all Ascendancers, except for Key and the peltarch Jaladar, a tough, silent, dark-skinned Mixtun who, after the custom of his race, wore his black hair in a single long braid. Mixtuns were natives of the islands far out in the Blue, where the Ascendancy had never ruled, and some of the rougher sort came to the mainland to serve in the Ascendancy's armed forces. They made formidable soldiers, even if they needed tight discipline to curb their taste for plundering civilians. Jaladar seemed of a different class; although he held only the rank of peltarch, he carried himself more like an exiled nobleman than a loot-grubbing mercenary. What his background really was, Key did not know.

He wondered what his father would think of his promotion to the Paladine Guard. He'd written home yesterday, reverting in his letter to his native tongue of Haema, though after his five years in the Ascendancy the spiky Haema characters were beginning to seem foreign. As soon as he could, he had to find a mail contractor and send the letter off.

They neared the end of the avenue. Just ahead were the russet-tile roofs and the blue facade of House Azure, and in front of the palace stretched a cobbled plaza where a bronze fountain splashed and bubbled. Key led his men into the plaza, halted them, and rode past the fountain to the portico. Beneath the portico was a bronze door inlaid with silver. A groom stood by the steps, holding a white mare whose coat shone like spider silk in the sunlight. The door-guard, at Key's approach, saluted.

"The luminessa's escort reporting," Key said.

The guard opened the door, and spoke to someone inside. Then he turned to Key, and said, "Please wait, sir. The luminessa is coming." He had left the door half-open.

Key dismounted. His mare smelled of warm horse. She

whuffled softly and studied him with one soft dark eye. He sighed, knowing he would never ride Rush, or likely any other hippaxa, again. There were none in Captala now, except for a score reserved for government couriers. With the hippaxas gone, the cataphracts and their traditions were finished for good.

The sun warmed his mail even through his Guards surcoat, and he pulled off his helmet and tucked it under his left arm. Soon he would be with Mandine again. The thought made him feel slightly giddy. He'd seen her only once aboard the dromon, when they talked briefly about the apparition that helped them escape the spell laid on the road. Though she was cordial, he'd been very aware, because of her father's presence, of the vast gulf between their stations. Then, as the squadron swept into the mouth of the Seferis, and the Water Fort's river wall loomed high above the mastheads, Bardas had informed him of his Guards posting and his promotion. He'd been inwardly exultant, though he wished it had been Mandine herself who told him.

He saw movement in the dimness behind the half-open door. A woman came out. It was Mandine. Wrapped about her was the gray cloak she had worn on the morning he rescued her, and her face was drawn and weary.

Mandine passed through the doorway into sunlight, and there he was: tall, sun-browned, his dark hair touched with glints of bronze. For an instant her riding boots seemed nailed to the pavement, and she went hot and cold at once. Her reaction startled her, the more so because she hadn't expected it. As she was dressing, her audience with the Perpetua had been so much on her mind that she'd barely thought about Kienan Mec Brander. Now he was here, and the sight of him had shaken her.

Perhaps it was because she wasn't feeling very well. Mandine collected herself, went down the steps, and took the mare's reins from the groom. Key stood two yards away, not quite looking at her. His face was hard and expressionless. She had believed that posting him to the Guards would please him; now she wasn't sure. Was he annoyed with the way she had arranged his life? He would not dare show it, of course, but he seemed very withdrawn. The comradeship they'd had at Essardene had evaporated. Some unspoken expectation in her heart lay unmet, and she felt a little saddened.

She said, hearing her voice as cool as the fountain:

"Good afternoon, Victurion Mec Brander."

He half knelt, following regulations exactly, and straightened. "My respects, Luminessa."

He was so very formal. But what else could he be? They were in Captala Nea, in the Fountain Palace, with others looking on. No immediate danger drew them together. For a moment she wished . . . what? That they could be again on the wall of doomed Essardene, talking almost as equals? No. That was in the past, and she was being foolish.

Mandine nodded briefly, then swung onto her mare. The mare pranced, and she stroked its neck. "I'm going to the House of the Sacred Marriage," she told Key. "I am to see the Perpetua."

"Yes, my lady." He mounted also, and turned his horse toward his men. They formed up, and the cavalcade set out along the avenue toward Guards' Gate. Key was riding well ahead of her. After fifty yards, Mandine dug her heels into the mare's flanks and moved up beside him. He had put his helmet back on, and his eyes beneath the steel rim were without expression.

"My lady," he said, "with respect, my standing orders are that you ride among the escort."

"I countermand the orders," Mandine said sharply. "If anyone complains, refer them to me."

"Yes, Luminessa."

Suddenly she wanted to reach out and touch his hand, to bring back something of the past. But that was not possible. It never would be possible. She was the daughter of the Dynast, and he was only the commander of her guard.

"I'm sorry," she said.

"My lady? For what?"

"For being troublesome about where I ride. But I hate being closed in, even if it's supposed to be for my own good."

He nodded gravely but did not answer. Mandine glanced over her shoulder. The escort was far enough away for their conversation to be lost in the clatter of hooves. "We can talk freely, Key," she said. "As we did at Essardene. No one will hear."

She saw a touch of life steal into his impassive face. "All right," he said, and she felt a flood of relief. Perhaps he wasn't angry at her, after all.

"Do you wish you were back with your old unit?" she asked.

"No, my lady, I don't."

Though she knew he would hardly say otherwise, Mandine thought he meant it, and was reassured. "In fact," she told him, "I'm going out today because I'm taking your advice. Back in Essardene, you said I should see a priestess about what was troubling me."

If this pleased him, he didn't show it. "It's still troubling you?" he asked.

"Yes, it is. I thought it was going away when we were on the ship. Then we got home, and I slept and slept. I thought I might be rid of it, but when I woke up this morning it came back. This time it's worse."

"What does it feel like?" He looked more than a little concerned for her.

"When it comes, I feel as if I've forgotten to do something terribly important, and something dreadful is about to happen because I forgot to do it. But when I *try* to remember . . . Key, I was walking across my room this morning, just after I got up, and I was trying to remember what it was I needed to do, and suddenly I was sure I'd just stepped off the edge of a cliff and was falling to my death. It almost stopped my heart before I realized there was still a floor under my feet. And later I tried to remember the thing again, at breakfast, and suddenly I couldn't bear to eat. It was as if the food would choke me if

I dared swallow it. I was able to drink some watered wine, that was all." She shivered. "Something similar happened yesterday. Falling. Only it wasn't as frightening or as clear as it was today. Whatever is going on with me, it's getting worse."

His alarm had plainly increased. "Do you think it's some aftereffect of the spell Erkai cast against us?"

"No, I don't think so. That was an illusion, outside me, and this feels so *real*, as if it were within me, somehow. But I don't know what it is, or how it got there. It's as if there were a . . . a wall in my mind, and whatever is doing this to me is behind it. And all the time, I feel that there's this thing I've forgotten to do. Something that I must, must, remember, so I can do it. Perhaps that's behind the wall, too." She shivered again. "And on top of that, I'm always cold. So cold I need a cloak even on a day like this."

"I noticed. Should we go back for a winter mantle for you?"

"No, even those don't seem to warm me the way this old cloak does. And it's comforting, somehow. Maybe that's because I wore it all the way from Bartaxa to the Inner Sea. Perhaps it's lucky for me."

He studied the cloak. "You don't suppose it's more than it seems? Where did you get it?"

"Here in Captala. It's just a traveling cloak. I've had it for more than two years. I—"

Abruptly, she had forgotten what she was going to say. Something about the cloak. She cast about for the memory. Nothing.

"My lady?"

Suddenly the words were there. "I looked in its pockets, just in case. But there's nothing in them."

"Ah."

"And there's another thing that's been bothering me, too. When we got away at Essardene, we both saw that huge bird, or something like a bird, just before the tree took fire. But Key, I don't think anyone else saw what we did. My father didn't, and neither did Bardas. They just saw a light, like a flame in the treetops, and they think it was part of the spell, and we were just lucky enough to ride free of it. What about your men?"

He frowned. "The same. I mentioned the bird to Melias, and he looked at me as if I'd lost my wits."

"It troubles me," Mandine said. "Something helped us, and I feel I should know what that was, too, but I don't."

"Here's Guards' Gate," Key said, and added in warning, "The passage will carry our voices."

They rode without speaking through the stone tunnel. "Why do you feel that?" Key asked, when they had emerged into the parade square.

"I don't know." Her fists clenched on the reins. "This is dreadful, the way I keep saying 'I don't know.' It's driving me mad. But something helped us against the sorcery, and it's important. I know it is."

"We don't have sorcery that powerful in the Elthame," Key said. "Not the kind to make a whole road go the wrong way, under the eyes of so many people. And I didn't think it was common here, either."

"It's not. I've never heard of anything that powerful, outside stories. Not even Erkai the Chain had that much of the Craft, back when he rebelled. But now he's made himself stronger, and he has the Tathars . . . Do you know if the news about him has spread in the city yet? In the House Azure I hear nothing of what's said in the streets."

"As far as I know, it's still only half-believed that he's come back. People don't want to believe it."

"Neither do I. But he has."

She fell silent, for they had reached the gate that led from the Paladine Barracks into the city itself. As they rode under the archway into the street, Mandine pulled up the hood of her cloak; if recognized, she would draw crowds, and she wanted to remain anonymous. Around them, hurrying people thronged the avenue leading toward the Sacred Way. Many carried bundles, or pushed heaped belongings on rickety barrows and handcarts. The air smelled of unwashed humans, cooking oil, and spices.

"Refugees," Key said. "The ones who don't have money or relatives in the city are camping in the parks."

"We're going to be under siege, aren't we? Is there enough food, do you know?"

"The barracks rumors say there's grain in the city for three months. But more supplies can come in by sea. We'll manage."

"That's true. And we'll have water from the cisterns, even if the Tathars cut the aqueducts." She sighed. "If only we'd won at Thorn River."

Key did not answer. *The worst of it is,* Mandine thought, *that we shouldn't have lost at all, and it's my father's fault we did. Key believes that, though he won't say it. In truth, my father should never have ruled. I realized as much in Essardene, and accepted it on the ship, as I watched him and listened to him. But who else is there? Me?*

They reached the end of the street and turned onto the broad reach of the Sacred Way. A mile ahead, the great sanctuary at the summit of Temple Mount reared into the sky. No one recognized Mandine, though her clattering escort drew curious stares, and she drew her hood a little closer about her face.

"Have you been to the House of the Sacred Marriage before?" she asked him.

"No, my lady. When I was training here, we didn't have much time to see the sights. But I can tell you we have nothing like it at home. Our temples to the Two are more"—he smiled wryly—"more rustic."

"Ah. But do you have the marriage-month tradition in the Elthame?"

"Not formally, in the way of the Ascendancy. There are a lot of marriages in the spring, but plenty of other couples wed in the rest of the year."

"They do that here, too, especially the poor. But we have a lovely ceremony to begin the month. And then there's the Wedding Festival afterward." She was about to describe it, but her cheeks warmed, and she stopped herself. In the ritual a betrothed couple, chosen by lot, passed their wedding night in the House of the Sacred Marriage. It was a great honor, for during that night the couple incarnated the transformation of the Youth and the Maiden into the Lord Allfather and the Lady Mother, and from that union sprang the fruitfulness of the world. On Temple Mount it was a decorous and sacred ritual, but in the poorer quarters of the city, the festival celebrations that followed were outright bawdy.

Key didn't pursue the subject. They rode on for a while, until they were passing the Necropolis of the Dynasts. The domed roofs of its ancient tombs, some almost as old as Captala herself, were half-hidden among the shadowy green of cypresses and yews. Above the treetops rose tall pillars, memorials to long-dead rulers. Among them, near the avenue, was a slender column of dark purple marble, crowned by a carving of a ship, with a crescent moon at its masthead.

Mandine pointed at it as they passed. "That's where the last dynast of the House of the Tessarids is buried. His son's there, too, Ilarion Tessaris. That's the Tessarid house crest on the pillar, the ship and moon. Ilarion died young, without issue, and the father had no other children. So old Lyrix Tessaris designated my great-great-grandfather to be his successor. That was how my family came to the diadem. By that time the House Tessaris had ruled for more than two hundred years. It was one of the longest-lived dynasties in our history."

"I've heard of them," Key said.

"They are well remembered here, and for some good reasons, I think—I've read the annals, and from all accounts, life was better then. The Tathars were much less of a threat, for one thing, because Galion Tessaris beat them so badly at the West Wall. It seems the whole Ascendancy was more prosperous—people were building roads and bridges and markets and temples everywhere. And many of our most brilliant painters and sculptors and writers worked during the Tessarid years."

He looked sideways at her. "You are very learned, my lady."

Was he being ironic? She preferred to believe he wasn't. She did know a great deal about history and governance, though now, in his company, it seemed so . . . so bookish. Reading about how people did things was nothing like having to do them yourself. If she didn't have a quicklight, for example, could she start a fire with nothing but flint and steel? She wasn't sure, and the uncertainty galled her.

"What's going on up there?" he said abruptly.

Ahead, where the Sacred Way crossed Optimates' Street, a large crowd was gathering. It murmured, exclaimed, then began to wail softly. As they rode closer, Mandine heard the words *Essardene* and *all dead* and *sorcery* floating on the sunlit air, and her stomach turned over.

"Key," she said, her throat tight, "find out what's happened."

As if in answer the crowd roiled, then flowed toward them. Staggering in its lead came a shirtless man in a breechcloth and ragged leggings, and in his hand was a wicker-covered bottle. At every few steps he drank from it. Tears streamed down his cheeks, into his filthy, tangled beard. He didn't seem to notice the horses ahead of him, and as Key halted the mare he almost stumbled into the animal. Key leaned from his saddle to seize the man's bare shoulder. "What's the matter?" he said, shaking him. "What's happened?"

"Key, wait," Mandine said. She drew her hood back a little. "Look up, citizen. Look at me. Tell us what's happened."

At her voice the man stopped weeping and hiccuped. "I'm not drunk," he said. His eyes were red-rimmed and looked mad. "Great Allfather pity me, I'm not drunk. I'm trying to get drunk, but I can't."

"Please, talk to me, citizen," Mandine said. "Essardene. Did you speak of Essardene?"

"I did, I'm from Essardene. Got away, three of us, found a fishboat. Nobody else—"

Key steadied him as he swayed. "You weren't *there*," the man blurted. "You don't *know*. At the city. All the stakes, and people on them, with no skins—" He choked, and drank again.

"And things coming out of the air. Like cold lights, sucking their lives out. Not clean deaths, worse than the stakes. There's a sorcerer there, he's doing it. The children, women—" He screamed, short and sharp. "My Lida, they split her, she was *inside out*, and she couldn't die, but they left her eyes, looking at me—"

He slumped against the mare, groaning and weeping. Mandine thought she would be sick. Her eyes met Key's. He was white around the mouth, but he dragged the man upright. "Who is it?" he demanded. "Who's this sorcerer?"

The man began to shake. "He spoke to us in the field where the stakes were. Before it began. He said, he said, 'Erkai the Chain.' "

Mandine looked up, saw people back away from the trembling figure. A frightened mutter spread among them, the name rippling away into the crowd. *Erkai. He said Erkai.*

The man pulled from Key's grip, dropped to the pavement, and sat with his head in one hand, the other clutching the bottle. A woman wearing the green stripes of a hospicess edged from the crowd and looked up at Mandine. "I'll see to him, ma'am," she said. Her eyes widened. "My lady?" she exclaimed. "My lady Luminessa?"

"Hush," Mandine said, but others had heard. The words whispered back into the throng now spilling across the width of the Sacred Way. *Luminessa. The Luminessa Mandine. She's come out to us. She's among us.*

Key yanked coins from his sabretache and leaned to thrust them into the hospicess's hands. "Here. See to his keep, and give him all the wine he wants." Straightening, he said, "My lady, we'd better hurry. They're frightened. They'll be all around us if we don't go."

Mandine knew he was right and kicked her mare into motion. Key led at a quick trot, and the crowd, still growing and murmuring, fell away behind them. The buildings along the Sacred Way flowed past—the Hemoticon, where priests and priestesses were trained, the Observatory of Celinius, the Pantechnion, with its great bell tower—but Mandine barely saw them. Sick at heart, she kept seeing Essardene in flames, and the horror that had awaited its people as she and her father fled.

They hurried past the Sacred Lake, to the foot of the ramp that climbed Temple Mount, and started the long ascent. The outer sanctuary's white walls drew nearer, and above the walls soared the greenstone columns and blue-tiled roof of the temple, the House of the Sacred Marriage. At the top of the ramp stood Pylon Gate, and Mandine, in an attempt to collect herself before entering the outer sanctuary, asked Key to pause a moment so she could gaze out across Captala.

From this vantage point she could see two-thirds of her vast ancestral city. Due west and beyond the seawalls lay the dark blue sweep of Chalice Bay, and at the bay's edge the naval harbor nestled in the stone embrace of the Water Fort. Nearer, the wandering line of Processional Way ran across her field of view, from its gate in the city's northern wall, past the Hill of Remembrance and the Obelisk, to join the great east–west axis of Central Street. Five miles to the southwest of Temple Mount, the broad estuary of the River Seferis joined Chalice Bay; she could see the white specks of sails on its gleaming waters, where fishermen trailed their nets and cargo ships sailed in to unload at the fortified merchants' harbor at the margin of the great river.

All this ancient wonder, she thought, so rich, so beautiful, so long in the building. How could it be destroyed? Who could bear to destroy it?

Erkai the Chain.

"Let's go in," she said, and touched heels to her horse's flanks. They rode through the Pylon Gate, into the broad plaza of the temple's forecourt. Scattered about it amid flower beds and ornamental trees were shrines to the aspects of the Two, each with its votive statue: shrines to Our Maiden of the First Flowering, to the Youth, to the Father of Fathers, to Our Lady of the Hearth, to the Maiden Bride. The air was fragrant with rose scent, from incense burning on the stone altar in the plaza's center. Two priests in blue, and two priestesses in green, stood with heads bowed at the altar's corners. A young woman in the white robe of an acolyte was walking toward Key and Mandine.

"We can't ride any farther," Mandine said, dismounting. "It's disrespectful."

Key slid from his mare as the acolyte reached them. She obviously had come to conduct Mandine to the Perpetua. Taking the reins of Mandine's horse, he said, "We will be here when you return, Luminessa."

"Why don't you come with me?" she asked. "You said you'd never been on Temple Mount. You could wait for me in the temple while I speak with the Perpetua. The inner sanctuary is beautiful. You'll need to leave your weapons behind, though."

He looked pleased, and the expression made him appear almost boyish. "I would be very happy to see it," he said, "if my lady the Luminessa is agreeable to my coming with her."

"Of course I am," she told him. But something about his words had made her uncomfortable. It was not until they were following the acolyte toward the entrance colonnade of the House of the Sacred Marriage that she realized the reason for it.

She wished he would call her simply Mandine, instead of addressing her always by her titles, and with such formality.

She blinked at the idea, for it was a little shocking. In the Elthame he might be a ruler's son, but here he was only a junior army officer, while she was a luminessa of the Ascendancy and the heir to the diadem into the bargain. She could not dream of asking a man of his rank to call her by her personal name. Such a thing was unheard of. He would be aghast if she asked him to do it.

But then, she *was* the luminessa. She could order him to call her Mandine, provided no one was within earshot, and he would have to obey.

But I couldn't order him to do it, she thought. *That wouldn't be fair. I'd have to ask. And he'd refuse, I know him that well. And suppose he did get used to calling me Mandine, and then he did it* by accident and someone overheard, and it got back to my father? We'd both be in trouble, but all I'd get is a tongue-lashing. Key might be flogged, and he'd certainly be dismissed from the army and then he'd have to go home in disgrace. Don't be such a fool, Mandine.

They were now halfway across the forecourt. So far she had managed to distract herself from the real reason she was here, but now it thrust itself again to the center of her awareness, and she began to be a little frightened. Might she, at any moment now, find herself stepping into the chasm she had imagined earlier this morning? And if it happened again, might not that terrible gulf under her feet suddenly become *real*? For a few moments she wanted to stop in her tracks, in case the abyss opened again before her, but she grimly forced herself to keep going, and allowed no expression to touch her face. The fear subsided, though she still felt it there, coiling its slow length deep within her.

They reached the broad shallow steps that led up to the House of the Sacred Marriage itself. Beneath the temple's colonnaded portico its golden doors stood open, and within them stretched the immense hall of the inner sanctuary. It was lit by crystal skylights, and at its far end the sun's radiance flowed like thick honey over the towering images of the Lady and the Allfather. As always, a shiver of awe and reverence touched Mandine as she walked into their presence. The Two stood as one, for the Lady's right hand held the Allfather's left, and on their heads they wore wreaths woven of the flower called silver amaranth, the crowns of the marriage day. Above the Lady's long green skirt her golden breasts were bare, and around them spilled garlands of fruitfulness: ruby apples, wheat of gold, lilies fashioned of emerald and mother-of-pearl. Beside her, the Allfather in his blue cloak gazed down from sea-dark eyes. About his shoulders hung a river of silver, the metal worked in all the forms of flowing water, and at his breast blazed the golden wheel of the sun.

The acolyte who brought them had slipped away, but awaiting them at the feet of the Two stood Orissi the Perpetua and her husband Taras the Continuator. Like those they served, the couple wore green robes and blue. Mandine was a little startled, for she had expected to see only the high priestess. She stopped in front of them and bowed. Key did likewise.

"The Luminessa Mandine," Orissi said, in her low rich voice. Her eyes in her plump face were grave, but there was warmth and pleasure in them. "Welcome to the House of the Two."

"May the Honored Lady and the Lord Allfather forever protect and favor us," Mandine responded. Then she stepped forward to embrace the Perpetua. The high priestess held her close for a moment, then kissed her on both cheeks. "Mandine," she said, "thank the Two you're safe. We thought the worst, when we heard about Thorn River, and you being so far off in Bartaxa."

Mandine smiled at Key. "As for that, Your Graces, this is Kienan Mec Brander of the Elthame, and I wouldn't be here at all, except for him. He's now the commander of my guard."

Taras bowed. "My lord Brander, I am Taras the Continuator. My wife is Orissi the Perpetua. We heard that a young officer had saved the luminessa outside Essardene, and we cannot thank you enough."

"Orissi was my tutoress when I was little," Mandine explained to Key, "before she was named Perpetua. We've been close ever since."

"The luminessa is fortunate," Key said. "I'm honored to meet Your Graces."

"Is it true," Taras inquired, "that Erkai the Chain has actually raised his head again? The rumor about him has found its way here, but we weren't inclined to believe it without some proof. We were hoping you might know more about it."

"It's almost certainly true," Mandine answered glumly. "There was a spell laid to keep us from escaping from Essardene, and it had Erkai's old marks on it. That's one of the things I'd like to ask you about, a little later. And we also just found out that Erkai has identified himself at Essardene. He was killing people there. Horribly."

Taras's gaunt countenance became gaunter still. "This is very bad news."

Orissi had been studying Key as Mandine spoke. "Very bad news indeed, but some good mixed with it." Her low voice rose with excitement. "Look at him, Taras—this must be the man! He's not of our race, and he's a soldier, and he's come with the luminessa!"

Taras blinked. "So he is. He *is*, it's true. He's probably the one you dreamed, Orissi."

"Why *probably*?" Orissi snapped at her husband. "He is, I tell you!"

"What?" Mandine asked, looked from priest to priestess. "I don't understand what you're talking about."

"I knew he was coming here," Orissi said. "I only didn't know *when*."

Mandine's eyebrows drew together in perplexity. "But I said nothing of lord Brander in my message to you."

"The knowledge came another way," said Orissi. "Yesterday, as I lay in the Lady's trance, the mirrors told me of a troubled woman who would seek us out, and a foreign soldier with her. I did not know who the woman was to be, Mandine, until I received your message this morning. But in it you spoke of unease, and then I knew." Her gaze rested on Key, then returned to Mandine. "And now you are here, and Kienan Mec Brander with you. You are the two foretold to me."

Key gave a muffled exclamation. "I?" he said. "With respect, Your Graces, I am not the stuff of prophecies."

"You don't yet know who you are," said Orissi. "If we could help you know, we would. But it seems this is for you to find out. It's enough for now that you and the luminessa are bound to one another."

"Bound?" Mandine asked, into Key's palpable silence. "How?"

"This isn't the place to talk," said Orissi. "And before anything else, we need to find out what's afflicting you, Mandine. Please, come with us."

She led them behind the statues, to a low door set in the

sanctuary's rear wall. Beyond the door was a tiny room, furnished with a cabinet, a small round table, and four wooden chairs. The table was of white marble, veined in blue and green, set on a pedestal of polished obsidian. A round light shaft lit the room from above, and the disk of illumination fell perfectly on the table's surface. A water clock plinked slowly in one corner.

The Perpetua closed the door, and said, "Mandine, my lord Brander, please sit at the table, not facing each other."

They obeyed. Orissi and her husband joined them, with the priestess across the marble disk from Mandine. There was a brief silence, into which Orissi said:

"Daughter, I can see fear in your eyes. What is troubling you?"

Mandine's throat was dry. "I feel that I'm supposed to do something terribly important, Orissi, and I'm terrified that something monstrous will happen if I fail to do it, but I don't know what it is. And I feel as if there's a wall in my mind, and that what I need to know is on the other side of it. Sometimes I can almost see over the wall, or through it, but then it stops me. And when it stops me, I get these terrible feelings. Falling into an abyss, if I'm standing up. Choking, if I'm trying to eat. And so cold. It's as if my blood were being drawn out of me."

Orissi and Taras regarded each other with troubled eyes. Then Taras said to his wife, "It's as you perceived. The Adversary has touched her inwardly."

"What?" Mandine asked. She heard her voice tremble. "You mean there's something evil inside me? The *Adversary* is in me?"

"Not that," said Orissi. "The Adversary Itself isn't within you, Mandine, or you would be . . . changed. Rather, it's an artifact of the Adversary. It's that which blocks your memory, I think. At some moment, you must have been vulnerable to such a taint. Do you remember any such time?"

"No, I don't," Mandine said wretchedly. "Sweet Lady, what am I to do? How can I drive it out?"

"The wall you perceive is an image your mind makes from

the evil," Taras said. "To remember what you've forgotten, and cleanse your spirit, you must bring down the wall."

"But I don't know how," Mandine said, trying to keep desperation from her voice. "There's nothing to grip. It's like trying to clutch water."

"But now you have us to help you," Taras said. "With us, you will be stronger, and in this sacred place the Adversary's barriers may be weaker. Will you try, with our help?"

Mandine lowered her gaze to the table's surface. The veining of blue and green looked like a map, like the whole world seen from the height of the sun. She took a deep breath, exhaled.

"Yes," she murmured. "What must I do?"

Orissi and her husband reached across the table and pressed fingertips to Mandine's forehead. "You must open your mind to us," Orissi murmured, "and walk to the wall you see. You must touch it. Close your eyes."

Mandine obeyed. She saw only a reddish blur at first, but it faded, then vanished, and suddenly she was alone in a dark place, and the wall was *there*, implacable, black, and strong. For minutes or hours or years she struggled toward it, though it seemed to recede with every laboring step she took. But at last she stood before its black, seamless face, and in her mind she put her palms to it. Artifact it might be, as Orissi had said, but it was no dead thing; though it seemed stone, yet it was also shudderingly like cold flesh, and around it hung a miasma of despair. Full of revulsion, she thrust against its strength. At the pressure its surface writhed under her hands, aquiver with monstrous life. Sickened, she summoned all her will, and thrust harder yet.

Her hands sank into the stone, and like manacles the wall seized her wrists. She struggled to draw back, but it dragged her closer, and in that instant she knew she would be engulfed. She heard herself scream, though whether in her mind or the world she could not tell. Then she was falling into an abyss, and she heard Orissi's voice, from far away: *Mandine, come back. Mandine, come back.*

The voice gave her strength. Somehow she arrested her plunge, and swam toward a distant light. The light grew, rushed toward her, and in a blink her eyes flew open and she was again in the temple room, her hands clenched on the stone table and her head lying on them. Taras and Orissi were holding her, and her skin was filmed with icy sweat.

"It almost took me," she gasped, and tried to raise her head. She was barely strong enough to do so.

"Bring wine," Orissi said. Taras went to the cabinet, and the Perpetua helped Mandine sit up. Key watched her, his face white and appalled. His concern warmed her, and she felt some strength flow back into her muscles.

"Your Grace, what happened?" he asked.

Taras came with a silver cup and put it to Mandine's lips. "Orissi?" he said.

The Perpetua's voice shook slightly as she answered. "I was too confident. I know something of the Adversary's wiles, but this—this thing it left in her has a concealed strength, something I have never encountered. A trap laid for the unwary. As I was unwary."

"But you have to help her!" Key burst out. "There has to be something—"

Taras and Orissi exchanged glances, and at the worried set of the Perpetua's mouth Mandine felt a whiplash of fear. "I'll try again," she said, as Taras put the empty wine cup on the table. "I'll do anything to make it go away. It's foul, and it's in me. I can't bear it."

"We must go deeper," Orissi said. "Into the breast of Our Lady Mother. Mandine, are you well enough to walk?"

The wine had brought back some of her strength, though her limbs still felt shaky. "I think so. Yes."

"Good," said the Perpetua. "Taras, help her stand."

✳ 10

THE GRANITE STAIRS WERE STEEP AND NARROW. KEY knew they had descended far beneath the House of the Sacred Marriage, and were now deep within the fabric of Temple Mount itself. He walked behind the Perpetua, whose lantern lit their way with a steady yellow glow; after him came Mandine and Taras. Key had worried that Mandine might be too weak to travel, but she was managing the descent well enough, with occasional help from the high priest. Neither Orissi nor Taras had said where they were going, and Key had not asked, because Mandine had not. Though he was growing impatient to know, he said nothing until the lantern's light fell across a worn inscription in the wall just ahead of him. The characters were not those of the Logomenon.

"Your Grace," Key said softly to Orissi, as they descended past the carvings, "what place is this?"

"The catacombs," Orissi replied. "This is where all the Perpetuas and Continuators are buried, back to the beginning of the city. Only priests and priestesses are supposed to enter here. I am trusting that the Honored Lady will not be offended, because of who you and the luminessa are."

At that Key fell silent. They went on, ever downward. Finally the stair ended at the mouth of a broad, arched passage, floored with dusty flagstones. Shallow grooves cut the paving and meandered away into the darkness ahead. They could only be wheel ruts, worn into the stone by countless years of traffic.

"This is a street," Key said. "Or," he added, "it was once a street."

"Yes, it was." Taras's voice echoed through the gloom. "A city stood here long ago, long before Captala did, perhaps long before the Old Dominion rose in the east. We walk its buried streets even now. But who the builders were, and what happened to them, no one knows."

"Who cut the stair?" Mandine asked, speaking almost for the first time since they began the descent. She had not known it existed, even by rumor, and despite her weariness and apprehension she felt a little curious about it. Orissi's lantern was leading them onward into the darkness.

"The first builders of Captala did, seventeen centuries ago. I suppose they sought treasure, or knowledge. But there was neither, as far as I know. Now we use the vaults and caverns for our own purposes. The air down here is dry and cool, and it preserves."

The lantern's light fell on a frescoed wall. In the painting, three young women with high-waisted skirts and bared breasts danced hand in hand beneath a flowering tree. They had long brown hair and long dark eyes; on their faded lips were small, secret smiles, and their skin was the color of pale sand. Near them three youths of the same race, naked but for loincloths, played on curious double pipes.

"They seem to have been a happy folk," Key said, as the painted dancers passed away into the gloom. Oddly, Mandine found no taint of the sinister in the ancient, long-dead street. It was merely very old, and tinged with a far-off sadness.

"Yes," said Orissi. "There was nothing evil about them. But they have been gone so long that even in the goddess's trance I can barely sense their traces."

They went on, until at last Orissi stopped before another fresco. The faded image was of a half-open door, painted so that the opening revealed a garden with a single flowering tree at its center. Orissi laid her palms on the tree's crown and pushed. Stone grated on stone, and a section of wall swung away. On its farside lay blackness.

They stepped over the threshold. The lantern illuminated a large, high-vaulted room, with an arched door in its opposite wall, and a dozen unlit bronze lamps suspended over a round stone table. The table was green and white and blue, like the table far above in the temple, but much larger. Orissi fired a taper from the lantern and lit the lamps. The room grew bright, revealing walls of rosy, polished stone. Along them Mandine saw many wooden chests, each as high as a tall man.

"This is where I enter the goddess's trance," Orissi said. "I am hoping that here, where she is so strong, the Adversary's work will be easier to undo. Mandine, how do you feel?"

"Not well." Mandine squeezed her palms together and knit her fingers. "I was almost all right when we set out, but now—" She shivered. "I'm cold again. I feel thin. And stretched, like a thread drawn too tight."

Taras said anxiously, "We must be quick."

"Why?" Mandine asked, looking from one to the other. "What's going to happen to me if this doesn't work?"

Orissi took her by her shoulders and held her gently. "I'm not sure. But I fear that what is in you has been aroused by our attempt to destroy it. A trap, as I said."

"And now that it's roused," Mandine said, "what will it do?"

"Daughter—"

"Tell me, Orissi. If you love me, tell me. Not knowing is worse than knowing."

The Perpetua's face was tight with pain. "I think it will try to drive you mad," she said. "That is its next defense, against your remembering what you must. If it fails in that, I believe it will try to make you kill yourself."

Mandine sagged, and Orissi caught her. "But it won't, daughter," the high priestess said fiercely, as she held the younger woman close. "We won't let it. You will lie here, where I lie in the trance, and we'll drive it from you. Lord

Brander, there are furs in that chest by the door. Bring them, she's too cold."

Orissi wrapped Mandine in a mantle of silvertip otter, and Key spread a bearskin on the table. Mandine stretched out on it, and closed her eyes. Despite the furs she was horribly chilled. She clasped her hands on her belly and waited.

Taras said, "Orissi, there may be some virtue remaining in the Diviner's writings. If Mandine holds them, perhaps they will strengthen her."

Mandine opened her eyes to see Orissi gazing thoughtfully down at her. "Yes, bring them," the Perpetua said. "They can do no harm."

Taras went to a chest, unlocked it with a heavy key he took from his robes, then drew something from the interior. He brought it to the table and gave it to his wife. Mandine stared at the thing in Orissi's hands. It was a book, bound in age-yellowed leather covers. Its binding was so narrow that it must hold only a few pages.

"This is the book called *The First and Last,*" Orissi said reverently. "In this are the words of Athanais herself, from her own hand."

Though she was growing colder and more afraid by the moment, Mandine felt a jab of astonishment. "The Diviner? But there's nothing of hers left. She destroyed all her works before she died."

"But not this," Orissi said. "This was the one thing she spared from the fire, and it has been hidden here ever since, by Taras's predecessors and mine, to the beginning of our history. Hold it close to you. Something of her strength may persist in it."

Mandine took the book and did as Orissi asked. Even the furs around her felt cold, but in the book, as it lay between her breasts, there seemed to be a faint quiver of living warmth.

"Now," Orissi said, "are you ready, Mandine?"

"I'm ready," she whispered, and closed her eyes. She felt Orissi's and Taras's touch on her brow, heard their breathing and her own in the stillness of the stone room.

And without warning, she stood again before the wall, but it was far more real now, as if both she and it were in the world, and her flesh opposed its stone. She knew she must walk to it, and she did. But she could not bear to touch it; the memory of its foul grasp sickened her. From the wall itself came a faint but horrible sound of laughter, as though it would take some amusement from her before it struck her down.

Go on, a voice murmured, from nowhere. It was Orissi, and she sensed Taras as well, and, farther off, a presence that could only be Key. And another, more distant yet, not a woman, but the memory of a woman, and a sadness beyond measure.

Mandine stepped forward and pressed her hands to the stone. The laughter quickened, became a howl, and again the manacles seized her with hideous strength. In her mind she cried out, and with her cry she heard Orissi's voice. *We are here. Only be strong.*

Suddenly her hands were filled with a power beyond her own, not only Orissi's but another's. She let it flow through her, into her fingers, and clutched at the inner fabric of the wall. With all her strength she tore at it. The wall trembled, stone squirmed. Agony tore at her hands and arms, as though the stone drew her tendons one by one from her flesh, and her inner sight darkened.

Now, said the Perpetua. *Now, Mandine Dascaris.*

Her skin and eyes and flesh burned in a torment of cold, but she threw herself against the wall. An icy voice snarled at her. Talons and jaws tore at her, as though they would strip her flesh from her bones. She gathered herself, threw all her strength and her borrowed power against the opposing will. It hesitated, quivered. The wall shook, and the darkness itself twisted hideously. A wail of fury pierced the darkness, dwindled into a far distance, and faded out.

The wall vanished.

Where it had stood, she saw a pool and a moonlit glade. *They* were there, and it was as if they again spoke to her, telling her what she must do. Then she knew again how the

Two had vanished, how the black wind swept down on her, how the pandragore and the hemandra sustained her mind and soul until she regained her bodily self. But since then the evil had lain within her, like the impregnation of rape. She had been defiled, violated, corrupted. Disgust and nausea filled her, and she knew then that she was in the world and in her body again.

The touch on her forehead lifted. "You are your own, Mandine," she heard Orissi murmur. "Daughter, be at peace."

Mandine opened her eyes. Above her, Orissi's face was drawn and exhausted. Taras, too, looked worn and used, but both he and his wife were gazing at her with wonder, and something close to fear.

"Did you see?" Mandine asked faintly. The nausea and disgust were fading, to be replaced by a trembling astonishment. *I have stood in the very presence of the Two,* she thought. *They have spoken to me. To me.*

"Yes, we saw," whispered Orissi. "Only a little, but enough. We saw *them,* and those who helped you—a woman of the Near Folk and a pandragore."

"What happened?" Key said urgently. "What's happened to the luminessa?"

"She's seen the living faces of the Lord and the Lady," Taras said, in a shaken voice. "They have called her."

Orissi passed a hand over her brow. "And the Adversary tried to make her forget that she was called. She was attacked right after the Two vanished, and it was then that the taint was put into her mind, to block her memory."

"But how could it get at her?" Key demanded, in astonishment and anger. "Why didn't the Two drive it away when it came for her?"

"When divinity opens itself to humankind," Taras said, "the way is also open to other entities, ones outside the orbit of the Two. When the Lord and Lady called her, they knew the risk, but they also knew they must accept it, or so I judge. To guide and help her they put the hemandra and the pandragore nearby. It was enough, but barely."

"I've remembered what I have to do," Mandine said abruptly, as if none of the others had spoken. "Orissi, you and Taras must have heard what the Lord and Lady told me. Didn't you?"

"No, my child, we didn't. We saw them with you, and what happened after, but heard nothing of what they said. But before you tell us, how are you feeling?"

Mandine sat up, Orissi helping her a little, though she didn't really need it. "I'm much better now. I don't feel so . . . so cold, and drained. And the dread has gone."

"The thing that was in you did that," Orissi said. "Now it's driven out, you have all of yourself again."

"I couldn't have done it without you, and the help I got from Athanais's book." Mandine found it in her lap and held it out to Taras. "I'm very glad you thought of it. *She* helped me, when I needed it most."

"So some of her power remains," Taras said pensively. "I wouldn't have thought it, after so long. Mandine, are you permitted to tell us what the Lord and Lady asked you to do?"

"I'm sure they want me to. But I didn't understand it completely when they said it, and I still don't. They said that Erkai was a tool of the Adversary, and then . . . then they said that we were to look for something that might be the salvation of our world. The *we* they spoke of is myself and a man whose path would cross mine. Key, remember when I said at Essardene that I thought I should know you? Now I understand. The man the Two told me about is you."

"Me?" Key said, aghast. "They chose *me*? My lady, choosing you I can understand, but I'm only a soldier, not a hero out of some legend. How can I be fit for such a task?"

"If they think you are, you are," Mandine said. "As for me, I don't feel very worthy, either. I wanted to refuse what they asked of me, but I just couldn't."

Orissi looked swiftly from Mandine to Key and back again. "You are both worthy, or you wouldn't be here. But worthiness aside, this news of Erkai is very ill. Think on what has happened. The Two warn you against him, then the Adversary tries to make you forget the warning. So Erkai the Chain and the Adversary are in harness together, or something like it." Her round face was flushed, and her voice had become harsh with anger. "Did they tell you what you and my lord Brander are to look for?"

"Yes. That's what I don't understand. They said we were to seek the place that contains all places, and the moment that contains all moments. And that was all."

Taras made a small exclamation of surprise, and Orissi's eyes widened. "Tell me again," she said, her tone softening a little. "There is no possibility you have misremembered?"

"No. I remember the words exactly. 'You must seek the place that contains all places, and the moment that contains all moments. In that may lie the salvation of your world.' "

Silence hung in the room. Then Taras said, "It's the Signata they speak of, Orissi. Just as *she* speaks of it." He looked down at the book in his hands, and Mandine saw his fingers tighten on the ancient leather. "Is it the same, do you think?"

"It can be nothing else," Orissi answered. Her voice was no longer angry, but grim. "What Athanais foresaw is here."

"I'm lost," Key said, looking from priest to priestess. "What under heaven is the Signata?"

"Wait, there was something else," Mandine said. In her mind the glade was again before her. The Two were speaking to her, then they vanished, and in the moonlit grass at her feet—

I put it in my pocket. But was it real, or vision?

She thrust her hand inside her cloak, searched frantically. Nothing. And then, deep at the pocket's bottom seam, her fingertips brushed a roughness. She drew it out and held it in the palm of her hand. In the lamplight, the ear of wheat shimmered as if newly reaped in the field.

"They gave me this," she said.

Orissi stared at the golden braid. "You've been carrying the Lady's token in your cloak all this time, and you never found it?"

For a few seconds, Mandine looked doubtful and confused.

Then her expression cleared. "I remember how it happened! Key, I told you I'd looked in my pockets, and found nothing, but now I remember that I never actually *looked*. I only thought I had. Orissi, did the taint in my mind do that to me, as well as the other things?"

Orissi gave a sharp, angry nod. "I'm sure it did, and someday its master will pay for what was done to you. You carried the Lady's gift all that time, and it was withheld from you. Sacrilege!"

Mandine gently touched the wheat. "But Orissi, I don't know what it's for, or even if it's for anything at all. It was just there on the ground, and I took it. But it isn't the Signata, is it?"

"No," Orissi answered, "but it shows that your vision was the true vision. Now there is really no doubt."

"I still don't understand," Key said. "What's this thing we're to look for?"

Taras smiled gravely at Mandine. "The luminessa is known for her erudition. She will have heard of it."

"It's a legend," Mandine said, "from the ancient world, from before the Flood. Or not even a legend, really, more like a rumor of one. Hardly anyone knows it now. The story told that there was a thing called the Signata, and that if you searched for it and found it, you would be given your heart's desire. But the Signata wasn't really an object, or not exactly an object. And even though it was supposed to give you your heart's desire, finding it was still supposed to be terribly dangerous. The story doesn't say why, or what the Signata was, except that it wasn't magic, not even the Deep Magic, and certainly not the Black Craft."

"Athanais knew of it," Orissi said. "She, like the Two, called it the place that contains all places and the moment that contains all moments. That's how we realized, just now, what you're supposed to look for. As for the Signata itself, much of what the luminessa says about it is true, though the part about it giving the heart's desire is a little uncertain."

Key said, "The legend says it was dangerous to find. Or to use, perhaps. Is it connected with Athanais's Ban?"

"In a way," said Taras. "Let me remind you how the Ban came about, my lord Brander, because that story's important to what we're about to tell you. Long before Captala was dreamed of, our Ascendancy was the western province of the Old Dominion. There were great magicians in those days, the White Diviners, but they grew too inquisitive and too sure of themselves, and finally overstepped their control of the Deep Magic."

"Thus the Flood," Mandine said.

"Yes. The mountains broke, and the New Sea covered Fallas Gaea and the heartland of our race, and all the White Diviners died but Athanais. She fled here to these six hills by Chalice Bay, and anointed the first Dynast, and with her help he founded Captala Nea. After that, she used the Deep Magic only twice more. First, she secured Captala's walls and gates against the Black Craft, for she knew its full strength, having fought in the White Diviners' wars against those we call thanaturges, the Deathmakers. They were the evil mirrors of Athanais's kind, and they were very few, but they were beings of dread.

"Then, in her remorse for the folly that drowned the Old Dominion, she worked her last and greatest spell, and sealed the Deep Magic away from the meddling fingers of humankind. That spell is the Ban, and it turns on and destroys anyone who tries to invoke the old power again." Taras looked down at the stone table, then up at Key. "She tested herself against it, to be sure it worked. A fire consumed her. A few others tried, in the first years of the Ban, and were likewise consumed. Now even the knowledge of how to raise the Deep Magic is lost. Unless . . ." He frowned. "Unless Erkai has somehow contrived to resurrect such knowledge. Above all things, I fear that."

"But why is that something to fear?" Key asked. "The knowledge is useless if Erkai can't use it in the face of the Ban."

Taras turned his gaze to Mandine. "I fear it, because the Two warned the luminessa against Erkai. I don't believe they would have done so if he were no more than his earlier self. That warning makes me afraid that Erkai may have found a way to counterspell the Ban and that he may be using the Tathars to help him toward that end. If he were to succeed, he would have the Deep Magic at his command. To go against the Ban is a great risk, but Erkai the Chain was never averse to risk."

"But if he succeeds, he'll become a thanaturge!" Mandine exclaimed.

"Yes," said Orissi, "he will. I do not know how such a one could be destroyed. The White Diviners could do it, if they united; by the time the Old Dominion fell, they had rooted out all the thanaturges, and the world seemed safe. But now Erkai is here, with the Adversary aiding him, it seems, and Athanais and her kind are gone."

"You told us she wrote of the Signata," Key said. "Could that help us know what to do?"

"It may," Orissi said. "I hope it can. Give me the book, Taras."

She opened it, and Mandine saw that the pages were heavy vellum and even fewer than the narrow binding had suggested.

"This, as I told you, is the book called *The First and Last*," Orissi said. "Our script and even our tongue have changed over the centuries, but these are the words of Athanais herself, and her meaning is still clear."

She began to read, in a strong, soft voice. The antique style made it seem as if the long-dead Diviner spoke through her; the back of Mandine's neck prickled, and the lanterns seemed to dim.

" 'I, Athanais of Fallas Gaea, write this, for the easing of my heart, for I have seen terror and beauty such as even I have never imagined. I have seen the Signata, the thing itself. I do not know why this has befallen me, for I did not seek it, yet it has sought me out. It was a worn copper coin, ordinary and of little worth, a sessos that I came by in no unusual way.

Twice I gave it to my servants, for the marketplace, and twice I found it again in the household coffer, unspent. Then, for no reason, it came to prey on my mind, and I began to see it as if it hung before my waking eyes. I feared for a time that it might be the sending of a thanaturge, though I could not believe this, for none of that power remain. With all my skills I assayed the thing and found it no more than it appeared.

" 'Then one morning at dawn I took the coin from the place I kept it, and set it on my hand. I looked into it, and saw nothing, and at last the sun rose, and with it a light that was not the sun. And then I did see.' "

"What?" Mandine whispered. "What was it?"

With trembling fingers Orissi turned the page. " 'I cannot speak clearly of it, no more than can those others who have crossed its path. For myself, I know only that within the Signata shines a light, of an abundance to break the heart. In that light is the place that contains all places, and the moment that contains all moments; the First and the Last, the Beginning and the End. But you who read this, be warned: Ponder long and hard before you seek the meeting that has befallen me. It is now only a shadow, for the human mind cannot hold such fullness, but even that shadow has bestowed on me a thirst I cannot quench and an ache I cannot ease.

" 'When in its mercy the Signata let me go, and its light faded and I came to myself at last, the sun stood as if time had not moved, and the coin was gone. What it means, I know not. No other strangeness has befallen me, though I ache and thirst without surcease, and dream of the Signata still.' "

"A coin?" Key said, dismay on his face. "*That's* what we have to look for?"

Orissi raised her hand to quiet him. "Those words she wrote before the Flood. These next she wrote after, and they are the reason the book is hidden." The Perpetua turned the page, and Mandine saw that the writing had changed to a ragged, urgent scrawl.

" 'I, Athanais the White Diviner, once of Fallas Gaea that is now under the sea, give this my testament, in the hour of my death. I have set my Ban over the Deep Magic, for through that power my colleagues and I brought ruin on ourselves and on our people. For this folly and madness, I have made what amends I can. Yet now I know why the Signata sought me out these thirteen years ago. For now in my dreaming of it, I see shadows of a dread to come, when the Adversary will find one to overthrow my Ban, though how this can be done I myself cannot understand. If that overthrow comes to pass, all will be again in ruin, as the old world was ruined, for a thanaturge will be brought forth to serve the ancient evil. So it must be, unless the Signata be found, unless its light shines from the Hill of Remembrance, through a man and woman linked. For in that light all other powers are set at naught. This I have seen, among the shadows that torment me.' "

"But what *is* the Signata?" Mandine said, as Orissi paused. "Is it the coin? Doesn't she tell us what to look for?"

The Perpetua sighed. "In no clear way. But listen, for here she gives what she can.

" 'You who take up the search, I can tell you only this: of the Signata, three occurrences are recorded. But you must know first of all that the Signata is not a *thing*, though it appears as such to our human awareness. It cannot be captured and held, and when it has done what it does, it vanishes. I myself believe it to be a manifestation of that which is neither the Created nor the Uncreated, that which is beyond our world and beyond the Lord and Lady, beyond even the Outside where the Adversary dwells. But I do not know why it comes and goes in this world as it does, and I suspect that its actions are beyond the understanding even of the Two, let alone that of humankind. To my knowledge it has appeared in three guises: in the first, a pottery cup, cracked along the rim, as was set down by Ybantus six hundred years ago. In the second, a stick of driftwood the length of a child's hand, according to the older account of Temonides. In the third, a coin of no worth, as it revealed itself to me.' "

"But—" Mandine broke in, aghast. "But it *changes*. If we

don't know what it is, how can we possibly find it? How can we even begin?"

"Yet finding it must be possible," Taras said, "or the Two would not ask you to do it. They do not offer false help or hope."

"Athanais only writes of three manifestations," Key said. "But that can't be all, can it? Surely it's appeared since she wrote this?"

"It has not done so, to anyone's knowledge," said Taras. "It has never been recorded in the seventeen hundred years since the Flood. And before that, in all the two thousand years of the Old Dominion, it was recognized but these three times."

"*Three times?*" Key's voice echoed in the stone room. "Three times, in thirty-seven centuries? What manner of aid is this?"

"The best we have," Orissi said sharply. "Do you question the advice of the Allfather and Our Lady Mother, my lord Brander?"

Mandine sent Key a slight, warning shake of her head. "No, Your Graces," he answered. "I spoke only out of disappointment. But the other two manifestations Athanais writes of—what happened in them?"

"No one knows, " Taras answered glumly. "The records, if there were any, vanished in Fallas Gaea with the Flood."

There was a silence. Finally, Mandine asked, "Then is there nothing else?"

"Little enough. Here she writes, 'Where you will find the Signata, and in what guise, I do not know, though as I have written, it was last in Fallas Gaea. Nor can I tell you how to use it in your hour of need. I have given you all I have, and little it is, as I know to my pain.'" Orissi faltered. "'Farewell. I, Athanais the White Diviner, last of my line, now go to test my Ban against myself. If all goes well, I shall die, and free the world from the burden of my footsteps.'"

She closed the book. "That is all," she said. "There is nothing else."

Another silence fell, this one longer. Finally Key broke it.

"So we don't know where the Signata is, nor what it looks like, nor what to do with it, if we find it."

"Yes," Taras admitted. "All this is true."

Anger flashed through Key, and would not subside. "Then I can't fathom the ways of the Two. To begin with, if it was so important for the luminessa to remember what she was supposed to do, why didn't they help her against the Adversary's taint?" His voice rose. "Why did they risk her mind, and her life? Was she nothing but a tool, to be used against evil while her strength lasted and thrown aside when she broke?"

"Hush, Key," Mandine said. "I have always prayed to serve the Lady. She and our Lord Allfather showed me how I could, and I agreed to it. It was my doing and mine alone."

"Lord Brander," Orissi said, "the luminessa is far more than a tool, just as you are far more than a tool. But as for your question, not even the Allfather and the Lady are omnipotent against the Adversary. They are of Creation, and rise from our world, and love it. But the Adversary came into existence at the Beginning, when the Silence was broken; It is no part of Creation at all, and It is not subject to the Two. Indeed our Creation is Its torment, for while there is Being the Adversary must know itself, as Creation knows itself. But the Adversary craves not knowledge but mindlessness; It seeks to return Itself and all created things to the Silence before the Beginning. Thus It works to annihilate our worlds of matter and spirit, and It works through what we call evil. And indeed It *is* evil, the evil from which all others spring, the oldest evil of all. It alone can challenge the Lord and Lady, and hope for victory, for It is from Outside, and beyond their powers."

"But the Two . . ." Mandine began. A gulf had opened at her feet, an abyss of terrifying silence. "But surely the Adversary can't *hurt* them. They are the Immortal, the Everlasting."

A silence. Then the Perpetua said, "Do not speak of this elsewhere. This is the hidden knowledge. They are not."

Silence fell. Mandine could not find words to break it.

"What do you mean?" Key said. "The Two can't die. Everyone knows that."

"Then everyone is wrong," the Perpetua said. "The Lord and Lady can indeed be driven from the world, if that is death, and in their departure the world will die."

"But then the Adversary can win," Mandine said. "But It can't. It *can't!*"

"But It can appear to, for a while," the Continuator said. "Yet though the Lord and Lady may die, they are always reborn, and the world with them. Even the Adversary's will cannot bring back the Silence for all eternity. No one knows why this is so. I suspect that even the Lord and Lady don't know, or if they do, they have no way to tell us."

Key's mouth drew tight. "So the gods can die and be reborn, somehow, sometime, and a new world with them. That's small comfort to those who live in this one, or to a mother who sees her child flayed alive by Tathars. Or worse, sees them fall into the hands of Erkai the Chain."

Mandine said, "But Key, even if that's so, I still have to do my best in the world we do have. I promised the Two I'd try to stop Erkai, and so I must."

"And I'm sworn as the commander of your guard," Key said. "Where you go, Luminessa, I go also."

"Because you have to? No." Mandine looked down at the book, then up at the glow of the lanterns. "In the name of Our Lady Mother and Our Lord Allfather, I release you from your oath. You are free to come with me, or stay."

Key looked at her face, pale gold in the lamplight, and saw her not as Archates' daughter, but as the brave, frightened young woman he had dragged across his saddlebow at Essardene. She would go, he knew, even if she had to go alone.

"I'm coming with you," he said. "By my own choice."

"Thank you, Key," she said, and in her eyes he saw the depth of her relief. *She draws me like rain to earth,* he thought, *but I have to put that away. She is heiress of the House of the Dascarids, and I am only a hill-king's son.*

"Something other than the Two seems to be on our side," he said. "The luminessa intended to ask you about it—it's what happened the night we escaped from Essardene."

"Mandine?" asked Orissi. "What was it?"

"A hemandra," she said, "or so I think." She told them how someone of the Near Folk appeared when they thought all was lost and of the birdlike thing that floated through the night as the tree broke into eerie purple flame. "I suspect now that it was the hemandra who took me to find the Two," she finished. "And what seemed a bird was really her familiar, the pandragore."

"It's said the Near Folk have their own adepts," Taras said thoughtfully. "It appears that's so, and that this hemandra and her pandragore helped you a second time. But I would not count on her aid in other places—the Near Folk septs each have their own haunts, and don't usually wander far beyond them."

"We won't," Key said. A moment of awe came over him. "So the pandragore is real. I've heard stories of the creatures, but I thought they were just that, stories. But now the luminessa has seen one, and I think I have."

"There may be more here than is immediately obvious," Orissi said. "The pandragore bespeaks the union of opposites, because it goes on its belly on the earth, and on its wings it is a denizen of the air. It signifies the gaining of hidden knowledge, therefore transformation of the knower. To encounter one foreshadows great change." The Perpetua smiled, without much humor. "As both you and Mandine have already discovered. That change, I suspect, is not over yet."

"Perhaps not, Your Grace," Key answered. He turned to Mandine. Sitting on the stone table, wrapped in the furs, she looked pale and terribly vulnerable. "Luminessa, I think we have to be on our way as soon as we can. The Tathars will be outside the walls before long."

"That's so," Taras said. "Moreover, you must tell no one about any of this."

"But my father," Mandine protested. "Surely I must tell him! He'll be relieved to know there's something we can do against Erkai. Especially if I tell him how the Two have helped us."

"And if the Dynast speaks of it to others?" Orissi asked. "We don't know how far Erkai's power extends, but he will be listening for any threat, especially a threat like this. A prophecy of Athanais, if he found out about it, is not one he would ignore. Luminessa, you and my lord Brander must tell *no one*. And you must slip from Captala so that no one knows of your leaving. You must not even tell *us* where you are going."

Mandine bit her lip. "I see. Very well, if that's what we have to do, we'll do it."

And if we're caught, Key realized, *I'll lose my head for taking her into danger. She'd say she ordered me to, but I don't think that would save me. But it doesn't matter. I've sworn to protect her, and I will.*

Already Orissi was locking away the ancient book, and Taras was extinguishing the hanging lanterns. "We will help as much as we can," he said. "You won't have to pass the city gates, for one thing."

"We won't?" Mandine said.

"No. Come here to the Mount after dark tomorrow, at the eleventh hour. From these catacombs there is an underground passage out of the city. It's an old secret, passed down with our office, and with our office alone. No one knows of the passage but myself and Orissi. It reaches the surface some four miles beyond the walls, to the east. I will guide you to the passage's exit, and have horses and supplies ready for you there. I will also provide the best maps we have of the Ascendancy. Suitable traveling clothes will be furnished, and you, my lord, have your weapons."

"Good," Key said, relieved at not having to run the gauntlet of the city gates. If a guard recognized Mandine, their search would be over before it began. "Wait, though. A way out is also a way in. When—if—we find the Signata, we're supposed to bring it to the Hill of Remembrance. If Captala's under siege, won't you need to seal the passage against the Tathars? If you do, we won't be able to get back in that way.

But perhaps we can use the sea approach, like the supply ships."

"The sea approach may be too dangerous for you. We will not seal the passage."

"But Your Grace," Key said, "cities have fallen that way."

"The passage will be guarded. My predecessors in other sieges found a method, though they never had to use it, for no enemy has ever found the outside entrance."

"What about when *we're* coming back?" Mandine asked.

"A password. I will reveal the tunnel to trusted priests, with the appropriate instructions. They will guard it till your return."

"That might take months," Key said, "even assuming we succeed."

"Yes," Taras said as he put out the last of the hanging lamps, "it might. But as long as Captala stands, and the tunnel is undiscovered, my sentries will be waiting for you." He produced a grim smile. "Do not forget the password. In memory of Athanais, let it be 'The Book of the First and Last.' The countersign will be 'Of Athanais the White Diviner.' "

They repeated the words, then left the darkened room and started the long ascent of the stairs. As they climbed, Key planned. He had to assume that Archates would send searchers after his daughter, so they would travel by night and stay clear of the main roads. As for direction, the Signata had last been at Fallas Gaea. So, lacking a better guide, they'd travel toward the New Sea that covered the lands of the Old Dominion, and trust to the aid of the Two, or to fate. The Temple Mount map would help, though he hoped they wouldn't need to travel all the way to the edge of the New Sea. Folk still called that wild and empty region the Cursed Shore, for after the Flood it was rimmed for a century with vast dunes and winddrifts of bones, the relics of the drowned. As well, the hills west of the Cursed Shore were once on the border of the Old Dominion, and in those shadowy glens the thanaturges had raised their strongholds. The White Diviners destroyed them, long before the settling of the western lands that later became the Ascendancy, but it was rumored that the ancient magic of that war still lingered in strange sights and sounds and in deceptive landscapes.

He was still pondering their route when they reached the iron door at the top of the stairs, and Taras led them through the small room and out into the temple. The sunlight falling through the skylights was already tinged with the old gold of late afternoon.

They paused to bow to the Allfather and the Lady, and Orissi embraced Mandine. "Remember the wheat ear they gave you," she said. "It is for some purpose."

"I will," Mandine said. "I'll keep it with me always. Until tomorrow, then, at the eleventh hour."

"Until then. May the protection of Our Lady Mother and Our Lord Allfather be on you both."

"Go with the Two," Mandine answered, and she and Key hurried from the temple. Its shadow was already lengthening across the forecourt gardens, and turning the altar smoke to silvery gray. Neither spoke as they rode through Pylon Gate, with the escort behind them, onto the head of the ramp leading down into the city. They had gone some distance before Mandine said, "My father will send soldiers to look for me, Key."

"I know, Luminessa. We'd best make ourselves look like refugees, heading east away from the Tathars. But, my lady, and forgive me for saying so, when the Tathars do get here, your father will have more on his mind than where you've gone. The search for you may slacken then."

"I hope so." A sharp bend in the ramp lay ahead, where it angled across the flank of Temple Mount; they were half-way down.

"How easily can you get out of the House Azure?" Key asked, and added quickly, "My lady." He'd almost forgotten to address her properly. Something indefinable between them had changed.

Mandine considered this. "I'll summon you to the House Azure at the hour before sunset tomorrow," she said. "But come alone. Can you get me through the Paladine Gate without the guards stopping us?"

"Yes. They might think it odd you don't have a full escort, but you'll have me. That should be enough."

"All right. Once we're outside the palace, I'll cloak myself, and we can go to Temple Mount. I'll tell my servants I'm doing a vigil, to pray for the city. With luck, no one will miss me till morning."

"Good," Key said. The turn in the ramp was at hand. They rounded it, and Mandine said sharply, "What's that?"

A vast crowd swirled at the ramp's foot and stretched along the Sacred Way as far as the Pantechnion. It saw Mandine and the soldiers, and its low murmur swelled.

Key swore under his breath. "Jaladar," he called to the Mixtun peltarch. "Form a cordon."

Jaladar saluted, and ordered a section forward, so that the Paladines formed a traveling wall around Key and Mandine. Key scrutinized the throng. It did not appear ill-tempered, but expectant. Arms rose, pointing up the ramp.

"There's no other way down," Mandine said. "We'll have to go through them. What do they *want*?"

"I don't know, Luminessa. Perhaps they're hoping the priests and priestesses will come down to bless them."

They continued down the ramp. One Paladine made to draw his sword, and Key stopped him with a sharp command. Then they were at the ramp's foot, with the crowd before them. Their horses reached its edge, and the people parted to form a murmuring avenue. Key relaxed very slightly, though his fingers were not far from his sword hilt.

"I don't understand this," Mandine said. "Why are they here?"

"My lady," Key said, suddenly reading the faces. "It's you. They want to see *you*."

"But—"

A cry from deep in the multitude cut her off. *"Luminessa! Luminessa! Pray for us! Intercede for us, in the Lady's name."*

The cry grew and spread. They rode on, in the center of a small open space that magically formed before them and drew in behind. Mandine smiled uncertainly, and at last raised her hand, waving in acknowledgment.

The crowd saw, and roared. *"Luminessa! The Luminessa Mandine! She will preserve us! Pray for us, our lady!"*

And then it changed. Key heard it first, a single voice a dozen feet from the horses.

"Dynastessa! Dynastessa!"

A chill went through him. He looked swiftly at Mandine. Her eyes had widened, her hand faltered. "No," she cried. "No!"

She might as well not have spoken. Voices took up the call, traveled.

"Dynastessa! Dynastessa! The Dynastessa Mandine!"

Mandine rose in her stirrups. "People of Captala," she shouted at the top of her voice. "Listen to me! Listen to me! I am not your Dynastessa! My father rules, I do not. This is wrong. I am the luminessa, only that!"

She cried it twice again, but they did not, would not, hear her. She dropped into her saddle and turned a frightened face to Key. "Get me to the palace," she called to him above the crowd's roar. "This is treason, and he'll blame me. Dear Lady, why now?"

"Escort," Key yelled, "make the slow trot, go!" Spurs went in, and the horses sped up a little. The slow trot was as fast as they could travel without overrunning people, but they were approaching the Pantechnion. Soon they'd be clear of the roaring multitude.

"Will he accuse you?" Key called to Mandine, knowing the guards would not hear above the pandemonium. "Should we go back to the temple? Get out tonight?"

Mandine yanked her hood over her face, a futile gesture. "No. If we do, he'll come after us as soon as he hears. Nothing's ready, we'd never get away. I'll try to explain to him that I didn't want this. He'll believe me. He *has* to believe me."

The crowd was thinning, though its tumult pursued them. Key thought he heard occasional shouts of *Archates, where's the army?* and found himself thinking, *Yes, where?* For an instant he had a mad impulse to join the crowd, proclaim her Dynas-tessa, and march on the Fountain Palace. The Paladine Guard might follow her. He knew his old cataphracts would. They hated Archates. But as they shook free of the crowd he thrust the wild vision away. If he tried it, she would never forgive him.

"Back to the palace!" he shouted to the guards. "Canter, go!"

Hooves rang on marble as they pelted east along the Sacred Way. Behind them, the crowd's roar dwindled to a sad, lost murmur, and diminished to brooding silence.

❈ 11

THEATANA WAS BEATING HER NEW MAIDSERVANT, NERissa, with a catwood switch. The girl crouched on her knees by the dressing table, and wept into her hands as the wand slashed across her thinly clad back. Theatana's cheeks were flushed with rage, her lips drawn back from her sharp little teeth, her dark eyes glittering in the lamplight. Kyris, her attiring woman, stood trembling against the tapestried wall, trying not to be noticed. Near Kyris, in their silver cage, the pair of whitethroat thrushes shifted nervously on their perch.

Theatana paused, then cut at Nerissa again. "Never, never, *never*, speak to me of my bitch-sister, unless I tell you to. Didn't Kyris instruct you in that?" She held the next stroke, switch raised.

"Yes, my lady, oh, yes she did."

"And being new, you forgot. Will you forget again?"

"My lady—oh, I'm sorry, my lady, I won't, I won't."

"Indeed you won't." The switch whistled, and seared a welt across the back of Nerissa's neck. The girl screamed and slumped forward, arms protecting her head. Theatana spat on her, then tossed the switch onto the dressing table, where it knocked over an open fragrance vial. The delicate scent of heartsease drifted through the room.

"You'll learn," Theatana said. She had lain awake half the

previous night, and as a result had slept most of the afternoon away and part of the evening. That had left her in a foul humor, and Nerissa's ridiculous tale, told without permission, had lashed her irritability to rage. Now, having vented her fury, she felt better. She reached down and stroked the girl's dark cap of hair. It was cut short, as was the hair of all the palace's servingwomen; Theatana's was long and black, hanging nearly to her narrow waist. Her slender fingers strayed to Nerissa's neck, where the welt burned, and she suddenly dug her nails into the reddened flesh. Nerissa cried out, and the female whitethroat chirped softly from her cage.

"*Have* you learned, Nerissa?" Theatana asked, withdrawing her hand.

"Yes, mistress," the girl said in a soft, broken voice. "Oh, yes."

"Good. *Now* you may tell me what the talk is about my sister."

"The steward said . . . said that the Lady Mandine was shouted as Dynastessa in the streets this afternoon."

"Rumors," Theatana snapped. "Where are your wits, slut? Do believe everything that's prattled around the palace?"

"No, my lady."

Theatana studied the softly weeping girl. The story was absurd. Mandine acclaimed as Dynastessa? That was treason. Mandine would never put herself in such a position. And yet, if it had really happened . . . Theatana felt a jab of excitement.

"Kyris," she said, "what do you know of this?"

"Nothing more, my lady. Only what Nerissa says."

Theatana considered summoning her steward for more details, then glanced at the water clock and realized she had no time to do so. Bardas would know more than the steward, anyway.

She poked Nerissa with the tip of her slipper. "Get out. You have leave to go to bed. You will resume your duties in the morning."

Nerissa fled. Theatana turned to Kyris, and saw the woman's eyes flick away from the switch. "What're you waiting for, Kyris? Come here and see to my hair."

"Yes, my lady," said Kyris, with relief ill hidden on her face. Theatana considered a cut of the switch to wipe that relief away, but decided against it. Kyris was the only maidservant who did her hair exactly as she liked it, and the woman would bungle the job if she were in tears.

"My lady wishes her hair to be up?"

"Yes. Close and tight. Then do my face."

If Kyris wondered why her mistress wanted her face prepared, she wisely did not show it. She deftly coiled Theatana's black tresses onto her head and secured them in a fine net bejeweled with tiny sapphires. Then she began work with rouge, lip paint, and fine green malachite dust for the eyelids. Black antimony powder darkened Theatana's eyebrows. When Kyris had finished, she stepped back and presented her mistress with a silver mirror. Theatana inspected her face with approval: the enormous dark eyes slightly uptipped at the outer corners, full lips, delicate pointed chin. *I look,* she thought with satisfaction, *a little like a dire-cat from the coastal hotlands. Good. Beware my claws.*

"It will do," she said. "Go to bed. Keep to your room unless I call you, and make sure that slut Nerissa does the same. "

"Yes, mistress."

Theatana waited until Kyris vanished behind the red-and-violet tapestry that concealed the door to the maids' room. Then she stood up and took the whitethroats' cage from its stand. The birds fluttered nervously as their perch swayed, and Theatana gave them a warm, lazy smile. Her blood was up, singing hot in her arteries. The water clock in the corner of her dressing room showed the tenth hour; one-half more division of the scale, and she would go.

She left the dressing room and took the cage into her bedroom. Its lamps had not been lit, and she left the door open behind her for illumination. Her quarters were in the Dynasteon, halfway up the flank of Dynasts' Hill, and had once been her mother's. They were the second-best apartments in the palace, surpassed in luxury only by those of Archates himself.

But the roof of the House Azure was visible from her bedroom window, and the constant reminder that Mandine had her very own palace to live in—even if it was only a small one—gave Theatana a canker. As a result, she rarely looked outside until night had made her sister's residence less of an eyesore.

It was dark now, so she did go to the casement, to gaze at Captala's scattered lights shining beyond the palace grounds. Miles away, the orange sparks of watch fires burned on the summits of the city's gate towers. The night breeze carried a muted clangor from the Armory, where the weapon forges pounded in the night.

Theatana put the thrushes' cage down on the sill, musing as she looked into the dark distances beyond Captala's walls. The Tathars were out there somewhere, and approaching by the hour. The servants shook at every word of the White Death, but she, Theatana, did not fear the silverhair scourge. Captala could never fall, and while the city stood, the Ascendancy would stand. And she would stand with it.

She silently rolled the words on her tongue: the Dynastessa Theatana. For the moment, she needed Bardas: to help her to the throne, and to raise new armies for her. But after she had defeated the Tathars and garlanded Captala's walls with their bloody heads, she would not need him, nor anyone else. Women without consorts had governed the Ascendancy in times past; as Dynastessa and sole ruler, she would march her armies west to destroy the Hegemon of the Tathars, then east to seize the rich highlands of the Elthame from the bronze-haired barbarians. She would build great new cities, and in every city she would raise a towering statue in her likeness. Men and women would sacrifice before it and worship her. The world would call her The Great, and at her name it would tremble.

The male whitethroat chirped uncertainly. Theatana went to the chest at the foot of her bed and took flint, steel, and a quicklight from a gold dispenser. She put the pine splint into its holder and struck metal on stone. Sparks showered over the fiber-wrapped tip of the quicklight, and the oily preparation in the fiber ignited. A yellow flame sprang up in the darkness, dimly illuminating the bedroom's scarlet-and-gold furnishings and the carved satinwood paneling of its walls.

Theatana kindled a bronze lamp with the burning splint, blew the quicklight out, and closed the bedroom door. After setting a chair against it, she glided silently into a corner, where she pressed upward on a carved lozenge, then slid it to the left. There was a click, and a section of wall paneling swung inward, to make a narrow door just her height. Beyond the door was a chamber, hidden within the wall's thickness. As far as Theatana knew, only she was aware of the secret room. She had discovered it a year ago, when in a fit of fury— over what, she didn't remember—she hurled a rouge box at the paneling. Its resonance made her suspicious, and after much tapping and investigation, she discovered the hidden latch.

Within the room, there was a treasure.

She had found it in the small wooden desk, which was all the furniture the room contained. It was a thin book, bound in green leather, and on the cover was written *This is the Compendium of Secret Affects.* Theatana had scanned its pages, and realized with growing excitement that the book was a manual for a dozen lesser spells of the Black Craft. Such works, even minor collections like this, were very rare, and she held one in her hands. With the excitement came curiosity: Who had known of this room and secreted the book within it?

She found the answer in a tightly rolled slip of paper nestled between the pages. Charred along one edge, it had obviously been used as a taper to light a lamp or candle. It was a personal memorandum, addressed by Latias to Theatana's long-dead mother, and stated merely that preparations were complete for the court's summer removal to Essardene.

So, Theatana had mused, *this was my mother's book, and now it's mine. I've dreamed of something like this, and now I have it.*

Under the law, she should have turned the book over to Temple Mount, for destruction. Even keeping it was an offense, and for actually exercising the Craft the punishments ranged from imprisonment to execution. Not all spells were black, of course; a few people in every community had the Kindly Gift of working charms that helped plants grow, that placated testy nature sprites, or soothed minor aches and pains. Such people were often local priests or priestesses, for men and women with the Gift were frequently drawn to the service of the Two. But the Black Craft was different. It began as the Kindly Gift, but its possessor turned it to darker purposes, and it forced events and beings along paths not natural to them. It required a death to empower even its most trivial spells, and it was dangerous to use, for errors in the castings could rebound on the user, with weird and unpleasant results. Also, its spells for a time left faint auras where they were cast, an aura that some people with the Gift, especially priestesses, could detect.

Such warnings filled several pages of the *Compendium*, and Theatana had studied them carefully before attempting the least of the spells, a simple change of appearance. To her delight, she worked it safely. So far she had used it four times, at the cost of three songbirds and a meerkit, and now she itched to try the *Compendium*'s more potent spells, such as the one that caused the victim constant nightmares. Unfortunately, their effects were odd enough to arouse suspicion, and a priestess might be called in to sniff out their source. Learning to use the other spells would have to wait till she was Dynastessa and too powerful to be touched.

Theatana brought the birds into the hidden room and set the cage and the lamp on the desk, next to a silver mirror already lying there. Then she opened the *Compendium* to the section she wanted, and took from the desk a bracelet made of Kyris's hair. She deftly removed the whitethroat female from the cage and settled the bracelet around the bird's neck. The tiny creature struggled in her grip for a few moments, then, paralyzed with terror, became still. Theatana composed herself, put her fingertips on the open book, and began to intone the spell. The *Compendium* vibrated under her touch, and she smelled an odor like that of moldy straw. The lamp flames sank to sparks, and the air thickened in her nostrils. The whitethroat's heart beat in a frenzy against her palm. Quickly, Theatana took her right hand from the book and wrung the bird's neck with a tiny *snap*. The bracelet squirmed slightly, then lay still as she finished speaking. The lamp flickered, brightened, and the odor vanished.

Theatana closed the book, and tossed the dead bird onto the desk. She felt dizzy and weak, as she always did after drawing out the spell, but from experience she knew the sensations would quickly pass. Drawing a deep breath, she slipped the hair bracelet over her wrist. Her vision blurred, and for an instant her skin seemed to shift and crawl over her flesh. She shuddered, picked up the mirror, and looked into it. From its silver surface, the face of Kyris gazed back at her. The illusion would last for as much as two hours, provided she wore the ensorcelled bracelet. Removing it during that time made her Theatana; replacing it would make her Kyris again.

This is the true power, she thought. *When I learn more—*

On a hook behind the door was a hooded brown cloak. She made sure the silver pass-tablet was in the cloak's inner pocket, then wrapped herself in the garment. After closing the secret room behind her, she left her quarters and set out through the darkened corridors of the Dynasteon.

It was a short walk to the door that led to the Green Colonnade, and she met no one on her way. The Paladine on sentry duty outside turned as she stepped into the night. His mail gleamed dully in the light of a brazier.

"Who goes?" he said.

"Kyris." Theatana showed him the pass-tablet.

"Go on, Kyris," the guard told her.

She passed him and hurried from the brazier's glow into the colonnade's shadows. Beyond the colonnade's end, across a stretch of lawn, stood the gate to the wooded Alia Gardens. Theatana went in. The gravel path ahead of her shone pale beneath the trees, and along its borders glimflowers spread their petals in rays of silver. The blossoms' fragrance drenched the night air; from afar, she heard the murmur of the fountain at the garden's center.

The path divided in a dark grove, at the crumbling marble statue of the poet Manoleon. Theatana stopped, listened, and watched. Her senses, as always when she used the spell, were preternaturally acute. She saw the shadow detach itself from the deeper shadows under the trees, and approach.

"Theatana?" came the whisper.

Quickly, she slipped the bracelet off, and swayed as the crawling sensation signaled her return to her normal appearance. She had never let Bardas know she used the Craft; it would give him too much to threaten her with.

"Yes," she called softly.

Bardas reached her. Theatana's arms slid around him, and his around her. They kissed deeply. In moments she felt him stiffening, and his breathing deepened. A soft heat stole over her skin and through her belly.

She pulled back and shoved Bardas away from her. "Enough," she heard herself say in a thick voice. "Enough, Tracien."

"God and goddess above and below," he muttered, "I want you."

He was malleable like this; it was so simple to direct men. "I know," she murmured. "And I lust after you." That much was true, for his hard soldier's body did draw her. And he had killed men, which she found fascinating. He was dangerous, unlike the young civilian nobles, whose soft flesh bored and repelled her. But unlike Bardas, she knew how to wait.

"You will enter me on our wedding night," she whispered. "Not before, Tracien." She put her hands on his shoulders and held him almost at arm's length. "What's this I hear about Mandine? That she was shouted in the streets a few hours ago, as Dynastessa? Or is it servants' babble?"

"Not babble at all," Bardas said. "It happened. Mandine went to the House of the Sacred Marriage this afternoon. On her way back to the palace, the city crowd acclaimed her."

Theatana's heartbeat quickened. "And? Did she try to hide it from our father?"

"No. She went to the Dynast and told him, and tried to

explain she had nothing to do with it. Your father flew into a rage, wouldn't hear her, and sent her away. He must have been brooding on it, because an hour ago he gave orders to put her under house arrest."

Delighted gratification surged in Theatana. "House arrest!"

"Yes, but it's supposed to be kept quiet. The guards she has now aren't her regular escort. They're from your father's personal bodyguard." Bardas laughed softly. "The ones he thinks he can trust."

"Tracien, this is perfect . . . no wait, there's a gall in it. Let me work this through."

"What's the matter?" he asked, as she thought hard. "I don't see that it changes our plans."

"But it does," she hissed. "Don't you see how dangerous this is for us? The people have no use for my father now, since he lost the army. If there's a rising, and he's overthrown, they'll put the diadem on Mandine, not on you and me. Worse, if Mandine thinks our father will execute her for treason, she'll have nothing to lose, and she'll try for the throne herself. I would, in her position. And the city's acclaimed her. She'd win. We have to strike against my father *now*, Tracien. We dare not wait."

"It's sooner than we'd planned." He sounded worried.

"There's no other way, my love." She put her arms around him and held him tightly. "Can't you see that? My father's going to lose the throne anyway, and if Mandine takes it, she'll get rid of both of us. I've told you how she hates me."

He made a guttural noise as she moved against him. "Yes. You're right."

"The other officers. Have you brought them around?"

"Enough of them. Dactulis let me know this afternoon that he's with us."

"Good. That's very good." With the support of the Paladine Guard commander, killing her father would be much easier.

"I hoped for Latias as well," Bardas added, "but when I sounded him yesterday, he refused to commit. There's no time to work on him now. I've had to be careful. He has spies everywhere."

Theatana stiffened and leaned away. "Latias!" she said, between her teeth. "That gelded no-man. He forced the Pargenes betrothal on me. When this is over, I want his throat opened."

"But he knows the government—"

"I don't care. Find someone else. I want him dead." Again Theatana pressed herself against Bardas. "Promise me, Tracien. He can't be trusted, and he likes Mandine. Kill him."

Bardas shook his head. "Not right away, my love. We're going to need him, for a while at least. With Archates dead, what's he going to do except support us? Latias knows where his interests lie. He'll come over."

She clung tighter, and against her belly felt Bardas's physical need for her. Yet she sensed he wouldn't change his mind about the chamberlain, so she whispered, "All right, but I don't like him, Tracien. Promise me, when we're secure, we'll kill him."

"Very well," Bardas said, his voice hoarse. "When the time is right, Latias dies. But not till then."

"And Mandine?" Theatana held her lover in her arms and swayed gently against him. "You know what must happen to her when we strike."

"I still don't like killing her," Bardas muttered. "She's too popular, and that's the knot in all our plans. Her blood on our hands—the city might rise against us."

"Tracien, while she lives we can't rule."

"We dare not kill her outright," Bardas said. "It has to look like something else."

"Yes." Theatana pondered the matter. Suddenly, excitement quickened in her. The answer was so obvious, why hadn't she seen it before?

"I have it," she said.

"You have what?"

"It's simple. We make it look as if my father killed her for trying to usurp the throne. People will believe it of him, Bar-

das. We say that he killed Mandine, and that you or Dactulis
or the others killed him in trying to protect her. It's perfect.
She'll be out of the way, and my father's death will be seen
as justice for the murder of my much-beloved sister. *We'll* be
acclaimed in the streets."

She sensed Bardas thinking. Then he gave a soft chuckle.
"You're right. It's perfect."

Theatana snuggled closer to him. "No one will stand in
our way, once my father and Mandine are dead. And if they
do, the Paladine Guard can deal with them."

"And then we marry," Bardas said.

"Of course, my love," Theatana whispered. *I may indeed
have to go through with the marriage,* she thought, *but it won't
encumber me for long. I have the Craft, and no one is going to rule
here but me.*

Half an hour after Kyris left the Dynasteon, the guard in
the Green Colonnade saw a woman's figure approaching. Kyris
again, he thought. He wondered if she'd had a lover, out there
in the Alia Gardens. If the younger luminessa found out about
her maidservant's night rambles, Kyris would pay for them
with a sore back. He felt sorry enough for the girl to open the
door for her. Kyris slipped through it without a word, and the
guard very quietly shut it after her.

He stretched. He would be off duty at midnight, and the
nondescript bald man would find him at the wineshop in
North Street, where the soldiers of the Paladine Guard did
their drinking. The sentry mentally added a line to his weekly
report: *The maidservant Kyris exited the luminessa's quarters at the
half after the tenth hour, and returned at the eleventh by the Pantechnion bell. She did not speak of her business.*

The sentry wondered briefly where his information went.
He did not much care, as long as the bald man gave him the
usual five silver minims for it. The money was a welcome
addition to a guardsman's pay.

✳ 12

KEY WAS IN THE BARRACKS EXERCISE YARD, DRILLING his men at sword work, when First Victurion Echius found him. The walled yard was sweltering, and sweat dripped from the Guardsmen's chins as they swung the double-weight practice weapons. Jaladar the Mixtun was the best among them, feinting and slashing with precision; perhaps because he came from the southern islands, he sweated less than the others.

"Warm work in this weather, ain't it?" said Echius, as he watched the red-faced soldiers. Like all Paladines he was tall, but he was running to fat, and perspiration glinted in his bushy eyebrows.

"It'll be warmer work when the Tathars get here, First," Key said. Echius spent most of his time in the administrative office, and Key wondered why the victurion had searched him out. The First did have his uses, though; he'd found a reputable mail contractor to handle Key's letter home.

"That won't be long," Echius said. "A courier came in two hours ago. The message was, the silverhairs' cavalry vanguard reached Phrax this morning. That puts less'n a day's ride between us and them. The Dynast will order the Diviner's sealbeams across the city gates tonight." The First spat into the dust. "Near fifty years since we've had to use the beams. Not since you-know-who rebelled against Maniakes."

But, Key thought, *Mandine and I will be gone before the Ta-thars arrive. Going we don't know where, searching for we don't know what. I would almost rather stay here and face the Tathar siege. At least a siege is something a man can get his teeth into.*

The waiting for night had seemed endless, but the sun finally was creeping toward the supper hour. He wondered how Mandine had pacified her father. Her escort had talked of the acclamation, of course, and yesterday evening the barracks was abuzz: *The people shouted her as Dynastessa, what will Archates do?*

Dactulis himself had grilled Key about what happened. Key tried to make it plain to the Paladine Guard commander that Mandine had not invited the acclamation, had indeed fled from it. He supposed his account of the incident had reached Archates almost immediately. He hoped it had helped her. No rumors had so far reached the barracks that the Dynast had acted against his daughter, and Key did not really think he would. Archates could not seriously believe that Mandine would seek to overthrow him.

"You wanted to see me about something, First?" he said.

Echius pulled a rolled paper from his sword belt and thrust it at Key. "This is a gate pass for the Numera. Chamberlain Latias wants to see you up at the Kellion offices. The executive officer's cleared it, so you'd better get going."

Key shouted, "Down arms!" at his sweating men, and took the pass from Echius. His mind raced. He knew of Latias the eunuch; everyone did. But the chamberlain would not be interested in a cavalryman. This summons could only be about Mandine. He glanced down at the blue surcoat that kept the sun off his mail. "Should I put on parade uniform?"

Echius ran a critical eye over the surcoat and Key's riding breeches, then shrugged. "Never mind the parade gear, you'll do. Now get moving—it's a good long walk up there, and I wouldn't keep old Latias twiddling his thumbs if I were you. You'll have to leave your sword and dag at the guardroom. And don't forget to take off your helmet when you go into the Kellion. Regulations."

Key turned to his laboring men. "Dismissed," he called. "Arms and kit inspection right after the sixth hour."

They did not quite grumble as they filed out of the yard. Echius watched them go, an expression of faint amusement on his face. "Train hard, fight easy, eh? But don't waste too much energy on them. Odds are you're all going back to regular duty."

"What?" Key said. Foreboding jabbed at him. "But this is the luminessa's escort."

Echius's furry eyebrows rose. "You haven't heard? No, I suppose you haven't—it's got a lid on it. The luminessa might not need an escort for a while. The Dynast's locked her up in the House Azure."

Key could not keep the shock from his voice. "He's *arrested* her?"

Echius nodded. "A jolt, ain't it? But not too surprising, when you think about what happened yesterday. The House Azure guards are supposed to keep mum, but the word's getting around. Some of the lads don't like it, so they talk, but they'll follow orders and keep the luminessa's doors locked. Archates pays their brass, after all."

Key's mouth was dry. "What will he do to her?"

"Who knows? I wouldn't like to be in her slippers, though, for all she's the luminessa and eats off gold." The First glanced at the westering sun. "It's getting late. You'd better take yourself up to the Numera. Latias has that wheely clock of his, and he runs the government by it. Also, he may not have his balls anymore, but he's got the Dynast's ear, which might be better. Don't make him mad at you."

In spite of the supposed urgency of the summons, Key had to wait for a long time in Latias's outer office. At the desk the chamberlain's secretary, bald, small, and wiry, ignored him. Key watched the man's pen travel, *scratch-scratch*, across one paper after another. The sound was maddening, and as the stack of completed papers grew, Key's worry grew with it. He did not have time for this. Somehow, within hours, he had to get Mandine out of the House Azure.

But how? I'm one man, not an army. But the chamberlain is powerful. If anyone can make Archates release her, it's Latias. Somehow I have to persuade him to act on her behalf. But it must happen soon, soon.

A bell chimed softly. "You may see His Eminence now," the secretary said, jerking his pen at the inner office. He did not look up from his papers.

Latias rose from his desk, as Key shut the door behind him. The chamberlain's smooth, handsome face was closed and watchful, but Key saw in it the exhaustion of a man who fought in a battle already long, and far from ended.

"My lord Brander," Latias said, pointing to a chair. "Please sit down."

The honorific startled Key a little, but he bowed, and sat. From over his shoulder came a slow *tock, tock, tock.* He looked around and saw the legendary clock. Its gold outer ring moved fractionally even as he watched it. Suddenly realizing that he looked like a staring bumpkin, he hastily returned his attention to the chamberlain.

Latias was already back in his chair. He put his elbows on the desk, and said, "I am aware of your background, my lord Brander. I am pleased to meet the son of the demarch of Oak Haeme, and the man who rescued the Luminessa Mandine from the Tathars."

He doesn't know I've heard about the arrest, Key thought. "Thank you, Eminence. Anyone would have done the same."

Latias regarded Key thoughtfully. "Yes, I'm sure. Now, my lord, I won't waste your time, or mine. Please tell me precisely what happened yesterday afternoon, when the luminessa was acclaimed in the streets. Leave nothing out."

Key did so, quickly and succinctly, as if presenting a battle report. When he finished, Latias said, "You have a field officer's eye for detail. You have also been close to the luminessa for some time now. Have you observed anything to suggest that Mandine wishes to replace her father on the throne?"

"No, Eminence. Nothing."

"I am relieved to hear it. This business yesterday—I'm glad

the luminessa wasn't the instigator. I had reports, of course, but I needed an eyewitness."

Key's mouth was dry. At any moment the chamberlain would dismiss him, and his chance would be lost. He said, "Eminence, if I may ask, why is the luminessa under arrest?"

Latias frowned. "You've heard of it?"

"Yes, Eminence. Soldiers talk."

"Ah. Very well, my lord, I'll tell you. It's because, unfortunately, she doesn't command her own fate in this. Through no fault of her own, she has become, shall we say, an alternative to the present rulership. Even if, as you have strongly proposed, she doesn't wish it."

"She doesn't wish it, Eminence." A faint hope rose in Key, for the chamberlain's tone suggested he stood on Mandine's side. "If the Dynast could have seen her face when it happened . . . Eminence, the luminessa doesn't deserve arrest."

But Latias was shaking his head. "My lord Brander, it is an unfortunate truth that rulers are suspicious and careful by nature. The arrest will stand, I think."

"Then what will happen to her?" Key asked, his voice hoarse.

"That is for the Dynast to decide."

Key's breath shortened. "Eminence, the penalty for treason is death."

"Yes, it is," Latias murmured. He sounded tired. "Now, my lord Brander, if you will excuse me—"

Key did the unforgivable; he raised his voice to the High Chamberlain. "But there's no treason here, Eminence! The luminessa doesn't want to rule. Would you condemn a woman for others' foolishness? We're hill-people in the Elthame, but we'd never—"

Latias cut him off with a raised hand. "Softly, my lord Brander. You skirt the edge of treasonous speech yourself."

Key subsided, breathing hard, hands clenched on the arms of the chair. "Eminence, you must intercede for her. She must be set free." He hesitated, then said, "You don't know how important it is."

Latias's eyes fixed on Key's. "Precisely what do you mean?"

Secrecy. Taras said it must be secret. But he didn't foresee this. I have to speak, if only a little. "The luminessa had a vision. No, more than a vision. The Lady and the Allfather spoke to her. There is something she has to find. I am to help her find it."

A long silence hung in the room. Then Latias said, "What evidence have you for this?"

"I was present when she spoke to the Perpetua and the Continuator about it. That was why she went to Temple Mount, to get their advice. They believe her. They say she—we—must start our search, and soon."

"This meeting with Taras and Orissi happened yesterday, before the incident in the streets?"

"Yes, Eminence, at the House of the Sacred Marriage. The luminessa had the vision some little while ago, but the Perpetua said it was a true one."

"Hm. You say Mandine must find something. What must she find?"

Key shook his head. "I'm sorry, Eminence, but I can't speak of it."

"You don't know, or you won't tell me?"

"Won't, Eminence. I have said too much already."

"I see." The chamberlain's face became remote, absorbed. The clock ticked. With great difficulty, Key quelled his urge to speak.

"Do you truly believe the luminessa has seen the Two?" Latias asked at last.

"Yes, Eminence. She is not a liar."

"I didn't suggest she was. But some people are, shall we say, prone to certain forms of hysteria. The problem is to distinguish a true visitation from an imagined one."

Key gave a harsh laugh. "The luminessa is the least hysterical of women. I was with her when we escaped from Essardene. She acquitted herself better than some who call themselves soldiers. If she says the Two appeared to her, then they did. The Perpetua and the Continuator had no doubt of it. You may ask them, if you wish, though I don't know how much they'll tell you."

"I don't understand this," Latias said, pulling at his smooth chin. "The gods concern themselves with the rhythms of the world, not with the everyday emergencies of humankind. They don't intervene in the affairs of mortals, except . . ." His face turned bleak. "Does this have to do with Erkai's reappearance?"

"Yes." Key paused. *How much can I say? But I have to move him.*

Latias said, "Go on."

"Eminence, the Two warned the luminessa against him. They were very clear that he is a terrible danger, worse than any of us could have believed."

A spasm of surprise crossed Latias's face. "The *Two* warned her against him? Specifically, and by name?"

"Yes, Eminence."

Latias collected himself and composed his features. "Few things surprise me, my lord Brander, but I confess that this does."

"Not more than it surprised me, Eminence."

"But why did they speak at all? What threat could be so dire as to cause the Lord and Lady themselves to intervene?"

Key hesitated, then said, "The high priest and priestess fear he will raise himself as a thanaturge."

The chamberlain stared at him. "What?"

"Yes, Eminence. A thanaturge."

"They said that?"

"Yes."

"Allfather above," Latias muttered. "If Orissi and Taras think this, and if the stories about Erkai at Essardene are true, it may be so. The Two help us, a thanaturge! Can he be stopped?"

"I don't know," Key said. "Neither did the Perpetua, nor the Continuator. I don't think he can be if the luminessa isn't free to act as the Allfather and Lady wished."

Latias closed his eyes, rubbed them with thumb and forefinger, then opened them again. "If I told the Dynast this much, he might lift the arrest. But then again, he is a suspicious man. He'd want to know where she is to go, what she's to look for. You won't tell me?"

"No," Key said, "I dare not. Erkai may have ways of finding things out. Even you, Eminence, know more than I like. Worse, the Tathar cavalry is at Phrax. By tomorrow morning they'll be here, and it will be too late for us to get away."

"You can always leave by sea. The Tathars have no navy."

Key shook his head. "We'd need a ship, a crew. There'd be no secrecy. Eminence, the luminessa and I *must* leave Captala tonight."

"This thing you're supposed to look for," said the chamberlain. "Will it help us?"

"It may, if we find it in time."

"But the Two gave no guarantee?"

"No. Now it is up to us."

Latias took a deep breath, let it out. "Very well. Our interests coincide, my lord Brander, though for different reasons. I also want the luminessa released, and soon. The Dynast is very unpopular, and if he takes some extreme action against Mandine, matters could go badly for him in the city. And with the Tathars at the gates, we can't risk an upheaval, even one in her favor. The Dynast, unfortunately, sees Mandine as a greater threat than either the Tathars or the city population. I will have to persuade him that his worst danger does not lie with her."

"But we have no time," Key protested. "You're a powerful man. Can't you take steps of your own to lift the arrest?"

Latias's face grew cold. "I risk much in going this far with you. I will not risk more until I must. In any case, I have no direct authority over you Paladines, and Dactulis, your commander, is not my friend. He would be delighted if I tried to order Mandine's guards to release her. He'd cry conspiracy and treason, and, with the Dynast in his present mood, I'd find myself in the deepest cell of the Numera. I'd be of no use to either of you there."

"I see," Key said. "What's to be done, then?"

Latias glanced at the ring-clock. "Archates is inspecting the harbor defenses. I'll go to the Dynasteon in two hours, when he returns, and see what can be done for the luminessa."

"And if he refuses?" Key said. "Eminence, you know what hangs on this."

"I know what you've told me. On more than that, I still reserve judgment."

"Eminence—" Key's grip tightened on the chair arms, and he forced himself to relax. "Eminence, the Perpetua and the Continuator will vouch for the truth of the luminessa's vision. Only ask them."

"I intend to," said the chamberlain. "Discreetly, of course." He touched his chin, stroked it. Then his fingers stilled, and he stared hard into Key's eyes. "My lord Brander," he said thoughtfully, "where exactly does your allegiance lie in this? To the Ascendancy or to the luminessa?"

"My oath is to the Ascendancy," Key said, "and the luminessa is of the Ascendancy. There is no discord of loyalties that I can see."

Latias smiled. "You chop logic like an adept." The smile vanished. "But I think differently. I think your true loyalty is to the person of Mandine Dascaris herself, and for reasons I am sure you would prefer not to discuss with me. But they explain why you are so determined to help her in this quest."

Key felt his ears grow hot, but he kept his eyes on the chamberlain's. He said, "A man's inner self is his own country."

"Indeed," Latias observed dryly. "Still, I'm relieved that she commands your devotion. She will need it. Now, to the business at hand. I do not want you to return to the Paladine Barracks. I want you here, where I can reach you easily."

Key sat back in the chair. "How am I to stay? I'm on duty."

"I will inform the barracks that you are being kept at the Numera for further questioning. Mandine's possible treason is a judicial matter, which is in the jurisdiction of my office. There will be no immediate protest from your superiors."

Key rubbed his forehead. "This is mad. The Tathars and

Erkai will be at the gates tomorrow, and we fight them by accusing each other of treachery?"

"It's a fallen age," Latias said wryly. "But no one thinks for an instant that Captala will fall. We have been besieged before. Each time the besiegers ate the countryside bare, then the rains came and they sickened, then they gave up and went away."

"This time is different. This time there is Erkai."

"Yes. This time there is Erkai." Latias rose. "Go and tell Phylact, my secretary, that you are to remain here. He will show you where to wait. And be patient, my lord Brander."

Key also rose, saluted, and left the office. Latias watched the door close behind the young cavalryman, then resumed his seat. *Damn Archates,* he thought. *The old saying's true: The tree of the Dascarids bears but two kinds of fruit, the sweet and the bitter. Mandine's the sweet, and look what it's brought her. Virtue fares ill in the world the Dascarids have made.*

The chamberlain shrugged the thought off; it was not the first time it had crossed his mind. Then he frowned. There was something he could not place about Kienan Mec Brander, a ghost of familiarity. But he was no longer young, and the older he became, the more people resembled each other.

His eyes burned with fatigue, and he massaged them. He had more immediate puzzles than Kienan Mec Brander. If he persuaded Archates to free Mandine, and she promptly vanished, the Dynast might assume she'd run away to raise a revolt. He, Latias, might be suspected of complicity. Could he survive that?

"But could we survive a thanaturge?" he muttered to the ring-clock, as dread coiled slow and cold in his gut. The Deep Magic had brought ruin even in the hands of the White Diviners, and in the hands of Erkai the horror would beggar description. If Temple Mount's fears were justified, Captala might fall at last, and everything go into the dark. How quickly could he get verification from Orissi or Taras? There was little time, according to Brander, and as the Elthamer had said, the luminessa was the least hysterical of women.

But a visitation from the Two? It stretched his credulity. To believe in it was almost as difficult as imagining that the Ascendancy itself could fall. As for that, no matter what the Two might have told Mandine, how could such greatness, such a long and brilliant history, simply . . . end? Surely it was not possible.

His gaze fell on a ceramic jar on his sideboard. It was glazed with strange sea creatures rendered in such flowing lines that they seemed almost to move, and was among his most cherished antiques. It dated from a good three centuries back, when such ceramics had, for a brief time, found their way to the Ascendancy from some mysterious source far beyond the islands of the Blue. What place that might have been, no one had ever discovered, yet its artists had been sublime. But the trickle of such objects had stopped, almost as soon as it began, as if some catastrophe had befallen their makers. It had never resumed.

What happened there, so long ago and so far away? Could it happen here? To us?

There was a soft rap at the door. "Come," Latias said, half-relieved at the interruption.

Phylact appeared, with a small, tight message-roll in his fingers. "This just arrived, under seal for you, Eminence."

Latias took the roll and dismissed the secretary. The symbol on the wax seal belonged to the agent who monitored the doings of the Paladine Guard. Latias spread out the roll and read. By the time he reached the end of the report, his hands were shaking.

Sometime last night, Dactulis had rearranged the Dynast's personal guard roster, effective this afternoon. Bardas had countersigned it. Furthermore, the Guard was to undertake night-combat exercises tonight, starting at the tenth hour. At the same time a detachment of Paladines was to go to the Armory, and a full securia of two hundred and forty men was to march to the Numera, with instructions to secure the treasury and the Kellion. Finally, a double guard was to be put at Theatana's disposal, as a further exercise in securing the younger luminessa's safety. All this on Archates' orders.

The paper slipped from Latias's fingers and wafted to the

carpet. He watched it fall. Archates had given no such instructions, and Latias knew it. This was not an exercise; this was rebellion. He'd been too confident in his spy network. He had always assumed he'd have all the warning he needed of a conspiracy, but now the soldiers had acted so suddenly they'd caught him unprepared. And Theatana was in the thick of it.

Or was she? Were they planning her death as well? But if so, why was there no mention of Mandine, for either good or ill?

The chamberlain swore violently under his breath. Then he pushed aside his fury at his failure, and thought hard. Warning Archates would serve no purpose now. The extent of the preparations showed that all the senior Guard officers were in the plot, or at least not against it; if he raised the alarm they would merely kill him along with the Dynast. Archates, though he still walked and breathed, was a dead man.

But what of Theatana? Latias bent to pick up the paper and stopped with his fingertips resting on it. A connection had formed in his tired brain. He cursed again, sat up, and searched his cluttered desk till he found the palace surveillance file. The topmost sheet said:

Guardsman at the entrance to Theatana's apartments saw Kyris leave by the Green Colonnade last night. She went in the direction of the Alia Gardens, was gone for a half turn of the glass, returned to the Dynasteon at the eleventh hour, did not talk. A man shortly thereafter came from the same direction, went on toward the Paladine Barracks. Informant suggests the man was the Treimarch Bardas. Report ends.

His mouth tight, Latias searched back in the file. Here was Kyris leaving the younger luminessa's quarters again, just before the army marched south to Thorn River. And again before that, twice, always by night. And another informant had seen Bardas near the luminessa's quarters on one of those occasions.

Latias thought: *Twice is coincidence, three times or more is a pattern. Theatana keeps her personal staff under her thumb, and she'd never countenance an affair between Bardas and Kyris. Nor would she let her maidservant wander the gardens at night, not without serving some purpose. So: she's been using Kyris to carry messages to Bardas, who is among the conspirators. That means almost certainly that she's a conspirator herself. The double guard Dactulis has ordered is for Theatana's use, not for her execution.*

He put his head in his hands. *So Theatana's in the conspiracy,* he thought. *She will have Mandine killed to clear her path to the throne, and Bardas will comply, because he believes Theatana is his path to the throne. The instant Archates is dead, Mandine will die. Unless I do something, and do it before the tenth hour.*

And how long would he himself live, with Theatana in power? He knew too many secrets, and the younger luminessa hated him. He himself would be wise to flee. For a while he would be safe on his estates in the south, and out in the Blue there were the archipelagos called the Blue Havens, well beyond the Ascendancy's rule.

Latias raised his head and stared at the wall, without seeing it. He would be even wiser to leave at this very moment, before Captala's gates were sealed. He could abandon Mandine and Kienan Mec Brander to the care of the Two; surely they would protect the couple?

I have lost my manhood. Did I lose my honor with it?

"No," he said into the silence. "That I have not lost."

The sunlight of early evening fell deep gold through his office window. *We need darkness to get Mandine away,* he thought, *and the plotters won't come for her till her father's safely dead. By just after the ninth hour, it will be full night. That's the time to take her from the House Azure.*

His eyes went to the base of the ring-clock. Within it lay the instrument he had hidden long ago, against just such a day as this, the instrument of a last desperation. Latias stood up and went to get it.

✳ 13

I MUST GET OUT. SOMEHOW I MUST GET OUT.

Mandine, nerves drawn taut, paced from room to room of her private quarters. Here she had always felt safe, but now her father had stripped that sense of safety from her, for he had made the House Azure's second floor her prison. Above her were the dark attics, where the castoff belongings of luminessas long dead slept among dust and cobwebs, and below on the ground floor were her guards, now her jailers. Normally the Paladine sentries never came into the house, but now that she was under arrest, two stood at the foot of the curved marble staircase that swept from the upper gallery down to the long inner atrium. Mandine knew this, because this morning she had slipped out onto the gallery to look. Other sentries patrolled outside; from time to time, from her windows, she had seen them tramping among the fountains and the flowering shrubs of the House Azure grounds. Her personal maids were not allowed near her, and her meals had been brought by a silent, frightened scullery boy accompanied by an equally silent guard.

Hardly aware of her surroundings, she passed again from her cool green bedroom, through the reception hall with its mosaics of blue and silver, then through her personal library to her favorite room, the solarium. It was walled and roofed by large rectangles of precious clear glass, and through these the light of the setting sun streamed in a dull orange flood, as though the palace gardens were aflame.

Her pacing accomplished nothing. Mandine forced herself to sit on a chaise in the solarium and think. Though she knew she should eat, she could not, and her supper remained untouched on the low table beside the chaise.

How could my father have done this to me?

She had hurried to the Dynasteon's Red Chamber as soon as she reached the palace, then knelt before him to confess that the city people had shouted her as Dynastessa. Looking back now, she believed that her action might have saved her from a worse imprisonment. If she had tried to hide the event, her father would inevitably have discovered it, and she might now be lying in a dank cell beneath the Numera.

As it was, his rage had terrified her. He had snatched a dagger from his belt, as if he might stab her there and then. But his officers were present, and that, perhaps, had restrained him. He ordered her not to leave the palace grounds, and sent her back to the House Azure. A few hours later a Paladine officer named Steilos invaded her personal quarters to tell her, apologetically but firmly, that she was under house arrest. She had half expected this, yet it left her with a sense of betrayal, bitter as sea brine. Her own father had locked her away, fearing a treachery of which she would never dream. How could he know so little of his daughter?

Theatana is gloating even now, Mandine thought. *She'll use this to her advantage. Will she try to persuade our father to execute me out of hand? Or will she be her usual devious self and bribe others to give evidence against me, now she's got this to work with? She might. She wants the throne, after all, and I'm in her way.*

Mandine shook herself. These distractions were profitless; she had to concentrate on escape. If Key knew of her arrest, he might be planning a desperate attempt at rescue. She hoped he wouldn't try; he was alone, and the Paladines were many. Perhaps he would go to Taras and Orissi, though she did not believe they could easily or quickly help her.

She went to the outer glass wall of the solarium. On its farside was an expanse of roof, whose russet tiles sloped away to the treetops of a walled ornamental orchard. One long-ago summer evening, when she was eight and a cracked pane of glass had been removed for replacement, she had crawled onto that roof, all the way to its edge. Then she'd wriggled into the upper branches of a sunsip tree, climbed down to the ground, and wandered among the cloudberry bushes and the smooth gray trunks of the sunsips. She had returned to the solarium the same way. Her maidservant caught her the second time she did it, and the open pane was quickly sealed. But she remembered that the surface of the roof could not be seen from the ground beyond the orchard wall.

Mandine knelt to inspect the setting of one of the glass rectangles. She judged that her shoulders would pass through the space it occupied, though she would be a close fit. But she dared not break the glass; someone might hear. She tested the join of glass to wood. Under her thumbnail the birch-gum seal was hard and unyielding. Still—

She returned to her untouched supper, found the fruit knife, and went back to the window. The gum resisted the slender blade at first, but then a short strip of it cracked away from the frame. Mandine looked at the sinking sun, then at the amount of sealing that remained. There was a lot, and she'd have to hide the debris in case someone checked on her.

She went to the library for quicklights and lit an oil lamp. Then she returned to the solarium. Taking her lower lip between her teeth, frowning in concentration, she set to work.

Archates Dascaris, Dynast of the Ascendancy, was dead.

His body sprawled loose-limbed in the chair where he had toppled in his last convulsion, his sightless eyes fixed on the scarlet-and-gold mosaics of the Red Council Chamber's ceiling. His right arm hung over the chair's back, index finger pointing at the floor. A drop of blood gathered tentatively at the finger-tip, hesitated, and fell to the growing pool on the pink-veined marble. Another followed, as if keeping time to the tick of the ring-clock in the council chamber's corner.

"I didn't know people had so much blood in them," Theatana said, wonderingly. "Is he really dead?" Her heart still pounded, and her skin felt hot and flushed. Moments ago she had knelt before her father, clutching his wrists as she beseeched him to reconsider her betrothal. Her grip kept him from drawing his dagger as Bardas and Dactulis rushed past her to strike him down. Dactulis's stab to the throat had cut off his scream before it reached his lips, and Bardas's blade had opened his heart.

"He's dead, my lady," Dactulis said, gazing down at the body. The Guard commander, a heavyset man with a thick neck and pocked skin, was breathing hard. Theatana suspected that the killing had shaken him, as if a Dynast's blood were different from any other man's. He had been in the conspiracy from the beginning, though, and if he was less clever than Bardas, he was equally ambitious.

Bardas was studying her. "You're not troubled by the blood, my lady?"

Theatana raised her eyes from the red spatter on her hands and arms. "No more than he would have been by mine, Tracien. He'd have cut my throat himself if he'd found out about us. Am I not to protect myself, just because he was my father?"

Bardas muttered an assent, and looked at the ring-clock. "We're ahead of time," he said. "It's not even the half before the tenth hour. Dactulis, you can go and start the Guard toward the Armory and the Numera."

Theatana smiled. "Yes, do. And Tracien, the sooner you bring my sister here, the better. I want to deal with her myself. Or perhaps those Mixtun guardsmen you gave me could spend an hour or two with her. That might be amusing."

"No," Bardas said, "they'd talk. Luminessa, we must stay with the plan. Everyone must believe her father killed her."

Theatana narrowed her eyes at him. Then she shrugged. "Very well. Hide the body before you go, in case someone comes before you return with her."

"No one will," Dactulis said. "The guards have been instructed."

"Hide the thing anyway," she ordered. "I don't want to look at it."

The two officers hauled her father's corpse and the stained chair to a curtained alcove. Theatana dragged a thick rug over the clotting blood puddles on the floor, then said, "All right, we're ready. Dactulis, off you go to your soldiers. Tracien, bring my sister to me."

Mandine's wrist and fingers ached, but only two short strips of gum now held the pane in place. On the horizon, a thin streak of deepest orange was all that remained of the day. For the past half turn of a glass she had been working by lamplight alone.

She hid the last few fragments of gum under the chaise and carried the lamp through the dark chambers to her bedroom. There she changed into black leather riding breeches, a dark green tunic, and soft, ankle-laced shoes. The Lady's ear of wheat was still in her gray cloak; after a moment's thought, Mandine took the garment from the clothespress, rolled it into a tight cylinder, and knotted it around her waist. It might serve as a rope if she needed one. Then she went to her writing desk, where she smeared her face and hands with the lampblack she used to mix ink.

She was as ready as she could be. Back in the solarium, she set the lamp by the window and held the pane steady while she removed the last two strips of gum. The glass shifted a little. Very gingerly, Mandine eased the heavy, brittle rectangle from its frame and laid it flat on the floor. Then she slipped the little fruit knife into her belt and blew out the lamp.

Her eyes adjusted slowly to the darkness. On the night air she smelled young grass, the tang of sunsip blossoms, and the fainter odors of the city: charcoal smoke, frying fish, the fragrance of the municipal bakeries. Somewhere out there, Key was no doubt wondering frantically what he might do to free her. How she would find him, assuming she escaped at all, she had no idea. The best measure she could think of was to reach Temple Mount and hope he would look for her there.

She could now see the texture of the roof tiles. With a silent prayer, she eased herself headfirst through the gap where the glass had been. Her shoulders scraped wood, and she had to wriggle, but after a few moments' exertion her hips followed her upper body onto the roof. She drew her legs after her and lay flat, listening for the tramp of hobnailed boots.

No such sound reached her, and she began to work her way down the roof, testing ahead of her for loose tiles. While it was still light she had marked the sunsip tree she would climb down, and in the dim sky-glow from the city's watch fires she could see its dark, motionless leaves. She longed for a breeze to rustle the foliage, to cover the sound of her passage down the tree, but the air was perfectly still. She heard dogs barking far off, and a horse's neigh from the Paladine Guard stables. More distant, the Pantechnion tower clock struck the half after nine.

At last she reached the sunsip tree's upper branches, where they lapped over the roof. She tried not to think of the twenty-foot drop that awaited her if she slipped. At best she would break a leg or ankle, and her quest would end before it began.

Sweet Lady, guide my grip.

The sunsip had grown sturdier since last she descended it, but she was no longer as light as an eight-year-old. Mandine searched with her feet and set them on the least-yielding limb she could find. Then she grasped a higher branch, summoned her nerve, and yanked her upper body into the top of the tree. The limb swayed under her, but she caught her balance before she slipped. The leaves shook and rustled, loud in her ears as a shout.

She listened, but heard no approaching footsteps or inquisitive hail. Breathing quickly, she worked her way inward to the sunsip's trunk and began to clamber down the branches. The noise of her descent seemed deafening, and by the time she reached the ground her heart was pounding. At the foot of the tree she listened again but heard no shouts, no thud of soldiers' boots outside the orchard wall.

The orchard gate was always open; Mandine moved silently across the grass to peep around the gatepost. Not far away, uphill in the direction of the Numera, she saw the yellow blink of a moving lantern. But nearer than that, pacing steadily toward the orchard, was a dark figure. The sky's glow shimmered on steel, the helmet of a guard.

Mandine ducked back, glad she had blackened her face. But for the moment she was trapped. She could see, only fifty yards away, the edge of the manicured woodland that stretched down toward the palace's outer wall and the Arsenal Gate. Though she still did not know how she might get past the sentries there, that was where she wanted to go. But if she ran for the trees now, the guard outside the orchard would be instantly on her heels. Very well, she would wait till he passed, then slip around him while his back was turned.

Her heart abruptly sank. Suppose the guards had orders to check the orchard on their rounds?

Perhaps he would not look up. She ran silently to the nearest sunsip tree, levered herself into its lower branches, and with as little noise as possible climbed into its concealing cloud of foliage. Now she heard the crunch of the guard's boots on the gravel path. Her fingers, with a will of their own, crept toward the handle of the little knife.

Key carried the lantern in his left hand, to leave his sword arm free. The yellow light danced along the flagstones ahead as he and Latias hurried down the hill's flank toward the House Azure. The chamberlain had said nothing since they left the Numera, and Key still did not know how he planned to manage Mandine's escape. He had asked, but Latias had said only, "If it works, you'll understand. If it doesn't, you won't need to. For the purposes of the moment, you are simply another of her guards."

But now, as the splash of the House Azure's fountain

reached his ears, Key could hold his tongue no longer. "Will it come to swords?" he asked, from the corner of his mouth.

"If it does, we are ruined. Keep your blade in its scabbard, and speak only if spoken to. I will give the luminessa any instructions needed."

"Yes, Eminence."

They went on in silence. Key wondered what the chamberlain planned to do after releasing Mandine. When they left the Numera, Key had noted that the man was wearing a dark green cloak, calf-length and voluminous. It was a traveling garment, though one of superior richness.

Is he going to run, too? Escape with us, through the catacombs?

That would be the only way they could flee from Captala. By now the city's gates would be closed against the Tathars, and sealed not only with their massive ironclad timbers, but also with the sorcery-laden stone beams set into the gate towers by Athanais herself. Those gates would not open again until the Tathars rode away, or were destroyed, or the city fell.

They were crossing the fountain plaza in front of the House Azure. Two gilt-iron oil sconces lit the entry portico, and below the lamps two Paladines watched them approach. The sentries saw Key's rank badges as he and Latias walked up the portico steps, and saluted.

Latias said to the taller man, "I am the chamberlain. Admit us."

The guard blinked nervously. "Yes, Eminence. But your pardon, sir, you'll have to make yourself known to Securion Steilos. He's inside, sir."

"Admit us," Latias said, as though the sentry had not spoken.

The man blinked again, cleared his throat, and swung the bronze door open. Latias stalked through it, Key following with the lantern. Inside was a large, brightly lit foyer, its floor paved in squares of white-and-blue tile. A Paladine officer, who could only be Steilos, sat at a small table. Behind him was a doorway that led deeper into the house.

"Eminence," Steilos said. He scrambled hastily to his feet and bowed.

"You are the securion in charge of the luminessa's guard?" Latias asked in a flat voice.

"Yes, my lord Latias. I report to—"

Latias cut him off with a gesture. Then he drew a slim white roll from his cloak sleeve. "We are to escort the luminessa from her quarters to another place. Where is she?"

Steilos fidgeted. "Eminence, I need authorization, or I have to clear it with my commander."

"Idiot," Latias said. He twitched the roll, and it fell open. Key saw that it was not the common reed-paper, but silky vellum. Steilos stared at it, and his eyes grew large.

"This writ bears the Dynast's seal and signature," Latias said, still in that flat voice. "His orders say, among other things, *immediately*. Would you have Archates Dascaris wait upon your pleasure?"

Sweat broke out on Steilos's upper lip. "No, Eminence, of course not. I mistook myself, great lord."

"Stop babbling. Where is the luminessa?"

"In her quarters, Eminence. There are guards at the stairs."

"Clear us past them," Latias said, rolling the vellum and pushing it into his sleeve. "I do not wish to wave this at every common soldier in sight."

They followed the securion deeper into the house. *Somehow,* Key thought, *Latias has persuaded Archates to release her. But when? When he came for me half an hour ago, he said nothing about seeing the Dynast. He couldn't have—*

You numskull, he thought, as he realized what must have happened. *Latias never spoke to Archates at all. The writ is forged. But when the Dynast finds out, Latias is a dead man. So he plans to flee, as I suspected.*

Steilos stayed behind with his men as Key and the chamberlain climbed the sweeping white staircase to the second floor. Latias never hesitated in the upper corridors; clearly, he knew the house. He stopped at a blue door with silver inlay and rapped softly. No answer. Latias frowned and rapped again, louder. When there was still no response, he opened it.

Inside, all was dark. Key raised the lantern as they stepped through the doorway, and Latias called quietly, "Luminessa?"

Still no answer. The chamberlain took a sharp breath and said, "Hurry. Bring the light."

Moments later, they stood in a room that seemed all glass. "She's gotten out!" Latias exclaimed, pointing to an unlit lamp on the floor and at the empty space in the glass wall. "Allfather above, what are we to do now?"

Key stiffened. Inexplicably, he *sensed* her. He knew as sure as he drew breath that Mandine was very near. He set the lantern down, knelt, and put his head and shoulders into the gap she had made. He didn't fit. He pulled back, drew his sword, and hacked at the wooden framing. The peal of shattering glass filled the night, and Key heard a man's distant voice raised in wordless surprise.

He slammed his sword into its scabbard. "Follow me," he said over his shoulder, as he thrust himself through the widened opening. He slid along sloping roof tiles, caught himself, and felt his boots strike something that yielded and rustled. A tree. She'd climbed down a tree. Heedless of height, he grabbed at barely visible branches, pulled himself into foliage. Half-falling, flailed by twigs and leaves, he let himself bounce noisily toward the ground.

"Who goes?" a harsh male voice called from the darkness.

"Latias the Dynast's chamberlain," Latias called back. From the sound, Key thought he must be out on the roof.

"What?" The guard's voice was shaded with surprise.

Key's boots hit grass. He walked quickly toward the voice, hand on sword hilt. "I'm Victurion Brander, the chamberlain's escort," he said loudly. He heard Latias coming down the tree behind him, in a rattle of leaves.

The guard's dark shape stood not far away. "What's going on?" the Paladine asked, his tone full of suspicion.

Key opened his mouth, not knowing what would come out of it, and a voice from the air said, "They've come for me,

guardsman. Wait, Victurion Brander, I'll come down peace-
fully."

Key looked up, mouth agape. Leaves thrashed above him,
then, miraculously, Mandine was clambering from the tree's
lower branches to the ground.

"You *have* come for me, haven't you?" she said wearily.
"You and the chamberlain together. My new jailers."

He realized she was speaking for the guard, and thought
quickly. "Yes, my lady. You must come with us, please."

She laughed bitterly. "Have I a choice, victurion?"

Latias arrived, breathing hard. "You," he snapped at the
guard. "I am the High Chamberlain. Go to Securion Steilos.
Tell him the luminessa almost got away, and that the lot of
you are under arrest for dereliction of duty. None of you is to
go anywhere."

Key distinctly heard the man swallow. "Yes, Eminence,"
he quavered. Then he backed away and scuttled into the night.

"Quickly," Latias said. "Along to Carmenal Gate and out.
We've very little time."

"Latias?" Mandine said. "It really *is* you?"

"Yes, my lady. Come, quickly, and be careful when we go
around in front of the house. The door sentries will still be
there, and you must seem a prisoner."

"Ah. This isn't my father's doing, is it?"

"No, Luminessa. I'll explain when I can. Quickly, I beg
you."

They got through the fountain plaza without incident, the
guards merely eyeing them from the portico. Moments later
they were in the avenue under the lindens, with the pale flagstones stretching into the darkness ahead of them. Key extin-
guished the lantern. Through the leaves he could glimpse the
Dynasteon rising on the hillside to their left, a massive shadow
against the city-glow in the sky. Few windows were lit.

"Why the Carmenal Gate?" he murmured to Latias. "It's
the long way around to Temple Mount."

"The others are too dangerous. Soon there will be military
movements, over on the barracks side of the palace grounds.

Archates' writ will take us past the Carmenal Gate sentries, and by the time an alarm's raised we'll be on Temple Mount. But the writ won't get us out of the city. I hope Taras has some plan that will."

"He does," Key said.

"You have my father's writ?" Mandine asked quietly. "But how have you made it work? It can't be to release me."

"It's not by his hand," Latias said. "It's by mine. For a long time I have kept a blank writ with your father's seal, and tonight I used it."

Key heard her draw a sharp breath. "But Latias, when he finds out—"

"He will not. Ever."

A pause. Then Mandine said, "What are you telling me?"

"*Who's there?*" someone called sharply from the darkness ahead of them. "Dactulis?"

"The Allfather curse our luck," Latias muttered, as they all stopped. "I think it's Bardas. No swordplay, my lord Brander. Let me talk. If there's noise, we're lost."

Key cursed himself as well. They should have kept to the trees, though the going would have been slower. He had been too ready to let the chamberlain lead. He should have watched better, seen the moving shadow before it saw them.

"This is Latias," the chamberlain called. "Is that you, Treimarch Bardas?"

"It is." The treimarch came out of the night and halted two yards ahead of them. In the faint sky-glow Key could make out his mail and helmet, and the senior officer's short sword in his hand. "Who's with you?"

"A guardsman, and the Luminessa Mandine," Latias said calmly.

"*What?* What's she doing here?"

"You didn't know?" The chamberlain sounded mildly surprised. "She's to be taken to the harbor and sent into exile. Archates gave me a writ to this effect."

A short pause. Then Bardas said, "I know nothing of such a writ."

"I can't imagine why he didn't tell you." The vellum cylinder was in Latias's left hand as he stepped forward. "I have the document. Here, look for yourself."

Tension hardened Bardas's voice. "I must tell you the Dynast has changed his mind. Just now he ordered her brought to him. The writ is invalid. I'll take her."

Key sensed the man's eyes on him and kept his hand from the hilt of his sword. He could not draw and close quickly enough for a silent kill. He dared not even edge nearer.

"But I can't do that," the chamberlain said in reasonable tones, taking another step. "I have the order in writing. A writ can only be superseded by another that cancels it. The paperwork must be done. Surely you see, Treimarch?" His left hand rose, and he let the roll spring open, a white patch in the dark. "The seal is here, my lord. How can I go against it? Please, look—"

"Damn your paper, eunuch," Bardas snarled, and slapped at the vellum with his free hand. Latias dropped it almost at the man's feet, and half bent to pick it up, his cloak obscuring his arms and hands.

He straightened quickly, very quickly. Without the slightest warning, his right hand came up and punched Bardas under the chin, just where the mail collar ended. The man gave a gurgling cough, dropped his sword, and stepped back. Latias followed him. Key saw the flicker of a wet blade go in and come out again. The treimarch staggered, made another strangled noise, and dropped to his knees. Then he fell loosely onto his face. On the dim flagstones by his head a black pool began to gather. Key let his breath out. Beside him, Mandine made a small shocked sound.

"He forgot I wasn't always a eunuch," Latias said softly. "The fool." He wiped the bloody dagger on Bardas's cloak, picked up the writ, and turned to Mandine and Key. "It may be fortunate we ran into him. Steilos back at the House Azure didn't seem to be expecting him, and that means we've some time before anyone realizes the luminessa's escaped. Lord

Brander, help me get him into the bushes, and we'll be on our way."

They moved Bardas out of sight, and returned to the avenue. Mandine was standing like a statue of dark gray stone. "Latias," she muttered.

"Yes, Luminessa."

Her voice trembled suddenly. "You said my father would never find out about your writ. Do you mean he can't find out because he's dead? Is that what you meant? That he's dead?"

The chamberlain's voice was gentle. "Yes, Luminessa. I think he is. Unless I am very much mistaken, Bardas and your sister have overthrown him."

Her shoulders sagged. Key caught at her arm as she swayed, but she shrugged him off, as if in anger. "I'm all right, Key," she said in a flat voice. "It does not surprise me. But Latias, did you know what they planned?"

"My lady, I knew too late. There was nothing I could do to avert it, without hazarding your rescue. I am truly sorry."

She drew herself straight, an arrow in darkness. "Yes. Now my sister will rule, and I must let her."

"Luminessa, if you proclaim yourself—"

"No," she said swiftly. "Key and I must go elsewhere, and the journey starts now. Come with us to Temple Mount, Latias. You've saved us, and now you need to flee as much as we do."

✳ 14

THEATANA PULLED BACK THE STAINED LINEN SHEET TO inspect the dandy-girl's ruined face. The dead prostitute's hair, spread across the couch and matted with blood, was as black and as long as Mandine's.

"Her build's the same as Mandine's," Dactulis said from behind Theatana. "She was wearing whore's dress, so I put a shift on the body when my men brought it in. But I didn't clean her up any."

Theatana yanked the sheet over the mutilated features. "She'll do," she said. A rusty odor of blood rose from the sheet, and she wrinkled her nose in distaste. "Did those islanders you sent need to make such a mess of her?"

"My lady, they're Mixtun barbarians, for all they're in Guard service. And you said she must be unrecognizable."

"She's that," Theatana agreed, and yawned. It had been a long, sleepless night. The Guard had secured the Numera and the Armory, as planned, but when Bardas had failed to return with Mandine, she'd become increasingly uneasy. Then she'd had a moment of real fear, when Dactulis brought the trei-march's body to the Red Council Chamber; he and some soldiers had found Bardas's corpse while searching the palace grounds for Mandine. But as the hours passed, it became clear that Mandine was not raising the city populace against the conspirators. Theatana could think of only one explanation for this: Mandine was no longer in Captala at all.

That was a gain for the moment, though it might mean trouble later. Otherwise, Theatana was satisfied; the Guard's loyalty, or at least that of its senior officers, was not going to be a problem. Dactulis had sworn faith to her, as had the three other senior men in the plot. These latter were out of the way for the moment, one in charge of the Armory and the other the Numera. The third had gone to the outer walls to see to the defenses, for the Tathars' cavalry advance guard had arrived outside the walls just before dawn. Only these four men, and Theatana herself, knew yet that her father was dead.

Now the gray dawnlight was edging through the windows of the Red Council Chamber, to lie dully on the blue cloak thrown over Bardas's corpse. Theatana glanced at the inert lump, then at the hanging that still concealed her father's body. Her father was dead, which was good, and Tracien was dead, which was annoying and inconvenient, though her quick mind had seen that even in death the treimarch could still serve her.

"The whore won't be missed," Dactulis said into the silence. "Or if she is, no one will bother about it."

A spasm of fury passed over Theatana's face, and she rounded on the man. "It doesn't matter if she's missed. What matters is that you and Bardas let Mandine get away. She had help, obviously from Latias and from that Elthamer who helped Latias take her from the House Azure. One of them must have killed Bardas, and Latias got Mandine through the Carmenal Gate under the guards' noses. *So where did she go?*"

Dactulis looked uncomfortable. "My lady, I don't know. But the outer gates are sealed, so they must be in the city. We'll find them."

Theatana's fingers curled into talons. "Dactulis, you aren't thinking. If my bitch-sister were here, she'd be raising the city mob against me. She hasn't done that. So she's *not here*, Dactulis, she's somewhere else. She's gotten out of Captala somehow, and for all we know she's on her way south with Latias. He's got estates down in the plantation lands, and that half-man has always hated me. He'd help her raise some ragtag army, and try for the diadem. So here's a question for you— if that happened, would the Guard follow me, or give the city to Mandine?"

"Line the Guard's pockets well, Luminessa, and they'll follow you. Captala has more riches than Mandine and Latias can ever hope to see. They can't buy the city from the Guard, and no army can take it. Mandine will never reign here, my lady."

"Nevertheless, we won't be truly safe till she's dead. Think like the soldier you are. Where has she gone?"

The officer pondered. "I see two possibilities. As you said, maybe she's gone south with Latias. But that Elthamer's also involved in her escape, according to the guards at the House Azure and Carmenal Gate. So she might have gone east, toward the Elthame, hoping to make an alliance there."

"All right. So it's south or east she's going. I want you to send men after her, Dactulis. Send those Mixtun butchers of yours, and pay them well. Half the money now, half when my sister's dead. Can you do that?"

"Immediately, my lady. I've got about twenty islanders I can use. I'll put them in two squads and send them out of Captala by the river port. They can take a light galley upriver to Salmoxis. The silverhairs won't be raiding that far yet, and the Mixtuns will reach Salmoxis by tomorrow evening. They can get horses at the posting station there. Then one squad will search east, the other south."

"Good. You're sure those braided savages will kill her? I don't want them rethinking their loyalty when they're about to put a blade to her neck."

"They'll kill her," Dactulis said. "Those islanders fight for coin, for all they've taken the army oath."

"See to it now." Theatana glanced at the ring-clock. "Then bring an honor guard to Accession Hall, in one turn and a half of the glass. I must assume the diadem and be proclaimed by the soldiers as soon as possible. Tell everyone that we have

Mandine's body, and that our father killed her. As to what happened to Bardas, have you got that straight?"

"He killed the Dynast in trying to defend Mandine, and took a mortal wound himself."

"Exactly. Spread it about as much as you can."

"Yes, Luminessa," Dactulis said, and turned to go.

"Guardsman," Theatana said in a low, hard voice.

The officer swung back to her. "Yes, my lady?"

"I am the *Dynastessa*. Down on your knees."

Dactulis sank to the floor, head bowed. Theatana watched him with a satisfied smile. She was only nineteen, and there were years of such delights to come.

Erkai, Duke Ragula, and King Hetlik halted their mounts at the edge of the grassy belt that separated the city fortifications from the outer ring of recently looted and burned suburbs. A quarter mile farther up the road, gleaming white in the noon sun, loomed the stupendous walls of Captala Nea. Even in the Hegemon's far-distant capital of Tatharkar, these defenses were spoken of as a wonder, but Erkai knew that the king and his generals had thought the tales exaggerated. Now, in the face of the reality, they looked awed and apprehensive. Triple-ranked the walls rose, the least and outermost equal to the girdle of a great fortress. Beyond the outer ring stood the even higher second rampart, and above that rose a white cliff, the titanic main wall, the Bastion of Athanais, its towers soaring into the summer sky. These were the land defenses, marching eastward on Erkai's left to blur into the heat-shimmering distance. To his right, they stretched downslope to the broad blue sweep of Chalice Bay. There they turned south to follow the shoreline for almost seven miles, past the city's impregnable naval harbor, until they reached the estuary of the Seferis.

Hetlik, sitting his dappled stallion ten feet from Erkai, cleared his throat. Erkai looked sideways at him. Near the king, Ragula leaned on his saddlebow, his eyes fixed on the nearest gate.

"What's that one?" Hetlik asked, pointing at the gate. It was broad enough for heavy traffic, but not as tall as one might have expected, given the height of the wall. It was sunk deep in the blue shadows of its defensive barbican and was clad in dark metal.

"Processional Gate," Erkai said. "It's probably the weakest, if there is a weak one."

"You're sure your Craft cannot help us?" Hetlik asked. "Now that you are here, do you sense any lessening of their wizardry?"

"Dread King, as I have told you from the first, Captala's walls and gates are protected against my Craft by the magic of a White Diviner. Only a like power can defeat that spell, and I have readily admitted that I do not yet possess such power."

"Yet?" the king said. "When will you?"

Ah, yes, Erkai thought, *when? I have posed that question to myself, many times. But now the answer is nearer. I am strong now, far stronger than when I last looked on these towers. Most important, I am someone the White Diviner did not foresee. But first I must make a path to her spell's source, and for that I need these white-faced animals. What a pity I didn't understand the chain long ago. Still, before this war and its fruits, I do not think I was strong enough to make much use of it.*

At Essardene he had completed all but nine links of the reversal spell, and at Phrax the rest. At both cities he had stalked through the glades of skinning frames and stakes, as thousands of prisoners gave up their life-energies in horror and torment. He had sucked that energy into him, and with it and his Craft had embedded each agony-charged symbol of the reversing spell into the chain, exactly as the shade of Spardas the Thanaturge had instructed him. The chain now clung snugly to his flesh, heavy and warm with power. If he were in a quiet place, and put his ear to the silver metal, he could hear a faint screaming, like the shrieks of a vast massacre. It was an effect he had noticed only recently, and it pleased him.

Suddenly he realized that Hetlik was frowning at him.

"When *will* you have such power, Erkai?" Hetlik demanded, irritation creeping into his tone.

Erkai knew the king was fuming again, at the failure of the lurking-spell to prevent Archates' escape from Essardene. The king misunderstood magic, like all the naive: He imagined it to be a craft as precise and predictable as sword-forging, which it was not. Black Craft lurking-spells sometimes faded or went awry for no obvious reason, no matter how adept the practitioner. Even if that didn't happen, they needed periodic renewal to maintain their strength. Such annoyances were to be expected, until he grasped the Deep Magic, and for that he had to get into the city.

"I will have it with Captala's fall," he said. "That is the long and the short of the matter, Dread King, as I have always admitted."

Hetlik scowled in annoyance, but declined to pry further. Instead, he studied the barbican, then turned to Ragula. "That gate's metaled against fire. A tough nut, and two tougher ones beyond it. If we heighten the siege towers, could we take the barbican and the gate as a base for an attack on the second wall?"

Ragula squinted against the sunlight's glare. "We could. But even when we had the barbican, we'd be under fire from the second rampart. I don't think we could hold if they sortied from the inside and came at us along the outer wall as well."

Erkai said, "Assault is not the way in."

"Then what is?" Ragula asked, curtly.

"Starvation and plague," Erkai said. "If you had a hundred myriads of men and did not fear to lose them all, you might take the city by storm; the White Diviner's magic protects only against sorcery, not against steel and fire. But no army has ever had such numbers. Your victory lies with sickness and famine inside the walls. You must break the defenders' will, then not even the Dynast's whip will keep them at their posts."

"But how are we to cut off their supplies?" Hetlik demanded. "You've been close-lipped, Erkai, and I haven't pressed you, but now it's time for an answer. I don't care to sit the army here for a campaigning season, when we have loot around us for the taking."

Barbarians and their loot, Erkai thought with disdain. "Dread King, their supplies come by sea, which their navy controls. But if their mariners see safe harbor by day, or homing beacons by night, where there are only shoals and rocks, those supplies will not reach the city."

"Your spells failed us at Essardene," Hetlik said irritably. "Why would you hope for success in this? Or do you intend finally to use that great spell we've been killing goldskins for?"

"No, Dread King. But the spell at Essardene was a lurking-spell, and not the sort I would use for this. In person, with a supply of captives to empower my Craft, I can keep all ships from reaching Captala by sea. After a disaster or two, they will be reluctant to risk their navy further. As for the approach down the Seferis, there are several islands fifteen miles up-stream. When our infantry arrives, garrison them with stone throwers, put log booms between them, and nothing will reach Captala from inland."

"Can't you use your illusions to help with an assault?" Hetlik said. "Make it look as though we aren't where we are?"

"Unfortunately, no. The Diviner's spell protects those on the walls from such attacks. If I did attempt a casting, it would rebound on us, to our great disadvantage."

"Very well. You know this city of old. How long to starve it out?"

"Dread King, their harvest was poor last year, and now in early summer the city granaries will be four-fifths empty. There are many refugees inside, as well." A cold smile stretched Erkai's lips. "We will wait till they are weakened and hungry, then let a ship drift ashore where the garrison can reach it. In the grain on board there will also be the seeds of a bleeding fever, which I can provide. By mid-autumn they will be abandoning their sick and dead in the streets, and soon thereafter they will open the gates in their despair, no matter how Archates protests. Captala will be yours."

"Mid-autumn, eh?" Hetlik said. "Ragula? Can we keep the

army here that long, before we run short of forage and have to move on?"

Ragula calculated swiftly. "Yes, my king. Just."

Hetlik nodded, satisfied. "Let's ride closer. I want to see what is to be mine."

The king trotted his horse onto the belt of open grassland that bordered the outer wall. Erkai, Ragula, and the royal guard followed. Erkai concentrated, and as the king's party approached Processional Gate, his Craft-sharpened mind sensed the aura of the Diviner's spell. Its strength, as he knew from long ago, was greatest at the inner Bastion of Athanais, but its effect extended across the whole curtain of fortifications.

Several helmeted heads appeared between the merlons of the outer battlements. Erkai could not perceive thoughts, but if he drew on deep reservoirs of will he could, from a moderate distance and for a brief time, sense states of mind. He considered trying this on the sentries, but rejected the idea. They were unimportant, and the effort would tire him greatly.

Hetlik reined in, and the party stopped. The king rose in his stirrups, took a deep breath, and bellowed, "The King of the Tathars is upon you! Open your gates, submit, and you will be spared."

No response came from the parapet, not even a flight of arrows. Then Erkai heard a shout from within the walls.

"Dynastessa! Dynastessa!"

Dynastessa? Erkai thought, a little startled. *What's this?*

He watched the ramparts. Rising into view above them, floating on the summer breeze, came the Dascarid banner, a white monogram on scarlet; beside it was the Great Standard of the Ascendancy, the sun disk with wheat garlands on a green ground. Between the merlons appeared a figure in crimson and silver. Erkai's eyes narrowed. It was a woman, and on her dark hair was the yellow glint of gold.

"What in Scyl's name?" Ragula exclaimed. "Why are they calling for a Dynastessa?"

"Archates is overthrown," said Erkai, suddenly understanding. "That must be one of his daughters. She's taken the diadem, or had it put on her. See, she wears it."

"By Scyl, so she does," Hetlik said. "Ragula, give me your spyglass."

The Tathars jabbered excitedly, but Erkai ignored them. This was important; he must try to sense the woman, despite the exhaustion it would inflict on him. Drawing on his deepest self, he felt toward her. It was very, very difficult. Not only did the effort drain his strength, but the protection spell's aura resisted him, as if he tried to push through a thicket of dense thorn. For a moment he believed he would fail utterly, but just before his strength slipped away he managed to touch her, just a brush at her innerness before the Diviner's magic thrust him back.

He swayed, then slumped over his saddlebow, his breathing hard and ragged, his vision a red blur. But he had learned something. The woman was prideful, exultant, and only a little afraid. Yet behind these, in a trace he barely sensed, lay something else: a darkness, a mark he knew.

So, Erkai thought, as his mind uncramped and his sight slowly cleared, *she's touched the Black Craft. Already she's corrupted. I may be able to use this.*

Hetlik was lowering the glass. "She's young. No experience. Must be depending on those donkeys who think themselves generals. I wonder who slit Archates' throat for us?" The king laughed. "If it was her, she's an ally, though not intending so. Should I marry her, Ragula, or skin her for depriving me of Archates' death?"

"Skin her," Ragula growled. "I—"

He broke off as a wind flattened the grass. It was no summer wind, but fanged with glacial cold. The sunlight turned pale, though the sky was unclouded. The horses squealed and shied, even Erkai's black mare. Still weakened, he fought her to a standstill.

"What's happening?" Hetlik bellowed. "Erkai—"

"Danger!" Erkai croaked over the wind's keen. "Go back, go back. This is not for you." He pulled his hood about his face as grit blew around him. What the others did he could not tell, for darkness came with the hood, like a sudden blindness.

Then there was silence, and from the silence came Its voice, soft and terrible and full of pain.

Erkai, my good and faithful servant.

In that lightless place, Erkai struggled to reply. Already weakened, he was shaken to his core, for he had not believed the Adversary could bring itself to strike into the world like this. Creation seared Its very being and essence; always, as far as Erkai had ever heard, It worked through human agencies to achieve Its ends. Yet now It was here, though he felt It straining as the power of Creation strove against It, to drive It back to the gulf from which It came.

"What do you want of me, Adversary?" he said, without breath or tongue or mouth. His strength was drained, and he knew he was in deadly peril. Only the power of his will stood between him and Spardas's fate of absorption, and he did not know if that will was enough.

I want nothing. I bring you aid.

"What aid?" Erkai asked, not convinced of Its disinterest. "I owe nothing for a service I do not request."

Nevertheless it is yours. A woman seeks your doom. She seeks the Signata, and you would do well to fear her, if she finds it.

"Then her search is the least of my concerns. No one can find the Signata. It finds them, and it has found no one since the drowning of Fallas Gaea. It may be altogether gone from the world. And it was no talisman of power. Why should I fear the Signata?"

Do not assume too much, Erkai the Chain.

"A Dascarid woman dabbles in my Craft. Is she the one you speak of?"

No. It is another.

"I act as your ally in Creation. Why do you not destroy this other woman, to assist me?"

The voice was weakening and fading. *It is not in my power. I struck once at her, when she crossed the bounds. But I could do no more than put a touch in her. She had aid, and I was driven out, and I suffer still for my intervention.*

"What aid did she have?"

The voice held despair, the longing for light and the hatred of light, and its own eternal torment. *That of Creation, that sears me even now. I must go. Your world eats my substance. Act. Find the woman who seeks your doom. Act.*

"How?" Erkai said, but he was suddenly gazing not on blackness but on green grass and the white walls of the city. The reek of the smoldering suburbs scratched at his throat. The sun was bright, the air warm.

He looked around. The others had not fled; frozen in place, perhaps. Hetlik's eyes stared fixedly at nothing, and his mouth worked. Ragula was bent double in his saddle, his shoulders and arms twitching. Men in the escort moaned softly and steadily; two had buried their heads in their arms, and several had vomited over their mounts' withers. The horses were silent, but fear-sweat gleamed wet on their trembling flanks, and foam dripped from their mouths.

Erkai summoned the dregs of his strength. "Dread King," he said sharply, "it is gone. Come back."

Hetlik's face worked. He wheezed convulsively, and said in a thin, strangled voice, "I saw . . . it was a black wind. You went into it. It sucked at my soul. Did you call *that*, sorcerer?"

Even in his exhaustion, Erkai thought: *There is advantage in this.* "It knows my voice," he said, and added, for good measure, "I have known It to show displeasure if my intentions are thwarted."

Hetlik looked away. Ragula, still shaking, unbent. "Lord Erkai," he blurted, "forgive me any offenses against you. I beg your mercy."

Erkai ignored him and looked up at Captala's ramparts. The woman still observed them from beneath the banners. With the wall-spell shielding her from the Adversary's visitation, she would have seen only peculiar movements in the Tathar party. But she was not the woman who sought the Signata; the Adversary had said as much, and when Erkai had so fleetingly touched her he had sensed no urgency that would suggest such a search.

Find the woman who seeks your doom. Like most of the information the Adversary had given him, this was obscure, incomplete, possibly a lie, possibly treacherous. And the Signata? Even if that ancient enigma awoke, nothing in Erkai's knowledge suggested it would resist either his Craft or the Deep Magic.

But to let him know of the threat, the Adversary had submitted to the agony of an encounter with the Created world, something Erkai could even now hardly believe. That suggested the threat was real, and dire, and much contrary to the Adversary's ends, if not to Erkai's. The encounter was also intimidating; if Erkai ignored Its gift of knowledge, might It strike directly at him? Previously he had not considered that a threat, but now . . . he might be wise to investigate further and take precautions if they were warranted.

Thinking this, Erkai studied the duke. The fool had been an irritant since the army marched from Tatharkar. "Dread King," he said, "I have learned something from the daemon who serves me. I ask for Duke Ragula's services, to be provided after I have made further queries into the matter."

Ragula's hands twitched on his reins. "It is yours," Hetlik blurted. "What do you want of him?"

Erkai said, "I will want him to find someone for me."

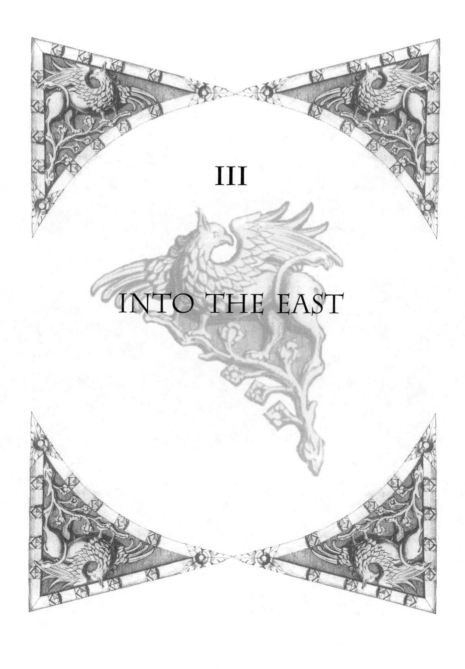

III

INTO THE EAST

✳ 15

THE WATER WAS SO COLD IT MADE KEY'S THROAT ACHE. He finished drinking and dipped the leather bottle into the stream again to fill it. The horses, their thirst now slaked, grazed placidly beneath the willows and river birch that bordered the watercourse.

A yard from Key, squatting like a washerwoman on a flat stone beside the brook, Mandine splashed water over her dusty cheeks. Late-afternoon sun glinted on the drops as they fell from her hands, and he found himself worrying about her again. Half a night and most of a day had passed since they exited from Temple Mount's hidden passage, well outside Captala's walls, and still she had hardly spoken. This was not how he had imagined them together, in this silence. Watching her, he wondered if she were grieving for her murdered father. He had seen the man only as a bloodily inept commander, but to her, Archates might have been different. Yet she had shed no tears.

"What are you looking at?" she asked in a harsh voice as she noticed his scrutiny.

He corked the water bottle. "Pardon, my lady. I wondered only if you needed rest before we go back to the road. We've been in the saddle since long before dawn."

"Oh, stop it."

Key stiffened. "My lady? Stop what?"

"That. *My lady. Luminessa.*" Mandine put her face in her hands. "Oh, please, just stop. I can't bear it. It makes me remember. Who I am, what I was, what I've done. What I haven't done."

Key rocked back on his haunches. "My—I don't understand."

She let her hands fall, and he saw anguish in her face. "I keep wondering if I should have stayed in Captala. I asked Latias if he thought so, just before we went down into the catacombs."

At that time Key had been busy with the map Taras had supplied, but he remembered Mandine and the chamberlain talking quietly, out of his hearing. "What did he say?"

"That only I could decide. He said he wasn't absolutely sure the Guard would support me, but he thought it would, and that the people of Captala had already acclaimed me Dynastessa, which is no small thing. And that he believed Theatana would be a worse ruler than my father ever was. He fears for the city, Key, and everyone in it. Not to mention what will happen to the Ascendancy if Captala falls to the Tathars, through my sister's misrule."

"His fear's reasonable," Key said. He wondered, briefly, where Latias was now. The chamberlain had accompanied them as far as the secret exit from the catacombs, but they had left him waiting for Taras to find him a horse.

"I know it's reasonable. He's usually right about these things, and he didn't want me to go, even though I told him I'd promised the Two that I would."

"That promise, I think, comes above all others."

Her hands clenched into fists. "But Key, I still feel as if I've run away. As if I've left my people to the Tathars, and to my sister and the generals, all fighting over the diadem. As if I were the traitor my father thought I was. My people needed me, and I've abandoned them."

"But you *haven't* abandoned them," Key protested. "The Lady and the Allfather said we had to find the Signata, on everyone's behalf. That's hardly abandonment."

"But look at us! What chance have we, just two of us? We

don't know what we're searching for or where to search for it. What if we've misunderstood something, and we're going the wrong way?"

They had talked over their direction before dawn, after getting well clear of Captala. "Do you think we shouldn't go east, then?" Key asked.

"How should I know?" She sighed. "I suppose it makes as much sense as any other direction—at least it's toward where the Signata last was seen. Though that was seventeen hundred years ago," she added, morosely.

"I know. I'm worried, myself. But I think we just have to keep going and trust to the Lord and the Lady."

Mandine grimaced. "I hope we don't need to go as far as the New Sea. You're from the east. You know the stories about the Cursed Shore."

"People do go there," Key reassured her. "Treasure seekers, men prospecting for metals. Trappers, sometimes, when furs are scarce in the Elthame."

"And do they all come back?"

"No," Key said reluctantly. "But the Allfather and Our Lady Mother are with us, Luminessa."

She raised her head, and her indigo eyes looked into his. "You're doing it *again*. Why don't you just call me Mandine? You have to get used to it, anyway. We can't avoid meeting people, and you can't make the mistake of calling me by my title in front of them. And it's a common enough name, anyway—after my name day, half the parents in the Ascendancy were calling their newborn daughters Mandine."

"Yes, you're right," Key said. "I'll remember." He slung the strap of the bottle over his shoulder and stood up. His chestnut gelding, still munching, raised its head and pricked its ears at him. "We should go on. We need to make Salmoxis before the sun sets, or they may shut us out."

"Yes," Mandine said, and dipped her water bottle into the stream. As it bubbled, she asked suddenly, "Are you wondering that I don't weep for my father's death?"

Discomfited, he said, "I don't know how you felt about him."

"I thought I felt very little for him. But he was my father, and he's dead. I had no one else, Key, except my half sister, and she wants to kill me. And now Theatana and I are the last of the House of the Dascarids." She stoppered the bottle and slowly got to her feet. "I feel bereft. I have no relatives who care for me. I don't even know if my father cared for me, though he might have, in his way. But now he's gone, and I'll never know. So that is what I feel. Regret. But not enough, yet, to make me weep. Do you understand?"

For an instant Key would have pulled her to him. But she was still the luminessa, though he might call her by name. "I think so," he said. "Though it's hard for me to understand, a little." He tried to imagine how he would feel if his father had treated him as Archates had treated Mandine and glimpsed an aching void. But there was nothing he could do to fill it.

Mandine was gazing downstream at the stone bridge that carried the Great East Road over the watercourse. "I'm ready to go now," she said, her voice dulled with weariness.

They mounted, and rode along the stream bank to the bridge, where they regained the road. No travelers were on it, though it was the main route to the east. The towns and villages through which they had already passed had been deserted as well; everyone within reach of Captala had either gained the shelter of the city's walls or had already fled eastward to escape the fury of the Tathar advance. Beyond the fields to Key's right gleamed a wide band of water, where the Seferis curved to within half a mile of the road. Usually the river was thronged with cargo broadboats, but now its slow current bore only a few high-prowed fishing craft. There was also a hemiolia, speeding upriver under both sail and oars; someone was in a hurry. At this distance Key could not tell whether the hemiolia was a rich man's pleasure craft, pressed into service for escape, or a naval dispatch-galley.

The river drew out of sight as the road swung north to avoid a stretch of marshland. A weathered stone block came into view, and Mandine pointed at the figures incised into the pink granite. "The sixty-first milestone. How far to Salmoxis now?"

Key pulled the map from his sabretache and unfolded it. It was Temple Mount work, and equal to the best military maps he had seen. Nor was it the only gift of the Perpetua and the Continuator. Taras had given Mandine a long dagger, and to each of them a money belt packed with silver minims and gold regnals, enough to feed a poor family for half a year. More precious even than these was the Perpetua's gift to Mandine: Athanais's book. Mandine had been reluctant to accept it, but Orissi had pressed it on her, saying that the Diviner's prophecy should go with those who were to fulfill it.

"Eight more stones," Key said. "We'll be there before sundown." *And none too soon,* he thought. The Temple Mount horses were good, but they weren't yet accustomed to endurance riding, and both Mandine's gray mare and his chestnut had begun to flag. He himself was tired and aching. Mandine was tougher than he had expected, and a superb horsewoman, but by now she must be on the brink of exhaustion.

He put the map away, and they went on as the sun settled behind them. The road was now climbing toward a range of hills whose tops were crowned with woodlots. It was a rich land; on both sides of the highway were fields of young grain and pastures dotted with russet auroch cows, valued for their milk as the auroch steers were for their meat. Salmoxis lay just over the far hill-line, but reaching it was only the first and smallest step of their journey. They had almost a thousand miles to go, across the plains and uplands of half the Ascendancy, all the way to the shores of the New Sea, where drowned Fallas Gaea slept in the cool silence beneath the waves.

Key thought: *And then, if we find nothing?*

If they decided not to continue the search, he could take her to Oak Haeme, his own country. The vast, mountainous plateau of the Elthame states rose mile-high on the north of the New Sea, and Oak's southern border would be within fairly easy reach. They could remain there. Mandine would be in exile, but an exile that in his company she might come to accept. . . .

"What are you thinking about?" Mandine asked suddenly.

He suppressed a guilty start. "A hot meal," he said quickly. "A soft bed."

She gave him a tired smile. "I thought soldiers were too hardy to bother themselves about such things."

Key grimaced. "On the contrary. Soldiers bother about them more than anybody else, because such things are so often lacking."

She smiled again, this time ruefully. "I didn't think of that. That's going to happen to us, isn't it?"

"Yes, it is."

Salmoxis stood on a bend of the River Seferis; it was a center of the wine trade, and famous for the sweet, heady vintages it shipped to Captala's cellars. Like most Ascendancy cities of the inner provinces, it was weakly fortified, though it had a walled commandery where its citizen-wardsmen trained twice a year. At the flimsy west gate, Key asked three such wardsmen for directions to a hostelry. They were of little help. Fugitives from down the river had filled the city, they said, and no room was to be had anywhere.

Their search for accommodations lasted until long after sunset. At last, Key and Mandine had some luck: An inn by the north gate gave them a place in the stable loft, for a price that should have bought three nights in a guesthouse of regal quality. Key gritted his teeth and paid. He was not unhappy, though, to be sleeping near the horses. As the times were, good mounts invited thievery.

He had not expected Mandine to help him unload the animals, but she did, cutting off his protest with a quick frown. They dragged their baggage to the loft, where Key at last could shed his mail. He had been wearing over it the gray-green surcoat Taras had provided; this he put back on, with a linen shirt. Orissi had cut Mandine's hair into a shoulder-length bob, such as the women of the minor merchant class wore, and her riding clothes were the tough breeches, boots, and tunic that such women would use for hard traveling. With the dust of travel on them, she and Key looked little different from many of the other refugees crowding Salmoxis. If anyone asked, Mandine was traveling to take shelter with her brother and his Elthamer wife in the east. Key was to pose as her brother-in-law, her escort on the road. In the commotion of Salmoxis, though, it seemed unlikely that anyone would show much curiosity about them.

They paid a groom a copper dandyprat to watch their gear, and went to eat oatcakes and fish stew in a dim corner of the inn's common room. It was crowded with refugees and townsfolk, and full of terrifying rumors about the Tathars, but no one mentioned Archates' death. The news of his overthrow had obviously not yet reached Salmoxis.

After eating, they returned to the loft, which was dimly lit by lanternlight filtering from the stable below. Mandine pulled off her riding boots, wrapped herself in her gray cloak, and was asleep seconds after collapsing onto the hay. Key, after making sure the groom hadn't pilfered anything from their gear, removed his own boots, hid his sword ready to hand under the hay, and likewise fell into oblivion.

A low groan woke him, much later. Already groping for his sword, he opened his eyes and saw pale dawnlight seeping into the loft. Again he heard the groan, softer this time. Key turned his head and saw Mandine levering herself to a sitting position. She looked blearily at him, ran fingers through her hair, and winced.

"Sore?" he asked.

"Very. Are you?"

He flexed his arms and legs. "A little. I'm trained to it. You're not."

"This will train me. I hope I survive the process."

"You will. The horses were having a hard time of it yesterday, though. Now that we're farther from the Tathars, we'd better ease back on them. If they go lame, we'll have trouble finding replacements."

"You're right," she said, yawning. "Do you really think we're out of the silverhairs' reach here?"

"For the moment. But I want to move on as soon as we

can. Once we're beyond Salmoxis, I think we'll be fairly safe. If they do come this way soon, it will be to sack the city."

Mandine picked up her sabretache and belt and gazed sadly at her sheathed dagger. "I saw that gate. There's no real protection for the people here, is there?"

"No." Key pulled on his boots and stood up, leg muscles protesting. "I'll bring bread and cheese and some small beer from the kitchen. We'll eat on the road."

She looked discomfited. "Where does one wash in these places? I was too tired to bother last night, and I feel filthy."

Key remembered suddenly that Mandine had never slept in an inn before, much less in a hayloft. On his own he would have used the well bucket in the innyard, but he said, "I'll ask for hot water and soapseeds."

"All right." Mandine was searching in the hay for her boots. "Thank you. I'll see to the horses while you're gone."

She was, he thought as he descended the ladder, adapting better than he'd expected. She'd gone from scented sheets and white wheaten bread to hay and oatcakes, in less than two days. And she didn't expect him to fill the place of her servants, either; he would have done so, but he knew he would have resented it.

In the pink-and-blue light of dawn the inn was already awake. In the yard, a chunky man with the corded forearms of a smith poured well water over his head, and a stableboy scooped stray horse dung into a wooden bucket. Key smelled the kitchen's breakfast fires, baking bread, and the tang of frying gammon. His mouth was watering as he went through the open door of the common room.

He stopped. Across the room, a man with his back to Key was speaking in a low voice to a potboy, the boy who had served up the fish stew last night. The boy's eyes were wide and fixed on his questioner. The man wore green-leather Guard breeches, military hobnail boots, and a mail shirt, and at his side hung an army-issue cavalry saber. From beneath the back of his helmet hung a thick snake of black hair, braided with fine silver wire.

Time slowed to a crawl. *A Mixtun trooper,* Key thought, *from the Paladine Guard. What's a guardsman doing in Salmoxis? A deserter? But if he were, he wouldn't wear soldier's gear.*

He is looking for someone.

He is looking for Mandine.

My sword is in the hayloft.

The potboy's attention was still riveted on the Mixtun, and neither had noticed Key. Key stepped back through the door and ran to the stables. Mandine was in one of the stalls, probing her mare's left foreleg for signs of laming. She looked up at Key's approach, and said, "She's fine. So is your chestnut. I was worried last night—what's the matter?"

"There's a Paladine talking to the potboy. A Guardsman shouldn't be in Salmoxis. We have to get out of here."

Mandine's hand went to her mouth. "Theatana."

He was already climbing the ladder. "I think so."

She was right behind him as he gained the loft. Key scooped his sword out of the hay, went to the wall that overlooked the innyard, and put his eye to a crack between the boards. He could see the door to the common room. Theatana wouldn't have sent a single guardsman, but how many Mixtuns were now at the inn? If only one, he would try to kill the man before he could summon his comrades from elsewhere.

"Do you see anything?" Mandine whispered. Key shook his head.

Abruptly, the Mixtun emerged into the innyard. The islander glanced at the stable, then hurried through the yard gate to disappear into the street beyond. He must have been the only one investigating the inn, but now he was out of reach.

"He's gone for help," Key said. "No telling how long we've got. Downstairs quick, saddles and bridles, go."

"But our supplies—the saddlebags—"

"It's only food and clothing. We can get more, and the money's in our belts. Have you got the Lady's wheat and Athanais's book?"

Mandine patted the sabretache at her waist. "Here."

"Good." He yanked his mail shirt over his head, buckled

his sword belt, and rammed his helmet on. Then he checked his sabretache for the essentials: the map, flint and steel, quicklights, ready coin. Everything was there.

In the stable they readied the horses in furious haste. The animals sensed their agitation and stamped and jittered. Key shoved the stable door wide, and they swung into their saddles. He could see the innyard gate, standing open just enough for a horse to pass. He drew his sword and held it low by the chestnut's flank.

"Let's go. At the trot."

The potboy and a groom were watching at the commonroom door, and their jaws dropped as they saw Key's naked blade. But neither called out, and in seconds Key and Mandine were through the gate and into the street. It was narrow, with awnings jutting over wineshops and food stalls on each side, and even at this hour it was busy with trade and traffic. Key knew from last night's wandering that the east gate was close by, and they headed for it, dodging the sausage-hawkers and watermongers as they rode. He saw no Paladines. The one at the inn wouldn't know he'd been spotted, and the Guardsmen would lose some time by going there. But they'd soon discover from the groom or the potboy that their quarry had fled, and they'd immediately set out in pursuit. If they didn't already have horses, they'd find some.

The street widened, and Mandine moved up on his left. "I don't understand how they got here so fast."

Key gritted his teeth. "My fault. I saw a hemiolia heading upriver yesterday. The Paladines must have been aboard. I should have thought of it."

"So should I. I saw it, too. What are we going to do?"

He remembered the map; it showed hills, marsh, and forest beyond Salmoxis. "It's not far to rough country. If we can reach that, we may be able to lose them."

"There's the gate," Mandine said. It was only fifty yards away, at the farside of a small square, and it stood open. Carpenters labored to strengthen it, spiking raw new planks to the old. A single sentry with a rusty pike loitered nearby, watching the men work.

Without warning, braids flying behind them, nine Paladines ran from a side street into the square. All were on foot, and all were Mixtuns. They saw Mandine, and yelled in excitement.

"Ride!" Key shouted at her. "Ride them down!"

His heels jabbed his chestnut's flanks. The horse gathered itself and lunged into a rolling canter. Pedestrians scattered like frightened birds. Mandine was beside him, her dagger out. Two Mixtuns ran across the square toward the gate; the carpenters and the sentry fled. Key's heart sank. The other seven, now rushing at him and Mandine, were too many. They'd saber the horses, and with the horses down the fight would be over.

He could still die an Elthamer. He aimed the chestnut at the enemy, and from his throat rose the ancient battle cry of the far plains, high, piercing, and harsh.

Four Mixtuns had outrun the others. Key struck at one, felt the blade bite, heard Mandine's horse scream. A sting on his calf. His animal shrieked and reared, and almost stopped. He dragged its head down, and hacked at the sword hand of a second Mixtun, who was trying to saber the chestnut again. The man howled and fell away. Key saw Mandine ahead of him, with blood in a sheet on her gray's flank, and the Mixtuns running after her. The two at the gate had almost closed it.

The chestnut was still on its feet, struggling against the bit to flee its attackers. Key used the horse's panic to send it after the running men. They heard the hooves and turned to form rank, sabers ready. Mandine spun her mare away from the Mixtuns at the gate and rode back toward Key, but her mount was barely trotting. Half-crazed with fury and despair, Key howled again the battle cry of the Elthame. It echoed in the street, from the gate, from the city wall. The Mixtuns awaited his onrush. He raised his saber.

And he heard the battle cry again, and saw three horsemen, bareheaded and yelling like fiends, charge from a side street into the square. They brandished the great curved swords of the Elthame, and the leader's hair was bronze. They rode over the Mixtuns at the gate and cut them down even as Key's chestnut slammed into the wavering rank of the five surviving islanders. One stabbed at him, but the others broke and ran into the shops lining the street. Key swiped at the remaining man, but he dodged under the chestnut's head and escaped into an alley too narrow for a horse.

A profound silence fell, broken only by the rattle of hooves on cobbles. The townsfolk had fled the street and square. Mandine had halted her bleeding, terrified gray, and was staring at the three horsemen. They stared back at her. Key collected the quivering chestnut and rode toward them. The bronze-haired leader turned at the sound. He was a huge young man, clean-shaven except for a ferocious mustache whose points swooped below the line of his jaw. Key blinked in astonishment, and the Elthamer's blue eyes widened.

"By the Lord's teeth," the man exclaimed in Haema. "Kienan Mec Brander. I thought you were dead!"

Key rode up to him, and they clasped forearms. "I nearly was. Great Allfather, what are you doing here, Cawlor Mec Skerris?" He glanced at the other two Elthamers, who nodded and grinned. One he didn't know, but the other, a redhead, had a familiar look. "Ardri Mec Ruaid? From Winterburn?"

"No, that would be my older brother," the young man said. "I'm Naevis."

Cawlor scowled at the four Mixtun corpses. "More of this later. If your horses will serve, we'd better get out of here."

Key leaned to inspect the wound in the chestnut's flank. The animal still trembled in pain and fright, but the flow of blood from the shallow gash was already easing. "It can be tended later," he said, straightening.

Mandine was at his side. "Thank you, my lords," she said. "All of you."

Cawlor bowed in his saddle, and spoke in the Logomenon. "My lady, it was nothing. A skirmish. How's your horse?"

"She's cut, but she'll bear me a while— *Key, another one, it's Jaladar!*"

The Mixtun of Mandine's old escort was astride a horse and trotting from an alley. Key was already turning his chestnut when Cawlor put out a hand to stop him. "This one's ours," Cawlor said. "He knows you."

Jaladar rode up and saluted. The somber eyes and the dark, sharp-chinned face were expressionless. "Victurion," he said. "My lady."

Mandine's face was full of confusion. Key looked at Jaladar, at Cawlor, then back at the islander. "You helped us?" he said. "But—"

"He did," Cawlor broke in. "He told us the others like him were looking for you and the lady."

"The ones who got away will bring others to hunt you," Jaladar said. "We must all go, and quickly."

Is he a lone assassin? Key thought. *There's no time now. Find out later.*

Keeping himself between Mandine and the Mixtun, he headed for the still-open gate. The Elthamers followed. No one opposed them, and in moments they were all beyond the walls, the horses galloping at full stretch. Key's mind churned with questions, but in the drum of hooves he could not ask them. He settled himself to the chestnut's rhythm and rode hard, Mandine beside him, the others bringing up the rear.

East of Salmoxis stretched wet lowlands and fens, where the engineers of the early Ascendancy had built miles of causeways and stone bridges. Beyond the marshes the ground rose again, and the road began to wind through thickly wooded hill country. Key's mount was laboring now, and Mandine's gray was blowing foam from its nostrils. He didn't feel safe yet, but they could not keep on in this blind rush. He slowed the pace to a trot, and waved Cawlor up beside him.

"We need to get off this road," he said. "We're too exposed."

Cawlor squinted into the early sunlight. "I saw a stream yesterday—can't be much farther on. We can get into the forest without leaving a trail. Follow me."

He put his horse into a canter. Two miles on, a shallow watercourse passed under the road. Cawlor walked his horse into the water and led the others upstream. Trees and underbrush closed over and around them, the brook changed course, and in minutes they were out of sight of the highway.

"Did you go this far?" Key asked Cawlor.

"No. Do you want to go on?"

Key nodded, and Cawlor fell back to let him lead. For some time the horses picked their way along the shadowy stream, through a green tunnel roofed by hornbeams and feather-pines. After a mile the roof thinned, and the undergrowth drew away from the banks to expose rough limestone ledges and mats of pine needles. Then the trees themselves parted, and the small band rode into a grassy hillside clearing, where the brook tinkled down a set of miniature rapids. Key stopped and let the reins slacken. The chestnut immediately put its head down and, despite the bit in its mouth, tried to graze.

"Our animals need water," he said, dismounting. "And forage, soon." He looked up to see Jaladar's dark expressionless face gazing down at him. "Peltarch Jaladar, you were with those others."

"I was with them, victurion. I was not of them."

Key considered this. During the short time he had commanded Jaladar, the peltarch had not behaved like most Mixtun rankers. He might, possibly, be trusted.

"How good are those others at tracking?" he asked.

Jaladar shook his head. "In this country? Poor. But they will keep looking."

"How many are there?"

"We were twenty all told," Jaladar said as he also slid from his saddle. "Ten took the ferry across the river early this morning, with horses, to look for you to the south while we searched in the city. Those ten will be called back, and all who still live will then hunt you. But for the moment we are safe enough, I think."

Everyone had dismounted by now. "Cawlor," Key said, "you I know, and Naevis I know of, but your other comrade has the advantage of me and—and my companion."

Cawlor grinned at Key, then gave Mandine a sweeping bow.

"My lady, I am your obedient servant, Cawlor Mec Skerris. My family's lands are near those of the Branders, which is how I know Kienan. This skinny person here is Naevis, of clan Ruaid, also from Oak." He waved the third man forward. "And this close-mouthed gentleman, as you'll find him to be, is Lonn. He's not from Oak, but he'll do in a pinch, for all that. He's from clan Mairid, up north in Ash Haeme."

As Cawlor spoke, Key pulled his helmet off and wiped his damp forehead. It was a vast relief to have reinforcements, if only for a while. Better yet, they were Elthamers. Naevis carried a stiff war bow on his back, and had a sparse red beard that did little to hide his youth. Lonn's left cheek was splotched with a ruddy fish-shaped birthmark, a sign of luck. The Ashman's gray eyes were heavy-lidded and distant, as though he watched within himself as much as without.

Mandine was smiling. "I am very pleased to meet you all," she said. "I cannot begin to thank you. And especially you, Jaladar, for telling these gentlemen that we needed help."

"I thank you, too," Key said, though he still did not quite trust the islander. "Can you tell us who sent you after us, peltarch?"

Jaladar bared his teeth, and for the first time Key saw that the incisors were inlaid with fine gold spirals. "Our orders came from the Paladine commander, my lord. But I think I know who spoke through him."

"Who?" Key asked, though he knew what the answer would be.

"The younger luminessa," Jaladar said in a bitter voice. "The woman who called me a dirty island savage when I was assigned to her guard, and cut at my face with her switch when I scowled." His tone softened, and he bowed to Mandine. "But you, my lady, when I was among your escort, you always looked kindly on me. You even knew my name. How could I willingly let you come to harm? Also, though this is less important, I am not the same filth as some other Mixtuns of the Guard. They are the scum of our islands. But I was noble, once, and I do not slaughter women for pay."

"So you decided to help us?" Key said. He wanted to believe Jaladar; otherwise, the man would have to die. That would be sickening. Killing in battle was bearable, but to become an executioner . . . He thrust the thought away.

Jaladar nodded. "I went with the others, hoping I might find you before they did. We reached Salmoxis by boat last night and began seeking you. This morning one of the others brought word he'd found you. I didn't know what to do, but then I saw these three in the street, and from their arms and bronze hair I knew they were your countrymen. I slipped away from my unit, and told the lord Cawlor that a man of his nation needed help. He and the others rode off, and I took a horse from a merchant who didn't need it and followed. The rest you know."

"Jaladar," Mandine interrupted, before Key could question him further, "you were in Captala yesterday morning, weren't you? What's happened there?"

"My lady, I am sorry, but the Dynast . . ."

"I know he's dead, Jaladar. But what's Theatana done?"

The Mixtun's face darkened. "When we left, the word was that she had taken the diadem, with the support of the Guard and the senior officers. There was a rumor that you, too, were dead, and that your father killed you." He laughed harshly. "The men I was with know you are alive, of course, but they are not about to sing it in the streets. They are too well paid."

The three Elthamers by now were staring in growing disbelief at Mandine. Naevis's eyebrows seemed about to disappear into his hairline.

"She planned it well," Mandine said softly. "May she have much joy of her prize."

Key studied Jaladar, as if by this scrutiny he could find the man's intentions in his face. Meeting his look, the Mixtun said, "I know what you think, victurion, and I do not blame you. You may kill me if you wish. But I swear to you on the Two and on all my gods, and on my honor, that the Luminessa Mandine is safe with me."

Key heard Naevis's sharp intake of breath and Lonn's soft

grunt. The brook chattered among its stones, and a bellbird sounded its metallic call from a distant treetop. Cawlor tore his gaze from Mandine and turned it on Key. "The Allfather preserve us," he stammered. "I didn't think I was hearing right, the last few minutes, but . . . is this really *her*?"

Mandine gave the three Elthamers a contrite smile. "I have been perhaps overreticent, and I apologize. But your suspicions are correct. I am the Luminessa Mandine, and despite the rumors to the contrary, I am very much alive."

No one spoke for a moment. Then Naevis sputtered, "Forgive me, Luminessa, if I've said or done anything to offend you." He sank to one knee, head bowed, face red as his straggly beard. Cawlor and Lonn did likewise, stumbling over their words, stuttering apologies for their earlier familiarity. Key watched his countrymen cope with their astonishment. At another time their discomfiture would have amused him, but he was too mindful of what lay ahead, and of the assassins who followed. Finally, Mandine said, "My lords, please forget who I am, for the time being. Think of me only as a traveler like yourselves. I am, however," she added gravely, though her eyes sparkled, "a very *hungry* traveler."

They were falling over each other to reach their saddlebags when Key stopped them. "I don't want to eat here. It's too close to the road, and if those Mixtuns pick up our trail somehow, we won't hear them over the noise of the brook. Let the horses drink, and then we'll go."

Jaladar nodded. "The victurion is right, my lords. They will not give up easily."

Well, Key thought, *if Mandine is willing to trust him, I can do no less.* "We've nothing for the cuts on our mounts," he said to Cawlor. "Is one of you carrying something to help them?"

Lonn had a horse surgeon's traveling kit in his gear. While the gray and the chestnut drank, he gently applied a healing salve to their wounds; he was deft with the animals, and they seemed to like him. "What now?" Cawlor asked Key, when Lonn had put his ointment jar away.

Key disliked asking for more help. His countrymen had

already risked themselves enough. "Where are you going, yourselves?"

Cawlor's eyebrows rose. "With you and the luminessa. Where else?"

"But surely you have your own destination?" Mandine said.

"What? Leave you and Kienan alone, with assassins on your heels?" Cawlor grinned savagely beneath his mustache. "Never. We'll stay with you as long as you need us."

Relief flooded through Key. "We'll welcome your company," he said, and turned to the Mixtun. "Jaladar, as matters stand, my authority over you is gone. You may follow your own path from here."

The islander's deep-set eyes went to Mandine. "I would ride with you, if the luminessa wishes."

"I wish it," Mandine said. "Come with us, Jaladar, at least for a time."

After a search around the clearing's edge, they found an overgrown trail leading away to the southeast. This they followed until the sound of the brook faded behind them, to be replaced by birdsong and the rustle of leaves in the green canopy high overhead. The trail had once been a road, for the worn corners of paving stones protruded here and there from the turf. Key asked Mandine if she knew anything about it, but she did not.

His stomach was agrowl when they came across the ruins. It was hard to tell what the place had once been, for its tumbled walls were mere ridges in the forest floor. It was large, and very old, for enormous black beeches and sagbark oaks grew from what had once been its interior. The only wall that stood taller than Key's waist seemed to be the remains of a huge square keep. The keep's gate had long vanished, but beside the opening a few massive granite blocks still thrust, head-high, from the invading greenery.

The place was a good defensive position, if by spectacular bad luck they needed one, and Key called a halt. Inside the keep's ruin only one tree grew, an oak with a trunk seven feet thick, and it had driven out all other vegetation except the wiry cordgrass. While the horses grazed, the humans gnawed on bannock and tough smoked sausage.

"We apologize for the poor fare, my lady," Naevis said, blushing again. "You must be used to better."

"Hunger's the best sauce," Mandine told him. She turned to Key. "Do all your countrymen speak the Logomenon with such grace and gallantry?"

Naevis turned even redder, and Key grinned at him. "Most of our landed gentry know the tongue, to some degree. It's part of our education. My father is very fluent, and so is my sister Ria. And our senior servants, too, my father's steward for example."

"Mine's a bit rusty, my lady," said Cawlor apologetically. "I was never a scholar."

Mandine gave him a warm smile. "It's much better than you think. But please, calling me 'my lady,' and especially 'luminessa,' is dangerous. I would prefer it if you would call me Mandine." She shot a glance at Key. "Key is learning to do so, though so far he has managed, usually, not to call me anything at all."

"But," Lonn said, "I don't understand what's happened to you. Surely, if your father the Dynast is—if the throne is empty, you should be the one to take it."

Mandine sighed. "My half sister thought otherwise. The rest is too long a story, and I mustn't tell you all of it, anyway. It's enough to say that Key and I must go east, to carry out a certain task, and only he and I can know what it is. But we would be grateful for your company, for as long as you're willing to give it."

Cawlor's expression showed that he wanted to know more, but he only tugged angrily at his mustache. "She's seized the throne from you? Your sister's a usurper?"

"Yes, but it doesn't matter. It may later, but it doesn't at the moment."

"I still don't understand," said Naevis plaintively. "Surely your people would follow you, if you proclaimed yourself? Why don't you?"

"Naevis," Cawlor warned, "mind that upstart tongue of yours."

Mandine gave Naevis a sad smile. "It makes no sense to you, I know. But I cannot make myself known. I would if I could, but I cannot."

"Even so," Lonn said, "you're the rightful heir. Look now, Cawlor, we'd planned to swear ourselves into the Ascendancy's service. We still can."

"Is that why you're here?" Mandine asked them. "To fight for the Ascendancy?"

"That's right," Naevis said brightly. "We three are younger sons, with little inheritance to look for. But we're good at weapon play, from the fighting up north—"

"The steppe riders again?" Key asked. His father's letter of five months ago had said that nomads from the northwest plains had gotten up onto the high plateau and caused some trouble in Ash.

Lonn nodded. "Last fall, and again in the early spring. They were looking for cattle and good horses, as usual, and three bands got into Ash from the Copper Gates. The other haemes sent us men, and we had some stiff fighting, but we fed the nomads a feast they'll not be in a hurry to eat again. It's been quiet since."

"But there's not much glory in chasing nomads, my lady," Naevis put in. "So we came to your country to fight your enemies the Tathars, and make our fortunes. We were on our way to Captala, but we heard last night the westerners have the city under siege. This morning we were trying to decide what to do next, when Jaladar happened on us. Let us swear our loyalty to you, as Lonn says."

Mandine raised her hand. "You do not need to swear. Your actions this morning are oath enough." She hesitated. "Also, my lords, Key and I are going to the New Sea, and it is not a place where I'd force you to follow."

The champing of horses' jaws was loud in the sudden silence. Then Lonn said, "You're going to the Cursed Shore?"

"Possibly," she said.

Cawlor's face became troubled, and he gulped down a mouthful of sausage. "Luminessa, that's no place for anyone. There were fearsome sorcerers there once, before the White Diviners ran 'em out and killed 'em. And remember about the old drowned people, too, washed up on the shore when the New Sea came in. Their ghosts are still there, it's said, and they're angry."

"Nevertheless," Mandine said, "that's where we may finally go."

"But my lady, it's not safe for you. Wouldn't it be better if you and Key came to the Elthame, instead? Oak would give you protection from the usurper."

"We appreciate your generosity," Mandine said, "but Key and I have decided to go to the New Sea, and we must."

Again the silence. Then Naevis said bravely, "If the luminessa's going there, so will I, ghosts or not."

Cawlor shrugged. "Well, I've never seen but one wraith, and it was of little consequence. I'll go, too."

"So will I," Lonn said, without hesitation.

"Jaladar?" Mandine asked. "I will not ask you to come with us. As Cawlor says, that part of my country has a malign reputation."

The Mixtun shook his head. "Where else would I go, Luminessa? My home is far across the Blue, and my enemies there would make me a ghost if I returned. I also will come with you."

"You're all sure?" Mandine asked.

They nodded, though their mood had darkened. "That's settled, then," Cawlor said, with forced cheer. "Naevis, Lonn, we wanted an adventure, and now we've got one. Enough of the matter." He turned to Key. "By the Allfather, I'm glad you're alive. We heard about Thorn River on the road, some days back. It was said the Tathars slaughtered the Dynast's army to the last foot soldier and cavalryman, and all the cataphracts. So I thought you were gone, too. What happened there, anyway?"

Key did not want to describe Archates' disastrous generalship in front of Mandine. "It was bad enough, but I'll tell you later. I wrote to my father about it, but I only sent the letter a few days ago. I suppose my father and Ria will think I'm dead, till they get it."

"They likely will," Cawlor said glumly. "I don't see what you can do, though, short of riding like a madman for home. But you won't get there before the rumors, not now."

Key took another chunk of bannock. "Speaking of home, what's the latest news?"

Cawlor told him: the crops thriving, the livestock fat and abundant, his sister and father in good health. Ria was not yet betrothed, though some thought she looked with favor on Tyrodi Mec Afrys. Naevis put in a few words here and there, Mandine listening with interest. Jaladar ate in silence, his gaze roving always across the tops of the ruinous walls.

Lonn finished eating before anyone else, and wandered away to poke among the fallen stones of the gateway. Suddenly Key saw him standing perfectly still near the opening, his eyes closed, his head tilted. Cawlor saw it, too, and thoughtfully pursed his lips.

"What's he up to?" Key asked.

"Lonn has a touch of the Kindly Gift," Cawlor muttered. "He doesn't like to talk about it. Sometimes he knows about things others don't. Sees them, too, maybe."

Key stood up and walked to the young Ashman. Lonn stirred and opened his eyes. "Did you hear something?" Key asked, as he peered through the gateway into the shadowy forest.

"Not with my ears." Lonn's voice was low. The wine-stain birthmark on his cheek had flushed to a deeper red. "I . . . ah, look. Straight ahead, deep in the trees. Do you see her?"

Key strained his eyes, but saw only paler greens where faint sunlight struggled down through the roof of leaves. Then a brighter patch shifted, and took on a wavering, misty shape. It was tall and slender, with the suggestion of flowing hair.

"She's a wood sprite," Lonn whispered. "An alsea, I think. Strange to see one in full day. I've only ever seen an alsea at dawn. I think it's lucky."

"I hope so," Key muttered. He'd come across nature spirits six or seven times in the wilder parts of Oak, and seeing them had never brought him either good fortune or bad. Wood sprites weren't usually mischievous, though, and rarely made themselves known around human habitations. "Does she want something? Is that why she's out in daylight?"

"I don't know," Lonn said. "If she comes close enough, I'll try to get her to speak to me."

"Speak to you?" Key was startled. Lonn had more than just a touch of the Gift if he could manage that. "You've talked with sprites?"

"A few times. They seem to like me. Ah, well, look there. She's noticed us. I wonder if she'll stay."

The alsea's hazy woman-shape glided out of sight, then reappeared a few yards closer, off to the right of the empty gateway. Lonn made a soft sound, then took a step toward her, then another. The alsea hung in the shadows, shining faintly, like mist lit by a new moon. Lonn went a little farther, and Key, though the hair on his arms rose and his skin tingled, followed him. He realized uneasily that they were now out of sight of the others.

Lonn stopped. The alsea was now only a dozen yards off. Key had never been so close to a wood sprite. Her face was indistinct, her body more so, though it was clearly a woman's. Then, for an instant, her translucent substance took on clarity, and Key's breath caught in his throat. She was beautiful, but no mortal woman had ever possessed a mouth so pale, nor eyes so haunted, nor fingers so supple and white. A cold sweat of apprehension crawled over Key's skin, and he prayed that she would not meet his gaze with hers. If he had been alone, he would have fled her presence as fast as he could.

Lonn raised his hand, and to Key's profound relief the

alsea wavered again into a hazy, luminous shape. She also might have gestured, but he wasn't sure. The Ashman bowed his head. A minute passed, as Key felt the sweat dry on his cheeks and upper lip. Then Lonn straightened, and the alsea drifted away among the tree trunks. Her form wavered and vanished. Key let his breath out.

"Were you talking to her?" he croaked.

"Yes." Lonn frowned. "There was something odd."

Key looked around. "Let's get back to the others. This is too uncanny for me."

"All right."

They headed for the keep gateway. Key said, "What did you mean, something odd? I thought everything about it was odd. Especially you being able to talk to her."

"I don't actually talk. It's more like feeling what they're interested in, or what they know about something. Most of it I can't comprehend. The oddity was that she seems worried. Even a little frightened. I've never sensed that before."

Key shot a look at him. "Frightened of what?"

"I don't know. Something enormous, it seemed. Very far off, not moving much, but visible. Like clouds hanging on a mountain peak, waiting to be a blizzard. That was all I got before she went away."

"Was there anything like a threat to the luminessa?"

Lonn looked puzzled. "No. It wasn't at all that clear. Why?"

"Forgive me, Lonn, but I can't tell you."

"Ah. Very well." The Ashman frowned again. "I wish I knew more about what troubled her. It's unsettling."

"Yes."

Cawlor was hurrying toward them as they reached the gateway. "What happened?" he asked. "We were getting worried."

"An encounter," Lonn said. "Something peculiar. A frightened wood sprite."

Cawlor looked uneasy. "Frightened of what?"

"I don't know. Nothing near, though. Nothing imminent."

"I think we'd better move on anyway," Key said.

✳ 16

FOR THE NEXT FOURTEEN DAYS THEY MADE THEIR WAY eastward, watching always for the Mixtuns, always uneasy that these might not have been Theatana's only assassins. They avoided the Great East Road altogether, seeking out byways and tracks at the price of slower progress, circling wide around cities and towns. It rained three times, but only during the day, so they slept each night under the stars. Twice Lonn slipped into villages for supplies and paid with Temple Mount's silver for bannock, smoked meat, cheese, and wine. On his first venture he also bought clothing to replace the garments Key and Mandine had abandoned at the inn in Salmoxis. Mandine still regretted the loss of her gray cloak, for it had seemed a lucky garment.

Each night and morning she looked into her sabretache, to make sure Athanais's book and the Lady's ear of wheat were still there. The wheat, wrapped in a square of fine-woven linen, neither withered nor shed its kernels, but seemed always like grain fresh-reaped in the field. No one but Key knew she carried either it or the book. The other Elthamers never asked why they were heading toward the Cursed Shore, though she sensed that Naevis was sometimes beside himself with curiosity. Jaladar rarely spoke and showed no inquisitiveness at all; he seemed content to ride eastward forever.

Their line of march was well north of the River Seferis, which from Salmoxis bent southward in a vast curve, then turned north to intersect the highway at the city of Baptisae, where there was a bridge. The Temple map showed ferry points along the great river's course, but Key did not want to use them; the landings were too easy for pursuers to check, and neither ferrymen nor hired boatmen would quickly forget a party like theirs. He also disliked entering Baptisae, but to continue east they had to cross the Seferis there, and he saw no way around the risk.

At the supper hour of the fifteenth day they reached the city. They were now more than four hundred miles from Captala as a bird flew, and with no sign of pursuit they relaxed their guard a little. Everyone, even Jaladar, was sick of living rough and of the monotonous travelers' food, and they decided to chance one night at an inn. Key and Mandine in particular wanted news of the capital and the Tathars. Lonn had gleaned only wild rumors from his expeditions into the village marketplaces, but in Baptisae they might get some reliable information.

It was an ancient city, older even than Captala Nea, for it stood by the easiest crossing of the Seferis for a hundred miles upstream and down. Three rivers and four roads met at Baptisae, and traders had settled there for time out of mind. Key had passed through on his way west from Oak five years ago, and its curious architecture had stuck in his memory. The cobbled streets were wide enough for two large wains to pass, but the houses' upper stories overhung the streets so that only a narrow band of sky was visible. The houses themselves were built of a yellow stone cross-banded with timbers painted red, blue, green, and black, producing fantastic patterns of lozenges, diamonds, hatchings, and stripes. The glass in the latticed windows was the old-fashioned type, thick, whorled, and greenish. The only true open spaces in Baptisae seemed to be the tree-shaded squares around the public fountains, and the esplanades and quays along the Seferis, where the broadboats moored for loading and unloading. Even the countless bazaars and markets were roofed.

Cawlor and his companions had been here only a few weeks ago, and headed for the riverfront and an inn Cawlor recommended. It was the dinner hour, and the smells of fried fish, roast auroch, stewed medlars, hot bread, and the tart South Shore herb called yellow sunfoil hung in the air. Key's mouth was watering as they finally emerged from the shadowy streets onto the West Esplanade.

"Look at the boats!" Naevis exclaimed. "Hundreds! No, thousands!"

He was right. Across the river's lazy breadth lay seven islands, linked like beads by the arches of the great bridge. It had been built in the time of the Tessarid dynasts, and people called it the Golden Necklace for its appearance and for the wealth it carried. Around the islands that supported the bridge's vast piers, and along the quays on each bank of the Seferis, river shipping clustered in great rafts, boat moored to boat.

"Nothing's moving on the river," Key said.

"There weren't many wains in the city, either," said Lonn. "Not like last time we were here. And I didn't see any real soldiers. Did anybody else?"

"No," Cawlor said. "Only the militia at the gate. Rusty pikes and bad armor."

"No trade, no trained soldiers," Mandine observed wearily. "The Tathar arm has stretched a long way."

"Yes," Key said. He was a little worried about her. For the last two days she had been withdrawn and quiet, but had pleaded fatigue when he privately asked her why.

"There's the inn," Cawlor said, pointing at a building whose facade was zigzagged with red, black, orange, and yellow, once garish, now faded. Its sign, equally faded, named it the House of Bountiful Transactions.

"It's where we stayed before," Cawlor said, looking doubtfully at Mandine. "The food's good enough, and . . . well, should we look for somewhere more suitable?"

"Not for me," Mandine said. "Only, do the beds have anything in them that bites?" They had been plagued by sand fleas at their last bivouac.

"I didn't notice any."

"That's fine, then. Let's go in."

"Wait," Key said, thinking of Salmoxis and Theatana's assassins. "Jaladar, go to the innkeeper and tell him you're looking for countrymen of yours. Ask if he's seen any."

Jaladar went in; the others waited, watching the boats. On the decks, tiles clicked and dice bounced as the crews played desultory games of escarlat or eyes-and-clouds. Key saw not one wagon loading or unloading at the quays. When he passed through before, the city had teemed with merchants, rivermen, cargo wains, and big dun-and-black carnyxes, the heavy draft animals favored by Ascendancy caravaneers. The lack of activity dismayed him. Trade was the lifeblood of the Ascendancy; if that stopped, all stopped.

After a while Jaladar returned, and said, "The innkeeper has seen no countrymen of mine, so I asked him if he has rooms. He does. He also complained that he is being ruined. The Tathars have burned Salmoxis, and trade to there and Captala has stopped. The rivermen have few places to go, and being frugal are living on their vessels. For these reasons, he says, the rooms are plentiful, the baths are unoccupied, and he offers the best price in the city for both."

"Salmoxis burned?" Mandine said unhappily to Key as they rode through the shabby gate into the innyard. "Those poor people."

They took one room for Mandine and two others for the men, all adjacent and with windows overlooking the innyard. Despite the shabby outward aspect of the House of Bountiful Transactions, the baths were clean, with plenty of hot water, and everyone was glad to use them. After that, a payment of six minims brought bread, wine, fresh greens, and grilled silverfin to Key and Cawlor's room, where they all ate.

The food was good, and they consumed it to the last heel of bread. With the meal ended and daylight fading toward dusk, Jaladar left for the quarters he shared with Lonn; Lonn,

Cawlor, and Naevis then decided to visit the taproom and seek news from the west. This left Mandine and Key in the dim, low-beamed chamber, with the empty dishes, a half flask of scarlet Imbria wine, and each other. The lamps had not yet been kindled, and the gilded light of sunset fell across the table and onto Mandine's face. To Key it suddenly seemed that she herself was aglow, as if from a light within, and she was so beautiful that his breath came short in his chest.

Mandine broke the silence that hung between them. "Don't you want to go downstairs, too?"

"No," Key said. "I thought of it, but I don't like leaving you by yourself. The others will bring us any news there is."

"I'll be all right alone." She put her elbows on the table, rested her forehead on her fingertips, and closed her eyes. He thought she was a little flushed. "You should share a cup with your countrymen."

"They'll enjoy themselves well enough without me. And there's wine here, as well as in the taproom. Will you have some?"

"Yes, please."

He poured two measures of water and a measure of Imbria into the mixing bowl, swirled it, then poured for both of them. Mandine sipped, then said, "Is it true that Elthamers drink wine unmixed? I heard that somewhere."

"Not often. It's considered the mark of a drunkard, just as it is in the Ascendancy."

Mandine's dark eyebrows lifted. "Does no one ever get drunk in the Elthame?"

"Of course they do," he said with a wry smile. "But it's on beer, usually. The best beer in the world is made in Willow Haeme. But it travels badly, so the rest of us make do with our own brews. Also, wine's expensive. The Elthame's too high and cold to grow the right grapes, so it's all imported."

She turned the goblet restlessly between her fingertips. "Do you miss your homeland and family?"

"Often," Key admitted.

"When we were in Essardene," she said, "you told me you

hardly remember your mother. Who brought you and your sister up?"

"Oh," he said, smiling with the recollection, "my father got a wet nurse for Ria. Her name was Hibby. Hibby took me over, too, and she and my father and my Aunt Amhuin raised the pair of us. Amhuin saw to my education, at least the part that wasn't woodcraft, hunting, horses, and weapons. My sister Ria got the same tutors. Her mind is very quick." He hesitated, then added, "I think you'd like her."

"I'm sure I would. Your father never remarried?"

"No. Amhuin said he loved my mother more than was perhaps good for him. He never looked seriously on another woman. Also, he had me, and he's a careful man. Stepmothers, inheritances, and half siblings are a recipe for trouble. As you know."

"Yes," Mandine said, with considerable feeling, "they are."

"And you?" Key asked.

"My mother died when I was only six months old. She was of the House Maraeis. It was a very old and noble line, older than the Dascarids, but it was dying out, and my mother was the last of it. But we had good lands in the southeast. My father married her because of her lineage, and because of her inheritance."

"But who looked after you? Theatana's mother, when the Dynast married her?"

"Her?" Mandine shivered. "Not at all. She was lost in a shipwreck when I was five, but I still remember how she hated the sight of me. Children sense that kind of thing. I think now I'm lucky she drowned before she had me poisoned. She wanted the diadem to go to her own blood, of course. No, I grew up in the House Azure with court ladies minding my deportment and training. I wasn't particularly unhappy, except when I wondered what having a mother would be like. I did have the best tutors, I'll say that for my father. Orissi was my favorite, as you'll have guessed. I lived in books much of the time. I even felt safe in the House Azure, until my father turned it into a prison for me." She sighed, and ran a fingertip around the rim of her goblet. "I seem to come at the end of things. My mother was the last of her house, and I'm the last of the Dascarids but for Theatana, and perhaps these are the last days of the Ascendancy . . . no, don't listen to me. I'm feeling sorry for myself, and I've no right to do so. Put it down to being tired. I'm really all right, or I will be in the morning."

He studied her weary face. "But you're not all right. I think something's wrong. It's not just being tired, is it? Luminessa—Mandine, tell me."

Her mouth tightened. "You can still hardly speak my name, can you, Key? Even after all this time you won't, unless you feel you have to."

He was startled that she cared about this, when she was so tired. Avoiding her gaze, he said, "I find it very difficult."

"Why?"

"Does it matter?"

"It matters to me. Is it because you think of me only as the Luminessa Mandine, heiress to the diadem of the Ascendancy?"

"I have to," he answered helplessly, "because that is who you are."

"Is that all I am even now, when we've traveled together day in and day out? We've faced *death* together, Key."

He looked up at the latticed window, where the setting sun brushed the whorled glass with tints of rose and ruby. What did she want him to say? He could not possibly tell her what he felt. He did his best to ignore it, though it had grown with every mile and day: that he ached to pull her to him, hold her in his arms until the sun dimmed and the Two slept. Yet he knew if he said so, she would be appalled at his presumption. Worse, she might pity him, and treat him with careful gentleness. He did not want pity or gentleness; either would sting his pride too much.

He said, "I can't explain it."

"Please. Try. Call me by my name again."

His mouth was dry, but he said, "Mandine," and looked down at the table.

"There, that wasn't so hard, was it? Oh, Key, *look* at me."

He obeyed her, and saw to his anguish that she was almost in tears. His tongue seemed frozen in his mouth.

"Don't you *understand*, Key? You're not my guard commander anymore, you haven't been since we ran from Captala. You're my friend, the only friend I have. Cawlor and the others, they're good men, but they're not what you are to me. We've been through so much together, and we must go through so much more, and I trust you with my life. But I'm not good at this, Key, I'm not good at having friends, because I never had any, except perhaps Orissi, and she was always more like an aunt, and so much older. I've never had a friend my own age. Until you. I don't know how to act, and I'm frightened I'll do something wrong or something stupid and you'll be angry at me and decide that you don't like me at all."

Her voice was shaking, her eyes wet. Key's throat was painfully tight. "Mandine," he said, "I'm sorry. I'm an idiot for not realizing what you meant. I *am* your friend. Always. Never forget it. And I do like you, I do, I always have. Please, Mandine, don't cry."

She dashed the back of her hand across her eyes. "I'm sorry. I hate women who weep. You do mean it? You do mean we're friends, Key?"

"The best," he answered, and on impulse reached across the table to grasp her hand. Her slender fingers clutched his, tightened. It was the first time they had touched each other since they fled from Essardene.

"I'm glad," she whispered, and smiled wanly. After a moment she squeezed his hand, and he very reluctantly released her. His heart was pounding.

Mandine suddenly passed her hand across her forehead. "I've been having dreams, Key. All last night. Bad dreams."

He was instantly alert, the painful hammering in his chest forgotten. "Dreams? What were they about?"

She shook her head. "I don't remember. I'd wake up with the feeling that something dreadful was going to happen. But then I'd realize I hadn't woken up at all, that I was still asleep.

Then I'd dream I was falling asleep again, and the feeling would come back. Every time it did, I tried to wake up properly, and I couldn't. It was horrible." She pushed her goblet away. "I shouldn't have any more wine."

"I don't like this," Key said. "Why didn't you say something this morning?"

"The sun was out, and the birds were singing. Everything seemed so—ordinary, and people do have bad dreams that don't mean anything. I didn't want to worry you, or the others. Perhaps it's what Lonn said, about the alsea being frightened. I keep remembering that, for some reason. But nothing's come of it, so maybe what she was afraid of has nothing to do with us. Not directly, anyway."

Key chewed his lower lip, released it. "You don't remember any details of the dreams?"

"No. I wouldn't have mentioned them at all, except . . . I'm uneasy. I have been all day, just a little."

Key got up and went to open the window. Below in the innyard, a white house-ferret tripped daintily across the cobbles. It carried a small dangling body in its jaws, a vole perhaps. A kitchen maid put her head out a door, clucked encouragingly at the ferret, and disappeared.

"Is anyone outside?" Mandine asked.

"No one who shouldn't be," Key said as he turned from the window. "Uneasy, you say?"

"Yes, but we all are." She gave a tired laugh. "It would be odd if we weren't, wouldn't it?"

"I suppose so." Key closed the window and shot the bolt. "I still don't like it."

"Now you'll fret. I shouldn't have mentioned it. But I feel better, now I've talked to you. It's just the vapors, and being tired." Mandine covered her mouth, and yawned. "We'll be up at dawn, again. I'm going to go to bed. I can wait till morning for news from Captala. It won't likely be good, anyway."

"I'll see you to your room."

"But it's just next door—oh, all right."

He took her to her chamber, made sure the window latch was both stout and secured, and checked the door's bolt. He was about to go when a boy of about fourteen came with tapers and a horn lantern to light the room's single lamp. Key waited until he left, then said, "I'll be on the other side of that wall. If anything happens, bang on it and scream. And keep your dagger by you."

"I will. Good night, Key."

He did not want to leave her alone; it felt dangerous. For a wild moment he considered offering to sleep inside her room, to guard her.

"Good night," he said, then he was on the other side of the door, closing it. He waited until he heard her thump the bolt home, and exhaled slowly. Then he returned to his chamber. The boy had lit the lamp, and was piling a tray with the supper dishes. He was skinny, with a narrow face and quick bright eyes.

"What's your name?" Key asked. He took a dandyprat from his sabretache.

The boy bobbed his head, eyes on the copper coin. "Skiptis, sir."

"Well, Skiptis, can you tell me who else is staying at the inn?"

"Here, sir? Only yourselves. There was a party of oil traders from the southlands last night, but they went on north this morning. Custom's very bad, with the war. Did you come in from the west?"

That was information Key did not want to give out. "Why?"

"Well, everybody wants news from there. It's said there's a sorcerer with the silverhairs at Captala." Skiptis's eyes got big and worried. "That he brings demons out of the air, and they take people's souls. They even say it's the man with the chain, the one it's unlucky to speak the name of. Do you know if it's true, sir?"

There was no point in frightening the boy. "Even if it is, he won't get as far as Baptisae."

"That's right, he won't. The new Dynast, I mean the new Dynastessa, she'll stop him, won't she?"

"Of course," Key said. "Who's down in the taproom at the moment?"

"Just the three Elthamers you came in with, sir, and some local folk who like to do their drinking here."

Key gave him the dandyprat, and he scuttled out with his tray and lantern. After the door had closed, Key pulled off his tunic and removed his boots and socks. Clad only in his breeches, he lay down and closed his eyes. He was half-dozing when the others came back upstairs.

"What news from Captala?" he asked, without sitting up.

"Glum," Cawlor said, and told him. Even with the wilder tales filtered out, the news made bad hearing. Theatana had made her ascension known by dispatches sent out through the naval port, and most of the Ascendancy now knew it had a new ruler. The story of Mandine's murder was accepted; Archates' ill reputation had made it plausible. Dactulis, now raised to the rank of treimarch, had sent officers by sea to raise troops in the Ascendancy's secure regions; one army was supposed to be training at the South Shore city of Kephelenia, and another at Pegae in the far north. This was as Key had expected. What troubled him was the rumor that while ships could get out of Captala Nea, few got in. Their navigation went mysteriously awry, the rumors said, and smashed hull timbers, broken masts, and the corpses of drowned sailors now littered the coast near the metropolis.

"That's Erkai's work, by its sound," Lonn added, when Key had heard everything. "Illusions and foul winds. Damn his soul to the Waste."

"If he has a soul," Cawlor muttered. "I'd put no bets on it."

"We've an early start in the morning," Key said. He rolled over onto his face. "I, for one, am going to get some sleep."

Mandine lay staring at the shadowy ceiling beams above her bed. She usually preferred to fall asleep in the dark, but tonight she had felt reluctant to extinguish the lamp. It glowed steadily in its bracket by the door, the small yellow flame motionless in its glass envelope. The delicate herbal tang of burning sunsip oil hung in the still air. A while ago she had heard muffled voices and thumps from Key and the others in the adjacent room, but now all was silence.

She put her arms above her head and stretched. The last time she had slept out of her clothes seemed eons ago, and even the coarse bedding felt delightful against her bare skin. And she was clean again, thank the Lady. Cold stream water and a handful of wild soapseeds were no substitute for real baths, even if those of the inn were crude by the standards of the Fountain Palace.

But those were my old standards, she thought. *I live now like one of the common folk, and it's changing me. I don't know who I'm becoming, but I'm different, not the old Luminessa Mandine, or not wholly so.*

She shifted restlessly on the feather mattress. This evening she had thought, just for a few moments, that Key felt more than friendship for her. Surely he had been a little reluctant to release her hand? What would she have done if he hadn't let go of her, if he'd drawn her up from her chair, and taken her in his arms. Would she would have let him?

Don't ask yourself false questions. You would have welcomed it.

But then she opened her mouth about the dreams, and the moment, if it had been a moment, passed. Perhaps it had existed only in her imagination. She had always thought he liked her, but why would she imagine that it was more than that? His words had been plain enough.

I am your friend. Always. Never forget it. And I do like you, I do. I always have.

Her eyes stung. He was the best, perhaps the only, friend she had ever had. She had meant it when she said she would trust him with her life, and she suspected that he would give his life to protect her. She hoped she would have a similar courage, to die if she had to, to save him.

But that didn't mean he loved her. There were lots of sto-

236

ries that told of men and women who gave up their lives for friends, not for lovers. And with that, there were also plenty of tales in which lovers—or husbands and wives—fell out and made each other miserable. And that didn't happen just in stories, either.

Friends, then. So be it. I mustn't ask the Lady for more, no matter how I ache. And I can't let him know about how I really feel. If he knew I wanted more from him, he might turn away from me. I couldn't bear that.

She turned over and rested her forehead on her folded arms. In spite of her feelings, she could still be clear-eyed and sensible. Key and she were the closest of friends, and that was one of the best things that had ever happened to her. Even more important, perhaps, they were allies in the search for the Signata. That was their real business. She had let her imagination run away with her this evening, but she wouldn't let it happen again.

She was oddly restless. Though she had just turned over, she wriggled onto her back again and made herself breathe slowly and evenly. Her eyes still burned a little. It was fatigue, she told herself; she was far more tired than she had admitted to Key. The stinging faded bit by bit, and eventually she slept.

Then, very slowly, she became aware that she was sleeping, as if one part of her mind had wakened to observe the rest. An indefinite duration passed, languid as the soft trickle of sand in an hourglass, while she drifted in this ambiguous state. Then a sickly dread began to insinuate itself into her awareness. She tried to push it away, but it grew remorselessly. It was like grit trickling into her throat, grain by grain, and it began to suffocate her. Mandine tried to move, shout, wake up, but the strangling grit multiplied with her struggles. Now it poured over her chest, her belly, her legs; crushed her, pinned her naked and helpless to the dream.

She opened her mouth to cry out. At first no words came, for she could find no breath. Then, at last, she managed a whisper.

Sweet Lady, help me.

The weight lessened, vanished. Her eyes flew open, and suddenly she was breathing in long, tearing gasps, as if she had swum a long way underwater. But she was still in her room, with the lamp flame burning clear and motionless. She was also truly awake and as alert as if she had not slept at all. Around her the room was silent except for the harsh rasp of her breathing, but her sick dread and her foreboding remained. Something was wrong. Something was coming for her. She had to reach the others. She stumbled out of bed to get her clothes, which were lying on the ark-chest by the door.

As she picked up her breeches, there was a noise at the window.

"Key!" she screamed, as she saw a flat white face pressed to the lattice. "Key!"

A huge fist smashed through both glass and leading. Blood streamed from the slashed fingers as they groped for the latch, found it, tugged, and threw the window wide. An icy breeze wafted though the chamber. The lamp flickered, but stayed alight. Mandine threw herself at the door, yanked at the iron bolt. It was cold, cold enough to burn her skin, and it would not budge.

Her dagger was under her pillow, and the bed was far away by the window. Through the opening clambered a huge man with glazed and staring eyes. His mouth worked, and spittle dripped from his chin; he moved in spasms, as if unseen cords jerked at his limbs. Now he was by the bed, and it was too late to reach her blade.

Her actions, and his, turned dreamlike and slow. Mandine saw her clothes on the ark-chest, saw her belt, and her sabre-tache. He was shambling toward her now, arms hanging gracelessly, in his left hand a long fish-gutting knife. She heard a shout from Key's room and feet pounding in the passage. Something struck the door a tremendous blow, but the bolt held.

She knew they would be too late. Her killer jerked toward her. Both his hands were bloody, and she saw white bone at his fingertips.

Hardly knowing what she did, she snatched up her sabre-tache and ripped it open. Now he was almost on her, but he lunged clumsily, and she slipped away from his knife. He made a horrible grating noise in his throat and flailed with the blade, herding her toward a corner. Blows thundered uselessly on the door.

She felt the angle of the walls behind her shoulders. He had her. She was trapped, and he would rip her open. His mouth hung agape, and she saw his twisted teeth. And then, dreadfully, his face changed. The features writhed, blurred, and she saw through them an abyss that could swallow her and the world with her, a lightless void that stopped the scream in her throat. But then the gulf was obscured by a new visage, as if another face grew in the vacant horror beneath the sickly skin. It was cold, pitiless, its dark eyes malevolent and searching, and she realized with new horror that they had found her.

Her fingers scrabbled in the sabretache, came out with Athanais's book. Without thinking, she hurled it at the face beneath the face.

The book struck hard. A harsh blue-white light blazed in the dimness, and the man shrieked as his features and those beneath them disappeared in a searing incandescence. He staggered away from her; the blinding light vanished, and the book thudded to the floor at her feet. She knew she should run past him, break for the door, but her arms and legs were gripped in sheaths of ice. Her knees gave way, and she fell dazed into the corner as he turned to stumble toward her again. His eyes were burned black, and the other eyes were gone, but the husk that remained had heard her fall. He knew where she was, and he still had the knife.

The door crashed open. Cawlor fell through it sideways. Key leaped over him, his sword naked in his hand. The blind man loomed above her, but Mandine still could not move. He raised the fishknife. She closed her eyes, waiting.

She heard Key yell, then a noise like a blow on soft wood, then another. There was a thump and clatter, followed by a heavy thud. Suddenly warm hands were on her bare shoulders, and Lonn said, "Give me her cloak, for pity's sake. She's frozen."

"I'm all right," Mandine said, in a croak. She had forgotten she was naked. She felt the thick cloth fall around her and opened her eyes. Key was standing between her and the body, but she saw the blood on the floor and on his sword. Her stomach turned over, and she looked away. Lonn put his arm around her shoulders and held her tightly. "What happened?" he said. "My lady, what happened? Are you sure you're all right?"

"He came through the window," Mandine blurted. "He broke the glass. I tried to open the door, but the bolt was stuck." She shuddered, in spite of her boundless relief. "I tried, but I couldn't get out."

"Cover that thing," Key said, and Naevis threw a blanket over the corpse. Cawlor was rubbing his shoulder, where he had hit the door with it. Jaladar was leaning out of the window.

"You're sure you're not hurt?" Key asked. He put his sword down and knelt by her. Lonn's arm was warm around her shoulders.

She could feel the book's corner under her cloak-covered knee. "He never touched me." She was about to add, *I had something that stopped him,* but she realized suddenly how sorcerous that might sound, and she didn't want to speak of it. "I heard you at the door," she said, "and I kept dodging. He was clumsy."

"Clumsy? Was he drunk?" Cawlor's face was puzzled.

There were noises from the corridor. The landlord stamped in, glowering, and saw the blood and the shrouded corpse. His jaw dropped. "What's happened here, then?"

"Someone tried to murder your guest," Key said angrily, as he got to his feet. "It's only by grace of the Two he failed. What kind of hostelry do you keep?"

"*Murder?*" the man yelped. His face went pale yellow with shock. "Allfather save us. Not in my house, never. Never had anything like this, I swear it—some foreigner, must have been—"

Cawlor twitched the blanket back. "Foreigner! He was in your taproom last night, and I saw you talking. You knew him."

The landlord's mouth worked. "Fornix. Shades of the Waste, it's Fornix."

"He came by the window," Jaladar said, drawing his head in.

"But he can't have," the landlord protested. "No way to climb, it's all straight up brick."

"He climbed," Jaladar said. He walked to the corpse, and pulled a bloody hand from under the blanket. "Look. His fingers are stripped to the bone, and there is blood on the wall outside. He drove his fingers between the bricks, into the mortar."

"Fornix did that?" the landlord wailed. "He couldn't have! No one could do that. And he was sick last night, had to leave. He's an odd one, I know, but—"

Key said, "The lady needs attention. Find another room for her, and light a fire in it, and bring her wine."

"Wait," Mandine said. Though she still trembled with reaction, she was strangely calm and clearheaded, and the terrible dread had vanished. "What did you mean, 'He's an odd one'?"

The landlord avoided her gaze. "Well, my lady, it's said that he, well, that Fornix knew a bit of the Craft. Nothing proved, you see, but, but, rumors." He was babbling now. "The temple here watched him, but they never caught him at it, if he did anything. 'Course, he might have done it other places, and cleared off before the local priests found him out. Fornix, he was a traveling man. He was only back here a few days ago. Didn't look well tonight, not well at all."

Mandine, still huddled on the floor, sat up straighter. Lonn took his arm from her shoulders. "He might have dabbled in the Craft?" he asked the landlord.

"Rumors. It was all rumors."

Mandine shuddered, remembering the glazed, staring eyes,

the spasms. "He wasn't drunk. He looked possessed. As if something else moved his arms and legs."

Key said to Lonn, "You know something of spirits. If a man had used the Black Craft, would he be open to another power using him?"

"It's said so." Lonn looked at Mandine, his face suddenly worried. "My lady, is your sister your only enemy?"

"No," Mandine said.

Cawlor looked savage. "Who else, then? Only tell us, and we'll deal with him."

"Enough, Cawlor," Key said quickly. "We've things to do here." He sent the landlord packing, with orders to have Fornix's corpse taken away, and to prepare another room for Mandine. For the rest of the night they would set a guard below her window, and a second outside her door. Though she felt no hint now of supernatural danger, Mandine did not protest. No one noticed when she slipped Athanais's book back into her sabretache. It didn't feel exactly as it had, being perhaps of less weight, but with the others around she didn't want to inspect it for damage.

Key took her to her new room. At the doorway, she said, "You'd better come inside for a moment. Fornix wasn't drunk, and I didn't dodge him."

With the door closed, she hurriedly opened her sabretache and drew out the book. "It was Athanais who saved me. I threw her book at him—oh, no!"

She had opened its covers. Inside there was nothing but a few scraps of charred vellum and a little fine dust.

"He destroyed it," she said desolately. "It saved me, but it's ruined." With a tremendous effort, she fought back her tears.

"Who destroyed it?" Key asked, taking the gutted binding from her. "Fornix? How?"

"Not him," she said, with shudder. "Remember what Lonn said, about something else using him? I *saw* the something else, Key—it wasn't Fornix, but it was *inside* him somehow, and I think it saw me, too." She swallowed. "I think . . . I think it was Erkai."

"Allfather protect us! Are you sure? How?"

"I saw his eyes, inside Fornix's eyes, and they were human eyes, but so . . . so *cold*, and they were looking for me. It must have been him, Key, it couldn't have been anyone else—no one else has that much command of the Craft. And I saw something else for a moment, too, something even worse than Erkai. It was like—" She shuddered. "I don't know. Like an emptiness that wanted me. I think it was the Adversary, and it was helping Erkai see through Fornix's eyes. Then I threw the book, and it blinded him."

"And now he may know where we are. Curse me for a fool, for letting us stop here."

"It's not your fault. We all wanted to. It was just our bad luck there happened to be someone nearby who used the Craft, so Erkai and the Adversary could use him. If we keep away from people from now on, maybe Erkai will lose us again."

"I hope you're right. We'll leave at dawn."

Mandine pondered for a moment. "Key, we can't ask the others to come farther with us, not after this. We must tell them so, in the morning."

"They'll come anyway," Key said. "I know my countrymen. And Jaladar is loyal to the death."

"But we have to give them the choice."

"All right, we'll ask them, but I know their answers. Whatever they decide, we have to leave here at first light. There's going to be talk, and that landlord will be babbling about Fornix being a Black Craftsman for climbing up the wall. We won't be forgotten in a hurry."

She sighed. "I'm so tired. I know you are, too. Will we ever feel rested again?"

"Someday," Key said. "But not likely tomorrow. Go to bed now and sleep. I'll be outside on guard till Jaladar relieves me."

"I know," she said. "I feel safe now, Key. Good night."

The door closed quietly behind her, and he was alone. The minutes and then the hours passed, one by one.

Far to the west, where Captala's walls rose into the star-spattered dark, Erkai stirred from his trance and opened his eyes. In the brazier before him the flames guttered low, their blue tongues edged with yellow. He sniffed, then breathed deep. The night air was cool and damp, tanged with the sea. Outside his tent a watch horn brayed, sudden and harsh. Dawn was coming.

He had found her now, the woman he sought. He had pondered for a long time over how to go about it, and more than once had almost decided to ignore the Adversary's warning. But as the days passed, the idea of a secret threat had nagged at him with increasing strength. He knew no more of the Signata than the fragmentary legend told, and he could not construe how it might be a danger to him. That troubled him, for he disliked a danger whose nature he did not understand. And with that, he was also a little uneasy about arousing the Adversary's possible displeasure by dismissing the matter out of hand.

So, guarding himself with every device he had, he entered trance and approached the Adversary for help. What happened next was still unclear, and he was unsure whether his protections had actually worked, or whether the Father of Lies had merely elected not to consume him. He was swept into a seeming vision, such as the Adversary had never yet offered him, though he realized quickly that it was not vision but an actual sight of a distant place. There had been a bridge across seven islands, and that was nowhere but Baptisae. Then he had seen through human vision, as the Adversary entrapped a weaker intelligence than Erkai's and attacked the woman. But somehow, It had been driven off; there had been a flash of light, and Erkai had sensed not only the pain of the possessed man, but a deeper, more terrible agony that struck deep into the Adversary Itself.

Then he was again in the cold dark place where he and

the Father of Lies had always met. The Adversary suffered, and Erkai knew that for the moment, at least, he was safe from Its appetites, for now It desired him to step in where It had failed. This pleased him. He could act in this world when It could not or dared not; therefore, his power was the greater.

Erkai stretched, to ease the ache between his shoulder blades. The woman was far to the east, but now he was much, much, closer to finding her. He did not yet know her name, but he knew what she looked like.

He reached out and opened a chest of gray wood. From it he drew a thin sheet of fine white leather, made from the delicate belly skin of a youth taken at Essardene. The aura of the boy's death torment still clung to the leather, enough for a minor work of the Craft.

Erkai laid the skin on the tent floor and stared at the brazier. His pupils shrank to black specks. The flames brightened, rose, shifted form and color, and flowed into a perfect miniature of the woman's face, the size of an outstretched hand. Erkai's lips moved soundlessly. The image drifted into the air, then settled slowly onto the skin and became one with it.

His pupils regained their normal size. He picked up the skin, inspected the result, and nodded in satisfaction. He would give the picture to Ragula and his hunters, then slip their leashes and send them east to track her down. The Tathar duke would protest furiously at riding so deep into enemy territory, but Hetlik would make him go.

Erkai's lips twitched in a tiny smile. No doubt the woman believed she was safe from Tathars. Far away in Baptisae, why would she think otherwise? But her belief was mistaken. In days Ragula and his men would be at her heels, for they would be riding hippaxas.

Until now, this was unheard of. The Tathars slaughtered hippaxas if they captured them, for they did not know the secrets of their breeding or training, and considered them useless. But the cataphracts who escaped from Essardene had left their mounts at Aptera, and Hetlik had finally decided, at Erkai's urging, that keeping the creatures alive might lead someday to a greater Tathar cavalry. His growing fear of Erkai had made him agree quickly to Erkai's request for a loan of the animals and riders to go with them.

Erkai had long ago ridden hippaxas, and with Hetlik's authority behind him he had, over the past fifteen days, made Ragula and fivescore other Tathars learn the skill. They were not as expert as the Ascendancy's veteran cataphracts had been, but they were riders by nature, and they would serve. Even deep in Ascendancy lands they would be safe enough; on hippaxas they could outrun larger forces than theirs and overwhelm any lesser.

Erkai permitted himself an inward quiver of satisfaction. If Ragula and his hunters set out this morning, they would reach the neighborhood of Baptisae in three days. The woman could not travel far in that time, and her much speedier pursuers would soon find her. The duke knew how to scout, and with him were the best trackers in the Tathar army. Even allowing for an extended search, Erkai judged that within fourteen days the woman would be here in the Tathar camp, where she would answer his questions: Why did she seek the Signata, who or what had prompted her to do so, and what power could it bring against him?

I don't believe I face a serious threat, he thought, *but if Ragula comes back with his fur bloody, or does not come back at all, I will have to take further precautions. Better, though, if he brings her to me; that will tell me much of what I need to know.*

He stirred the fire, seeing again in the flames the face of the woman he sought. It was a beautiful face. When he had sucked her dry, he would, for the trouble she had caused him, give her a death of his most elaborate invention.

✳ 17

FOR THE FIRST TWO DAYS OUT OF BAPTISAE THEY RODE
through rolling farm country, where strip-fields of wheat and
barley alternated with sunsip groves. There were only a few
small villages, whose folk spoke the Logomenon with a flat
twang, instead of the fuller accents of the west. Captala was
now so far behind that Key risked trading secrecy for speed,
and they kept to the main road. Because of the attack at the
inn they were trying to conceal the fact that Mandine was a
woman; her hair was now bound back, and she wore a hooded
cloak so that she could pass for a young man of delicate features, at least at a distance.

Using the road, they made good time, and both Key's and
Mandine's spirits rose. The New Sea was still almost five hundred miles away, but even allowing for rougher going to the
east, they might be nearing its waters in ten or twelve days.
Neither of them was willing to think farther ahead than that.
After the attack at Baptisae they'd told the others everything,
because it was so clear that whatever the Adversary had
known about their search, Erkai now would know also. As
Key had expected, the threat only strengthened his countrymen's resolve to help. Jaladar had merely shrugged, and
said, "Where the luminessa goes, I go."

By the fourth afternoon they had left the farmlands for

harsher country. The landscape grew rough, its limestone foundations thrusting from hills clad in dark mantles of columnar oak and black beech. Now and again Key heard axes ringing faintly in the narrow valleys, or saw a thread of smoke that betrayed a solitary homestead. This was timberland, where a sparse population lived by floating logs down the rivers to the cities of the south. Since entering it they had come across only two hamlets, huddled within timber palisades. According to the map, the hills brooding above the road were the western outriders of a range of ancient, eroded mountains, which stretched eastward to the New Sea. To the north of the mountains rose the high plateau of the Elthame, and far to the south, six hundred miles from the travelers' line of march, the mountains reached the coast of the Blue. The far margin of the range stood along the Cursed Shore itself.

The country they now traveled had once been populous, but four centuries ago a plague from the southern islands had visited the mainland and killed multitudes. The sickness was worst in regions neighboring the ill-reputed lands of the Cursed Shore, and many who escaped believed that the specters and entities of those sorcerous battlefields were wandering farther than they once had done. So even after the sickness burned itself out there was little resettlement, and the deserted farmsteads and the empty towns and villages had returned to wilderness. Here the Great East Road, though gangs of workers maintained it once a year—at least, they did in normal times—was under assault from the forest. It would have been allowed to go to ruin long ago, except that it still served the wagon caravans that carried goods and travelers between Baptisae and the south rim of the Elthame plateau. But the war was affecting trade even this far from the Ascendancy's heartland. Since leaving Baptisae, the party had met only three such caravans, and those were small.

Two hours before sunset they found an open space beside the road. The remains of fires and a broken wheel spoke showed it to be a caravan bivouac, and when they found a spring back among the trees they decided to make camp. Steel, flint, and dry moss soon started a fire—they were saving the quicklights for bad weather—and Naevis slipped into the forest with his bow. An hour later, four ruffed partridges and a brace of tree-hares were grilling over the coals, and Cawlor was making pan bread. Mandine deftly basted the partridges with sunsip oil as Lonn turned them on their spits.

Key watched her covertly as he and Jaladar cleaned the horses' tack. Since they left Baptisae, much of the tension between him and Mandine had dissipated. They were true friends and comrades-in-arms now, and as far as he could tell, to Mandine that was enough. As much as he could, he tried to accept it for himself also, and much of the time, as they traveled, he was almost content. But never fully. His yearning for her was always with him, however distant, like the muted ache of an old wound.

He scraped moodily at a harness leather. Such longings were hopeless, of course. Even if she did fall in love with him—and she showed no sign of doing so—and even if they somehow defeated Erkai and the Tathars, so that she might take her rightful place as Dynastessa, she would necessarily marry into a noble house of her own race. She could never take as husband a man so far below her rank as Key, and an outlander into the bargain. And as for himself, he did not want to gain a throne, even the throne of the Ascendancy, by riding at the back of his wife's saddle.

Be content with what you have. Until she's Dynastessa, she's your friend. Even after that, perhaps it won't fade.

He looked up from the harness leather. She was kneeling by the spit, and the curve of her cheek in the firelight and the grace of her slender hands suddenly hurt him so piercingly that he almost dropped the strap.

Jaladar looked sideways at him. "Something troubles you?" he asked quietly.

"No. Clumsy, a little." At the fire, Lonn spoke to Mandine, and she laughed. Key's fingers tightened on the leather.

"There is more than one kind of clumsiness," Jaladar said. "Why do you not tell her?"

Key stiffened. "Tell her what?"

"What you are feeling for her."

Denial sprang to Key's lips. Then he heard himself say, "Is it so obvious?"

"It is to me. But I am older than you and the others. Perhaps I see more."

"You know who she is," Key said. "We're comrades, and that has to be enough. She would not thank me for speaking."

Jaladar raised one thin black eyebrow. "Are you so sure of that?"

"Yes."

"Perhaps you are sure, but perhaps you are also wrong. I have seen her look at you."

"How?" Key asked reluctantly.

"The way a woman looks at a man, when she wishes he would tell her what she wants to hear."

"I've told her everything she wants to hear," Key muttered. "She needed a good friend, and I'm lucky enough to be one. As for her looking at me, I think you're imagining it."

Jaladar shrugged. "I've said enough. The rest is up to you." His mouth tightened. "But don't let your pride silence you too long. I did, and I and others have paid for my silence ever since."

Key stared at the Mixtun. This was the most Jaladar had ever said about his past. "Why—"

Jaladar suddenly pointed to where the road entered the clearing. "Look. We have company."

A man on a dun horse was riding toward them through the russet evening light. Key swore to himself, for Mandine had earlier shed her cloak, and she was very clearly a woman. He dropped the harness, and with Jaladar walked swiftly to the fire to greet the newcomer.

The rider was lean, heavy-jawed, dressed in dusty brown breeches and a yellow tunic, and he wore a leather cap that sported a sweeping red firedrake's plume. A short sword hung at his side, and his right hand was near it but not too near.

"Good evening, messires, madame," he said, and touched

his cap with his left hand. "I am Pellico, caravan master. My caravan and escort are a little behind. We are peaceful men, as I hope you are also."

Key raised his hands, palms outward. "We're travelers, as peaceful as yourselves." In courtesy he had to introduce himself. "I am Terl," he said, giving a second cousin's name.

"Where bound?" Pellico inquired. "If you don't mind my asking."

"Up to Thunderhead, and then into the Elthame." It was the usual route. "And you?"

The caravan master swung down from his horse. "Baptisae, though I don't expect much good of it, from the tidings I've heard. I've been up-country since the spring thaw. Do you have any news out of the west?"

"Some," Key said. "We'll be glad to pass it along."

Pellico scratched his long nose. "Elthame furs took most of my trade wine, but I've got a few flasks of vintage for my own use. As soon as I've settled my men and beasts, I'll be pleased to exchange some of it for whatever you can tell me. We'll camp over yonder, so my men's belches won't offend the lady. Could you spare me an ember?"

Lonn gave him a smoldering stick, and Pellico led his horse to the farside of the clearing, where he unsaddled it and started a fire. A few minutes later a caravan of six wagons rumbled into the clearing, and the drovers bullied their hulking brown-and-white carnyxes to a stop. Trotting alongside the wagons were four rough-looking horsemen in jerkins of hardened leather, armed with javelins and sabers. Cawlor and Key watched them discreetly as they and the drovers made camp, but decided after a while that Pellico's group posed no threat of banditry. Given the near disaster at Baptisae, however, Key resolved to set a double guard over Mandine during the night. For Pellico, they would stick to the story that Mandine was Cleophano, and was traveling to her brother and his Elthamer wife in Oak. As before, Key was her brother-in-law; to account for the others, he had supposedly hired them as escort.

By the time Pellico arrived at their fire with three wine

flasks, darkness had fallen and they had finished eating. As it turned out, they had little new information for the caravan master; he had heard about Thorn River in the Elthame, and the news of Archates' death and Theatana's accession had reached Thunderhead by the time he got there. He seemed less concerned about these events than about the Tathar invasion's effect on trade, though he appeared to assume that the disruption was temporary. That it might not be so, that Captala and the whole Ascendancy might fall, had not apparently occurred to him. It was the Ascendancer overconfidence Key had seen before; they had been mighty for so long that they could not conceive of their ruin.

Finally, as the caravan master paused to refill his horn drinking cup, Key said, "You've been up in Oak?"

Pellico gulped and nodded. "My train's on the way from there, just got down to the lowlands the other day. By the by, we saw something odd after we made the flat. Never come across its like."

"What?" Key said.

"We spotted four hemandri together, just this side of the Thunderhead junction. All my travels, and I've never come across more than two of the Near Folk at once. I thought they wanted to trade, but they faded off into the trees, the way they do. You'd swear they had the spell of invisibility."

"Four males?" Key said, thinking hopefully of the hemandra who had helped Mandine.

Pellico looked puzzled at the question. "Of course. Nobody ever sees a hemandra." He pondered for a moment. "They must exist, though. I heard somewhere that the females grow their young in belly pouches, and birth 'em from there, already walking and talking. Probably a fable. It's said there're true villages of the Near Folk way east of here, but nobody I know's ever seen one. They're not like us, that's certain. They're lucky to meet, though." He belched. "Maybe trade will have opened up by the time I reach Baptisae."

"One of the Near Folk helped my grandfather," Cawlor put in, "when he was a young man. He was winter hunting up-country, way past the Long Lakes, and an avalanche hit him and his party. All the others were killed, and a rock broke his leg."

"What happened?" Pellico asked, with interest. Tales of the Near Folk, true or not, were always popular.

"A hemander found him, made a sledge, and hauled him all the way home to the manor gate." Cawlor's brow wrinkled. "My grandfather's father would have given him gold, but all he would take was a brace of steel knives. Went away and never came back. A strange folk. But lucky to meet, as you said."

"Were you anywhere near Amalree?" Key asked Pellico. "Where the demarch has his Oaken House?"

"Oh, yes. I was up there, let me see, eighteen or twenty days back." Pellico sat up straight and slapped his forehead lightly. "Ah! My apologies, my brains aren't what they used to be. Of course you wouldn't have heard yet, being on the road. You said you're an Oakman?"

"Yes. Heard what?"

"Terrible thing. The Two raise us up, and cast us down." Pellico spilled a few drops of wine on the ground as a libation. "Blessed be the Two."

Key's mouth went dry. "What terrible thing?"

"I didn't see it myself," Pellico said. "The day before I left, it was. The talk was all over the Amalree marketplace after it happened. That's where I heard it." He swigged more wine. "It seems the demarch's only son was a cataphract with the Dynast's army, and the cataphracts were all killed at Thorn River, or so it's said. Anyway, the demarch was giving justice in the Amalree high court when the news came in. He stopped the proceedings to listen to the messenger, and when he heard about the cataphracts, he jumped up." Pellico poured another libation. "He jumped up, put his hands to his head, and cried out his son's name, and fell senseless. The son's name . . . I can't remember."

There was a silence. Key saw Mandine watching him, her

eyes huge and dark. "Is he alive?" he asked, through numb lips.

"Well, maybe he is. I heard on my way south he was still living, but the word was he didn't speak, or open his eyes, though he'd eat and drink what was put into his mouth. That was a good fifteen days back, so he may have gone by now. A pity, if he has. He was a good and just ruler, by all accounts."

"He was," Key said, somehow keeping his voice even. He heard a horse whicker softly in the darkness and got up. "My apologies. I have to see to our mounts."

He walked away from the fire. The animals had been hobbled to graze, and he found them munching the grass between the campsite and the forest margin. Key's chestnut whuffled at him as he stroked its warm neck. The moon had not yet risen, and starlight lay ghostly on the crowns of the trees.

My father is dead? Or nearly so? What am I to do now?

He should go home. Ria would need him. His father would need him if he still lived. And if the demarch were dead, someone had to rule Oak. Everyone would assume that Key was dead, too, and the rulership would fall to another clan, perhaps to Cawlor's father.

But I can't go home, he thought. *I have to go with Mandine. Lady, Allfather, why must I turn my back to my family, on my homeland? My place is there. Give me a sign, anything, to tell me it's right to turn away.*

Mandine's voice came soft out of the darkness. "Key?"

"Yes."

She was suddenly there, a slender shadow beside him, her face a pale oval in the starshine. "I'm so terribly sorry about your father," she said. "Truly sorry, Key."

Key said, "I should never have gone away. But he's not old, you know. Not old at all. There was no reason to think . . . that something might happen before I came home."

"Pellico didn't say he had died, Key. He might be recovering even now."

"Perhaps," Key said, not believing it.

"You want to go to Oak, don't you?"

"Yes."

"Will you?"

"How can I?" he demanded, as anger welled in him. "The Two have said that you and I must look for the Signata. Why do you ask such a foolish question?"

He heard her quick indrawn breath, like the gasp of one slapped. Her voice trembled slightly as she said, "I won't speak against it if you decide to go home. Perhaps you should."

But she doesn't need to speak against it, he thought, feeling her conviction like a hill's weight on his shoulders. To her it was plain what he should do. But it was easy for her to feel that certainty; what were his family and homeland to Mandine Dascaris? After all, the Two had chosen her, face-to-face. What did she have to lose?

Shame swept through him. *What are you thinking, fool? She's lost everything. She has no one now but you.*

"I'll go to Oak," he said, "but not till this business of ours is finished. However long it takes."

"If you decide to go to home first, Key, I'll come with you."

Taken utterly aback, he could only say, "You will?"

"Yes. I know you love him. I would never keep you away from someone you love."

He imagined himself home again: Ria, the halls of Oaken House, his father's proud, stern face. He and Mandine could go on later, after he had done whatever was necessary.

It felt wrong.

"No," he muttered. "We can't. Not yet."

"Are you sure?"

"I'm sure. Mandine, I'm sorry I spoke angrily. It wasn't a foolish question at all. Please forgive me."

Mandine looked up at him, her face brushed by starlight. He took a tiny step toward her, and suddenly her arms were around him, her forehead pressing his shoulder. His arms encircled her. They stood together in the darkness.

"Key," she whispered.

"I love you," he blurted. "Mandine, I love you." But she didn't respond, and he realized he had not spoken the words, only imagined speaking them. He felt cold sweat on his brow, and his knees shook.

Her arms tightened about him. "Your father. I'm so sorry."

"I'm sure he'll live," he managed to say. "He's a strong man. This won't defeat him."

He straightened, drawing away a little in case she wanted to let him go. But her arms were still around him. He didn't know what to do. Release her? Or forget everything he had sworn to do and not to do, and turn her face up to the stars, and find her mouth with his?

"I'm very glad I have you," he said, fighting for control of his voice. "You give me strength."

"You give me strength, too," she murmured, and looked up at him. Then, so quickly that he was utterly unprepared for it, she went up on tiptoe and kissed him.

He thought for an instant that she had meant her lips to meet his, but instead they brushed across the corner of his mouth and onto his cheek, light as a moth's wing. Delight warred in him with bitter disappointment; it was a kiss, but not the kiss for which he yearned.

She dropped back onto her heels, and even in the dim starlight he saw that she was flustered. But she was still in his arms, and she was breathing quickly. His pulse throbbed in his temples.

"Hai! Key, are you there?" It was Cawlor's voice, a few yards off. Mandine's embrace fell away, and Key let her go, and she stepped back.

"I'm here," he answered furiously.

Mandine said, "That's settled, then, we go on eastward." She turned away, and started back toward the fire. Cawlor mumbled a greeting to her as she passed. Then he lumbered up to Key. "That's ill news of your father," he said, and gave Key a rough pat on the shoulder. "I'm sorry. But these merchants, they exaggerate everything. When you get home, you'll find he's himself again. You *are* going home, aren't you?"

"No," Key said. "I can't."

Cawlor absorbed this in silence. "Very well," he said after a moment. "I can't fault you for it, seeing what you and the luminessa are supposed to be doing. By the by, if you want more of Pellico's wine, your luck's out. He's finished it, and gone."

Key grasped at the present; it was easier than the future. "Did he swallow our story, do you think?"

"Most of it. He spotted the luminessa for highborn, though. He called her 'my lady' once, after you were gone. But don't fret over it. He's carrying a skinful. By tomorrow night he'll have forgotten what she looks like."

"I hope so," Key said. "But we'd better get an early start tomorrow."

"You're sure you're not going home?"

"I'm sure."

"Your father will be all right," Cawlor said, and together they tramped back to the campsite. Mandine was sitting on a log by the fire, staring into the flames. She looked up at Key's approach, but said nothing, only smiled a little sadly as the other men offered him rough reassurances that his father would recover.

Key was in turmoil. He desperately wanted to be alone with Mandine, to be close to her again as they had been close out in the darkness; but the others were there, and they felt like a multitude. There was no hope of sharing even a moment of privacy with her. And with all this was the misery of knowing his father might be dying, or already dead.

"I'll take the first watch," he said, aware that he wouldn't sleep even if he tried to.

"You wanted double sentries," Cawlor reminded him helpfully. "I'll keep the guard with you."

So much for the last chance of private speech with Mandine. But Pellico and his men were on the farside of the campground, and no matter how harmless they seemed, Key would not forgo the double guard.

"I'll welcome the company," he said, and looked across

the fire. But he could not tell what Mandine was thinking, for she had turned away from the flames, and her face was concealed in shadow. There it was, then. She offered him no encouragement, so he could take none. She had kissed him from compassion, not from passion, and with that he would have to be content.

Duke Ragula reined in his hippaxa and counted the bodies sprawled around the two cooking fires. There were eleven, as far as he could tell in the crowd of mounts and cavalrymen that milled around the enemy campsite. A few survivors might have escaped through the sunsip grove behind the fires, or into the fields across the road, but most had fallen to the sudden attack from the darkness. One point in favor of the cataphracts' hell-beasts, Ragula thought, was how quickly and quietly they ran. The surprise was so complete the enemy hadn't gotten anywhere near their horses, which were now being cut loose and driven into the night.

None of his squadron had gone down. A dozen riders were out searching in the darkness for fugitives, but the other seventy-five were around him. He'd lost four men since leaving the goldskin capital, though not from fighting; their mounts had thrown them, then gored the troopers as they lay stunned. Despite the hippaxas' speed and endurance, Ragula would be glad to get back to horses.

A body lay faceup a few feet away. Something was odd about it. The duke dismounted, and made a closer inspection. The man wore Ascendancy military issue, but he wasn't a goldskin. A thick braid of hair curled in the dust beside the gashed neck.

"Look at this," Ragula said as Balik, his second-in-command, joined him. "Islander mercenaries?"

Balik tipped his head in agreement. "I just looked at the others, lord Duke. They're all like that."

"Might be deserters, out raiding." Ragula thought about it. A day ago, just before they seized the ferry and crossed the Seferis, they'd seen a score of mounted militia ride out of a town at their approach and quickly ride in again. That showed that the goldskins could still handle small parties of bandits. Then why would these raiders, if that's what they were, camp next to a main road?

"Did we get any alive?" Ragula asked.

Balik pointed toward the field. "It seems so, lord Duke."

A helmetless captive stumbled into the firelight, two hip-paxas behind him, the riders prodding him on with their lances. He also was an islander. Balik grabbed his braid and threw him on his face at the duke's feet. Ragula studied him, then said, "Do you speak the Ascendancy tongue?"

The man's accent was different from Ragula's, but his speech was understandable. "Yes, great lord. Grant me my life, great lord, and I will tell you of a treasure."

The mercenary had spine, Ragula thought, trying to bargain with a Tathar noble. "Perhaps. Where are you coming from?"

"From Baptisae, great lord. A day's ride west."

Ragula pictured the map Erkai had given him. The city was the one they'd avoided by ferrying the river. "What treasure is this? Don't make something up, dung."

"*Not* made up, great lord. It's a woman. New Dynastessa wants her head. She's important. Very important."

"So you would have me believe. Who is this female?"

The man hunched, as if expecting a fist or a blade. "The Luminessa Mandine. The scum Archates' eldest daughter."

Knowing Balik would not understand, Ragula said in the Logomenon, "Stake him for speaking lies."

The islander's hands shot out, clamped around the duke's armored ankles, and his voice rose in fear and horror. "No, please, great lord," he gabbled, "please. By your gods, I speak truth. We were tracking her from Captala—this morning we find she's in Baptisae not long ago. Lord, five men protect her, and we heard that she fought a magician in the city and won. But her magic is nothing against you. Take her, great lord, and your king will give you lands and gold!"

Fought a magician? Ragula thought. The female Erkai

wants would have magic, wouldn't she? Why would he want her otherwise?

Ragula kicked the man's hands from his ankles. The islander groveled before him, quivering. The duke opened his pouch, took out the skin Erkai had given him, and seized the mercenary by his braid. He jerked the head up and thrust the skin before the man's eyes. Firelight flickered on the image embedded in it.

"Is this the one you're looking for?"

In a strangled voice the islander said, "Yes, great lord. That is the luminessa."

"How do you know?"

"I was in the Paladine Guard. I have seen her in the Fountain Palace."

Ragula put the skin away. "Where is she going?"

"East, great lord. Always east."

"Do she and her party follow this road?"

"I think so, majesty. Before Baptisae, she went across country, and we could not come up with her. But this afternoon a traveler told us he saw five warriors and a youth on the road east of here. Perhaps the youth was the luminessa."

Ragula felt a profound satisfaction. Soon he would be through with this errand-running for Erkai, sooner than he had hoped. Five nights ago the necromancer by his arts had seen the woman in Baptisae, and in the following dawn the king had set the duke on her trail. Now, from the islanders, it was clear that she was traveling due east. How far ahead of them could she be? The duke calculated swiftly: horses traveling fast, the speed of hippaxas. She could be little more than two days' ride away, assuming she kept to her present course. Soon he would have her. Then he could return to Captala, give her to Erkai, and resume his proper business of war.

He considered riding through the night, but rejected it as an unnecessary risk; besides, his men were very tired. "We camp here," he said in Tathar to Balik. "At graylight we go on. The goldskin female's two days ahead of us. Standing orders: we don't stop for anything except westbound goldskins, to persuade them to say if they've seen her. Tell the men."

Balik inclined his head. "Yes, my lord Duke." He kicked the islander. "What shall I do with this?"

The shrieks of a staked prisoner would keep everyone awake. "Slit its throat," Ragula said.

✳ 18

BY MANDINE'S RECKONING, TWENTY-THREE DAYS HAD
passed since she and Key escaped from Captala. The road was
empty now; since meeting Pellico three nights back, they had
encountered no caravans and no travelers. Even where the
road split, its north fork leading toward Daras and the great
waterfall of Thunderhead, they had seen no one, though the
fork had a good spring and was a regular stopping point for
wayfarers. Mandine was beginning to feel that everyone else
in the world had vanished, leaving their small band to toil on
in a search without end.

Key had been morose and quiet all the day after meeting
Pellico, obviously worrying about his father. She desperately
wanted to ease his pain, but she was not sure how to do so.
She was not sure, in fact, of exactly what he was feeling toward
her. On the night he received the bad news, she'd kissed him,
and she had thought for a moment he was going to kiss her
back, and do so with passion rather than friendship. But then
came Cawlor's hail, and she'd gotten flustered at the prospect
of being found in Key's arms, and had fled back to the fire.
When Key returned from the darkness, she'd hoped he'd find
a way for them to be alone again together, perhaps when he
was on watch. But then Cawlor had offered to stand guard
with him, and he had accepted without demur. That suggested

that he wasn't especially interested in having her company to himself, which made her fleeting earlier impression—that he'd been about to kiss her passionately, out beyond the firelight—seem rather ridiculous.

And anyway, what would she have done, or said, if they'd found themselves the only ones awake among their sleeping comrades? Key was torn between his need to find out what had happened to his father and the need to go on in their quest, and she could hardly ask him to deal with her tangled feelings as well as his own.

For her emotions were indeed tangled; in Key's presence she sometimes felt a deep, securing warmth and sometimes a wretched sinking under her breastbone that was very like despair. But those feelings were not so tangled that she didn't know what lay beneath them. *That* was simple enough. In spite of her best efforts to keep a level head, she had fallen in love with Kienan Mec Brander. In fact, as she now recognized, she had already been half in love with him by the time they fled from Captala.

But she had no idea what she should do about it, or even if she should do anything about it at all, and as a result she had spent the last three days acting as normally as she could manage. As for Key's behavior, the embrace and the kiss she had given him might never have happened, and whatever his deeper feelings were toward her, he had so far revealed not a hint of them. Which might mean that they weren't there, except in her wishful imagination. Whatever the case, she had never known a man who was so hard to read. It made her want to shake him.

At least his mood had lightened after they passed the Thunderhead turnoff, two days back. It was as if he were no longer pulled in opposite directions, once the road to Oak was behind him. He even joked a little with her and with Cawlor, and her spirits had risen with his. She had then begun to hope that circumstances might allow them some time alone together, a time when she might perhaps summon her courage and ask him if he felt more for her than he would admit—though she was not sure she could bring herself to speak into his silence, even if she had the chance.

But as it turned out, no such opportunity presented itself. During the day the others rode too close to her and Key, and when in camp they and the horses stayed near the fire, and always set two sentries on each watch; for they were in wild country now, with the mountains closing in around them, and the road's disrepair had increased until it was only a half-overgrown track winding through the forest. No caravans went east of the Thunderhead turnoff, and few travelers. Most of these, Cawlor and Naevis told Mandine, were hunters or trappers, and they did not willingly venture near the Cursed Shore. The others were scavengers, looking for valuables in the tree-shrouded, ruined villages emptied long ago by the plague. Often these men did not come back, and the few objects the survivors did recover were said to be unlucky to own.

Mandine found the accounts unsettling. Cawlor and Naevis treated their possible destination with bravado, for they were the kind of young men, Mandine judged, who would endure red-hot pincers before admitting to a woman that they were apprehensive. Lonn seemed more thoughtful, but if he felt any uneasiness about where they were heading, he did not express it. Jaladar kept to himself as always, though recently he had opened to her a little. He had indeed been a noble in the Mixtun islands, but there had been some unspecified trouble over a woman, and people had died by the sword as a result of it, and Jaladar had either fled or been exiled. More than that, he was unwilling to say.

With the sun at zenith, they stopped for rest and food. Huge trees crowded the road on both sides, so old and so thickly canopied that the only underbrush was dimfern and lacewort, growing from a carpet of dry leaves and cordgrass. As they ate, Jaladar and Key considered the forest with soldiers' eyes, and agreed that they could get the horses through its dim green aisles without much trouble, if they kept to a trot and were careful of deadfalls.

Cawlor swallowed some cheese, pulled thoughtfully at his

mustache, and turned to Lonn. "Is there anything around here but us? I mean, like that sprite you and Key saw?"

Lonn pondered, eyes half-shut. "Oh, they're here," he said. "I feel them, just a little."

"Wood sprites?" Naevis said, looking around. "Very many?"

"More than in tamer places. They're asleep, I think, since it's midday. Or drowsy. They're likely not fully aware we're here."

"They don't mean us harm, do they?" Cawlor said. "We're getting nearer the Cursed Shore, after all. Maybe they're different out this way. Not so agreeable."

"I don't think so," Lonn said. "I don't sense any anger at us. I wouldn't want to chop down a tree, though, not without the rite of permission."

"I don't intend to chop trees," Cawlor said. "But at the Cursed Shore, *will* they be dangerous?"

"I don't know," Lonn said. "I've never been there."

"It's not the sprites that worry me," Naevis put in. "It's what people say about the old black sorcerers that lived there. That some of their magic's still about, or somebody's is, because of that war the White Diviners fought to get rid of them, and you can still get trapped in the leftover magic and never get out. You know how those treasure hunters vanish. Some of them do, anyway."

"People alone in the wild vanish for all sorts of reasons," Lonn told him. "Sickness. The bad luck to fall and break a leg. Avalanches. Remember Cawlor's grandfather?"

"I suppose that's true," Naevis said, and added hopefully, "Most of those stories are just made up, anyway."

It was time to go on. As they set out again, Mandine drew her mare alongside Key's chestnut, in the lead. Ahead, the road's remains curved away to the right. Here the cordgrass completely covered the paving, and their horses' hooves made little sound. Above, the sky was a narrow blue ribbon between the crowns of the trees.

"We're getting closer," she said brightly, as they left the

curve behind, and the road straightened before them. "How long now, do you think?"

"Not many days, if we can keep to this pace. Assuming the map's right."

"It's never been wrong, so far."

"No, it hasn't." He was preoccupied, his gray eyes ceaselessly scanning the trees ahead and to their flanks. She wondered what it would be like to be with him when he was not wary, not on guard. She could barely remember when she had last seen him relaxed. It must have been the night at Baptisae, when they all ate together in the inn, before Erkai's attack.

"After we leave the New Sea," she offered, "we'll go to Oak."

"If we don't find the Signata, we might as well. Although I can't imagine why we'd find it in the Elthame."

"I suppose we'll find it when and how we're meant to." She looked over her shoulder. For a wonder, the others had dropped back, and if she kept her voice low, they wouldn't hear her. This wasn't the opportunity she'd envisioned, and it might be too brief to say all that needed to be said, but she was so tired of *not knowing*. It had to be now. Now, before she lost the impulse.

Her heart pounding, she said, "Key, there's something we have to talk about. I—"

"Listen!" Jaladar called suddenly. "Someone is behind us."

Her words forgotten, Mandine whirled in her saddle to look back at the receding curve. She heard it, too, a muted drumming, a faint jangle of metal. Then, impossibly, a huge horned animal, its black coat frothed with foam, hurtled around the bend and onto the straightway behind them. Its rider's face was bone white, and from his waist flew a silver sash. Behind him poured a flood of hippaxas, their riders bent low over the long, plunging necks, lance heads glittering against the forest's gloom.

"Tathars!" Cawlor bellowed.

"Into the trees, turn right," Key shouted at Mandine. Mandine swerved to obey, ducked as a heavy branch swooped at her head. Thick trunks flew past, one scraping her right calf, and her mare nearly rammed a massive beech. Mandine slackened the reins, jabbed heels into the mare's flanks, and gave the animal her head. Key, flying through the dimness on her left, had drawn his sword.

The hot metallic taste of fear filled Mandine's mouth. They could not outrun hippaxas. They were outnumbered, doomed. And she knew in her soul that this was none of Theatana's doing, but Erkai's. He had found her out at Baptisae, as they had feared, and put the Tathars on their trail.

She had her dagger. She would kill herself before she let the White Death drag her before him.

She glanced over her right shoulder. Jaladar and Lonn pounded through the gloom a dozen yards away, Naevis just behind them. She could not yet see the Tathars, but their high, wavering battle yell howled through the forest. Now the trees were closer together, and dodging them slowed her mare. Would the hippaxas, so much bigger than horses, be held back enough to let them get away?

No. The ululation was already closer. She shot another look behind, saw black shadows, white faces, closing fast. The ground was rising now. Jagged stones thrust from it; her mare slowed even more, barely trotting. Then Key swore, and to her horror she saw a sheer wall of rock looming through the trunks ahead.

Trapped. No escape. Now we have to die. Sweet Lady, I'm sorry. We tried.

Almost together, the six of them reached the cliff base. The rock wall was only thrice a man's height, but it was too smooth to climb. It might as well have reached the clouds.

"Get behind me," Key told Mandine, and she did. The men turned their horses to form rank and face outward, and Naevis strung his bow and nocked an arrow.

Their pursuers had also slowed. "Too bad they've got lances," Cawlor said, sounding merely annoyed. "Gives them more reach."

The Tathar vanguard appeared before them and halted.

There were so many. Mandine drew her dagger, and rested it across her saddlebow.

One of the Tathars rode forward. He was older than the others, with long, sweeping mustaches as silver as the rank sash about his waist. To Mandine his white face, with its dark red mouth, looked like a skull hanging in the forest's gloom. She touched her sabretache, but she knew that the Lady's wheat had no power against steel.

"I am Duke Ragula," the Tathar said in his hard, high accents. "Give us the female and live."

"No," Key said. "Try to take her and die."

Ragula snorted, then gazed hard at Key. "Ah, you. I have seen you before, worm, outside Essardene. I missed you then, but this time I will have your skull on a pole." He reached behind his saddle and tossed an object onto the turf. It rolled to lie faceup, and Mandine saw that it was Pellico's severed head. "Like this one," said Ragula. "We met it on the road, and it told us where you were before it died."

"Then come and cut mine off, too," Key said, "if you can."

Mandine stared in horror at Pellico's dead face, and thought: *But the Tathar wants me alive. He hasn't attacked us yet because he can't risk killing me.*

She raised the dagger and put its point to her breast. "Duke Ragula," she said, in a voice so calm it surprised her, "if you come a step nearer, I will kill myself. Your master Erkai will not like that."

Ragula's mouth twisted in something like a smile, but Mandine saw a moment of uncertainty in his eyes. "Erkai is not my master," the duke said, "but your corpse will satisfy him, even stinking."

"Will it?"

Ragula ignored her, and spoke over his shoulder in Tathar. Mandine saw movement back among the trees. They would work their way to the top of the cliff, perhaps try to drop on her before she could use the dagger. And if she killed herself now, Key and the others would die immediately. It was hopeless.

And life is so sweet. I clutch at even a few moments more of it.

Lonn, just ahead of her on her left, suddenly made a low noise in his throat. Mandine's gaze slid to him, and to her shock she saw that he was trembling like a wind-shaken birch. Lonn, showing fear?

The Ashman stared fixedly at the Tathar duke, but his eyes were wide and seemed to gaze elsewhere, and sweat gleamed on his face. He grunted again and raised his left hand. Then he spoke a low, guttural word, and made a summoning gesture.

Ragula laughed. "Hedge-magic? Dung, save your trouble." He edged his hippaxa a step forward and watched Mandine. "Go on, cow, strike."

He did not believe she would. And would she? The dagger's point had pierced her tunic, and its steel pricked sharp against her flesh. To drive it in—

She saw a mist forming in the gloom above the Tathars. Not rising from the ground, as mists should, but drifting out of the heavy boughs, thickening from the air itself. Lonn's head dropped forward, chin on chest. Above Ragula the mist congealed, took on form: an alsea's translucent woman-shape, long white fingers reaching down for the steel helmet.

A Tathar screamed, *"Faraq!"* and Ragula looked up. His face contorted, his mouth opened, but no sound came out. A wave of cold swept from the mist, and Mandine's face and hands went numb. Fear clutched at her, the primeval, unreasoning terror of the inhuman. Hippaxas bellowed in fright, the Tathars wailed. Ragula threw up his arm as if to ward off the specter above him, and thrust clumsily at it with his lance. The shaft appeared to twist at midpoint, and the blade went wide. The alsea touched his helmet. The duke cried out, and as his hippaxa reared he dropped his lance. Other wood sprites condensed from the mist: more alseas, a callista, syliads. Mandine sat frozen, rooted to the spot on her shaking mare.

Ragula screamed in Tathar, drew his sword, and spurred toward her. Key met him, blade on blade. A few of the duke's men mastered their fear and surged forward. Lonn's head came up, and he raised his shield. Then the mist rolled over everything, glacial and luminous. All around Mandine raged the shout and clangor of men fighting blind, but she saw nothing.

A hippaxa loomed from the whiteness beside her. It rammed her mare. The mare screamed and staggered sideways. Mandine lost her seat, the mare was falling, she was falling. As she fell she glimpsed a green shadow, a lithe something that raced past her into the mist. Then she hit the ground, and her head, and plunged into blackness.

She opened her eyes to leaf-dappled sunlight.

I'm dead, she thought. *I've died. But it wasn't as bad as people say. Perhaps the Two have already judged me, and I've reached the Serene Fields. I wonder if Key's here, too?*

Then her head and her shoulder began to hurt, and that didn't seem right. She stirred, and realized she was covered with a cloak. A face intruded between her and the sunlight. It was Key's face. On his left cheekbone was a bruise, and his eyes were full of pain. Naevis leaned over Key's shoulder, looking distraught.

"It's all right," Key said harshly, as she tried to find her voice. "They've gone."

"What happened?" Mandine's throat felt rusty.

"Your horse must have thrown you. Can you move your hands and feet?"

Mandine experimented. "Yes."

"I thought you were dead," he muttered, and looked away. Mandine saw his throat move as he swallowed. She put her hand on his, and squeezed it. After a moment he returned the pressure, then drew his fingers from hers.

"Well, I'm not," she said. "Help me sit up."

Key put his arm around her shoulders and eased her to a sitting position. Mandine winced and tried to hide the wince as dizziness swept over her. When her head stopped spinning, she looked about her. They were still at the foot of the cliff, but the mist and the wood sprites had vanished. Pellico's head, now mercifully facedown, lay in the scattered leaves next to

Ragula's lance. Four of their horses stood trembling nearby, but Lonn's bay stallion lay at the cliff's foot, obviously dead, and Mandine's mare had vanished. A few yards away, Lonn was stretched white-faced on the turf. Jaladar was wrapping his upper leg with strips of cloth, and thick bandaging covered the crown of Lonn's head and his left eye. Swatches of the bandage were stained crimson.

"What's happened?" Mandine groaned. "Where's Cawlor?"

"He's dead," said Key in a flat voice.

"Oh, no. Oh, sweet Lady, no."

Key held her closer. "It was quick," he said. "He didn't suffer."

"Key, I'm so sorry. So far from home."

"He died fighting, Luminessa," Naevis said desolately. "That's what he would have wanted." He moved and winced.

"Are you all right?" she asked him.

Naevis was growing pale as she watched. "A bang in the ribs from a mace. Didn't get through my mail, but I felt something snap."

"Jaladar and I were only scratched a little," Key told her. "Naevis, go and lie down. Carefully. If you've got a broken rib, you don't want the sharp end in your lung."

Naevis moved away, favoring his right side. "He and Lonn won't die," Key said. "But they can't go on. Also, your mare's run off."

"But the Tathars. They'll come *back*."

"They will not," a lilting, liquid voice said from nearby. "The Quiet Dwellers have broken their courage, and in their fear the death's-heads flee back toward the stone path. Not all will find it. We have killed many, and will kill more before nightfall."

The accent was strange, sibilant. Mandine looked around to see a hemander standing by the trunk of a black beech. His skin was olive green, with tan-and-russet highlights, and his golden eyes had oval pupils. His curly hair was dark chestnut, and he wore a sleeveless brown tunic that reached to mid-thigh. On his arms were strange, swirling tattoos, and over his shoulder was a short, thick bow of black wood.

"That's why the silverhairs won't come back," Key said. "The hemandri fought for us, and they're out there now, chasing Tathars."

Mandine remembered the shadow that had flitted by her as she was falling. "I saw you. You came when the mist did."

The hemander raised his narrow chin, an apparent affirmative. "We would not have interfered, except that—" He hesitated. "Except that you and this one bear the mark of the Shining Ones. It was wrong for you or those with you to die, and I am sorry we could not save you all. Also, your companion over there has a rare summoning power, and that drew us to you, as well."

"Lonn does? You mean, you didn't bring the alseas and the others?"

"No," said the hemander. "He did."

"I didn't know he had so much of the Gift," Key said.

"Neither, I suspect, did he," answered the hemander. "But when life hangs by a wisp of grass, the summons may leap forth." He looked over his shoulder, and Mandine saw movement beyond him. "Now we will help you further, for the sake of the Shining Ones. My kinsmen will carry your wounded, and the man who died."

"To where?" Key asked.

"To a safe place," the hemander said. "My name is . . ." He trilled liquidly.

Mandine gingerly shook her aching head at him. "I don't think our throats can say that."

"Call me Speaker," he said. "I know your tongue; the others of my sept do not. Follow. It is not far."

The summer evening drew down over the hemandri settlement. Mandine had slept the afternoon away; she was still weary and heartsick, but a hemandra had brought her a sweet herbal drink that banished the ache in her head and limbs. Now she sat on a flat stone by the doorway of a hemandri cote. The dwelling was a frame of light wood covered with animal skins, and the skins were painted with intricate patterns of curves and spirals. If Mandine fixed her gaze on the patterns, they shimmered into the forms of curious animals and birds, then into images that were neither animal nor bird but strange minglings of both. There were faces in the patterns, too, somber and beautiful faces with tilted eyes and streaming hair, visages not quite either human or hemandri.

So this is their hidden place, Mandine thought. Before she arrived she had expected the settlement to be in a clearing, but it wasn't; the hemandri village was simply a collection of cotes scattered beneath the trees. From where she sat she counted nineteen dwellings, but she suspected that many more lay out of sight. How many Near Folk might live here, Mandine had no idea. They moved gracefully among the cotes, tending their cooking fires, and their slim children darted about the adults in strange flitting games.

Only one of the Near Folk had approached her since she woke up, the hemandra who brought the herbal drink. Mandine had spoken to her, but the woman only smiled fleetingly and dipped her chin to show she did not understand. She carried an infant in the birthing-pouch beneath her kirtle; its tiny head peeped above the kirtle's waistband and regarded Mandine with puzzled golden eyes. The woman had worn nothing above her waist, and her flat chest did not have even vestigial nipples. The tales seemed to be true; if hemandri infants suckled, they must do so within the birthing-pouch.

She was musing halfheartedly over this when Key appeared from around the cote and, wordlessly, sat down next to her. He looked worn out and miserable.

"How are Naevis and Lonn?" Mandine asked. On their arrival at the settlement, Speaker had put the two wounded men and Jaladar in a large cote by themselves. She and Key had been given the one at her back. A reed screen partitioned it into two small rooms. Cawlor's body lay not far away, in an enclosure under a vast ironwood tree.

"Better. Lonn may keep the eye. Naevis has three broken ribs, but he'll recover."

"I wish Cawlor were here," Mandine said wretchedly. "I miss him. I miss his mustache that he was so proud of. He laughed so well. I wish we hadn't let them come, and he'd still be alive."

"Cawlor was a fighting man," Key said. "You couldn't have stopped him from coming. Or any of them. You'd sooner have kept the sun from rising."

"I know. I just wish he were alive." Grief caught at her throat, grief not only for Cawlor, but for herself and Key who might soon follow him, and suddenly and to her dismay she found herself in tears. They wouldn't stop, and after a moment she felt Key draw her to him. She wept in his arms for what seemed a long time, and as her weeping at last quieted, she thought, *It's not just Cawlor and our fate that hurts me so. It's loving Key. Why can't I speak? Why can't I just blurt it out?*

But how can I, with poor Cawlor still warm?

Her throat tightened again, but she managed to say, "What will happen to Cawlor now?"

"It's our custom to burn the body on the second day after death. Speaker will see to it and keep the ashes for Cawlor's kin."

"And poor Pellico. Why did the Tathars have to murder him? He was only a merchant, no threat at all."

"Tathars like killing. I did the Ascendancy rites for him while you were asleep."

She drew her cloak closer about her. "Were any of the hemandri killed or wounded?"

"Apparently not. Speaker told me the mist and the wood sprites followed the Tathars for a long way, and the hemandri picked off scores of them with arrows. They missed the duke, unfortunately."

Mandine shuddered. "Erkai must want us badly if he persuaded the king to send a duke so far east."

"Yes, so we can't stop here long. Ragula himself doesn't have enough men now to keep up the hunt, but there might be reinforcements coming. Even if there aren't, Erkai won't give up looking for us in whatever ways he can. There's a little good news, though. The hemandri found your mare while you were asleep. So there are still mounts for all of us, though it hardly matters. Lonn and Naevis won't be fit to ride for days."

"That leaves Jaladar fit, and you and me."

"Yes. But I don't like leaving badly injured men by themselves."

Mandine watched three Near Folk children playing a complex game with pebbles and a small basket of woven grass. "The hemandri seem willing enough to tend them."

"That's true, but the hemandri know most about healing their own folk. They may know much less when it comes to humans. And Jaladar is good at battlefield medicine. I'd like him to stay with Lonn and Naevis until they can ride. Speaker said some of his people will escort them to Thunderhead when they're fit to travel."

The light was waning swiftly; a small constellation of firebrights appeared and took up a dance over a patch of ferns nearby. Mandine watched the glowing sparks. "So we go on alone?"

"I see no choice. It's not far to the New Sea now. A few days."

And then? Mandine thought. "Do you think we'll find it there?" she said. "And if we don't, what will we do then?"

"I don't know." Key looked down at his hands. "Mandine—"

She waited. He seemed to be having trouble getting his words out. At length he said, "I told you I thought you were dead. But I didn't tell you how I felt when I thought that."

"Oh," she said, in sudden confusion and faint hope.

"You were dead. The world had ended. There was nothing left, only shadows and ashes, and me wandering among them. Nothing mattered anymore. I wanted to die."

"Oh, Key," she said again, hearing her voice quaver.

"So I have to tell you this now, because we *may* die, and

I don't want to die without letting you know. I hope you'll forgive me for speaking, with Cawlor dead, but he'd have been furious if I kept silent on his account."

Why was he torturing her like this? "Tell me, Key."

He clenched his hands together, and said, "I love you."

An extraordinary feeling of release swept through her, as though the hard-drawn knot she carried under her breastbone had suddenly been loosed. It took her breath with it, and she seemed to have lost the gift of speech.

He said, "If I've offended you, I'm sorry. But I couldn't keep still any longer. It was driving me mad."

She turned to him and put her hands on his shoulders. The touch gave her words. "Key," she said simply, "it's the same with me. I love you."

Astonishment stood in his face, and he seemed tongue-tied. Finally he managed, "You do?"

"Yes, of course." Another curious sensation was rising in her. It was something like happiness, though it was not the joy she had hoped to find in the awakening of love. There was too much death and pain around them for that, and too long a journey yet to go. "Couldn't you tell?"

He looked confused. "No. I thought we were friends, and that was all it could ever be."

"Why?" she asked. "Because I am Mandine Dascaris the luminessa, and not just Mandine, a woman?"

"Yes. It seemed wrong. Your rank—"

He stumbled into silence.

"What do you truly feel for me, Kienan Mec Brander?"

Key closed his eyes, opened them. "I need you forever. I've needed you since Essardene."

"I know," she said softly. "So Key, how can this be wrong, when it feels so right?"

He rested his forehead against her dark hair. "You really do care for me?"

She gave a choking laugh. "I feel as if I've loved you since I was born."

"I would kiss you," he murmured, "but there are three hemandri children watching us."

Mandine looked around, and there they were, golden eyes wide and wondering. "Hello," she said, smiling. They did not return the smile, only looked more solemn, if possible.

"They wonder what on earth we're doing," she said. "Perhaps to the Near Folk, it's rude."

They released each other. The children flitted away, visible one moment, vanished the next. Mandine leaned against Key. He had taken off his mail, and she felt his comforting warmth through cloak and tunic. She was happy, in a subdued way and in a small corner of her being, but what she felt was not the ecstasy the romantic poets wrote of.

It's hardly surprising, she thought. *Our friends are hurt, and one is dead, my homeland is in flames, my people have been slaughtered in thousands, my capital is besieged. Key and I are bruised and sore and exhausted, we're deep in the wilderness and aren't sure where to go next, and we're searching for something that may not even exist. No wonder love seems of such slight account, beside all that. But to us . . .*

"I'm glad we care for each other so much," she said. "It makes what we have to do a little more bearable."

He squeezed her hand. "Yes, it does. Look, here comes Speaker."

The hemander squatted on the turf before them. "Are you well?" he asked Mandine.

"Much better than I was. Thank you."

"Food will be ready soon. If you wish to bathe, that is also possible."

"I'd like that very much," Mandine said fervently. "But Speaker, may I ask you a question?"

Speaker tilted his chin. "Ask."

"When we were at the cliff, you said you saw the mark of the Shining Ones on Key and me. Are your Shining Ones what my people call the Two? The Allfather and Our Lady Mother?"

"Yes. I believe this is so. The Shining Ones are joined, as are the earth and the sky."

"I'm curious about what else you meant. What mark did you see?"

With a narrow fingertip the hemander traced a circle in the grass, then bisected it. "So, and so."

Mandine frowned. "I don't understand."

"Perhaps not," Speaker murmured. "Nevertheless it is there." He shifted his shoulders in a strange, fluid movement. "Your people and mine have different ways of seeing. You and Key are . . . warm with light. In my tongue it would be easy to say. In yours, not possible at all. So I draw you a picture on the breast of our mother."

Mandine thought, *I don't feel warm with light. I just feel worn-out, and short of sleep, and grubby.*

"How did you reach us so quickly?" Key asked. "When the Tathars caught us by the cliff. You couldn't have had much warning."

"One of our folk saw your camp last night, and brought word. Today many of us were between the road and our hidden place here, though you didn't see us. We do not interfere in the affairs of you long-birthers, but then I saw the mark on you, and it became necessary."

"This isn't the first time one of your folk has helped me," Mandine said.

"It is not? How so?"

"Sometime back," she told him, "I was alone in the west, and I saw one of your women. She and her familiar helped me escape a terrible danger. The familiar was a pandragore, a plumed and winged serpent. I didn't believe they existed."

Speaker drew a hissing breath. Mandine thought she had startled him, but his face was harder to read than a human's. "You were aided by a *heksera*. They are like Lonn, except that they use their gift at will. They are very rare, and those who can call the plumed snake as an ally are rarer still. There have been none such in this region for more than my lifetime. How did this come about?"

Mandine hesitated, wishing she hadn't spoken of it. Speaker saw her hesitation. "Be still, I asked without forethought. It is not something I need to know. But I am happy that the Shining Ones saw fit to help you, through one of my people."

"So am I," Mandine agreed, with feeling.

"I'm sorry we brought the Tathars so close to you," said Key. "If they'd found your village, could you have defended it?"

Speaker's upper lip moved, exposing sharp white teeth. His expression might have been a smile or a snarl. "There are many of us here. With all our craft bent against them, the death's-heads would have seen cliffs and gorges where there are none, and turned aside."

"You have powerful magic," Key said.

Speaker pursed his lips. "I know your word, but I have never been sure what your people mean by it. We do what we do, just as the rowan bears fruit. Some of us can do more than others, just as acorns grow oaks while fern spores grow ferns. Where do you go when you leave here?"

The question caught Mandine off guard. After a moment Key said, "Eastward, to the shore of the New Sea."

"Ah. None of your race live there now, and the old stone places have gone back to the earth. Therefore, I judge that the Shining Ones have asked you to do this."

He was very perceptive. "Yes," Mandine answered.

"And the death's-heads pursue you to prevent you from carrying it out."

"Yes."

Speaker half closed his golden eyes and seemed to deliberate with himself. "There may be more death's-heads than we know of, so you would be unwise to use the road. Also, farther toward sunrise the road vanishes; the trees have taken it back."

"If I can see the stars or the sun, I know which way to go," Key said.

Speaker's eyes opened. "Is there no other path?" he asked softly. "I would not see you go there. The salt shore is an unlucky place."

"So we've heard," Key said. "Can you tell us what the dangers are?"

"In our tales it is a deceptive land. There was strong magic there once, and it is still easy to become lost. More than that I do not know. We do not go that way."

"I think we have to," Mandine said. But Speaker's reluctance disturbed her. If hemandri, with all their wood skill and magic, disliked the place, what might await her and Key?

"If you must, you must," Speaker said. "But you would travel more quickly with our aid. Would you accept one of us to show you part of the way? I am the only one here who knows your language, but I am needed and cannot myself go with you. You and your guide would have to talk without words."

It was more than Mandine had dared hope. "We are already forever in your debt, Speaker. But if you offer this, we accept gladly."

"I am sorry we cannot bring you to the salt water, but we do not range that far. That country, as I said, is uneasy for us. Still, we can take you two days' march toward the sunrise."

"Thank you," Key and Mandine said together.

"Good." Speaker rose. "Tonight I will ask for a guide among our people. Now there is food. Please, come and eat."

✳ 19

THE GUIDE WAS A YOUNG HEMANDRA, AND SPEAKER had said they should call her Flute. She knew the forest as Mandine knew the courts and avenues of the Fountain Palace, and for two days she found fords in racing streams and paths through tangled thickets, where Mandine could see no ford or path at all. The hemandra's ability impressed Key. Like most Elthamers, he was skilled at woodcraft, but Flute was more than his equal, and he, Mandine, and the two horses trudged and waded and clambered stoically along behind her. The horses carried supplies and gear; the ground was so broken that walking was as fast as riding and less risky for the animals.

Flute turned back at midmorning of the third day. She suggested, by gestures and drawing on the ground, that she was willing to go on, but Mandine sensed that the hemandra was apprehensive about doing so. Also, according to Speaker, she would be unfamiliar with the country ahead, and it seemed pointless to ask her to enter it. They made their farewells, and their last sight of Flute was her slender form dissolving like mist under the beeches and hornbeams.

"They just vanish," Mandine observed, as she and Key resumed the march. "It's as though they each had a cloak of invisibility."

"It's their coloring," Key spoke over his shoulder; they were proceeding in single file. "Maybe a touch of their magic, as well. Remember what Speaker told us about the way they conceal their village?"

"Yes. It shows how little we know about them."

"I think they prefer it so," Key said.

Without Flute's guidance they traveled more slowly, but Key kept an easterly course by observing the angle of the sunbeams that penetrated the thick leaf canopy. By late afternoon the going became easier because the narrow valleys began to run mostly along their line of march rather than across it. Speaker had given Key a hunting bow and arrows, and while they rested the horses he stalked and shot a woodcock for supper. Somewhat later they passed a cluster of stony hummocks where two valleys met, and realized from the regularity of the mounds that it was a ruined village. But there was no aura to the place; its ghosts had vanished long ago.

Several miles past the ruin they found a deep pool, fed by a spring that tinkled from a crack in a limestone shelf. The heights above were still sunlit, but the light in the valley was fading quickly, and they decided to make camp. They had done this so often now that the preparations were routine and almost wordless. Key found a patch of bellberry plants while he was gathering firewood, but the fruit-bearing flowers were still only tiny hard buds.

They sat together by the fire while the woodcock roasted, their fingers entwined, but speaking hardly at all. They were so close now that there seemed little need for words; indeed, Mandine felt that speaking much of what was between them might endanger it, as if hostile ears listened for such talk and would use it to find them. Moreover, their task was to find the Signata. No love could relieve them of that pledge. Especially now that they were alone, and nearing what they hoped was their goal, it hung over them like a mountain's weight.

After their meal, Key scoured the cookware with water and soapseeds while Mandine built up the fire for the night. They gathered dimfern and spread it on the turf to make two narrow mattresses, which they covered with spare cloaks. That done, they sat side by side in the fire's dancing glow. Insects chirred, the spring chuckled unseen outside the tiny circle of light. They talked a little of Cawlor, and then of more ordinary matters, such as the state of their supplies and how long they should search the Cursed Shore before going on to Oak.

"If this is as strange as the place ever gets," Mandine observed, "I don't see why the hemandri are uneasy about it."

"We're not quite there yet. That ruined village was likely from the old plague, so I think we're still in country that was once populated."

"How much farther to the sea, then?"

"As near as I can tell from the map and dead reckoning, two or three days."

She sighed. "I wish we knew if we were going where we need to."

"This direction's as good as another, at the moment." Key leaned over and poked the fire, raising sparks.

"We'll find the Signata sooner or later," she said. "The Lord and Lady wouldn't tell us to look if we had no chance."

Key opened his pack and took out a whetstone. "I'm sure you're right. What I can't quite understand is, if the Signata's divine in itself—and Athanais's writings suggest it is—why don't the Two know where to find it? You'd think they would." He slipped his dagger from its sheath and began to touch up its edge.

"I don't know. Perhaps the Signata is some other order of divinity. Separate from the Two." The long, narrow blade whispered softly across Key's whetstone. Mandine watched the brightening steel glide back and forth.

"Key," she said suddenly.

"What?"

"Teach me to fight. I've learned a lot since we met, but not that. Remember when I threw the knife at Ragula, back at Essardene? I didn't kill him, and I wish now I had."

He pursed his lips thoughtfully, then nodded. "You're right. We should have done this before." His hand moved, so quickly she barely saw it. The dagger's blade flashed orange, and it was suddenly hilt up in the turf by her feet.

She looked down at it. "Not a sword?" she asked, a little disappointed.

"No. My cavalry blade's too heavy for your wrist, and we don't have a stabbing sword. This will do to start with."

"All right." Mandine pulled the dagger from the turf and held it in her fist, point down.

"Try to kill me," he said.

"But you took your mail off. I might hurt you."

He grinned. "No, you won't. Go ahead."

"Shouldn't you be standing up, at least?"

"No. Pretend you've surprised me."

"You mean I should really try to stab you?"

"Yes, I mean it. Imagine I'm Ragula."

Mandine got to her feet, stood uncertainly, then lunged at him, her arm swinging up to strike.

He was so quick she hardly saw him move, but she glimpsed a stick in his right hand. It hadn't been there an instant ago. It smacked the dagger aside, and he was on his feet with his left hand clamped around her wrist, forcing the dagger around behind her back.

And the tip of the stick was at her throat.

His eyes were dangerous and intent, and only inches from hers. "I'm dead, aren't I?" Mandine said shakily. For an instant she was very frightened of him. If she had been his enemy, those eyes would have been the last things she ever saw.

"I'm afraid so," Key said. He let go her wrist. "The first thing is, you never hold the knife point down. Hold it point up, like this." He demonstrated with the stick. "And never come at your enemy with the blade wide of your body. Keep it between you and him. It's your shield if you don't have a real one. He has to get past your point to get at you. Make him work for it."

"All right."

He showed her how to place her feet, how to balance, how to feint. He used the stick to parry her attacks. The work made her feel flushed and hot. Key was like quicksilver; no matter how she tried, she couldn't touch him.

"Watch his blade. Never mind his eyes, they can't hurt you. His blade can."

His bare brown arms and his hands began to fascinate her. They seemed to move of themselves, as if he didn't need to consider where they should go to defend him.

"That's it. Better. Be patient. Let him make the first mistake."

At last she drew back, breathing quickly. Key was flushed, and in the fire-glow his eyes were bright. "What do I do if he has a sword?" she asked. "His reach is longer. How do I deal with that?"

"Run, if you can."

"And if I can't?"

"Then you're dead, if that's what he wants."

"Isn't there *anything* I could do?"

He pondered. "Maybe. Most men don't have much regard for a woman's fighting skill." He dropped the short stick, picked up a longer one from the woodpile, and pointed it in her general direction. "The reach is better, but once you're inside it, he's at a disadvantage till he can back away. Also, he's got one hand busy with his sword. If you can keep your knife hidden, he won't see you as a threat until too late. Look terrified, and he might be overconfident enough to let you slip inside his guard."

"Like this?" Mandine said, and as the words left her she was past the stick's point, darting at him. She was already bringing the dagger up, and in the blink of time that followed she realized that he was truly startled. Horrified that she might actually hurt him, she dropped the dagger even as his hand closed on her wrist. She slammed into him as Key shoved her arm down and away. He staggered slightly, but he had bested her. Then they were standing locked together, length to length.

"I knew you had it, you see," he said huskily. "You mustn't let him know."

He had not released her. "I dropped it on purpose," she said. Her voice was shaking. "I didn't want to hurt you."

Neither of them moved. Mandine felt him trembling against her, or was it her body trembling against his?

We've never touched like this. Sweet Lady, my knees are water.

A soft noise on the turf: the stick had fallen. Without warning, his arms enfolded her. She put hers around his waist, clung to him. "Mandine," he said, in a harsh, breaking voice. "Mandine."

"I'm here," she whispered, her head buried between his neck and shoulder. "I'm here."

And she felt another presence, suddenly, and raised her head to look past his shoulder. For an instant she believed it was a wood sprite, but then she saw them both, and she knew. The Youth's face was warm, and on the Maiden's lips was a grave smile.

"Key," she whispered, "it's *them*."

He turned and saw, and she had to support him as his knees almost gave way. "My Lord," he said, in a shaking voice. "My Lady."

Their light a dim glory, they reached out to each other, and their hands clasped. They inclined their heads, and Mandine saw what they wore in their shining hair. Then, like candle flames vanished in a gust of wind, they were gone.

"I saw them," said Key. "I *saw* them. The Two." He sounded terrified, and exalted, and almost in tears.

Mandine realized that she was trembling like an aspen leaf. "But Key, did you see what else was there? They wore the marriage crowns. They want us to do the same. Don't you *feel* it?"

After a pause he answered, "I feel it. We're together like them, forever and forever."

Mandine tightened her arms around him. "Forever, till the sun darkens and the stars go out. Key, love me. Love me now."

His arms tightened about her. "Mandine, dear heart, you're sure?"

"Yes. We're supposed to." She looked up at him, half

weeping. "I know it as I know the Two. It's the Great Marriage. They are in us."

"Mandine Dascaris," Key said, his face grave, "will you marry me?"

She laughed through her tears. "Kienan Mec Brander, I will."

He smiled, as she had never seen him smile before. "Then," he said, "we must be married. Now and here. Is there a way to do that, under your laws?"

She held him tighter. "Yes, there is. We have fire and water, and the Lady's wheat for the grain. We need only swear ourselves to each other, in the sight of the Two. But we should have garlands, for the vows and for the fire."

"We'll find something," Key said, as he reluctantly let her go. "The water, first."

A burning branch served as a torch, and by its light they took a bronze cup to the spring. As Key filled it, Mandine touched his arm. "Look," she said, pointing into the shadows on the farside of the pool. "Look, there."

In the undergrowth were glints of white. Together they went around the pool's margin, and Mandine parted the tall fronds of dimfern. Beneath them were masses of small white flowers, with gold at the center of each bloom. From the flowers rose a sweet and delicate fragrance, like that of rain on young grass.

"What are they?" Key asked.

"They're silver amaranth. They're very rare. We use them to crown the Lord and Lady, at the start of the marriage month."

"I don't remember seeing them here earlier. Do you?"

"No, but they're here now. I think the Two have given them to us, for our wedding." Mandine stooped and began to break off the stems. Key thrust the butt of the flaming branch into the earth and helped her. The fragrance of the amaranth grew heady as wine. Then, deftly, Mandine wove a crown of flowers, and with less adeptness, Key did the same.

"Now we can begin," she said gravely, when the garlands were finished.

With the cup and the flowers they returned to the fire. Key said, "Do you know what to do?"

"Yes. It's like the rite we use when the betrothed couple stand before the Lord and Lady, in the marriage month. Put the water down. Oh, and I need the wheat."

She brought her sabretache, opened it, and set it on the grass beside the cup. "Now," she said. Her voice trembled. "Key, I can hardly speak."

He touched her mouth. "Speak."

"I'll try." She took a deep breath. "In your names, Our Lord Allfather and Our Lady Mother, Kienan Mec Brander and Mandine Dascaris stand before you as one in two. We beseech that our union be crowned with blessing, as yours is crowned with blessing."

She reached up and set the circle of amaranth on Key's hair. "You must do the same," she murmured.

He did so, a little clumsily, with shaking fingers. "Now the water," she told him, and stooped to pick up the wheat. Key took the cup.

"This may be a little complicated," she said. "Usually the priest and priestess do part of it."

Key smiled. "We'll manage."

"Take some water on your fingers and touch my forehead and mouth with it."

As he did so, Mandine said, "This is the Father's rain that calls forth life. Let it bring forth life in us and for us, and for all those who are given under our care. Key, say, 'Let it be so,' with me."

"Let it be so," they said together.

She raised her right hand and with the ear of wheat brushed Key's forehead and lips. "This is the Mother's grain that gives life to the living. Let it be fruitful and nurture us, and nurture all those who are given under our care. Let it be so."

"Let it be so," he said.

She put the grain back in her sabretache and motioned for him to set down the cup. Then she took his right hand in her left. "Say this with me, Key."

He nodded solemnly. Their voices spoke together into the circle of firelight, murmured into the darkness beneath the trees.

"Before Our Lady Mother and Our Lord Allfather, we two declare that we are husband and wife, in love and friendship and trust, as they are husband and wife in love and friendship and trust. We declare that we are bound as one in two, in this life and all others, in this world that is, and in worlds that are to come. If I break this bond, may bread be as ash in my mouth, and water as dust in my throat. Let it be so, and so say I, Mandine Dascaris, in the name of the Two."

"Let it be so, and so say I, Kienan Mec Brander, in the name of the Two."

Mandine took the crown of amaranth from her hair. "This gift of the earth we give to the sky, in symbol of our marriage."

She cast the garland into the flames, and Key did likewise. The flowers did not char, but flared blue-white as summer lightning, and spears of fire leaped as high as the branches of the trees. Sparks soared in constellations toward the stars, and as the flames sank again the night air filled with the scent of rain on grass.

Mandine turned to him. "Now we are one," she said, and her arms went around him, and his around her. Then Key picked her up, and took her to the marriage bed. There his weight on her was a sheltering roof, and Mandine opened to him. Gently he entered her, and she drew him within her, like rain into the furrows of the earth. At last she heard him cry out, and arched herself to meet him, and as ecstasy swept her there was nothing but him, and her, in the ancient garden at the turning axis of the world.

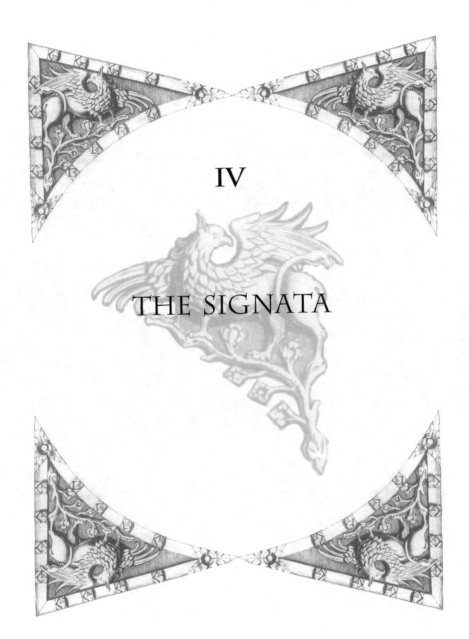

IV

THE SIGNATA

✳ 20

A RAIN CROW WOKE THEM AT DAWN, ITS HARSH CRY reaching down from the heights above their camp. Despite their few hours of sleep, they both felt fit and exuberant. Even the dim valley seemed suffused with a newer, richer light. They ate breakfast, then bathed together in the pool by the spring, which led to a rather lengthy delay.

"I can't help wishing," Mandine said a little wistfully, as she helped Key pack the saddlebags, "that we were just ordinary people. And that the Tathars were peaceful, and there were no Erkai, so we could just get on with being ourselves. Together."

"I admit this isn't the way most couples begin marriage," Key said. "Is it? Wandering around a wilderness."

Mandine took her time closing the last buckle. "Do you still want to be married to me?"

Key shot her a startled look. "Of course. What in the world makes you ask?"

"Well, soldiers, as I understand it, sometimes prefer not to be burdened with wives."

"The more fools they." He knelt by her and took her hands. "We're married in our eyes and in the sight of the Two."

"But do you *want* to be married to me?"

"Yes," he said, kissing her lightly. "Don't be foolish. You are my beloved wife, and I'm your husband, till the sun darkens and the stars go out."

"Don't say that," she murmured, with a sudden shiver. "We don't know how long that might be. Remember why we're here."

"I know." His face was somber.

"If we do win," Mandine said in a rush, "if Erkai and the Tathars and Theatana are all defeated . . . If we win, Key, you and I will rule the Ascendancy together, as Dynast and Dynastessa."

He rubbed his forehead. "I thought of that this morning. I can imagine governing Oak Haeme. But the Ascendancy? I'm reluctant even to think about it."

"My poor husband. You've taken up more burdens than just a wife."

"You're no burden. You make my burdens lighter. But as for the rule of the Ascendancy—Mandine, please believe me, I never sought that through you. I would have married you if you were a drover's daughter."

She gave his arm an emphatic pinch. "I'm not such a poor judge of character as you seem to think. I know why you married me, and it was not for the diadem. Until last night, you did all you could to avoid me."

"I regret to admit it."

"You were a little foolish, and so was I, I suppose. But we mustn't worry about the throne. For now, we should take what happiness we can, day by day, until we win or lose."

"You're right." Key kissed her, then peered at the screen of leaves above. What little sky was visible was still blue, but from the east the rain crow called again. "Now we've settled that, wet weather's coming. We'd better go."

For some two miles the valley sloped very gradually downhill; then its floor began to climb. Key scrambled up a columnar oak to reconnoiter what lay ahead, but the skyline to the east had vanished in a thick haze. The sun itself was growing indistinct, and the sky was no longer blue but a misty, luminescent gray. When he returned to the bottom of the tree, the light at ground level had faded perceptibly.

"Are we going to get a storm?" Mandine asked.

"I'll be surprised if we don't."

They trudged onward, Key in the lead, with the valley floor still tending steadily upward. They heard the rain crow again, far off and ahead of them, and almost simultaneously a sullen peal of thunder boomed from the east. The first drops pattered on the foliage overhead, and Key stopped to pull their foul-weather gear from the saddlebags. By the time they had the leather cloaks on, the patter had turned to a heavy drumming. The leaf canopy resisted at first, then surrendered and let the rain through. The downpour hissed around them, thumped on their hoods, and set the sparse undergrowth dancing. The aisles of the forest became misty with spray, and the already-dim light dimmed further as the air grew chill. The horses plodded miserably through the deluge, heads low and tails dripping.

After a while the lightning and thunder slowly flashed and rumbled away to the southeast. The rain slackened, then settled into a monotonous drizzle, and, to add to their discomfort, they found themselves walking into a thick, cold fog.

"Upland mist," Key said over his shoulder. "We've climbed quite a way."

Mandine brushed rain from her face. "Then I hope we start going down soon. This feels so shut in."

But the mist steadily thickened, until they trudged along in a small, moving chamber bounded by wet gray walls and a dripping gray roof. Tree trunks and bushes loomed out of the fog, then vanished within a few yards. The drizzle showed no sign of stopping.

"The ground's leveled out," Key called at last. He halted the chestnut and came back to her. "Are you cold?"

"No." She smiled up at him. "You know, you wouldn't be suffering through this if you hadn't met me. Aren't you sorry?"

"Idiot," he said, and kissed her lightly.

She tilted her head as their lips parted. "Thunder again. Do you hear it?"

Key listened. "No."

"I thought I heard it, a long way off ahead of us. Maybe it's my imagination."

They went on. The ground soon began to descend. Visibility was so poor that they could no longer tell whether they were in a valley or not. The trees thinned, and the spectral oaks and beeches gave way to shadowy alders and larch. Then the scrub vanished altogether, and they saw only walls of mist. The turf became patchy and stunted, and eventually gave way to rock and rounded stones, as though they were in an old riverbed. There had been little air movement in the forest, but now Mandine felt a slow, dank breeze in their faces, as though they might be in the open. Key went very carefully, for in the mist they would not see the brink of a precipice until they were a few strides from it. The rain drizzled on.

"I *do* hear something, Key."

They stopped. From ahead a faint, resonant booming made its way through the fog. It was too steady to be thunder.

"It's water moving," Key said. "It must be rapids. A biggish river."

"I don't remember one on the map."

"I don't, either. I hope we're still going east."

"Well, if we're near the New Sea, the river's likely flowing there. If we find it, we'll know which way to go."

"Right."

The breeze dropped, but the sound continued. It faded, returned, faded, muffled by the fog but never dying away altogether. Now the ground was loose stones interspersed with swatches of coarse grit.

Suddenly there was nothing underfoot but sand. The drizzle stopped abruptly. Mandine felt an instant of vertigo and stumbled. When she regained her balance they were still moving, but Key was shaking his head as if to clear it.

"Did you feel something peculiar just now?" she called.

"Something. A dizziness."

"So did I, but it went away. Are you all right?"

"Yes."

Whatever had caused the sensation did not recur. The breeze rose again and became a wind. Now the sound of moving water came from just ahead, slow and dull: *hiss, thud, hiss.* A familiar tang was suddenly in Mandine's nostrils, and ahead of them the fog abruptly parted before the wind.

They stopped short, staring in disbelief. A few yards away, low gray waves swept out of the thinning mist, broke in knee-high surf, and sent sheets of foamy water hissing across the sand. The air smelled of salt and sodden weed.

"It's the sea!" Mandine exclaimed. "The New Sea! It can't be anything else. Can it?"

Key dropped the chestnut's reins, went to the water's edge, tasted, walked back to her. "Brine," he said.

"But we can't have reached it yet. I thought we had two days to go. Is our navigation *that* wrong?"

The wind was steadily dispersing the mist. A brighter patch glowed whitely overhead: the sun. "It's not that wrong," Key muttered. "We shouldn't be here yet. I don't know what's happened."

"I don't much like this," Mandine said, with a quick little shiver.

The fog was evaporating rapidly, as if the sun were a lens burning it away. The watery horizon became hazily visible, pale blue and far off. There was no sign of a far shore, or islands.

"Key, sweet Lady help us, *look!*"

He spun around to face inland. The fog there had gone. Long tawny dunes, bare of any green, marched to the north and south as far as the eye could see. Beyond the dunes, where he and Mandine had been only hours ago, parched and barren mountains rose against a hot sky. There was no forest, no cloud, no sign of rain. The dry riverbed that had led them here groped westward into the sand hills, and vanished into a shimmering film of heat.

"Where are we?" Mandine whispered.

"I don't know." Key looked around. Sea, beach, dunes, mountains, sky. There was nothing else.

"Should we go back the way we came?"

He gauged distances. In the shimmer the mountains were indefinitely far. "No. It's not where we just were, and it's very rough ground. We'd be better off to keep to the shore."

"This place looks awfully dry. Should we worry about water?"

"We'd better, till we know where to find some." He calculated silently. "We've got about three days' supply on the horses, if we ration ourselves. But the horses will need to drink today, and we need grazing for them." He scuffed the sand with his boot. "This looks real enough. Do you think this is some illusion of the Adversary?"

"I don't think so," Mandine said, frowning. "I think it would feel more evil than this. This just feels . . ."

"Ominous."

"Yes."

"There were thanaturge strongholds west of the Old Dominion, once," Key said. "If that's where we are, could some of their magic be lingering?"

"The White Diviners destroyed the last of them more than two thousand years ago," Mandine reminded him. "But I suppose it's possible."

"But maybe," Key said, "maybe this is the old battlefield of that war. A battlefield that sorcery made, that looks like our world but . . . but is somewhere else. And we've slid into it. That's one of the stories about the Cursed Shore, the stories Naevis was talking about, remember? On the Shore, people wander into weird places. And there was that moment when we both felt dizzy. Maybe that was when it happened."

Mandine grimaced. "I don't like that idea at all. If we're not in our world, it might be easier for the Adversary or Erkai to attack us. That's how I lost my memories the first time, when I was in an in-between place. And if we're somewhere else, how are we going to get home?"

"We could go back to where we were dizzy and see what happens."

She hesitated, then said, "That doesn't feel right. We've never retraced our steps yet. I don't like staying here, but I think we should go on."

He trusted her instincts, though he wondered if plunging on would take them any closer to the Signata. Whatever this place was, it felt utterly empty, as though its air had never been breathed.

"We'll go on, then." He pointed along the beach. "If this is part of our world, or a shadow of it, that's north, and the Elthame plateau's up there somewhere. It should only be about two days on horseback, but looking for water and grazing will slow us down. We'd better get moving."

Now, on clear ground, they could ride. They mounted and set out, keeping close to the low surf, where the waves had packed down the sand. It was not a lifeless sea, for ropes of damp emerald weed lay here and there, but there were no small fish cast up in their fronds, as Key would have expected. Nor were there the usual shoreside scavengers like crabs, nor any seabird, and inland the dunes and mountains rose treeless, stark, and dun.

They paused in early afternoon for a sip of water and a few mouthfuls of bannock. The horses showed no distress yet, but by evening they would be suffering. Key began to worry about his water-rationing estimate. His mail was making him sweat too much, and he exchanged it for a linen tunic.

When the sun was a handbreadth above the mountains, they moved away from the tide line to halt for the night. They unloaded the horses, and Key trudged across the first few dunes behind the beach, in the hope of finding firewood. There was none to find, and after a fruitless search he gave up and headed back to the sea. The dune nearest the beach was higher than the others, and he paused at its crest to stare north, then south. The landscape was exactly the same in both directions.

He looked down. Below on the beach, Mandine was unpacking saddlebags. She looked up, saw him, and waved.

Key's throat tightened. How long would they last, if the beach went on and on, if the Elthame plateau wasn't there? And if it *were* there, would it be changed, as the mountains had changed?

He knew how their deaths would come. The horses would go first. Mandine would follow them before he did. He wondered how he could watch her die. Or he could make sure she got extra water, but then he might die before her, and she would be left alone in this desolation.

Key shook himself. Thinking this way wasn't like him; perhaps something about this place sapped the will. He started down the face of the dune, and his foot struck a hardness just under the sand. It rolled, dislodging itself from its burial place. Key looked down and saw a leather mask.

But it was not a mask; it was a mummified face, teeth brown and bared, eye sockets full of grit. He recoiled, then looked toward Mandine. Her back was to him. Quickly he used his boot to shovel sand over the dead face, and accidentally uncovered part of a dried rib cage. He concealed that, too, and came down the dune in long, loping strides.

"No wood?" she asked, as he reached her.

"No. It doesn't look as if anything's ever grown here." *But other people have found themselves here,* he thought, *and they never got out.*

"Did you see something from up there? You were looking around."

"Nothing. But we're still too far south to see the plateau."

"Yes." She did not say, *If it's there,* but she might as well have.

They ate and allowed themselves a little water. The horses had to go without, and stood dispiritedly over their ground ties, heads drooping. Night fell, and as the stars came out Key saw that the constellations resembled the old familiar ones, but they were not quite in the right places. As best he could tell, north was indeed the direction they were going, which gave them both some comfort. As the air grew colder, they wrapped themselves in their cloaks and curled up in each other's arms.

Neither thought of lovemaking; they were both too thirsty and exhausted.

"We'll go another half day's march," Key said. "If we don't find water by then, we'll wait out the afternoon and evening, and start traveling by night. We won't lose as much moisture that way." He remembered the wizened mummy's face and shivered.

"Are you cold, my love?"

"No. Go to sleep." He knew they should stand watch in such a place, but she was too tired. She would need all her strength to reach safety, if there were any safety to reach. So would he. He commended himself and Mandine to the care of the Two and closed his eyes.

On the second day they traveled on foot to spare the horses and sucked pebbles to keep their mouths from drying out completely. Key knew his first water estimate had been dangerously wide of the mark, but he had never been in air so desiccated as this, air so dry it sucked moisture from the lungs. He thought now that there might be enough in the bottles for another day after this one, but there was none for the horses, and they were flagging badly. At noon he still saw no shadow of a plateau on the northern horizon, though with the heat dance of the air it might be only ten miles away and still hidden.

"We'd better stop and find shade," he said. "We'll go on after dark, when it's cooler." *As we should have done before now,* he thought. *I hope I haven't killed us.*

"All right." Her lips were cracked, her eyes red-rimmed, as he knew his must be. "Where?"

He pointed at a distant shadow. "I think there's an overhang up that hill, back of the dunes."

They struggled through the soft, clinging sand for ten minutes before reaching the end of the dune field. Twenty feet up a rubble slope a ledge jutted out from bedrock, forming a shallow cave. There was just enough shade to cover them and the horses. The animals stood listlessly, heads drooping. Key unsaddled them, then he and Mandine huddled against the rear wall of the cave, where they shared a few drops of water. Even with that, their mouths were too dry to eat the hard bannock or the flinty sausage. Talking was difficult, and they soon gave up words and sat very still, eyes closed, dozing. With agonizing slowness, the sun declined finger width by finger width toward the west.

At last the shadows of the mountains crept across the dunes and the beach, and Key roused himself. Mandine had fallen asleep, and he hated waking her. When he did, she looked confused for a few moments. He tried to smile. "I'm sorry, love. But we have to go on."

"I was dreaming," she said. "It was a garden, Key, and there was water. Pools and pools of it, and streams. A water-fall." She sat up, wincing. "I didn't want to wake up."

That frightened him a little; it sounded like a touch of delirium. "We've got to eat something," he told her. "Then we'll go on. We'll have to leave everything behind we don't absolutely need, including the saddles and tack, and my mail and shield. The horses will last a bit longer without the weight."

She looked around the brooding landscape. "Not your sword, though."

"No. I'll bring the bow, too, in case we ever see any game. And I'll keep my helmet."

They choked down some bannock moistened with a little water. Then, in the gathering dusk, they slung the lightened saddlebags on the horses and struggled back to the beach. Mandine's mare was faring badly, and the chestnut's eyes were dull and rolling. Key didn't think either animal would last much beyond sunrise.

They set off northward along the shore. With the sun down, the air cooled rapidly, though it was still arid. A faint breeze blew from the sea, as it always did there, but there was no moisture in it. Key still hoped for a drizzly shore fog, like the one that had shrouded their arrival, but so far there had been no sign of one.

After an hour's travel they stopped to rest. In three more hours they could have a little water. Darkness had fallen completely, but they could see a silvery glow on the eastern horizon, where the dark sea met the dark sky.

"The moon's coming up," Mandine said. "Was there a moon last night?"

"I don't know. We were asleep just after dusk and didn't wake till dawn."

They watched as the shimmer became brighter, and a silver thread appeared at the rim of the world. It thickened, became an arc.

"Is she the same moon as ours, I wonder?" Key muttered.

"When she's risen maybe we can tell. If she is, we'll see the Dreamer."

They moved on, plodding along the packed sand and pebbles near the waterline. The sea was very calm, breaking on the shore in ripples rather than waves. The sound of their fall was hardly louder than the crunch of boots on shingle and the harsh breathing of the horses. The moon broke free of the horizon, and they both saw the Dreamer, but she appeared slightly out of place on the luminous disk.

"It's as though we were in a world almost like ours," Mandine said, "but not quite. Our world in a different time, perhaps?"

"Maybe." Key was keeping an eye on the dunes and the foothills beyond them; if there were danger, it would likely come from there. Suddenly Mandine exclaimed, "Key!"

"What?" He spun around. She had stopped and was pointing.

"Look at the sea. Look."

Beneath the moon, the sea was not quite *there*. It was indistinct, like a mirage of water, and through the wavering film a moonlit landscape slowly took shape, sweeping away to the horizon: fields, woods, a white ribbon of road, the broad silver band of a river. And in the middle distance appeared a vast white city, vaster than Captala Nea herself, real and solid in the gossamer illumination, garlanded with lights.

"Do you hear?" Mandine whispered, her voice full of awe. "Do you hear the music?"

"Yes." It was faint but distinct, citterns and cembalos and a bawn drum, the melody bittersweet, with a lovely melancholy in its dying fall.

"I know it," she murmured. "It's an old song, so old. It's 'The Stone and the Maiden.'" In a voice so soft he could barely hear her, she sang with the music.

> She's found at last her true love's tomb,
> And the bloodred stone where his heart lay,
> And she's lain her down beside his dust,
> And taken the stone upon her breast,
> And with his heart's love passed away.

She trailed off, though the music did not. It remained, a silver thread of melody in the moonlight.

"Are we looking at the past?" he asked in a hushed voice. "At a ghost city?"

"I don't know. It looks so *real*." He heard her breath catch. "Sweet Lady, I know what it is. It's Fallas Gaea, the old drowned capital."

"But how can you—"

"It is. There's a picture in the Pantechnion. I see the High Temple, and the Silver Palace, and the river. It's Fallas Gaea herself. Key, maybe we could go down there. We could walk the streets the White Diviners walked. Maybe this is a place where the Deluge never happened. Maybe the Signata's *there*."

"We can try." He let go the chestnut's lead rein and took her arm. Together they walked toward the moonlit landscape. Now the ghostly sea lapped almost invisibly at their feet, but Key felt the wash of cold water at his ankles. How real was anything here? Were the sea and the barren strand the illusion, and the white city the reality?

The music faded and whispered into silence. The lights of Fallas Gaea dimmed, and one by one began to go out, like stars before the coming dawn.

"No," Mandine cried out. "Please, no." Key felt the cold reach his knees and stopped, still holding her arm.

The silver sweep of the river darkened and disappeared, and slowly the city itself turned mistlike, insubstantial, and dissolved. The road and the fields became a glimmer on water, and then only the waves, silver-tipped by the moon, stretched restless and desolate to the far horizon.

"It was a ghost," Key said. "Though I would have sworn it was real."

"I was so sure," she said dully. "I was so sure the Signata was there."

They turned and made their way to the beach. Key helped Mandine sit down, then squatted on the sand and took her hands in his to warm them. Suddenly he looked up.

"What's the matter?" she asked.

"I thought . . . just for a moment, I thought the hills had forests on them. But they don't. They're the same as yesterday."

"This is a very strange world," she said. "As though times and places were all mixed up together."

There was a moment of silence. "What did you just say?" Key asked.

"As though— Key, is that it? Are we *inside* the Signata somehow? It's supposed to be the place that contains all places, and the moment that contains all moments. Have we already found it?"

"But I thought it appeared as a thing, that you could find and carry around. For Athanais it was."

"Yes, it was. It was for the others who saw it, too." Mandine rummaged in the cloaks, found her sabretache, and opened it. "I wonder if the wheat might tell us something. It hasn't changed since we've been here, but we just saw something magic." She searched in the pouch, and suddenly her hand stopped moving. Her face in the moonlight was stricken.

"What's the matter?" Key said in alarm.

She opened the sabretache wide and held its open mouth

to the moon. "It's gone," she said in a shaking voice. "The wheat. It's gone."

"What? It can't be."

Already Mandine was half in tears. "You look. The wrapping's there, but the wheat's not."

She was right. The scrap of linen lay in the pouch bottom, empty. Not even a dried husk remained.

"Please don't hate me, Key," she said, in a voice full of despair. "Please. I look every night and every morning, to make sure it's safe. Except I didn't, this evening just past. I was so tired, and so thirsty. But it was there yesterday morning. I know it was."

He could not be angry at her. "The straps were buckled?"

"Always. I'm very careful."

He felt along the seam of the pouch bottom. "There," he muttered. "The stitching's come out. There's a slit." He could just work his fingertip into the gap. "But it's small. I can't imagine how the wheat could get out of the wrapping and slip through it."

"But it did. Have I doomed us, Key?"

"Of course not," he said, with false confidence. "We know where we were yesterday. We'll backtrack and look for it."

"But you said we've only water for another day. If we go back a day's march, and there's nothing to save us, we'll never reach the plateau."

He sat down in the sand beside her. "We don't know if the plateau's there. Even if it is, it might be as barren as this."

"But it's a chance. Maybe our only chance."

"I think," he said slowly, "that we have to go back. The Lady gave you that gift for a reason. We can't turn away from it."

"If we don't find water, we'll die. And there's no water back there."

"But the wheat must be. We have to go back, Mandine. Anyway, it would have taken time to work its way free of your pouch, so maybe it's not far." *But the onshore wind was stronger yesterday,* he thought. *If we lost the wheat on the beach, it could be anywhere, blown inland.*

"Maybe," she said, with desperation clear in her voice, "maybe the city was some kind of sign for us. I wouldn't have looked for the wheat, otherwise."

"Maybe," he answered, though he didn't know whether to share her hope. In a place like this, things might happen for no reason at all.

"So we go back," she said.

"Yes, as soon as it's light enough to see what we're doing. Come here, love. It's cold."

They made a halfhearted camp, then huddled miserably together in the bitter night. As they tried to settle down, Key said, "That song, 'The Stone and the Maiden.' Do you suppose there was something in it? A message for us?"

"I don't remember the words, except the ones I sang. Let me see, how did the story go . . . it's about a maiden who lived in an eastern country, and a prince from the west came there, and fell in love with her. He went home to get his father the king's permission to marry, but the king wanted him to marry another woman. The prince refused, and his father threw him into a dungeon, where he died."

Key grimaced. "Oh."

"So when he didn't come for her, the maiden set out to find him, because he was her one true love, as she was his. She searched for years and years, till she was an old woman, and finally she came to his tomb and knew he was dead. So she entered the tomb and in his dust she found a red stone where his heart had been, and she knew it was his love for her, that had waited for her all those years. So she lay down beside him, and put the stone next to her own heart, and so died."

"I don't like that song much," Key said, after a moment. "There's too much death in it. People shouldn't have to die for love. They should be able to live it."

"Yes. I know. But she was given no choice, was she?"

Because of the cold, neither slept well. Dawn came at last,

as the moon passed its zenith and began to sink slowly in the west. When there was enough illumination to tell a black pebble from a white, they loaded the horses and set out, treading in their earlier footsteps, eyes scanning every speck of ground near their path. Soon the sun broke over the horizon, and flooded the mountains, dunes, and shore with a hard white light. The sea glared at them from a surface like molten blue glaze. The sun itself seemed peculiar, as if it were not a blazing disk at all, but a flaw in the sky that admitted a savage incandescence from another realm.

"I keep thinking of that pool up in the mountains," Mandine said, her voice cracking. "Remember how cold it was? How wet?"

He had been doing the same, and trying not to, for the memory was an exquisite torture. "And I was annoyed about the rain. If I'd known what was coming, I'd have blessed it."

"So would I."

A hundred yards farther on the mare groaned, shuddered, and sank to her knees. As if her collapse had taken the last strength from him, the chestnut also staggered and fell. Key and Mandine stood looking at the two horses. The mare was gasping, the chestnut's flanks heaved. Key pulled off the saddlebags and put everything into one.

"We can't just leave them," Mandine said, in a breaking voice.

"I know. Go on a little way."

He drew his dagger, and Mandine walked twenty yards along the beach and turned her back. She heard nothing but a faint gasping. In a few moments Key was beside her again. The last saddlebag was slung over his shoulders.

"Could we have . . . drunk their blood?" she asked.

"I tried it. Too much salt. They were too thirsty."

They tramped on. Hours passed, until the sun was almost above them. By now their tracks of the day before were blurred, almost gone in places, and what little hope they had had was fading. On their right the mountains were uniform in their raggedness, and any dune could have been any other.

On their left, the sea lapped almost soundlessly at the shore. The sand glared into their eyes, and bright and dark specks began to swim in Mandine's vision. She looked up, but the specks didn't go away. One in particular floated differently from the others. She blinked rapidly. All the specks but that one disappeared.

"Key, there's something flying up ahead. Look."

He squinted. "You're right. Great Allfather, I think it's a bird."

"A bird? Here?"

"It can't be anything else." He stopped, pulled the hunting bow from its sheath on his back, and strung it.

"Should we kill it? It might be the only creature besides us in this dreadful place."

"We need its moisture," Key said.

The bird called, faint and distant, but the cry was unmistakable. "A rain crow?" Mandine exclaimed in disbelief. "In this desert?"

"It sounds like one." Key had an arrow out, and was setting its nock to the bowstring.

"Wait. We heard a rain crow in the mist, on the way here. It moved ahead of us."

He glanced at her, and his brows knit. "Are you suggesting it was keeping us company, and this is the same one?"

"I have no idea. I just don't think we should kill it."

"All right." Reluctantly, he put the bow and arrow away. "It's closer. It's just over the dunes there, look."

The bird cried again, harsh and long-drawn. Now it was recognizably winged, and dipped and soared above the dune field, as if awaiting them.

"It's hovering," Mandine said. "It's really a rain crow, Key. I think we should follow it. Maybe it's found water."

"They're carrion eaters," Key reminded her. The mummified corpse of two days ago leered at him from his memory, and he did not want her to encounter something dead or nearly dead. But Mandine was already angling away from him, toward the nearest dune. Key followed. The rain crow circled on the hot updrafts as they struggled to the top of the first dune. In the trough behind it they saw nothing but sand. The crow called once, as if in encouragement, and glided farther inland. It soared above the back of the dunes, where a narrow valley cut into the outer rank of foothills.

"I'm sure it's leading us," Mandine said.

"Into what?" Key muttered, and drew his sword, though he didn't don his helmet. The blade felt too heavy, and he realized how weak he had become. Mandine would be faring as badly.

"Do you think you'll need that?" she asked.

"I hope not. Come on."

They trudged up and down the dunes until they reached the valley entrance. Beyond it the valley angled off to the right. Here, away from the sea, the air was like the inside of an oven, and a hundred yards ahead of them the valley's floor and slopes disappeared in a turbulent shimmer of rising heat. The rain crow swooped in and out of the wavering draperies, vanishing, then reappearing.

"Should we go on?" Mandine asked.

Key nodded. They trudged into the valley. Its floor was rough, ridged with windblown sand and dust and patched with deposits of gravel. The flickering veils receded slowly as they walked, revealing only more dry rock and slopes of rough pebbles. The rain crow disappeared again, but this time it did not come back.

"There's something up there," Key said. "Something bright."

Part of the shimmer became a gleam, hardened, took on blurred form. It was huge, strangely regular in outline for this wild place. Then, without warning, the veils seemed to part, and they saw it, not a bowshot away.

"It's a building," Mandine said.

✳ 21

IT WAS A COLOSSAL TOWER, AS HIGH AS CAPTALA'S IN-
nermost and greatest wall. Its crown showed gaps where a
few smaller stones of the parapet had fallen away, but its main
shaft was perfectly intact. As they came closer, Key saw that
its tightly fitted masonry had neither windows nor arrow slits.
There was no sign of a surrounding wall or other outworks;
the tower rose naked, white, and solitary, from the valley floor.
It did not look like a fortification; it did not look like anything
he had ever seen. He watched carefully as they approached,
but everything about the tower suggested age and emptiness.

"I don't see a door," Mandine said.

"Maybe on the other side," Key suggested. If they could
get in, the interior would give them shade. What they would
do then, he had no idea. He didn't think they'd find the wheat
now, so far from the beach. Even if the wind had blown it up
the valley, they had no chance of locating it among the rocks
and crevices of the valley's slopes.

They tramped around the tower to its farside, and there
by its foot they saw the husks of two human beings.

The bodies lay near each other, mummified like the dead
man Key had found. Rags of clothing hung about their
shrunken ribs, and their limbs were dark brown sticks. The
eye sockets gaped black and empty, and lipless grins bared

yellow teeth. The tower's entrance was there, too, and the leathery fingers of one corpse clutched at the mortared blocks of pale marble that sealed it closed. A notched sword lay by the dead hand, as though its owner had hacked at the stones in his last despair.

"Others died here," Mandine said, her voice faint with shock.

Key put his arm around her. "They did. We won't."

She sat down quickly, on a block that had fallen from the tower's pinnacle. Her face was averted from the dead men. "How . . . how did they get here?"

"Maybe they're what Cawlor was talking about, treasure seekers who vanish on the Cursed Shore. I found another body the first day, when I was looking for firewood."

"You didn't tell me," she said.

"It didn't seem necessary."

"You don't need to protect me that way, Key. We're together in this."

She was right, and he nodded. "Yes. I'm sorry. I won't do it again."

She seemed to be regaining her composure. "But why did these two stay by the tower? Why didn't they go on, when they found they couldn't get in?"

Key also was wondering at this. He went to the body farthest from the sealed door and looked down at it. He noticed a metallic glint under a swatch of rag, and used his boot to push the cloth aside. The jeweled hilt of a dagger protruded from the ribs.

"Have you found something?" Mandine called.

"A murder, I think."

She stood up but came no nearer. "Somebody killed him? Maybe the other man?"

"Maybe." Key went to inspect the second body, though he knew his curiosity was a waste of time. The corpse lay outstretched, its fingers still clawing in hopeless supplication at the blocked doorway's indifferent stones. Beside the sword was a leather pouch the size of the dead man's head, and as round and desiccated. Key nudged the pouch with his boot. The leather split open, spilling its contents in a glittering flood onto the sand.

The flood was jewels: white, emerald, yellow, ruby, purple. Key gaped down at a golden bracelet studded with enormous pearls, at a necklace like a sapphire waterfall, at a crown of roses, except that the roses were cut rubies on gold stems.

"This one found the treasure he was looking for," he called.

Mandine hesitantly came over to him. "All that," she said, glancing first at the corpse and then at the shining heap, "and it couldn't buy him a cup of water."

"I suppose one killed the other for it, then died of thirst."

"It's cursed. We shouldn't touch it."

"Are you sure? There's a demarch's ransom here." It would, Key thought, equip a lot of soldiers, if they should need them.

"I'm sure. Please, before we do anything else, let's get these poor creatures out of sight, and the jewels with them."

"All right."

Key moved the corpses a little farther up the valley, with the jewel trove. He would have liked to build cairns for them, but he didn't think he could spare the strength or the sweat. Then he returned to the tower. Mandine was standing by the sealed door, staring dully at it.

"Someone didn't want anybody to get in," she said.

"It looks that way." Key began to inspect the joints and the mortar. Suddenly he tilted his head. "Do you hear something?"

Mandine listened. "I'm not sure. I didn't hear it earlier. Is it inside?" She stepped up to the wall and put her ear to the stone. Several seconds passed.

"It's *water*," she said faintly. "Falling water. It's in there. Oh, Key, I'm so thirsty."

He also listened. The faint splashing sound was unmistakable, the sound of rivers, cataracts, cold mountain streams. Perfect torture. His mouth felt full of dust.

"There's a way to enter," Mandine said desperately. "There has to be. We wouldn't be here, otherwise."

But for all their searching, they found no entry. They could not tell whether the tower roof had fallen in, but even if it had, they could not possibly have scaled that sheer, smooth wall to reach it. Key hammered at the door, using a piece of broken marble fallen from the battlements, but his efforts barely scuffed the stone. Running water meant there might be an outflow from beneath the tower, but when he dug a test pit he found nothing but dust and gravel, then bedrock. The splash of water inside the tower was maddening; they seemed to hear it, ever louder and more alluring, as the afternoon wore on.

"Is this hopeless?" Key asked her, as they sat against the wall by the door. "Should we give up here and go searching for the wheat while we've still got some light?"

"No." Mandine knit her brows. "There's a way in. We just can't see it."

Wings fluttered suddenly, high above them. The rain crow, black against the harsh bright sky, hovered at the tower's summit. Then it flapped down to settle on the sand, a few feet away. The bird stood there, head cocked, watching them sideways with a gold-and-ebony eye.

"It helped us before," Mandine said in an undertone. "What does it want us to do?"

The rain crow regarded them with an enigmatic stare. It opened its yellow beak and closed it. Then it did it again.

"It's thirsty," Key said.

"Give it some water. Give it some bannock, too. There's nothing for it to eat or drink in this dreadful place."

"It's almost the last of our water."

"Give it to the poor creature, anyway. It's as doomed here as we are."

Key got his helmet from the saddlebag and dribbled water into it. The rain crow hopped away while he put the helmet and some crumbled bannock onto the sand, but as soon as he returned to Mandine it fluttered to the helmet and drank a beakful. Then it quickly pecked up a few fragments of bannock. It didn't seem especially hungry; if it had been human, Key would have said it ate out of politeness.

The crow stopped eating, and returned to the helmet. It fixed Key and Mandine with one bright eye, then hopped onto the helmet's rim. The helmet teetered.

"No!" Key exclaimed. "If you don't want it—"

The bird sprang into the air with a flurry of black wings. The helmet rolled away, spilling its precious mouthful into the dust. Key swore and leaped to his feet as the rain crow flapped up the tower's wall. Then, at the moment it vanished around the stony curve, he thought he saw not a rain crow but something else. Something like a slender green iridescence, wings with a feathery sheen of gold, a hooked beak.

He blinked, eyes dry. "Did you see that? When it went round the tower?"

Her voice betrayed a faint excitement. "I thought I saw *something*. As if the rain crow had a green body and gold plumage. For just an instant."

"I thought the same. And a beak, like an eagle's."

"A pandragore? I want to believe it, but . . . it might have been heat shimmer, or we're thirsty enough to see things. Have you been seeing things?"

"Nothing except what we think we just saw. And the rain crow didn't act like a pandragore, whatever that's like. It acted like a rain crow, unfortunately."

Her shoulders sagged. "Yes, it did. Maybe we're starting to hallucinate. Don't worry about the water it spilled. There wasn't enough to make a difference, anyway."

Key retrieved the helmet. The water was a damp splotch in the dust, already disappearing as the parched earth drank it. "I suppose not," he muttered glumly as he came back to sit beside her.

"I hope it finds its way home. I'm sure it doesn't live here."

"I could say the same for us."

"Key," she said after a long pause, "I have an idea. You won't like it."

"Tell me, anyway."

"You're stronger than I am. Leave me just a little to drink, and go on. If you're by yourself, you can make it past where we saw the city. But with me holding you back, you can't."

He was appalled. "I won't leave you alone."

"Key, you must. One of us has to try to live, to find the Signata, and I don't think I'm strong enough to do it."

"No."

"Key, we'll both die here, if we both stay. Then we'll have failed. Please."

"No. I won't live without you, and I won't die without you, either. I won't go, Mandine."

She leaned forward, arms around her legs, and put her head on her knees, facing him. "It may be the only chance for one of us to live, Key. Even leaving the Signata aside."

"Mandine, I won't leave you, even if the Lord and Lady themselves demand it. If we die, we die together."

"You love me so much?" Her eyes were wet.

"Yes." He kissed her. "Stop crying. It's a waste of water. Anyway, don't you remember what Athanais wrote? A man and a woman have to use the Signata together."

"Maybe the woman isn't me."

"It's you. It can't be any other. You can't argue me away from you, Mandine."

She tried to smile. "All right. I wouldn't have left you, either. We belong together too much. The Lord and Lady will understand, won't they? They're in love. They've been in love since the Beginning, and that's what makes the world flower."

The injustice of her dying enraged him. He leaped to his feet. "What do you *want!*" he shouted, and kicked hard at the stones.

"Key, that won't help. Why don't we—"

They heard a dull rumble, like rock falling, and Key felt the ground vibrate. "Get up!" he cried, and grabbed Mandine's arm. They scrambled away from the door as its mortar split with a series of staccato cracks. The bottom course of masonry shivered, sagged, and slowly began to collapse inward. Stone grated on stone, and a thick cloud of dust shot from the doorway and enveloped them. Mandine saw rubble tumbling in the murk; then the dust blinded her. She and Key stumbled out of the cloud, coughing, as the rumbling and crashing stopped.

"The door," she said, after getting her breath and wiping her eyes on her sleeve. "I think the door fell in."

The dust was settling. It slowly revealed the empty and gaping doorway, and from the shadows within came the hiss and splash of water.

"It's open," Mandine said, her voice almost breaking. "But how? What happened?"

"Water first," Key said feverishly. "Questions after."

They made their way gingerly to the opening and looked in. The tower's roof was intact, but daylight filtered past them into the interior, and in the dimness they saw that the granite door-seal had fallen inward to scatter its rubble across the paler flagstones of the tower floor. On the tower's farside was a huge stone basin, and in its center was a bronze fountain, in the likeness of a flowering tree. Water poured from each bloom, rollicked into the basin, and tumbled from there to a channel cut into the floor.

They ran to the basin and drank as they had never drunk in their lives. The water was cool and strangely sweet, and their very flesh seemed to soak it up. They plunged their heads into it and came up with their hair dripping, and drank again. Finally Mandine gasped, "I've never tasted water like this. Is it because we were so dry, or is it really different?"

"I don't know." Key rolled the liquid over his tongue. "But it brings the strength back. There's something more to it than water, I think. But whatever it is, it doesn't feel evil."

"Look at the basin's rim," she said abruptly. "There's an inscription."

Even in the dimness Key could tell the carvings were in a foreign script. "Can you read it?"

"No. I've never seen anything like it before."

Suddenly, as they watched, the incised glyphs seemed to flow, as if cut stone could move in slow, thick eddies. The shapes of the glyphs did not change, but through them, somehow, Key saw the spiky characters of his mother tongue.

"It's Haema!" he stammered.

"But it's the Logomenon, too," cried Mandine. "Sweet Lady, look what it says!"

They read the words, each in their native tongue.

Athanais built me, her Tower of Guard in the War of the Thanaturgai. If you serve not the Fathers of Bitterness, drink of her blessing and pass from this shadow of the world.

"Athanais!" Mandine exclaimed. "This is hers!"

Key backed a little away from the basin. "There's magic in the stone. Be careful."

"But it's *her* magic. We don't need to be afraid, unless . . . Who were the Fathers of Bitterness?"

"The thanaturges, I expect."

Mandine touched the lip of the basin. "Athanais made these letters. She was *here*, in this very place. I think the Signata must be nearby. She was the last person to find it, and here in the east is where that happened."

"But somehow we have to get out of this place, with the Signata or without it." Key looked around. "We've drunk from the fountain, but we're still here. How exactly do we pass from this shadow of the world, then?"

"Maybe we have to leave the tower. Find another mist, perhaps." Mandine splashed water over her arms. "But even if we have to go a long way, we've got water now. How much will our bottles carry?"

"Four days' worth. I wish we hadn't lost the horses. We haven't much gear left."

"It will be enough. Perhaps the rain crow will lead us again." She looked puzzled. "But I still don't understand why the door fell down all of a sudden."

Key was studying the channel that carried the water away

from the fountain. The trough disappeared under the stones of the fallen door-seal. "Look there, where the water goes. It must have cut away the foundation under the door. Maybe it was ready to collapse, and my kick was the last jolt it needed."

"You gave it heavier jolts before that."

He pursed his lips. "That's true."

"Maybe the crow's a spirit of this place, that helps travelers if they help it, and when we did, it opened the door for us. I don't suppose we'll ever know." She wrinkled her brow. "Unless you did see a pandragore, and the crow wasn't really a crow at all. That would put a different aspect on things, wouldn't it?"

"It's still not one I'd recognize."

"Well," Mandine said in a practical voice, "no matter where we are, we need food." She unbuckled the saddlebag and searched inside it. "There's quite a lot of dried sausage left. Now we've got water, it'll go down more easily."

From far above, they heard a faint, eerie sigh. Mandine looked up in alarm, as the sound came again. Key listened, then gave a short bark of nervous laughter. "It's just wind around the battlements," he said. "It must be blowing harder than it was."

Mandine sighed with relief and busied herself cutting up sausage. Key dipped his helmet into the basin and poured water over his head. Again he sensed the strangeness in the liquid, and his skin prickled. Then he set the helmet on the basin's rim, and, eyebrows and hair dripping, went to the doorway to look out. The wind was indeed rising, stronger than he'd known it yet in this dire place. His gaze skipped across the dust and sand before the tower's entrance.

"Mandine," he said. "Come here."

"What is it?" she asked, with a trace of alarm.

"Just come."

Quickly, she joined him in the doorway and peered around his shoulder. "Look," he said, pointing. His hand trembled. Where the rain crow had eaten and drunk, there was a stand of young grain.

"It grew," he said haltingly. "While we were inside. In not even the turn of a glass."

"It's the Lady's wheat." Mandine held tight to his arm. "Key, we've found it."

They walked out of the tower to look at it. The grain was indisputably there, real and solid. Mandine reached out to touch a stalk. "If we hadn't given the rain crow water," she murmured, "we never would have known it was here."

"It must have blown into the valley, and been buried. But why?"

"It's to bring us to the Signata," Mandine said. "It's near us, Key. Or I think it is."

He looked around. Nothing had changed, except that the wheat had grown. "But there's nothing here."

"I'm sure I'm right. We just have to *look*."

"All right, but what is it? The wheat itself?"

Again she touched a green bud of grain. Nothing happened. The wheat was just wheat, or appeared to be. She shook her head. "I don't think so."

They searched the area and found nothing but sand, stones, and gravel. "I don't understand this," Mandine said, as they returned to the cluster of plants. "It must mean *something*."

"Maybe it marks the spot where something's buried."

They knelt and began excavating. Neither wanted to disturb the roots of the grain and risk killing it, so they dug around the fine tendrils. The plants had grown in a pocket of fine sand, which kept sliding back into the hole, as if fighting them. A foot down they reached solid rock, and Key's hope turned to bitter disappointment. Still he dug, farther out. Sweat stung his eyes.

Suddenly Mandine straightened. "Stop."

He stopped. "What's the matter?"

"We haven't been thinking. If the Signata's here, it's right under the wheat. The wheat marks the exact spot." She wrapped her hand around the base of the green clump.

"Maybe we shouldn't pull it up—"

But she was already doing so. The wheat came easily out of the earth, its mat of roots shedding sand. Key and Mandine looked into the hole left behind. It was empty.

"Nothing," he said dully. "Nothing at all."

"Wait!" Mandine exclaimed. "There's something here." She frantically brushed clumps of sand from the roots. Key cupped his hands under them.

An object was caught in the tangled fibers. Mandine's trembling fingers dislodged it, and it dropped into Key's hand.

"This?" Key said. "This can't be it."

"But it *must* be." She shook the roots. "Look, it's all there was."

They stared at the object in disbelief. Lying in Key's palm was nothing but a small white stone.

✳ 22

"A STONE," KEY SAID, TRYING TO KEEP HIS VOICE LIGHT. Despite what he knew of the Signata, he had hoped for more than this. "Well, I suppose if it's been a cracked cup and a worthless coin, why not a pebble?"

"Oh, look!" Mandine burst out. "Key, it's dying!"

The wheat was withering in her hands. Its shoots went tawny, then dun, and before their eyes it crumbled into fragments, then into dust, and sifted from her fingers onto the stony ground.

"Gone," she whispered. Then her voice strengthened. "But we must have found the Signata, Key. We *must* have. The Lady's token wouldn't have crumbled away if it hadn't served its purpose."

The wind had strengthened, and a gust blew grit into Key's eyes. "Let's get back into the tower and think about it."

They brought the stone inside and examined it more closely. It was a disk Key could hold within his circled thumb and forefinger. It was very smooth and white, with no discernible markings. It could have been any of the flattened, water-burnished pebbles he had skipped across Cauldron Creek when he was a boy.

"Is this really the thing itself?" he said, turning it over and over in his fingers.

"It has to be."

"You'd think there'd be something more," he muttered. "An aura. Something."

"Athanais said it looked like an ordinary coin when she found it, remember? It didn't act as the Signata until later." Mandine took the stone from him and examined it. "She did say that after it was in her possession for a while, it preyed on her mind."

"But not in this short a time. Is it preying on yours, though?"

"Not the way I think she meant. I keep wondering about it, but that's to be expected. Is it bothering you in any strange way?"

Key shook his head. "I'm the same as you. Puzzled. Frustrated. We've come so far, and we're still trapped, and this is all there is?"

"We must keep faith," she said, and gave it back to him. "It will do something when we most need it. Put it in your sabretache. Mine's got the hole, and we don't want any more accidents."

He did so, then observed, "Except I don't think it was an accident, losing the wheat."

"Even so." She cocked her head, then looked around at the gaping doorway. Outside, the sun was westering, and the light on the valley walls was yellower. "Did you hear something?" she said apprehensively.

His gaze followed hers. "No. Did you?"

"I thought—like metal on stone."

Key drew his sword and turned to face the door. A long shadow fell across the ground outside. In three strides he was at the entrance, waiting.

The shadow moved, and suddenly the dead jewel thieves were before him.

Mandine screamed. Key stumbled back in horror. The corpses' leathery legs were clumsy as they shambled into the tower, and their bony arms swung without the grace of life, but one gripped its sword and the other the knife that had killed it. Their eye sockets were empty, but they saw, and in them something gleamed. Then the hardened skin of their faces crawled and blurred, and in each Mandine saw the face from Baptisae.

"Erkai!" she cried, in horror and fear. "It's Erkai!"

Key steadied, his saber's point centered between the two dead men. They lurched forward, and the swordsman clumsily raised his weapon. Key struck. His saber hacked across the corpse's throat, but the beheading blow went awry, as though the sword had twisted in Key's hand. He danced back, hissing between his teeth. Far above, the wind sobbed in the tower's ancient crown. Mandine drew her dagger.

The dead men stopped, as if Erkai assessed his next attack. His face flickered in and out of existence on the mummified skulls, intent, remorseless. "What can I do?" Mandine called.

"I don't know." Key sounded desperate. "My sword won't bite." His left hand went to his sabretache.

"No, Key!" Mandine cried. She knew instinctively that the stone would not help them in this. "He's not really here." Without realizing it, she had backed to the basin. There was nowhere else to go.

"What, then?"

Before she could answer, the dead men lurched toward him, much faster and much less clumsily this time. Key swung at the sword, and astonishingly it flew from the dead hand and clanged away among the stones. Its owner halted again, and so did the one with the knife. "I can get at their weapons," Key called to her. "But he's learning."

The swordsman had retrieved his blade. Key moved to their left, and Mandine knew he was trying to maneuver their attackers away from the door. If he succeeded, there was a chance of escape. She got ready to run, but Erkai was not to be fooled. His dead servants also shifted left, still blocking the path to the doorway. Then they shambled apart. They were going to strike at him from both sides.

"I'll try to disarm them," Key called, without taking his

eyes from the pair. Now he was only a few strides from her and the basin. "Break for it when you can."

They rushed at him. Key parried the sword, then the knife, but the attackers were closing. He jumped back two strides, his bootheel caught on a flagstone's edge, and he fell almost at Mandine's feet.

She cried out as the dead men lurched toward him. In their eye sockets she saw Erkai's eyes, ablaze with triumph. She threw her dagger at the swordsman, but it glanced harmlessly from the leathery chest.

Key was on his knees now, but they reached him before he could stand. On his knees, he parried, and parried again. Mandine looked for a stone to throw, anything that would help him, and her elbow hit something on the basin rim beside her. It was his helmet, already toppling into the fountain. With one sweep of her arm she caught it up, half-full of water, and hurled it at the dead men in a plume of spray.

The water sluiced over their faces. For an instant they froze, blades raised to strike. Then the gleaming in their eye sockets went out, like torches plunged into a deep pool, and Mandine thought she heard a faraway howl of pain and fury. The sword clanged to the stones, and the knife fell from the skeletal hand. The dead sinews loosened, and the corpses toppled to the tower floor.

"Athanais's water," Mandine gasped. "It stopped him."

Before Key could reply, the floor shuddered. He struggled to his feet. The ground shook again, so hard that Mandine swayed and nearly fell. Above, the masonry groaned, and mortar sprang from the chinks and tumbled clattering around them. Light blazed through the doorway, and the floor heaved and buckled.

"It's coming down!" Key shouted. He seized her arm, and in a staggering run they raced for the door. Mandine could hardly keep her feet; stones thrust and heaved from the earth, and she heard a terrible cracking from above as the tower's fabric sheared and split. The door lintel sagged and began to fall as they stumbled beneath it into the open. But there was no escape; vast blocks from the tower's walls crashed all about them. Slivers and shards of rock stung Mandine's neck and face, and she squeezed her eyes shut as she staggered blindly onward, waiting in dread for the stone that would crush her and Key.

All was suddenly quiet.

Still at a half run, Mandine found herself squinting against a wash of dazzling orange light. She gave a wordless exclamation and stopped in her tracks, blinking as her eyes adjusted to the brilliance. Beside her, Key gave a muffled curse.

She looked around in astonishment, for the outside had changed, changed utterly. They stood on a rocky height, and the nameless sea had vanished. Below them was a lake, half-hidden in mist, and on its farside was a notch between two green hills, where the sun, cloaked in haze, was either rising or setting. High above it gleamed a bright point of light.

"The tower's gone," Key said.

She spun about. Where the tower should be was a low, circular mound of broken stone, tufted with the pink blossoms of heartsease. Beyond it, the ground fell steeply away into a pearly mist, but in the mist she saw shadowy forms of enormous trees. For several moments they stood speechless. Then Mandine said hesitantly, "Are we home, or somewhere even stranger than we were?"

Key stared at the sky. "If I could see the stars . . . but it's too bright. But there's the Day Star, or one like it. It's dawn, by the Allfather!" He gazed into the north. Mist hung there, shrouding the distances. "If we're not home, at least it's a lot better than where we were."

"Erkai found us." She looked around. "I hope he can't find us here."

"So do I. What made you throw the water at him? I'd never have thought of it."

"It was your helmet I threw. The water was an accident."

He laughed. "We thought there was something different about it, remember? We were right. Whatever it was, it didn't suffer evil." He pulled her to him. "You saved us."

"Saved our lives, perhaps." She leaned her head against his chest. "But we've lost everything else, except your sword and our clothes. And the money in our belts. But that won't help us out here."

"We've got the important thing, though."

She nodded wearily. "That we have. I hope Erkai didn't sense it, somehow."

"His reach has gotten long," Key muttered. "I hope it's not as long here as it was there. We'd better look around and try to work out where here is."

The mist below the height was slowly thinning, and they could see the edge of a forest. They trudged down to the tree line, where Key studied the vegetation. "The trees are what they should be," he observed. "This looks like the country we were in before we slipped into that other place. I'm starting to believe we're home."

Mandine suddenly knelt and untangled a patch of serrated leaves from the cordgrass. "What?" Key asked.

"There's something peculiar here. Look at these bellberry plants."

Key examined them with her. The bellberries they had seen in the hills a few days ago had been just budding into flowerlets. But these bore only a few wizened fruits.

"Could a blight have done this in the time we were away?" Mandine asked.

"That's not blight. These have fruited, but they've dried up."

They looked at each other in consternation, then got up to search beneath the trees for more bellberries. They found several patches, each with a sparse scatter of dried fruit. On closer inspection of the underbrush they discovered nut grass, some of whose pods had burst.

"This can't be right," Key said. "Nut grass doesn't ripen till late summer or early autumn." He poked the plants with his boot. "At least we can eat it."

"We've been in such an odd place," said Mandine. "Maybe

this is another strange one. Maybe here the plants are different. Key, maybe we're *not* home, after all."

He looked around. "The mist's burning off. Let's go back up where we were and see if anything looks familiar."

When they reached the height they briefly inspected the mound. It had been a round building once, but whether it was the ruin of the windowless tower they could not tell. There was no sign of a spring, or a statue. Key tried to make sense of what had happened, and failed. They had reached the New Sea—if it had been the New Sea—two days before they should have, and now they were in a place where the sea was not. And here, from the evidence of the vegetation, the season was late summer at least. Had they traveled from one time to another, as well as from one place to another?

He loathed the possibility, but it was beginning to look as if Mandine were right: they weren't home, after all.

From the height above the lake, they gazed into the north. The haze had dissipated with the rising sun, and Key saw on the horizon a long reef of flat-topped, slate gray cloud. He studied it for several minutes. Its shape remained fixed; it had a solidity clouds lacked.

Not a cloud, then. A vast upland.

"Mandine," Key said, trying not to sound too hopeful, "I think that's the Elthame plateau, or one very like it. If we're anywhere near the New Sea, that's the South Rim. It *looks* like home."

"It may look like it, but not be."

"We'll have to find out. Let's go back down and harvest some of that nut grass. We'll think better with food in us."

Wearily they retraced their steps. As they neared the forest margin, Mandine saw a green flicker of movement, as if a sapling had lifted its roots and walked. She blinked, and the emerald-and-brown pattern took on form.

"Key, it's a hemander!"

In fact it was two hemandri, watching them from the edge of the forest. Suddenly, one waved. "It's Flute," Mandine cried. "And that's Speaker! Sweet Lady be thanked, we *are* home."

Flute bounded toward them, chestnut hair flying. When she reached them she threw her slender arms around Mandine, who was crying and laughing all at once. Speaker stopped a yard away and smiled his sharp white smile. "Welcome back," he said. "We believed you lost."

"We *were* lost," Key said. "Very, very lost."

Flute released Mandine, who wiped her eyes with the back of her hand. "But Speaker, how did you know you'd find us here?"

"I dreamed five nights past that you were returning, and I dreamed a high stone place of the kind your adept ones made long ago. This is the only one whose ruins we know, though I believe there are others closer to the salt water. I sent Flute to watch it, then came here this morning, to find out if she had seen anything untoward. And here you were."

"Adept ones?" Key said. "Do you mean the White Diviners?"

"Is that what you call them? If you mean those who fought the darkness in the mountains long ago, yes, it was them, before the sea covered the white cities."

Mandine's face suddenly became perplexed. "Wait. Speaker, you said you dreamed of our return five nights past. But five nights ago we were still on our way to the Cursed Shore."

Speaker's thin eyebrows rose. "There is something amiss here. Five nights ago you had already been long gone."

"Long gone?" Key said.

"How long?" Mandine asked apprehensively. The berries and the nut grass, she thought, in rising alarm.

They held their breaths as Speaker appeared to calculate. "Last night, the moon was the same as the night you slept under our roofs."

"A month?" Key said, aghast.

"No," Speaker said. "Something is amiss, indeed. You have been gone these sixty-five days."

The hemandri villagers were preparing the evening meal, and savory odors drifted from the cooking fires into the cote where Key, Speaker, and Mandine sat resting. The journey from the ruined tower back to the settlement had taken them all day.

"Two *months*." Key said. He glanced at the cote doorway as a hemander child peeped in, blinked at the two humans, and flitted away. "Two months gone here, and some three days in that other place. The Allfather knows what's happened in the west by now. Speaker, do you know where we were?"

The hemander made a gesture of negation. "None of my people have ever seen such a region. All we know is that for all our woodcraft, those hills are deceiving. Easy to enter, sometimes hard to return from."

Mandine sensed that he would prefer another subject. "Thank you again for caring for our friends," she said.

Jaladar, Lonn, and Naevis had left the settlement twenty days after the fight with the Tathars, when Naevis's and Lonn's wounds had healed enough to bear travel. According to Speaker, Lonn had regained partial sight in his injured eye, though in strong sunlight he needed a patch over it. The hemandri had guided the three humans almost to the town of Daras, which was near the foot of Thunderhead Falls. By now they would have been a month in Oak.

"You are welcome," Speaker told her. "We do not turn away the sick or hurt, if they are of goodwill."

"But I *wish* we knew what's been happening," she went on. "In two months, could Captala have fallen?"

"There'll be news at Daras," Key said. "Though it'll be old news."

Speaker glanced at Key's sword lying on the grass matting. "The man Naevis, when he left, talked of raising the high country against the death's-heads."

"That sounds like an Elthamer," said Key, and laughed, though without much humor. "We prefer the most direct path to any goal."

"Will it be done?"

"I don't know. I'm not sure it's a good idea. It's a matter

of numbers and of experience in major campaigns. The Tathars have more of both than we do."

"Perhaps an army is not the answer," Speaker said. He studied them obliquely. "I would ask, though you need not answer, if you found what you sought?"

Key hesitated, but Mandine said, "Yes, we did. Show him, Key. Maybe Speaker can sense something we can't."

A little reluctantly, Key took the white stone from his sabretache and gave it to the hemander. Speaker turned it over in his long fingers. "It is a stone," he murmured doubtfully. "I find nothing in it. What is it supposed to be?"

"It is the place that contains all places," Mandine said quietly, "and the moment that contains all moments. Or we think it is. In my tongue, it is called the Signata."

Speaker took a quick, deep breath. "Ah," he murmured. "The All-Seer. That was what you were charged to find?"

"Yes. You know of it, then?"

"Only as legend. That it goes always to and fro in the world, but few encounter it. Those who do are changed." He frowned at the white disk. "Yet it is only a stone."

"But the Shining Ones showed us the way to it," Mandine said. "That must mean that it does *something*."

Speaker handed the stone back to Key. "Perhaps the time for it to act is not ripe."

"Perhaps." Mandine sighed. She had hoped the hemander would find an obvious power in the stone that they had not.

"Where will you go now?" Speaker asked. "To the westlands?"

"That's the next step," Key said. "We're supposed to take the stone to Captala. What we do with it there, I don't know."

"By which path will you travel?"

Key rubbed his newly shaven chin. "I'm not sure yet. Do you know if any more Tathars came to help the others?"

"None have come as far as our lands. Those who escaped us rode west, the day after you left, and we have not seen them since."

"But there might be more on the way," Mandine said.

"Key, if we take the Great East Road, we could run right into them. And we'll be on foot."

"Do you know where we might find horses?" Key asked Speaker.

The hemander rose to his feet in one liquid movement. "I have something that I hope will please you better. Come."

Puzzled, they followed him out of the cote and along the edge of the settlement. After a few minutes' walk they came to a thorn fence as high as Key's head. He peered through the closely spaced branches and glimpsed the forms of huge black animals.

"Hippaxas!" he exclaimed in astonished delight.

"There are four," Speaker said. "We found several beasts wandering after the death's-heads ran away. The man Jaladar said you knew how to ride them, so we kept these in case you returned to us. We have their gear also."

"Speaker," Key said gratefully, "you don't know what you've done for us."

"If we took the East Road with them," Mandine asked doubtfully, "could they get us past any Tathars we might meet?"

Key pondered, thinking of ambushes and what the White Death might do. "Possibly. But the Tathars may have more hippaxas. It could be chancy."

"We daren't take chances," she said. "We have to reach Captala, even if we take a longer way."

After a moment he nodded. "You're right. We'd be better advised to go around. Up through Oak, then west from there into the Ascendancy, and go cross-country well north of Baptisae."

"That seems better to me," she said. "After all, the Tathars can't be everywhere. And Key, we must visit Oaken House on the way. We need to find out about your father."

He looked torn. "Can we afford the delay, especially now?"

"Yes." She hated to see him suffer. "It won't take long, Key."

"No, it won't, I guess." He brightened a little. "Anyway, if my father lives, I'd like to tell him what we're doing. We need supplies and clothing, too. And for all we know, all six demarchs have raised their clans, and the army's about to head west." He turned to Speaker. "When we go, will you guide us as far as the road?"

"We will take you farther, to the great fall of water. The road is not the most direct path; we know quicker ways."

Key put an arm around Mandine. "On hippaxas it won't take long to reach Thunderhead, and then it'll be one day more to Oaken House. My love, we'll sleep safe inside four walls again."

"When will you wish to leave?" Speaker asked.

"Tomorrow," they said, together.

✳ 23

THEATANA'S PALMS WERE DAMP WITH SUPPRESSED EX-
citement. She folded her arms, and with her fingertips stroked
the brocading of her cloth-of-silver sleeves. Below the window
where she stood, the small paved rectangle of Penitential Yard
lay cold and gray in the dawn. The courtyard was deep in the
oldest part of the Numera, next to the prison beneath the Bucelon Ravelin, and in the courtyard's center stood a double
gallows.

"What's it going to take to stop this, Tefraos?" she asked.
"These are the fifth and sixth rumormongers you've had up
here in the last eight days, unless I miss my count."

"I've been working very hard on it, Dynastessa," Tefraos
said. His voice echoed from the stone walls of the room behind
her. It was his office; he had been one of the Paladine conspirators, and since her accession he had been building a network
of informers and spies for her.

Theatana turned around. Tefraos was a squinting man, his
left hand crabbed from an old wound. "You'd *better* be working hard," she said. "These malcontents are spreading rumors
that my sister's alive. I want it stopped."

"It will be, my lady. Perhaps they should be done away
with in public. Make an example."

"No. It's better that they just disappear. People are more

afraid and obedient if they don't know what might happen to them."

"The Dynastessa knows best."

"Yes," Theatana said, "I do." For a moment, a violent rage shook her. The commoners' whispers about Mandine were undermining her authority, and this in the face of the enemy. *If all the people of Captala together had one neck,* she thought, *I would without hesitation put a noose around it.*

She returned to the view from the window. A door opened below, and the Mixtun executioner stalked into the courtyard. All the Mixtuns of the Guard were now quartered in the Numera, and these seventy-three islanders had become the enforcement arm of Tefraos's secret police. He used them for arrests and executions, since they would have no fellow-feeling for the native Ascendancers they dragged to the Numera's cells. The Mixtuns' assignment had been Dactulis's suggestion. When he made it, Theatana had asked him sharply if he suspected the loyalty of the native-stock Paladines, but he assured her that that was not in question. Theatana believed him. After all, she was Dynastessa, and the Guard had sworn to serve her. More to the point, she had fed them well during the three months of siege, though food was now very scarce in the city.

The Mixtun mounted the scaffold and positioned a stool beneath each rope. The door opened again, and four other islanders brought out the condemned, a young man and a slightly older woman. Theatana breathed a little faster. She liked executions; they stimulated her, and she felt energetic and decisive afterward.

If only it were Mandine down there, she thought: Mandine tortured, gagged, and chained. She still hoped her assassins might bring back Mandine's head, but there'd been no sign of them since they went upriver at the start of the siege. Still, they might have caught and killed her long ago and been unable to get back into Captala to claim their reward. This was possible, for the Tathar blockade was impenetrable by land, and by sea it was just as tight. Tefraos found out why, a week into the siege; a half-drowned rower, lashed to a broken oar, had been picked up at the naval harbor's water gate. When revived, he babbled a tale of a strange fog—this in summer—and of misplaced landmarks that had led his grain ship and its escorting dromon onto Axa Shoals. There had been *things* in the fog, too, he said; when they took form, men shrieked and raved and cast themselves into the sea. It was Erkai's work, of course.

Tefraos had had the rower strangled, so the man could not spread alarm about the grain supply. Two more survivors had washed into the port since, with similar stories, and were similarly disposed of. But with no ships coming in, the word of Erkai's sea blockade got out anyway. The news caused a near riot in Mileon Square, but a Guard detachment broke the crowd up before it became a real mob. But now, although everyone knew that the Diviner's spells secured Captala against the Black Craft, Erkai's ominous presence hung over the city like a cliff about to fall.

Erkai the Chain. Theatana's pulse quickened. *He knows the Craft I want to know. If only his power were mine. Has he discovered how to use the Craft to stay young? I'd like that. I wonder what sort of man he really is? He's partly of my blood, Ascendancy blood. So he can't find much to love in the silverhair barbarians, can he?*

She returned her attention to the scene below. The condemned were on their stools, the nooses already around their necks, the ropes tight. Without ceremony, the Mixtun executioner pulled out the stools. Theatana watched until the jerking and squirming stopped, then turned from the window. Tefraos was standing at his desk, flicking through a sheaf of papers. His face was set in a dark scowl.

"What's the matter?" Theatana said amiably. "You look as though I'd just ordered you to swallow baneroot."

Tefraos's scowl vanished, and he managed a smile at her little joke. "It's not that, my lady. As I said, I've been working hard, and I've been looking through these reports all night. Some of the stories about . . . about *her* survival appear to come from Temple Mount. Several people we've interrogated say they heard it from someone who spoke like a priest or priestess, or acolyte. Or just that they heard it first near the

Mount, or another of the city temples. Never any names, of course."

Theatana's amiability fled. "Did you ask them *thoroughly* about names?"

"Yes, Dynastessa. Three died."

"So Temple Mount may be behind these lies."

"It seems very likely, my lady."

"That's treason."

"Yes, Dynastessa. Of the blackest sort."

Theatana pondered. Since her accession, Temple Mount had behaved toward her with distinct coolness. So far, she hadn't cared. But now . . . Mandine had always been on cordial terms with the Mount, and Orissi had been her tutoress and her friend. Was Mandine alive, and Temple Mount knew it, and was secretly preparing the ground for her return?

That's foolish, Theatana thought. *If Mandine lived, she'd have proclaimed herself by now. She's dead, and it's just Orissi making trouble because she doesn't like me. That stupid old woman. I'll show her who rules here. I must speak to Dactulis.*

"Watch the Mount carefully," she said. "I'll take measures when it's fit." The rumormongers would have a harder time, she reflected, if she could declare a dusk-to-dawn curfew. But Dactulis objected that he didn't have enough soldiers to guard the walls and enforce a curfew as well. It was all very annoying.

"I don't suppose you've had any word of Latias's whereabouts?" she said.

"No, my lady. We've looked everywhere, but found no sign of him. I think he must have slipped out of the city when your sister did."

She would deal with Latias eventually; for now, he was not a threat. "Very well. What else does the city mob gabble in the markets?"

The officer spread his hands dismissively. "Nothing of great consequence, my lady."

"Tefraos," Theatana said in a cold voice, "I will be the judge of what is consequential."

Tefraos flinched. "Yes, Dynastessa. They . . . I'm afraid that people talk of omens. There was a story of the images in the Lady Temple on North Street weeping blood. I sent men to look; it wasn't so. And other things, smaller ones, like medlar trees withering in full fruit. There's been some sickness among the refugees, and people mutter that the soldiers throw bread to dogs while children go hungry."

"But they speak nothing against me myself?"

The man would not look at her. *"Tefraos!"* she snapped.

"Dynastessa, forgive me, but it's been scribbled on walls around the grain markets that you arranged the death of your sister, and of the Dynast. We haven't found the scribblers yet."

Theatana laughed harshly. "So one rumor has my sister alive, while another says I killed her. Before you know it, the whisperers will have her rising from the dead. Omens, is it? That sounds like Temple Mount's work again. Catch these people, Tefraos. Perhaps it's time for public examples, after all."

"Yes, my lady. I'll catch them."

"See that you do." If only, she thought, she knew more of the Craft; likely there were ways it could be used to track her enemies down, and dispose of them. But she had so little time nowadays. Still, when life was normal again, she could quietly search out more spell-books, and settle down to develop her skills. Being Dynastessa opened so many possibilities.

"Listen," Tefraos said.

Theatana listened. The sound was distant, but unmistakably an alarm horn. Others joined it, and suddenly she heard also the distant, hollow boom of Tathar assault drums.

"They're attacking again," she observed calmly. "Dactulis said they were showing signs of it, in front of Processional Gate last night. Maybe they hope they'll be luckier the second time."

"The more fools they, my lady," Tefraos said. "With you leading us, we have nothing to fear."

"Indeed," Theatana said, her mood slightly improved by his words. The attack did not trouble her, though during the first Tathar assault everyone had feared that Erkai might try to assist it with sorcery. But he hadn't; Athanais's protections obviously kept him at bay. Theatana decided to visit the walls later, when the attack ended. Her soldiers would be there, and the officers always got them to cheer her. Besides, she could look at Erkai's tent again. She did that quite often now. It was rather fascinating, knowing that a man with so much power was right there, just out of her reach.

The attack failed, bloodily. Theatana came out in midafternoon to see the aftermath, and from the parapet of the outer wall watched the Tathars lick their wounds. Their main camp lay just beyond the siege lines, slightly out of range of the wall stone throwers, but when she used Dactulis's spyglass the enemy seemed right below her. She could clearly see Hetlik's tent, identified by its enormous size, and by the red-and-black running-horse banner above it. Clustered nearby were the lesser tents of his nobles, each with its personal standard. Only one tent in that assembly lacked a banner, as if its owner saw no need for one, and Theatana soon turned the glass in that direction. The tent was of a cloth so black that it appeared to darken its surroundings, and the other dwellings seemed to edge away from it.

He was there, sitting on a stool by the tent's entrance flap, as usual doing nothing but studying the walls. Theatana had come to expect his presence; he was there nearly every time she visited the ramparts. Even without the evidence of the tent, she'd known from the first that this was Erkai because he was the only person in the camp who wasn't Tathar. He always wore a gray robe, with the hood thrown onto his shoulders, and his hair was still black. In fact, Theatana had come to think him handsome. He also didn't look as old as he must be, which was encouraging.

"There he is again," Dactulis said beside her. "Damn him to the Waste." To their left, the Dascarid and Ascendancy banners flapped slowly in the wind. Theatana always took the standards with her when she watched the Tathars; it was a point of honor. It also let Erkai know she was there, defiant and unafraid.

Theatana almost told the treimarch to show respect for someone of Dascarid blood, even an enemy, but thought better of it. Dactulis would not understand; people without experience of great power could never know its loneliness and its weight, and the treimarch might think she felt a sympathy for Erkai. But Erkai would understand her, she thought. She and he were of a kind: alone in their greatness, as far above others as the stars were above the earth.

Theatana touched up the focus of the glass, and as she did so Erkai raised his eyes and looked directly at her. It was as if he spoke, saying he knew her thoughts, and agreed with them. At the idea of such affinity she felt a rush of pleasure, and the glass trembled. He was so powerful, stronger than anyone she had ever met. Her heart cried out suddenly for the secrets he knew, the sweet black knowledge that would make her great.

If only I could make him teach it to me.

Yet I possess what he wants: Captala. If I opened it to him, and to him alone—

Her hands shook so badly that she lowered the glass. Could she control him? Still, he was a man, and she was beautiful. She knew how old men could be besotted by young women. She had controlled Bardas, and he had been almost her father's age.

It needs more thought. I don't know yet how he would respond. But an alliance between us seems so natural. Surely he would see it, too?

Down in the siege lines, a Tathar archer loosed an arrow at her. The missile fell hopelessly short. Theatana said, "They'll tire of this when the autumn rains come. They'll lift the siege by the turn of the year."

"The poor will be eating grass and house voles by then, my lady. If Erkai persuades the silverhairs to stay on past that, we'll be in very serious trouble."

"Let the poor eat each other, as long as my soldiers are

fed. But of course, Treimarch," she went on sweetly, "there are always those relief armies you keep promising me. Surely they'll be here by the year's turn? Won't they? Or don't you *know*?"

Dactulis flushed. "My lady, raising men is only a start. We lost our professionals at Thorn River, and the recruits have to be trained and properly equipped, or the Tathars will beat them flat."

Theatana reflected on this. If only she knew what was happening in the outside world. At the beginning of the siege, a few couriers had used the sea route by night, in small boats beneath Erkai's notice. But then the Tathars collected a dozen sailing cutters, learned to use them, and now patrolled the two-mile-wide entrance of Chalice Bay. The fleet dromons would have demolished the cutters in minutes, but Erkai's sorcery kept the navy far away.

"We'll hold till the armies come," she said, "even if we have to drive our useless mouths outside the walls." She grimaced with disgust. "All those dirty refugees in the parks."

"The Tathars will kill them," Dactulis pointed out, "if we drive them outside."

Theatana shrugged. "Then they will give their lives for their Dynastessa and for the Ascendancy. Soldiers do it all the time. And speaking of soldiers, Dactulis, I want you to put a guard around Temple Mount. Seal it off. No one goes in or out."

The treimarch's jaw dropped. "But Dynastessa, people will want to sacrifice, to pray."

She glared at him. "The city has other temples. Let them burn their incense there. Tefraos says the Mount is working to undermine me, and I think he's right. It has to stop. Tell the Continuator and the Perpetua that, when you set up the guard. Then we'll see what happens. If the subversion goes on, I'll have to rid myself of that meddlesome pair." Her voice sharpened. "And wipe that reluctant look off your face, Dactulis. They're my enemies, and if I were to fall because of them, you'd fall with me."

The treimarch composed his features. "Yes, Dynastessa. I'll see to it immediately. The Guard's committed to the walls, but I've got those last few cataphracts in reserve, the ones that got away from Essardene. I've put them under Guard officers. I can use them to seal off the Mount."

"Don't vex me with the details," Theatana said wearily. She looked over the rampart again. Even without the glass, she could see that *he* still watched her. He was too far away for their eyes to meet, but she felt that they met. His presence called to her sweetest, most secret self, or perhaps that hidden self called to his. She suddenly felt as though she opened to him, and suddenly a tide of lust rose in her, more compelling than she had ever felt, lust for the man, and for the power in him. Heat flushed her skin, her breath caught in her throat, and she swayed.

Since her appearance on the outer wall, Erkai had exerted all his power of mind and will to sense the heart of the woman. The Diviner's spell resisted him fiercely; sweat beaded on his forehead and trickled beneath his arms. But now, in the instant before his strength failed, he suddenly felt Theatana Dascaris embrace her idea of him, and felt her lust like a soft, devouring mouth.

Then the contact broke. Erkai closed his eyes. His mind was cramped and aching, like a muscle driven past exhaustion, and his temples pounded. But he was inwardly exultant. *I will soon have her,* he thought. *Theatana Dascaris thirsts after the Black Craft, and she will barter herself and all she possesses for it. She corrupted herself more quickly than I dared hope. Already she looks for a way to bargain with me, and I will make sure she has it.*

He opened his eyes and studied the battlements. She watched him for a few seconds more; then she moved away, and her banners disappeared with her into the gate tower. But she would be back. For two months she had observed him, and he had expended much energy on assessing her growing fascination. That fascination was an unlooked-for gift, a way to his goal that did not depend on the siege. And he needed such a gift; he was growing uneasier as the days passed.

His disquiet had sharpened when Ragula returned empty-handed from the east, fifteen days after setting out, with his dozen surviving troopers babbling of forest demons, specters, ghosts, and hemandri arrows. Hetlik had been furious at Ragula's failure and banished the duke from his table for two weeks. Erkai considered inflicting a more stringent penalty but decided that it would serve no real purpose. But he now knew that it was Mandine Dascaris, of all people, who searched for the Signata.

Her identity, however, was a matter of near indifference to him. What was much more troublesome was the woman's elusiveness, and his suspicion that some enigmatic, subtle power might oppose him through her. The first evidence was that she or some unknown agency had defeated the Adversary's attack on her at Baptisae. Then she had been snatched from Ragula in a most unusual manner; hemandri were not warlike, and nature spirits paid little heed to human strife, and it bothered Erkai that either had intervened.

Finally, and most alarming by far, was what had happened to him some twenty days ago. Fretting over the slowness of the siege and the possibility that he was under threat, he had risked going into trance to contact the Adversary. There in the cold darkness he found not It, but the wisp of Spardas the Thanaturge, and the wisp showed him where Mandine Dascaris was. To Erkai that place was a shadowy region, a realm not in the world nor yet out of it. But it reeked of ancient magics both dark and light, and in it she and the man with her were vulnerable. He found angry ghosts nearby, and his will drove them back to their bodies and raised them up to destroy both the Dascarid woman and her protector. He had already won, or so he thought, when she summoned one of the old magics against him. It swept him from her presence, and he fled raging through tides and depths of emptiness such as he had never known. Most frightening, he had sensed a stealthy assault on his will, as though the Adversary were tiring of his independence and sought to enchain him. Only after a long struggle did he regain himself, and when he broke from the trance he could hardly move or breathe, and the sweat on his forehead was not sweat, but blood.

Since then he had not dared the deep entrancement that made him vulnerable to the Adversary. As for the Dascarid woman, he still did not know to what realm she had penetrated, nor what might have given her the power to do so. Still, she did not appear to have found the object of her search, for the force she wielded had been defensive. He was sure that the Signata would manifest itself as an attack, not a defense, though he could not guess what the nature of the attack might be.

Knowing so little, he had to make haste. Theatana Dascaris was his gate to the city, and he must bend all his power toward opening her.

A Tathar edged into his field of view: one of Hetlik's bodyguard. The soldier kept a wary distance, and controlled fear showed in his expression.

"Speak," Erkai said.

The soldier averted his eyes. "Lord Erkai, the king would be pleased if you would attend him in his tent."

"When?"

"Now, great lord, if your needs permit."

Erkai smiled a little. Hetlik would summon no one but him in this diffident manner. The Adversary's visitation under Captala's walls had frightened the king out of his wits, though he would never have admitted it. Three months had not lessened his belief that Erkai could summon such horrors at will, and Erkai had not disabused him of the notion.

"My needs permit," he said, and got up from his stool.

The king's booming, furious voice reached Erkai well before Erkai reached the tent. The second attack on Processional Gate had been savagely repelled, just as Erkai had warned, and the Tathars' nerves were wearing thin. They were unused to the grinding tedium of a long siege, and this morning's attack was more the result of sheer frustration than any real hope of victory. Still, the defeat was humiliating, and Hetlik was making his officers pay for it. Erkai slipped through the tent doorway and waited patiently while the king bellowed abuse at them.

Hetlik saw him after a moment, stopped in mid-curse, and told his officers to get out. They obeyed, looking whipped. Erkai remained by the doorway until Hetlik acknowledged his presence with a brief nod. Erkai bowed, slightly less than Ragula would have.

"Well, my lord Erkai," Hetlik said, with forced cordiality, "what do you think of this morning's try?"

"Your soldiers fought valiantly, Dread King," Erkai said blandly. "They deserved better success. But no one has ever taken Captala by storm, nor by any other means. When the time is right, you will be the first."

"Hah!" Hetlik stalked to a campaign chest and poured wine into a silver cup. "When the time is right, hey? So how long is that, Lord Erkai? What about this plague ship you've been promising to send the goldskins? The rains will be here in fifty days, you say, and I want the city by then."

Ah, Erkai thought. *He's going to push me. He worries that his men fear me more than they do him, and today his blood's up and he's going to try putting me in my place. I weary of this petulant barbarian. We're alone, and it's time to let him know who governs here.*

"You will have Captala when it pleases me," he said.

Hetlik's eyes bulged. "When it *pleases* you?"

"Exactly so."

The king opened and closed his mouth twice before he could speak again. "And when might that be, sorcerer?"

"In my good time." Hetlik would never have Captala, of course, not if Theatana acted according to her nature.

"Do you defy *me?*" Hetlik said, his voice aquiver with rage. The wine cup shook in his hand. "I am the Dread King, sorcerer."

"And I am the sorcerer, Dread King." Erkai drew back his sleeve a little to expose the bright links of the chain.

Hetlik's eyes went to it, and his mouth twitched. "No. No need for that. And my guards are outside."

"They would not hear you," Erkai told him softly. This was not true, but Hetlik would not know it.

The Tathar made a strangled noise of fury. Then he croaked, "Do you threaten me?"

Erkai let the silence draw out. "Hetlik," he said at last, "I am master here. I will let you speak as king to your army, but do not speak so to me." He dropped a loop of the chain from his wrist, and let it swing gently. The metal slowly twisted and writhed. The king watched it for a long time. Erkai needed no craft to read Hetlik's thoughts: *I should have rid myself of this demon long ago. I never should have listened to him, never brought him to war with me.*

Finally Hetlik said, "There's something you fear. A talisman of power. You sent Ragula to kill the woman who looked for it. He failed. Someone will bring it against you. Then I will put you on a stake."

Erkai laughed. "But *you* do not have it, if it even exists. Bend with the wind, Hetlik. I will take care not to make your men scorn you, if you don't force me to."

"They won't follow you in battle. They will desert without me."

"If I need them in battle, you'll command them for me. Be easy, Hetlik. No one but you and I will know."

With a trembling hand, Hetlik set his cup on the campaign chest. "I will kill you someday, sorcerer."

The chain crawled to Erkai's wrist and slithered around it. "But not today. Nor the next, nor the next. Until you can kill me, you will obey me."

"You need my men. If I refuse to obey—"

"There are worse fates than flaying and the stake, Hetlik. You saw what I summoned at Mallia, at Essardene, at Phrax, and outside the walls here. I can prepare a place where you will live in torment forever."

Hetlik shuddered, but he said harshly, "Until I can kill you, I will obey. Now get out of my tent."

Erkai shrugged. "Since I know you understand me, I need not remain. One small matter, however. I need the use of a long-range arrow thrower, with crew."

Hetlik swallowed, so loudly that Erkai could hear the saliva gurgle in his throat. But he said nothing.

"Hetlik," Erkai murmured into the silence. The chain writhed slowly.

The king seemed to diminish. "It shall be done," he said.

❊ 24

THUNDERHEAD FALLS WAS THE WELLSPRING OF THE
river Seferis. From a cavern's mouth a thousand feet beneath
the rim of the Elthame plateau, a great underground torrent
roared into thin air and plunged straight and free to a spume-
shrouded lake half a mile below. East of Thunderhead lay the
town of Daras, and the only easy ascent of the cliffs of the
Elthame's South Rim. There the ancient engineers had built a
road that led, by switchback and hairpin turn, up the sheer
face of the precipice.

After a long climb, Key and Mandine were nearly at the
cliff's top, on two of the hippaxas, with the second pair on
leading reins behind them. Controlling a hippaxa was more
difficult than Mandine had expected; they were far more powerful than horses and needed a much firmer hand and leg. Key
was pleased with her progress, however, and after two days
her mount was getting used to her and she to it.

At the last hairpin before the top, they encountered the
rear wagon of an upbound caravan, the only caravan they had
seen since meeting Pellico. Rather than edge the hippaxas past
the vehicle, they followed in its rumbling wake.

"It's not so bad going up," she said. "But it must be heart-
stopping to get the wagons down."

"They hitch the carnyxes to the wagon's rear drawbar,"

Key told her. "That way, if the brake levers crack, the carnyxes can act as anchors. If the wagon still gets away, the drovers cut the traces, and they don't lose the animals."

So much I still don't know, Mandine thought as they neared the plateau rim. *When I wore Elthame furs in Captala's cold months I never wondered how they got to me. All my life I was so shielded by my birthright, yet I believed I knew the world. That was my real ignorance: not knowing that I knew so little.*

But I'm so happy just being with him. As he's happy, being with me. If only this fate of ours were not hanging over our heads.

The incline eventually flattened out, and they followed the wagons onto the plateau. "Now," Key said to her as he halted his mount, "you really are in the Elthame. In Oak Haeme, to be precise. Welcome to my homeland, beloved."

They paused to gaze southwest, where the green country stretched away into the limitless distance. There gleamed the silver thread of the Seferis; eight hundred miles to the west, as a bird flew, it flowed past the walls of Captala and into the Inner Sea.

"I wonder what's happening in the city now," Mandine said, her happiness fleeing with her words. In Daras the latest news from the west was twenty-six days old, from which they had concluded that the military dispatch system had broken down. That was a bad sign, though the reports did say that Captala was still holding out, while the Tathars ravaged the Ascendancy's heartland far and wide. But there was one truly frightening piece of news, and it was not rumor: Erkai's Black Craft had severed the great city from her sea supply.

Key reached out to squeeze her hand. "When we left, Captala had three months' worth of food."

"But that was just for the normal population, Key. There were so many refugees. They're hungry by now."

"Yes, I'm afraid they are."

"At least we had one piece of good news in Daras," she said. The innkeeper had told them that Key's father was alive, and said to be recovering, though apparently he could not walk. After some discussion, they had decided to tell him the whole tale of their journey, including the finding of the Signata, and what they were supposed to do with it. Once he knew all they had been through together, and how strong the bonds were that joined them, they'd tell him of their marriage.

"It was better news than I'd hoped." Key forced a smile. "We'd best move on."

They turned their mounts and set off northward along the road. The caravan drovers gaped and pointed at the hippaxas as they passed, but soon the wagons fell behind, and the hippaxas settled into their ground-devouring lope: fifteen miles every hour, steady and tireless. The countryside was mixed forest and farmland, growing crops much like those around Baptisae, but the woodland had more pine and hemlock and birch than Mandine was used to seeing. These were cold-weather trees, but Key told her that this was in fact the gentlest region of Oak. In the east and northeast, around the Long Lakes and the border with Aspen Haeme, the country was much wilder. The silvertip otter furs and the white pelts of ermine, both highly prized in the Ascendancy, came from there.

"So the people of Oak are great trappers, then?" she asked.

"Not as much as in the northern haemes, like Ash and Redwood. We are the Elthame's great breeders of horses, rather."

Here was something else she had never known, or had learned once from Orissi and promptly forgotten. "Tell me."

"I will bore you with geography."

"No, you won't," she said, laughing. "Anyway, I should know about my husband's country, shouldn't I? Besides, it's interesting, and it makes the miles shorter."

"All right. But tell me if it makes them longer." Key cleared his throat loudly, shamming scholarly pretentiousness. "Well, then, Oak's southeast corner is very high and windswept, and it's bitter when the snows come. Hardly anyone lives there, because the soil's no good for farming, but it grows a steppe grass that makes strong horses. On its south the plateau drops right into the New Sea, a mile straight down. You can look at the tops of clouds floating by. You can find places to look down on the Cursed Shore, too, if you care to. The horse-herdsmen stay clear of the Rim there."

The air was balmy, but Mandine said with a shiver, "I don't wonder."

The miles fled by as they talked. There were few villages, and no place large enough to be a town, by Ascendancy standards. When they did speed through a settlement, the hippaxas raised astonishment and alarm. Few Elthamers had ever seen the Ascendancy's heavy cavalry mounts, and to villagers the animals must have seemed like creatures from a nightmare. On the road a few travelers drew hasty swords, but Key shouted at them in Haema, and the men gave way.

"What are you saying to them?" Mandine asked, the first time it happened.

"That we're on the demarch's service. It's true enough."

"No one recognizes you. Will you be known when we get to Amalree?"

"We don't actually go into the town. My home is this side of it." He smiled at her. "It's your home as well, now that we're husband and wife. Though it's a far call from the House Azure."

"I was a prisoner in the House Azure. I have no love for it now." She cast back in her memory. "Didn't you say once that your father and sister speak the Logomenon?"

"They do. You won't have trouble with language."

They reached Key's home just before the hour of the evening meal. The demarch's residence stood atop a long, wooded ridge overlooking the town of Amalree, which lay in a river valley between that ridge and another to the north. Mandine was very tired after nearly eleven hours in the saddle, but Key's apprehension was showing in his face, and she made herself keep her wits about her.

They turned off the main road and headed up a flagstone lane that led toward Oaken House. The residence was half-hidden by ironwoods and weeping birch, but Mandine could see that it was unwalled, and constructed of golden wood and a honey-tinted stone. As they drew closer she realized that it was not really one structure but many, joined in a long ramble along the ridge crest. Its buildings were from one to three floors high, with dozens of diamond-paned casements and green-shingled, steeply pitched roofs; the steepness was, Key told her, to shed heavy snow. The floor beams of the upper stories extended beyond the walls, and the beam ends and gable eaves were carved with intricate patterns of plants and animals, all gaily painted. Mandine had never seen anything quite like it. Beside the splendor of the Fountain Palace, Key's home was a simple country manor, yet it radiated a warmth unlike anything she ever had felt, even from her once-loved House Azure.

The lane forked, one branch leading to the rear of the manor, the other to a portico at the main entrance. A middle-aged man in Elthamer boots, breeches, and tunic hurried out of the portico and made toward them, hand on sword hilt. Then he stopped short, and his mouth became a dark O of astonishment.

"Don't look so surprised, Goivni!" Key called in Haema. Despite his worry over his father, he felt a rush of happiness. He was home at last. "My father's steward," he told Mandine in her tongue. "A good man."

The steward yelled over his shoulder, "It's the lord Kienan!" and ran toward them. Key swung down from his hippaxa, and as Mandine did likewise a young woman, bronze-haired and wearing a green skirt and brocaded over-mantle, burst from the portico. "Key!" she shouted, "Key, you're home!"

"My sister Ria," Key said to Mandine. "Brace yourself."

"My lord?" Goivni said. "My lord, it's really you? Chillip saw these beasts coming up the hill, and ran to tell me, but I thought he was seeing things. Monsters, it sounded like. Or ghosts, he was so a-dither."

A cluster of excited servants had appeared on the portico steps, and faces were peering wide-eyed from windows. "I'm no ghost," Key said. "Close to it, once or twice, but not there yet. By the way, Goivni, my companion is of the Ascendancy, and doesn't speak our tongue."

"Your servant, my lady," Goivni said in the Logomenon, and bowed to Mandine.

Before Mandine could answer, Ria was upon them. Without a sideways glance, tears streaming down her cheeks, she flung herself into Key's arms. "Key, you brute," she cried, "where have you been? We got your letter from Captala, but then Naevis Mec Ruaid came and said you—" Suddenly she noticed Mandine, and her eyes widened as she released her brother and stepped back. She went pink, and switched to a liltingly accented Logomenon. "Oh, my lady, I've forgotten myself."

She began to kneel, but Key caught her arm. "No, Ria. We'd prefer not to make a show of who she is. Did Naevis tell you?"

"Yes," Ria said, blushing deeper. "He wasn't supposed to, but he let it slip, though only to me." She turned to Mandine. "My lady, poor Naevis isn't to blame for me knowing about you. I was pestering him, just a little."

"I don't think it matters, now we're here," Key said. "Anyway, Mandine, this hoyden is my sister, Riata Min Brander. Ria, this is Mandine Dascaris."

"I'm honored," Mandine said, with a smile. Ria had Key's high cheekbones and gray eyes, though her hair was redder, and her nose was pert and upturned instead of straight.

Goivni had emitted a muffled exclamation at the name of Dascaris. "My lord?" he said to Key. "Did I hear rightly?"

"Yes, Messire Goivni," Mandine said, "I'm of that family. But please, treat me only as you would treat the lord Kienan's sister."

"Stay on your feet, Goivni," Key told the steward, as the man made to kneel. He turned to Ria. "Our father. How is he?"

"He's alive. But Key, he's not who he was. He's speaking now, but he can't use his left arm, and he can't feel his left leg, so he can't walk. He mended quicker after he heard you survived that battle, but the doctors don't know if he'll recover much more than he has."

Key's shoulders sagged. "It's less than I'd hoped, but thank the Two it's not worse. Naevis was speaking to you, you say. How much did he tell you of Mandine and me?"

"Only that you both were fleeing enemies, and you were away to the Cursed Shore. He said you were looking for something to help against the White Death, but he wouldn't say what it was. I didn't tell Father that, or where you were going—I was afraid of what it might do to him. He thinks you've been traveling here alone, by a roundabout way." Her face saddened. "It was bad enough when he learned that Cawlor was dead. At least Naevis and the others were able to bring Cawlor's ashes home."

"Were there two others? Are they still here in Oak?"

Ria nodded. "Yes, they're all staying at the Ruaid manor. There's that Ashman, Lonn, with the eye patch, and a *real* foreigner, with a braid, from the islands. Naevis says they're waiting for you to turn up. He said he was sure you would."

Key grinned. "Well, we did." Behind him, Mandine's mount rumbled. "What *are* those things?" Ria asked, as she stared up at the horned black head. "No wonder Chillip was frightened."

"They're hippaxas," Key told her, "and we're very lucky to have them. We'll tell you about it, but not right now. Can I go to Father?"

"Key, he's just fallen asleep. He does that for two or three hours, then wakes up for a while. While he's sleeping you'll have time to wash and eat. And it might be a good idea if I went in and told him you're here, before he sees you. I'm not sure that too much of a surprise would be good for him."

"Then we'll wait. Mandine, I'll show you where you can clean off the dust, find some decent clothes—"

"I'll show her," Ria broke in excitedly. "And I'm sure we're of a size—my gowns will fit."

Key gave a snort of laughter. "Mandine, will you submit

yourself to my sister's pitiless management, while Goivni and I see to the hippaxas?"

Ria looked uncomfortable. "I'm sorry, my lady. I didn't mean to be forward."

"You aren't, at all," Mandine told her. "You're the first woman I've talked to for a long time, and I'd love to get out of these man's riding clothes. And please, Ria, among us I am just Mandine."

Three hours passed, and Key's father awoke. Ria came out of the retiring room, into the Summer Hall, and said quietly, "I've told him you're here, Key, and safe. And I said you have a noblewoman under your protection, but that you would introduce her."

"How is he?"

Ria smiled, her gray eyes suddenly bright. "He's well, considering. Sometimes he sounds almost as he always did, and he's that way at the moment. Thank the Lord and Lady you're back. Maybe now he'll mend completely."

"Are you sure I should come in?" Mandine ventured. She was anxious to meet her new father-in-law, but nervous about it in spite of all the poise she had learned at court.

"Our father wouldn't neglect a guest, under any circumstances," Key said. "If you didn't come, he'd be annoyed with both me and Ria."

They all went in. The retiring room was large, paneled in richly carved amber oak, and lit by the violet light of evening and the gold flames of oil lamps. At its far end it opened into a small courtyard where a rose-tree grew, its yellow blooms luminous in the dusk. Key's father sat in a high-backed armchair, next to a writing table with a marble top. He wore a simple brown tunic with short sleeves, and a russet blanket of capy wool lay over his lap and legs.

"Key, my son," Liachan Mec Brander said.

"Father," Key answered, with a catch in his voice. He bent and kissed Liachan on both cheeks. Mandine watched as Liachan's good right hand rose to grasp Key's shoulder and give it a powerful squeeze. Key straightened, and the two men gazed silently at each other. Mandine searched for the likeness between them, but while it was there, it was not strong. Liachan's face was broader and rougher-hewn than Key's, and his eyes were green instead of gray, and his hair was redder. It was his wife's clan, Mandine thought, that had left the deeper mark on their son.

"So you survived Thorn River, after all," Liachan said. "The news made ill hearing, let me tell you. Thank the Two you're safe." He gave Mandine a crooked smile, and gestured with his good arm at a nearby couch. "Madame, my manners are at fault. Sit there with my son. Ria, bring yourself a stool and stay with us."

They all sat, and Key cleared his throat. "Mandine, may I present my father, Liachan Mec Brander, Demarch of Oak Haeme. Father, this is my traveling companion." He hesitated, then said, "You may find her identity . . . startling. She is the Luminessa Mandine, of the House Dascaris."

There was a silence. Mandine could smell the fragrance of the rose-tree wafting in from the garden.

"The elder luminessa herself?" Liachan said at last.

"Yes, Father."

Liachan regarded Mandine closely. "But the story from the west is that the elder luminessa is dead. That Archates' younger daughter now rules in Captala, and holds the city against the Tathars."

"The last is true," Mandine said, "but only that."

"Father," said Key, "I understand your doubt, but this truly *is* Mandine Dascaris. I was with her at Essardene, and I was commander of her escort at the Fountain Palace. She is no impostor."

Liachan made an apologetic gesture. "Forgive me, both of you. I did not mean to suggest doubt. Surprise, I admit. I never expected to have someone of House Dascaris under my roof. But with respect, my lady, I do not understand why you are here. Is this by some arrangement between you and your sister?"

"No, my lord Demarch. Theatana has usurped the diadem."

"A usurper." Liachan nodded slowly. "I see. The tale of your death comes from her."

"It would have been more than a tale," Mandine said, "if it weren't for Key. Theatana was intent on my death. Your son was chief among those who saved me."

"Ah." Liachan's intent green eyes moved over her face, and his watchful expression softened. "Well, then, Mandine Dascaris, you have the guest-protection of my house. No one will harm you here, if it's in my power to prevent it."

"Thank you, my lord Demarch." Despite the softening, Mandine knew that Liachan would still assess her carefully; it would surprise her if he did not. Given the political implications of her presence in Oak, he would want to determine quickly what manner of woman she was.

And he doesn't even know about the marriage yet, she thought.

Liachan again gave her the lopsided smile. "Has my son treated you fittingly?"

"I owe him my life, as I said. And more than once."

"Ah. Tell me how this came about, then."

"It's a long tale," Key warned, "and not for any ears outside this room."

"The night has only begun, and no one is listening, not even Goivni. You can speak as you will."

So Key and Mandine told the story, as dusk deepened to night and the yellow roses folded their petals into sleeping buds. As they spoke, Ria gazed at her brother and Mandine with growing awe. Liachan listened closely, clearly fascinated, though not as outwardly affected as his daughter. But better than his awe, to Mandine's mind, was his obviously increasing regard for her, and as the story ended she saw a warmth and admiration in his eyes that had not at first been there. Her relief at this, to her inward surprise, was enormous. She had not realized how much this man's approval meant to her, not only for Key's sake but for her own comfort. If only, she thought, her own father had been like Liachan, and had seen her so clearly and with such warmth. But Archates Dascaris had never even bothered to look.

They finished. A lamp guttered, and Ria rose to trim the wick. As she resumed her seat, Liachan said, "So you found what the Two wished you to find."

"One of us always carries it," said Key. He took the stone from his sabretache and let it lie on his palm.

"Only a white stone." Liachan gazed at it with something like perplexity, then looked up at Mandine. "And this is what the Diviner called the Signata?"

"We think it is. The legend's very old. Hardly anyone knows it now. I wouldn't have believed the Signata really existed, except for the Lord and Lady, and Athanais's book."

"But you don't know what to do with it?"

"No, we don't," Mandine admitted, as Key put the stone away. "If you have any ideas, sir, we'd be glad to hear them."

"This water is too deep for me. I have never spoken to anyone who has encountered the Lord and Lady as you have. I have never even heard of it happening, except in the old tales."

"I sometimes wish it had never happened," said Mandine. "But the Two brought me to Key. He is . . . we . . ." She trailed off, knowing she flushed.

Expressionless, Liachan scrutinized them both. "Ah. There is something else, perhaps, that happened on the way here, that you haven't mentioned?"

Mandine heard Key take a deep breath. "Yes, my lord Father," he said formally. "It is no secret. We intended to tell you tonight, once you knew what we'd been through together."

"Then speak," Liachan said. "I have my suspicions, but tell me."

"Mandine and I love each other. We are man and wife in the sight of the Two, by the rite of grain and water. Father, we ask your blessing on our union, and that our marriage be recognized also by the rites of Oak."

Ria gave a little squeak and sat up straight. Mandine held her breath, until Liachan at last smiled. "I approve this marriage," he said. "I approve it without reservation. Mandine

Dascaris, you are a daughter now of the House Brander. Our roof is your roof, our fire your fire, our bread your bread." He raised his right hand in the sign of blessing. "So be it."

Ria clapped her hands, her face shining. "I should have guessed! And a wedding, in Oaken House! Key, I'm so glad. Mandine, you'll be so happy living here—"

"Wait," Liachan said, and Mandine's heart lurched.

"Father?" said Ria plaintively. "What's the matter?"

Liachan passed a hand over his eyes. Alarmed, Key half stood, but his father waved him back to his seat. "I know something of the laws of the Ascendancy," Liachan said. "Key, if Mandine regains the throne, you will be Dynast to her Dynastessa. Is this not so, Mandine?"

"*Dynast?*" Ria squeaked. "*Key?*"

"Yes, it's so," Mandine said. "Key and I would rule together. But it's not something we are much concerned with, just now. The Tathars, and Erkai, and my sister all stand between us and the diadem."

Liachan was staring into space. "Dynast," he said.

Key rested his elbows on his knees and leaned on them. "Yes, but as Mandine says, the diadem's not greatly in our minds at the moment. But sir, one other matter I haven't mentioned yet, because, well, it didn't seem to fit with the rest. The Perpetua told me I didn't know who I really am. I still can't understand what she meant." He looked down at his hands. "Except that it may be part of all this. I would be glad of your help, if you can give it."

No one spoke for a while. Liachan seemed a great distance away, as if he looked inward to some memory of the distant past. His silence lasted so long that Mandine began to be afraid that his illness was suddenly becoming worse.

But then he said slowly, "Yes, I can give you that help. As matters stand now, with you and the luminessa married, it is right that you should be told, in any case." He seemed to draw himself together, as though about to shift some great weight. "Key, go to the corner of the room, there by the door. In the carving you will see a shape like a two-barbed fishhook. It is not fixed. Draw it from the wall."

Key obeyed. Mandine looked on, in perplexity mixed with apprehension.

"Now," Liachan said, "near the hook is a cluster of acorns. Push them aside. Behind them is a hole like a knothole. The hook is a key, and it opens a door. Use it."

Key did so. With a click and a soft creak, a small section of paneling swung outward to reveal darkness. He peered inside.

"Bring the box," Liachan said. "There is nothing else."

Key took it from its hiding place and put it on the marble table by his father. The box was unadorned dark wood, the size of a jewel case. Liachan laid his good hand on it and said, "This was your mother's. If the world had gone as it should have, I would never have known of it, for she would have passed it on to Ria. Key would never have known what it contains, either. But your mother was dying, Key, and Ria, you were a baby, and there was no grown woman of the clan Arvoran bloodline to take it. So your mother gave it to me, and told me that if Ria did not live, I was to destroy it."

"But I don't understand," Ria said. "Why was it to go only to me? Why not to Key? He's the elder."

"You will see." Liachan ran his fingers over the dusty surface. "In fact it was in my mind, not long ago, to destroy what it contains. It seemed a pointless knowledge to preserve, after so long. That is why I never told you about it, Ria. But now Mandine Dascaris is Key's wife, and the Lady's high priestess spoke to him of his ancestry, and who am I to oppose the will of the Two?" He pushed the box toward Key. "Open it. There's no lock."

Key took the box onto his lap and gingerly lifted the lid. Inside was a folded sheet of vellum, tinted yellow with age. As he took it out, two small heavy objects slipped from its folds, and dropped into his palm. He looked at them. One was a thick gold seal-ring, the other a painted miniature of a young man.

"Who is this?" Key asked, staring at the miniature. The

back of his neck prickled. The face was not unlike his, though the hair and eyes were darker.

"He is Ilarion Tessaris," Liachan said. "The son of Lyrix, who was the last Dynast of the Tessaris line, a hundred years ago. The ring you hold was Ilarion's personal seal."

"What are you telling me?" Key asked in a low voice. Mandine's gaze flicked from the miniature to his face, then back. Her eyes were wide.

"You will know, in a moment. But first, the paper. It is a writ of betrothal between Ilarion Tessaris and your mother's great-grandmother, Critalli Min Banain. It is impressed with his seal over his signature, and Critalli's signature as well."

"What?" Ria exclaimed. "Our ancestress was to marry the Dynast's heir?"

"Yes, she was. Ilarion was a young man who liked to travel, and on one of his travels he came here to Oak. He and Critalli met and fell in love. He intended to go to Captala, tell his father of his intentions, and after that return here and marry her. Just before he left, Critalli discovered that she carried his child, and in his love for her, Ilarion added a confirmation of his paternity to the writ of betrothal. They were secretly married here, under our rites. But Ilarion fell ill on his way home to Captala, from drinking bad water or so it was said, and died in the city of Lidion. So Critalli had no marriage, and the child had no father."

"But . . ." Key trailed off, then said, "But you mean that—"

"I do," Liachan said. "Ilarion Tessaris was your great-great-grandfather. You and Ria have the blood of the Tessarid dynasts in your veins."

Key could not speak. Ria was white, her hands clasped tightly in her lap.

"Your marriage is fitting," Liachan said. "It's the blood of the two houses joined."

"But why was it kept secret?" Ria whispered. "Why?"

Mandine wrapped her arms around herself, as if suddenly chilled. "I know," she said, "though I wish I didn't. There is a wickedness in too many of the Dascarids. When Ilarion died, his father the Dynast named my own ancestor, Rabanes Dascaris, as successor. Rabanes was a savage man. He would have killed Ilarion's child to keep his claim to the throne. Perhaps Ilarion warned Critalli to beware of Rabanes, if anything happened to him. As it did, in Lidion." Mandine bit her lower lip. "I read in the old archives that some people were executed back then for saying that Rabanes poisoned Ilarion. Maybe it was true."

"No one knows now," Liachan said. "But whatever the truth, the women of my wife's line did their best to protect Ilarion's descendants. Critalli's mother and father must have known the child's parentage, but after that generation was gone, only the eldest daughters of the bloodline were told of it, never the sons. There were no sons in Key's mother's generation, and her two uncles are dead, so he is the last male of the House Tessaris."

Key had been staring at the miniature, trying to grasp what had happened to him. The earth had shifted beneath his feet. He was still partly Kienan Mec Brander of Oak, but he was also a descendant of the great house that had ruled in a golden age of the Ascendancy. It was very difficult to put the two people together.

"Why were only the daughters told?" he asked, though he thought he knew.

Liachan gave a wintry smile. "Out of fear for the Elthame. The sons, knowing their ancestry, might have been tempted to raise an army against the Dascarids and try for the throne. Your Great-uncle Shehan was like that, hotheaded and overconscious of his honor. That would have been disaster for Oak, and all the haemes. No army of ours could have defeated the full might of the Ascendancy. So the women of your mother's line protected both their children and our homeland, in secret."

"Key," Mandine said sadly, "my family has much to answer for. The Dascarids should never have worn the diadem. None of us was worthy of it, and it's because of us that Erkai and his horrors have come into the world."

"*You're* worthy of it," Key told her sharply. "It's your

mother's blood that's strong in you, not the blood of House Dascaris."

"Isn't it ironic?" she murmured. "All those times you pushed me away from you because I was the luminessa, and all the while the diadem was really yours."

"I don't feel as if it's mine," he said. He turned Ilarion's seal ring in his fingers, examining it for the first time. The gold was bright and warm and massive, the seal a huge emerald. He turned it to catch the lamplight, and there, carved deep in the green stone, was a winged serpent. Mandine saw it also, and her breath caught. "Look," she whispered, "it's a pandragore."

Key shivered with the eeriness of it. "But that wasn't the Tessaris insignia. You told me theirs was a ship, with a crescent moon."

"Then this must have been Ilarion's personal emblem," Mandine said. "Wheels within wheels. The pandragore protected me from the Adversary, and we thought we saw a pandragore at Athanais's tower, and Ilarion's emblem was the pandragore."

"But Key," Ria asked, "what are you and Mandine going to do? You won't actually go back to Captala Nea, will you? Surely you'll stay here, where you're safe?"

"We have no choice, Ria. We've found the Signata, so we have to go."

"Alone?" Liachan asked. "Or will you do what Cawlor's father wants to do and raise the clans?"

"I'm not sure," Key said. He had only begun to absorb the knowledge of his ancestry; it felt like a story told about somebody else. But he could get his teeth into the problem of their next move, and with relief he turned his attention to that. "Mandine, what do you think?"

"It doesn't seem right," she answered. "I know we must take the Signata to confront Erkai, but Athanais said nothing about an army."

Ria sat bolt upright on her stool, dismay on her face. "But you *can't* go without an army. What about the Tathars?"

"One enemy at a time," Key said. "Without Erkai, the Tathars are somewhat less. We must destroy Erkai, above all else."

Liachan leaned forward in his chair. "Very well, but if Erkai the Chain falls, will the Tathars then turn to dust?"

"If they believed our magic destroyed him, it might shake their confidence. We'd need that, Father. I've fought them, and beating them will take every advantage we can find. But would the other haemes join an expeditionary force if we raised one here in Oak?"

"There has been much talk of Tathars lately," Liachan said. "Everyone's afraid that if the White Death overthrows the Ascendancy, they'll come here. The other haemes would indeed join us."

Key chewed his lower lip. "Even so, getting an army from here to Captala would take at least a month. And there's our harvest to see to. We couldn't send more than half our force. That's far too little."

Mandine had been listening, her brow knit in concentration. "But it's Erkai's magic that keeps the grain ships from supplying Captala. If we destroy Erkai, the ships can get into the city. The Tathars can't take Captala as long as she's supplied, and they can't live off the land around the city indefinitely. Also, they can't move their army farther east, because that would leave Captala to threaten their rear. So when they run out of forage and plundered food, they'll have to raise the siege and withdraw west. That will give us time to train new armies, and if the Elthame sends its horsemen to us in the spring, after planting, we can defeat the White Death in the field. The key to it all is to destroy Erkai as soon as we can, and for that we have the Signata."

Liachan and Key stared at her. Then Liachan burst out laughing. "Your wife's a soldier," he said. "I have seldom heard a military situation so clearly put."

Mandine was nonplussed. "It just seems to make sense," she said. "Doesn't it?"

"That it does." Liachan's glee vanished. "Does this mean

that you intend to go to Captala alone? Surely you should take someone to guard your backs."

"We've considered it," Key said. "We have four hippaxas, so we can take two men with us."

"Have you decided who?"

"Jaladar, for one," said Mandine. "Also Lonn, if he'll join us," she added.

"Not Naevis?" Liachan asked.

Key shook his head. "He's very brave, but he might fight when he should hide. We'll be doing a lot of hiding, but even allowing for stealth, hippaxas will take us to Captala in six to seven days. Tomorrow I want to send to Winterburn to have the others join us here. We'll rest for a day if Ria can see to collecting supplies for us. Then I'll need a day to show Jaladar and Lonn how to stay on top of a hippaxa, then we'll go."

"But aren't you going to be married here, first?" Ria asked, disappointment plain on her face. "With witnesses, and the rites of the Elthame?"

"It takes time to do that properly," Key said. "I'm afraid we don't have time."

"All right. But promise it, for when you come back."

"When we come back," Key said, with a lightness he could not feel, "I promise, Ria, that we will."

They set out from Oaken House two days later, in a misty autumn dawn. It was a sad departure; Naevis was desolated that he couldn't join them, and Ria wept. Liachan, sitting in his chair beneath the portico, had raised his good hand in farewell, and as Oaken House disappeared into the mist Key muttered a prayer to the Two that it would not be the last time he saw his father.

It was not many miles from Oaken House to the lip of the West Rim, and they descended from the plateau by the narrow switchback path called Cloudsplitter Way. At that point Mandine felt that their journey had truly begun, for they were again in the Ascendancy. They had found mail and a helmet for her, that had belonged to some slightly built ancestor of

Key's. The helmet fit, though the mail was a little large for her, and was an unaccustomed weight on her arms and shoulders. She now carried the Signata, in a strong sabretache with a thick belt buckled around the waist of her mail.

They traveled well away from the Great East Road, crossing the Lithadi River, a tributary of the Seferis, a hundred miles north of Baptisae. This far east there was no sign of Tathars, and the farming folk were bringing in the harvest. All looked peaceful, as though the invasion had never happened, but the country towns along their route were trying to strengthen their defenses, even if it was only with earthworks and palisades. Jaladar, when he first saw these, shook his head morosely, and muttered, "It will delay the slaughter a little. The Tathars will have to finish laughing, first."

After the second day they took to traveling by night. They were still a long way from Captala, but Key worried that Tathar raiding parties might be ranging far from the siege to seek loot. In this he was right, for the next morning showed them a deserted countryside; only a few farms had been burned, and one village they saw, but this had been enough to send the inhabitants fleeing with their livestock. After that they moved only after full dark, and found shelter from hostile eyes well before the first light of dawn.

Then, two hundred miles from Captala, they entered the devastated zone. In her worst imaginings Mandine had not dreamed that such ruin would be inflicted on her people. The reek of ash was always in her nostrils, for the Tathars had sacked and put to the torch almost every human habitation and destroyed what they could not carry off. Wheat fields that should have been silver in the starlight were burned black; a plantation of sunsip trees showed pale bands on the trunks where the Tathars had ringed the bark to kill them; those indistinct reeking humps were a slaughtered auroch herd; and the shattered walls of pillaged towns haunted the darkness like sad gray ghosts.

But they found no trace now of Tathar foraging parties: no campfires, no fresh horse dung or tracks, or newly slaughtered human beings. The raiders' absence was hardly surprising, Mandine reflected bitterly, for the region had been so thoroughly raped that nothing of worth remained. She hoped that most of the inhabitants had escaped to the east or into the hills, but from the carrion stench that wafted from time to time on the night wind, she knew that not everyone had gotten away. And if Erkai and the Tathars won, Mandine thought with a shudder, they would spread this ruin across the whole length and breadth of the Ascendancy, and later across the Elthame.

With the Day Star at last on the horizon, Jaladar scouted ahead and returned with news that the farm ahead had been burned, but the fire had not taken hold on the outbuildings. They reached the place not long before the eastern sky showed its first tint of gray, slipped into the stable, and after settling the hippaxas made a meal of their cold, monotonous, travel provisions. Key took the first watch, and Jaladar and Lonn curled up in their cloaks, with swords unsheathed and ready to hand, and fell asleep.

Mandine was far from sleepy though her body was weary. She sat by Key where he peered through a chink in the stable wall. He put his arm around her shoulders but never took his eyes from the outside.

"We're almost there," she murmured. "Tonight, we will be."

"If everything goes well." He held her closer. "After dark, it's straight west till we reach the Rushwater River. If our navigation's good, we'll strike the river valley soon after midnight, about ten miles northeast of Captala. Then we work downstream, till we find that island we saw when we left the tunnel three months ago. It had that old temple on it, remember?"

"Yes. The little one. It should be easy to spot."

"Barring Tathar interference."

There was a long pause. "Key," Mandine said, "do you wish we'd stayed in Oak?"

"I wish we'd been able to. But we couldn't."

"I know." She sighed. "I keep remembering that one day

we took just to rest, after we reached Oaken House, and before the others came. I wish it had lasted forever. I was so happy, knowing we had a few hours when we didn't have to think about going on."

"We'll have other days like it," he told her. "And better."

"Will we?"

"Of course. We'll win, Mandine."

"But what will be the cost of winning? I couldn't bear to lose you."

"Don't talk of that. It won't happen."

She remembered him on the walls of Essardene, and what he had told her then: *It's not good to talk of one's fear, especially before a battle. It only makes the fear worse.*

But I am afraid, she thought. *I'm terrified. Not so much for myself, but for him. And afraid of being without him. Sweet Lady, sustain us now, and if we die, be with us at the hour of our deaths.*

"No," she whispered, "it won't happen."

✳ 25

LATIAS RAN AS FAST AS HE COULD, BUT STILL THE wardsmen were gaining on him. He hurtled around a corner and saw the black mass of Temple Mount rising into the night sky ahead. His pursuers were close, but if he could reach the Metradora Cistern fifty yards ahead of them, he might yet escape.

He saw the alley mouth on his right, raced into it, and heard a shout behind as the wardsmen called out at his disappearance from the street. The alley stank of garbage; refugees were sleeping in it, and Latias slowed to avoid tripping over them. A few woke at the yelling behind him, and somebody grabbed at his ankle. He yanked himself free and kept running.

The alley ended at a small square and a public water basin. Dark bundles on the pavement betrayed more refugees, but these still slept. Latias ran down the short flight of steps to the pool, plunged into the thigh-deep water, and waded to the far wall. There he took a deep breath, and submerged. At the pool's bottom was the mouth of the basin's feed channel; it was a foot high, and just wide enough for his shoulders. He pulled himself into it, thrust hard with his knees and elbows, and with groping hands at last found the slimy stone edges where the channel entered the cistern. In seconds he was standing in the near dark, shaking water out of his eyes and wheezing. The cistern's floor was lower than that of the basin outside, and here the water was up to his breastbone.

The close-hooded lamp, which he had left behind him on his way out, burned with a faint glow on the ledge above him. Fearing that light might leak to the outside if he unhooded it, Latias used the lamp as it was, and very carefully made his way farther into the vast cavern. The Metradora Cistern was one of ten in Captala, its water a huge underground reserve against drought, or, as matters now were, against enemies who had cut the aqueducts. Its forest of supporting columns marched away into the blackness around him, and Latias sloshed along in a tiny puddle of light. Few things made him shudder, but the thought of dropping the lantern did; in the pitch blackness he might feel his way to a service stair, but then again he might not.

His decision to stay in Captala had defied good sense and self-preservation. Still, he did not regret it, though if there'd been a spare horse when Mandine and Kienan Mec Brander left, he probably would have gone, too. But there wasn't a horse, and just after the couple departed he changed his mind about escaping. His oath was to the Ascendancy, and Mandine Dascaris was its rightful ruler. That being so, it was his duty to prepare the ground for her return. Moreover, Theatana must know he had helped Mandine escape. If the false Dynastessa prevailed against Erkai and the Tathars, she would hunt him down. And then she would kill him, slowly. His best defense against Theatana was not flight, but attack.

After he made this decision, Orissi and Taras hid him in the catacombs. With their help, and that of a few trusted acolytes, he had campaigned against Theatana with the only weapon he had, which was rumor. His most recent whisper was that Mandine was alive and would soon return. Latias hoped she might because he couldn't continue his nocturnal expeditions much longer. Every time he went out there were more of Tefraos's wardsmen-thugs in the dark streets. Sooner or later they would catch him scrawling on a wall, as they almost had tonight, or he'd whisper a rumor to a provocateur.

Or an informer would recognize him, despite his grayed hair, straggling beard, and the wax mouth pads that plumped his cheeks. He'd had a network of such people himself, and knew from experience how dangerous they could be. The irony of this reversal might have amused him if coping with it weren't so profoundly uncomfortable.

He paused to brighten the lantern, and saw the cistern's east wall and in it the black maw of the rainwater drain. Cursing Theatana, he waded toward the drain. If she hadn't sealed off the Mount, he wouldn't be slopping through the guts of the city like this, and the acolytes would still be whispering his rumors to the crowds that came to the sanctuary to pray. Even that had been getting dangerous, though, with people disappearing after repeating the stories. Tefraos hadn't arrested any of the priesthood yet, but if Theatana pushed him to it, he would.

But, Latias told himself as he reached the drain, his efforts were affecting people. For example, there was that scratching of *Dynastessa, tyrantessa* on a wall in Pallion Street tonight: a clumsy word-yoking, not his style at all, but it made the point. And two days ago, refugees had rioted for bread in Mileon Square. It was the first civil outbreak since the siege began, but Latias was sure it would not be the last. He would do his best to encourage more, though insurrection in a besieged city was a dangerous business. But Theatana ruled so cruelly that the sooner she went, the less damage she could inflict, and the less damage she inflicted, the longer the city could withstand the Tathars' army and Erkai's sorcery. That was the imperative, that Captala somehow hold; hold, though no supplies had gotten in for months; hold, though the city granaries were scraped bare even of chaff. Orissi, Latias knew, dreaded Erkai's entry into Captala even more than she dreaded that of the Tathars. She believed that if he found a way in, he might succeed in breaking the Ban, though neither she nor her husband knew how he could achieve that. But the possibility clearly frightened both her and Taras, and *that* frightened Latias.

The floor of the rainwater drain, where it entered the cistern, was almost level. Latias clambered into the opening and set off into the dark. The drain's low ceiling forced him to walk doubled over, and the lantern's sway threw weird shadows ahead of him. After a while the drain began to climb, ever more steeply. Latias's back throbbed and burned, and the ache in his knees became excruciating.

At last he saw the rope and the leather sling. Latias grabbed the rope, ran the sling under his armpits, and tugged twice. The rope jerked twice in response, and tightened. He climbed, the lantern bobbing. Only with the rope's help could he manage the last three hundred feet, for here the drain was nearly vertical. Finally he smelled fresh night air, the rope gave him a last heave, and his head and torso popped out of the drain mouth. Above him loomed the rear facade of the House of the Sacred Marriage. Beyond, the Day Star was a handbreadth above the horizon.

"You're all right, Eminence?" The three male acolytes smelled even worse than usual from their exertions. One took the lantern, and the others helped him scramble out of the drain.

"I'm fine." Latias slowly unbent himself against the pain in his back. His clothes were dank and cold; autumn was at hand. The acolytes were already laboring to slide the massive grating stone over the drain entrance. *The Allfather be merciful,* Latias thought, *I've been down that hare-run three times in six days. I almost wish Taras hadn't known where it went. I'm twenty years too old for this, and my luck's running out. I must think of some other way to give Theatana a canker. Whatever it is, though, I have to keep at it till Mandine's return.*

If she returned. "Your Grace," Latias had said to Orissi ten days ago, "can't you ask the Two if Mandine's coming back, and when? Or if she's dead, at least to tell us that?"

"I can only dream," the Perpetua had told him. "Sometimes it's the true dream. It's always hard to separate the truth from the wish. I believe Mandine is alive. That is all I can say."

Priests, Latias thought bitterly as the grating stone clunked into place. *Never a clear answer when you need one.*

He took the lantern and went up into the temple's rear colonnade. Taras was waiting there for him. So was Orissi, which was unusual. Latias's heart jumped; perhaps Mandine—

The Perpetua's face in the lanternlight was too grave for good news. "They almost caught me tonight," Latias said. "Tefraos is working harder."

"We'll see more of his work very soon," Orissi said. "I've just come from the east parapet. Torches are coming up the lower ramp, and I saw metal gleaming. I think we'll have soldiers here in a few minutes."

Latias felt a sickening in his belly. *Theatana's found out I'm here,* he thought. *Ah, well, at least the bitch won't be able to castrate me.*

"I'll go out to them," he said. "I'll tell them you never knew I was still in Captala."

"Don't act in haste," said Taras. "It may not be you they're after. It may be us."

"What? Take you in the temple sanctuary? That's sacrilege!"

"Theatana Dascaris is past caring about sacrilege," Orissi said. "Go to your hiding place, Latias. If the soldiers say you're on the Mount, we will deny it, even if we must swear it on the altar of the Two. The Lord and Lady will forgive us, I think."

"Thank you, Your Graces," Latias answered, with feeling. Few people would risk swearing falsely on the great altar of Temple Mount, even in the best of causes.

"Go now," Taras said. "The soldiers will be here soon."

Tefraos's forehead was damp under his helmet band. He didn't like doing this, but he had no choice. This evening, Theatana had finally lost patience with the subversive rumors that seemed to emanate constantly from Temple Mount, and she had decided to put a stop to them. Her orders to him had been very explicit: take a detachment of his Mixtuns, go to the Mount, and arrest the Perpetua and the Continuator. With them out of the way, she said, the rumors would be cut off at their source.

Tefraos was not so sure of this. But he hadn't considered refusing the order because doing so would land him in his own cells under the Numera's Bucelon Ravelin, and he suspected that Dactulis would be glad to see him there. The treimarch would like to have the security service under his own direction.

He led his twenty Mixtuns under the shadowy lintel of the Pylon Gate, into the plaza before the temple. The sacred flame burned on the high altar in the sanctuary's center, and by its light he saw the Perpetua and the Continuator. It was the hour before dawn.

Tefraos halted the squad ten yards from the altar. The Mixtuns' torches cast his shadow before him as he strode forward. Without apparent alarm, the high priest and priestess watched him approach. Then the Perpetua raised her hand, palm outward. Tefraos stopped. Was she about to curse him?

"You have brought swords to the high altar," she said. "That is impious, Tefraos Epicato."

"I don't want trouble," he said roughly. "If your people interfere, there'll be trouble."

"We have sent everyone out of the sanctuary," the Continuator said, "as you can see. No blood will flow here on our account. Why have you come in this manner?"

"You're under arrest," Tefraos said.

"And the grounds?"

"Don't act the innocents. Sedition, collusion with the enemy, high treason, inciting of mutiny. I could go on."

"You needn't," said the Perpetua. "What you've already said sounds quite enough." She seemed unafraid, and her stare was unnerving. Tefraos tore his gaze from her eyes, motioned brusquely, and the Mixtuns clanked forward to surround the high priest and priestess. The islanders threw coarse brown cloaks around them, to conceal their Temple robes from early-rising citizens who might be in the streets.

"Will you walk," Tefraos asked, "or will they drag you?"

The Continuator laughed. "We'll walk, of course. Where would you like us to walk to?"

It was an absurd question. "The Numera," Tefraos said.

✳ 26

GREAT LADY, MANDINE THOUGHT, *THANK YOU FOR making the moon cooperate. You've given us just enough of her, not too much.*

The thin silver crescent rode low above the eastern horizon and shed little light on the devastated countryside around the farmstead. Mandine was glad of the near darkness, for now they were less than fifty miles from Captala and the Tathar army.

"On we go," Key said, and she heard Lonn answer, "Yes." The men kept their voices down, though the day just past had revealed no living creatures except birds and a few hares.

They rode from the farm's lane onto the narrow country road. Jaladar's memory was proving valuable, for the Paladine Guard had trained in the area east of the Rushwater River, and he knew the ground to within a mile of its banks. The territory downstream would be unfamiliar even to him, but Mandine told herself that even in the dark they could find the temple island easily enough, then the cave that hid the tunnel entrance. She shifted her shoulders under her mail, and smelled charred wood; for better concealment, they had blacked their faces with soot from the burned farmhouse. *If only,* she thought, *the tunnel's still open, and Taras's sentries are still waiting for us. We can't likely get into Captala by sea, and the*

*Signata has to go to the Hill of Remembrance. And it has to go there
soon, for my heart tells me our time's running out. I couldn't bear it,
after all we've been through, to be too late by a day, or by a moment.*

At an hour past midnight they reached the Rushwater, as
they had hoped to do. It was a respectable river, sixty yards
across, that ran through a steep-sided valley toward the Seferis.
The valley walls were shale and limestone, honeycombed by
caves and by the ancient shafts of the iron mines that had once
fed Captala's foundries. The ore had given out two hundred
years ago, but the slag heaps from its smelting, spiked with
claw-thorn and mantled in ragged underbrush, remained in
drifts along the valley's slopes.

They halted at the top of a slag incline that descended
almost as far as the riverbank. "Are we where we should be?"
Lonn asked.

"I hope so," Key said. When he and Mandine had left the
tunnel's concealing cave three months earlier, they'd gone
south from there to the Great East Road. Now, however, they
were approaching from the north, and he wasn't sure how far
upriver they were from the island.

"No Tathars, at least," Lonn said. "But they'll have pickets
out, closer to the city."

"Yes, they will. Let's hope the sentries are beyond the island, so we don't run into them. Mandine?"

"Yes, Key?"

"We're almost there." *If only,* he thought, *she could have
stayed safe in Oak. But what's to be done we must do together. Our
fates were twined from the moment we met at Essardene. And now
I'm a Tessarid, and the diadem is mine as well as hers, and I'd give
the thing up to keep her from harm.*

"At last," she said. She must have guessed what he was
thinking, for she added, "Don't be afraid for me. This is what
we're supposed to do."

"I know. Well, we'd better get on, and do it."

The undergrowth would hide pits and open mine shafts,
so they dismounted and led the hippaxas carefully down the
slope. Thorns raked at them, penetrating even the tiny rings

of their mail, and the slag shifted treacherously underfoot. But they reached the valley floor unscathed except for thorn scratches, and from the moon Key judged that they had about four hours before first light. If they couldn't find the island within three, or if they spotted a Tathar patrol in their path, they'd find somewhere to hide and try again the next night. He hated the thought of that, for like Mandine, he sensed that their time was running out.

The Rushwater was a placid river, and the stars reflected clearly on its smooth black surface. They mounted and set off along its bank, the hippaxas moving with no more than a faint crunch of gravel under their pads. After a few miles the valley's sides steepened and became cliffs, with long slopes of brush-grown slag heaped at their feet. A light wind sprang up, blowing from the southeast. Key's alertness, already sharp, became razor-edged. By now they must be near the island.

Suddenly, he smelled woodsmoke. "Stop," he hissed, and the soft noises behind him ceased. "Somebody's burning something up there."

Jaladar and Mandine eased up beside him. "It will be Tathars," Jaladar said in an undertone. "What now?"

The starlight showed a sharp bend in the river valley, about a hundred yards ahead. The fire must be out of sight around it, but they needed to know exactly where. "I'll go up and look," Key said quietly, and dismounted.

"Be careful," Mandine whispered from above him.

"I will." He patted her knee, then made for the bend, keeping near the brush for concealment, and moving in a crouch. When the bend's farside was just in view he pushed his sheathed sword around to the small of his back, went down on his belly, and crawled. The smell of smoke became stronger, but he heard no voices and saw no fire. Then he spotted a dark, angular shape that appeared to be standing in the water. His vision suddenly made sense of it, and the shape became the small island temple, only a long bowshot away.

Without warning, a glow appeared on the island. It was rectangular, and Key realized that he was looking at firelight through an open doorway. Someone had just poked a campfire to life inside the temple, and from near it he heard the whicker of a horse. It was a cavalry picket, then, guarding the river approach to the Great East Road. And it was directly below the cave that hid the tunnel entrance.

He wondered whether the Tathars had listening posts on the riverbanks. Or would they have grown careless after three months of picket duty? It was impossible to know. But even if the urgency allowed, hiding until tomorrow night would solve nothing. The sentry post was not going to go away.

He crawled back to the bend, then hurried toward the others. "Trouble?" Lonn said, as he reached them.

"Yes. There're Tathars on the island. We'll have to crawl past on the farside of the river, through the brush."

"What about the hippaxas?" Mandine asked.

He'd thought about this on the way back. "We'll swim them over the river here, then leave them. They won't wander far till it's light. The Tathars won't find them till then."

"So we burn our ships?" Jaladar asked. He spoke everyone's thought; without the hippaxas, there was no way back.

"We burn them. Let's go."

The lanterns and food were in the saddlebags, and they draped these over their shoulders before riding the hippaxas into the water. Once on the farside of the river, they sorted their equipment and supplies, taking what was essential and concealing everything else in the undergrowth. Any gear that might clank, like the lanterns, they muffled in spare clothing before putting the items into their packs. The hippaxas seemed content to stay put; one lay down by a bush and began to chew sleepily on the tough leaves.

They started out. When they reached the river's bend, they plunged waist-deep into the brush and started working diagonally up the incline toward the foot of the cliff. The ground was slag and broken rock, and the going difficult; thorns and twigs caught at them, and they were constantly untangling themselves. Worse, the brush was dry and brittle, and it protested at their passage. Key hoped desperately that the breeze would carry the sounds away from the Tathars.

When the Tathar watch fire finally came into sight, they were halfway up the slope. They got right down into the brush and began to crawl, tending always upward. It was warm work, in spite of the cool of the night, and sweat ran stinging into Key's eyes. Occasionally he raised his head to peer down at the Tathar camp. On his third inspection the starlight revealed a dark figure moving along the riverbank on their side, obviously a patrolling sentry. Key ducked and wriggled on upslope, testing the slag for looseness before he put his weight on it.

At last a shadow crawled across the starlit sky above him. It was the overhang of the cliff, and beneath it the underbrush petered out. That made for easier travel, but their screen was gone. If the sentry looked at the cliffs, and looked carefully, he might spot movement.

Either he didn't look up, or if he did, the shadow beneath the overhang hid them. Finally they reached the top of the rubble slope and huddled together against the stone of the cliff face. Now they had to find the cave entrance, black in near black.

"Do you remember exactly where it was?" he breathed to Mandine.

"Not exactly. To the south, I think."

They worked along the base of the cliff, which rose only six feet vertically before it thrust itself out to become the overhang. Loose stones skidded under their knees and elbows, but mercifully did not trigger a slide. At last Key saw a dark seam, like a cleft, but when he felt into it the opening was too narrow to enter.

"Is that it?" Mandine whispered.

"No."

They went on. A second shadow was more promising than the first, but led only two feet into the rock. As Key crawled on, a chunk of stone slipped from beneath his knee and grated its way thirty feet down the incline before it stopped. They all held their breaths, but no cry of alarm came from below. Key had lost sight of the sentry, and he was now badly worried about spending so much time in the search. The overhang continued a long way both behind and in front of them, and their luck wouldn't hold indefinitely; a stone would fall, the sentry would hear it. But the entrance *had* to be close by if he could trust his memory at all. When they came out, with Taras, hadn't the temple been directly below them?

"Key, I think I see it!" Mandine's whisper was sharp with excitement.

"Where?"

"There, that lighter streak in the rock. I think I remember it."

Key didn't, but he crawled toward the pale band. Just beyond it, and three feet above him, was a pitch-black vertical shadow in the cliff. He gingerly got to his knees, put his forearm into the shadow, and found emptiness.

"This must be it," he whispered. Unfortunately, they would have to stand on the loose rubble to climb into the cleft. He tested the slope beneath it, and found a mass of shale that seemed stable. "There's good footing, I think, but be careful when you climb in." He looked down at the temple. Someone had fed the fire, for it was brighter, but he still couldn't see the sentry. "Mandine, you go first, then the others. I'll follow."

"All right." She reached up and grabbed the lip of the cleft, and Key boosted her into the opening. "I'm sure this is it," she whispered. "It opens out, and I can't feel a back wall."

"We're here," he murmured to Jaladar and Lonn. "Go ahead."

They scrambled over him into the cave mouth, packs bumping against stone. Key's pack straps had loosened in the climb, and he paused to tighten them as he looked for the sentry again. Firelight glinted on metal below, and he spotted the Tathar as the man's helmet caught the light. The sentry stood motionless by the riverbank, as if watching the cliff. Key held very still.

The tiny reflection vanished as the Tathar moved. Key let

his breath out and hauled himself into the cave mouth. As his right boot left the ground outside, rock shifted under it. There was a scrape, three sharp clacks of tumbling stone, and suddenly part of the slope let go with a clatter. Over the racket came a sharp yell from the riverbank.

Key was too furious with himself to curse. "Everybody get a few feet deeper in. Be careful. Don't knock your head on the roof. Lonn, prime a lantern."

More shouts came from outside, as the Tathar camp woke up. Key edged deeper into the blackness, unslinging his pack and digging in it by feel until he found the sheaf of quicklights in their oiled pouch. He yanked some out, knelt, and bunched them on the rock floor.

"Do I keep on?" Mandine asked, her voice echoing nearby.

This might not be the right cave. There might be a mine pit deeper in. "No, wait. The lantern first."

"It's here," Lonn said, next to him. "It's primed."

Key snatched striker and steel from his sabretache. Stone and metal rang in a shower of sparks, and four quicklights ignited together in a bright yellow burst. Lonn opened the lantern's front pane, Key thrust a quicklight at the wick, and the lantern caught. He took it from Lonn, and stamped out the rest of the quicklights. From outside there was more shouting, orders by the sound of it.

"They may have seen a glow at the entrance," said Mandine urgently. "We've got to hurry."

"How far?" Jaladar asked as they began to trot along the passage.

"Two hundred yards," Key said. "Then we have to open the door."

"There's dust," Lonn said, "but your footprints from before aren't here. Are you sure this is right?"

"Taras said he'd brush them out on his way back." But they had no time for that precaution now. If the Tathars found the entrance cleft, they'd know exactly where their quarry had gone.

The passage opened into echoing darkness. The lantern

cast a wavering bubble of light as they ran through a cavern. In the cavern's far wall were half a dozen irregular openings, natural clefts.

Do not, Taras had said, take the wrong one. The others lead no one knows where, and they branch. If you go far into the wrong one, you will never come out.

"There," Mandine said, pointing at the second opening from the right. A huge round boulder almost blocked it. "The big stone."

They squeezed past the boulder into the next passage, which thrust deep into the living rock. After a hundred yards it led them into another cavern, smaller than the last, so that the lantern threw fitful illumination on its walls. "The door's here?" Lonn said doubtfully. "I don't see it."

"You're not supposed to," Key answered. He hurried to the other side of the cave, where irregular slabs of stone, apparently joined at their backs to the cave wall, jutted from the floor. He handed the lantern to Mandine. The rock face was webbed with fissures, some the breadth of a man's thumb. He searched for the right slab. Taras had given him and Mandine time to memorize the patterns in the cracks, but many days had passed since then.

"It's this one," Key said. "One of you help me." He seized the edge of a chest-high sheet of stone. Before leaving the cave the last time, he and Mandine had made sure they alone could open it; they'd succeeded, but only just. "Haul left," he ordered, as Lonn joined him.

"I hear voices," Mandine said, as they strained at the slab. "They've found our tracks."

They heaved at the rock. A dull rumble sounded from deep in its roots. "Keep it moving," Key grunted.

They redoubled their efforts. The slab shifted a little more, then, protesting on its stone rollers, began to lumber aside. Behind the stone was the mouth of the tunnel. A gentle breeze blew out of it, and on the breeze was the faintest hint of burning sunsip oil, the smell of a lamp or torch. Taras's men were still at the sentry post, then. Or someone was.

The gap was wide enough. "Through," Key said. As the others squeezed past him, he looked behind at the footprints that betrayed their passage. Finding out how the door worked would delay the Tathars for a little, but they would get it open. He and the others had to get in earshot of Taras's sentries and call the password before the priests heard the Tathars coming and started the poisonous smoke that was part of the tunnel defenses. He didn't know if they could do it. Four miles of tunnel lay between them and the sentry post. He tried not to imagine their fate if the priests on watch panicked and released the huge stone that would seal the tunnel forever.

Everyone was through. Key slithered through the gap into the tunnel. "Get it closed, quick."

The ancient craftsmen had cut handholds into the door's reverse face. Jaladar and Lonn hauled on them, and the slab grumbled home. Key wiped gritty palms on his mail, took the lantern from Mandine, and said, "Run. They may be on our heels."

They ran at full speed at first, to put as much room as possible between them and their pursuers. Then Key ordered a slowing of the pace, one he hoped Mandine could sustain till they reached the sentry post. He listened for noises from behind, but for a time heard nothing but the thud of their boots on the tunnel floor and the hiss of breathing.

Lonn gasped, "A light, far back."

The Tathars had breached the door much sooner than he'd hoped. But he said, "Stop. We need to spell ourselves a moment."

They halted, breathing fast, and he peered into the dark reaches of the tunnel behind. The spark was dim and distant, but as he watched it grew a little brighter. But there were no yells. The Tathars were saving their breath to run. "Mandine, we've got to get you out of that mail," he said. "It's too much weight."

He helped her, and in moments she was in her undertunic. The helmet went, too. Then he buckled her sabretache, with its precious contents, back around her waist.

"You should carry the Signata," she said. "I can't run as fast."

"No. It might protect you somehow, who knows? Quick now, they're coming."

The passage flew past, and they entered a long curve. The bend hid the light behind them. Key was unsure how far they had come. Halfway, perhaps. Mandine, even relieved of her armor, was breathing hard.

"Can you keep going?" he panted, between breaths. His lungs were beginning to rasp.

"Yes."

"Keep heart—you'll get—second wind—"

His own came a few moments later. But he knew that when that energy passed, they'd be done in, too exhausted to fight. The only consolation was that the Tathars would be as winded. But what he feared most, just now, was the poisoned smoke, and that the guards might release the seal-stone.

He looked over his shoulder and saw the light. It was brighter, much brighter. He cursed Tathar stamina. He, Lonn, and Jaladar could run faster than they were, but Mandine could not. She was gasping now.

They were in another curve. Key wished he had counted the bends on the way out, for by now they must be nearing the sentry post.

"These sentries," Jaladar wheezed. "Will they panic?"

"They'll wait for the password," Key answered, hoping they would.

The tunnel ahead must have straightened, for he suddenly saw a tiny orange spark hanging in the blackness ahead. It moved slightly, then steadied.

They'll have seen our lantern now, Key thought.

A larger glow bloomed in the dark. A torch, to light the brazier of oil mixed with the crushed fibers of baneroot. *Wait,* he prayed. *Wait, just a little.*

The torchlight ahead was brightening fast. Then a voice echoed down the tunnel, distorted by distance and reverberation. *"Who goes?"*

To Key's despair, voices rose behind, in the unmistakable *ulululu* of the Tathar battle yell. Ahead, the torch swung down. Key yelled, as loudly as his burning lungs would let him, "The Book of the First and the Last!"

The countersign didn't come, but the torch wavered. *"Who goes? Speak, or die."*

"Mandine Dascaris! The Book of the First and the Last!"

The torch bobbed uncertainly. *"Say again?"*

He repeated the call. Then, to his unspeakable relief, a male voice shouted, "Of Athanais the White Diviner! Advance, and be recognized."

They raced forward. Ahead, someone lit a second torch, and by its light Key saw two junior priests peering anxiously into the tunnel. There was a brazier at their feet. "Luminessa?" one called.

"Yes," Mandine called back, and they heard her, though she barely gasped the word. Then she stumbled. Key grabbed her arm, dragged it over his shoulders, and together they half fell into the square room that was the tunnel's antechamber. Lonn and Jaladar were at their heels, but so almost was the enemy. The Tathars howled again, the yell of the kill.

The second priest jabbed his torch into the brazier. Black smoke billowed into the passage mouth. Key heard many running feet, the jingle of mail and weapons. Then there was a choking wail, and a Tathar, clutching his throat, staggered into the chamber.

"Back!" the priest shouted. "Back to the seal-stone."

They stumbled from the chamber into the next passage. Key heard more Tathars gasping, then a clang as the brazier was overturned.

Ahead were the two stone pillars that held up the seal, and the deep cleft that would receive it. Key and Jaladar dragged Mandine to the cleft's farside, and Lonn collapsed, wheezing, to the passage floor next to them. The priests seized heavy sledges, and swung them at the pillars. The first pillar cracked under their frenzied blows, then the second, and both fell in fragments.

For an endless instant nothing happened. Then a grating rumble came from the roof, and Key saw a huge block of granite slide from the tunnel ceiling. It moved slowly at first, then faster, and the earth shook as it moved. Then it fell free and, with a tremendous *boom*, rammed into the cleft. Flagstones split and shattered, fragments of rock fell from the roof, and a cloud of choking dust flew into the air. Then there was silence.

"I'm thirsty," Mandine said weakly. Key held her up, opened her water bottle, and put it to her lips. She drank, coughed, and drank again. Her gasping eased, and her breathing became more regular.

"Are you all right?" he asked.

"I will be." She sat up and wiped sweat from her eyes. Key took a long pull at the water bottle.

"Luminessa," the taller priest said, "it's really you?"

"Yes, it's me," Mandine answered, her voice stronger now. "Let us recover a little. Then you must take us to the Perpetua or the Continuator, as quick as you can."

The shorter priest looked distraught. "Luminessa," he said wretchedly, "we can't."

"You can't? Why not?"

"My lady, they've been arrested."

"*Arrested?* On whose orders?"

"On the Dyna—on your sister's, my lady." The young man's voice cracked with barely suppressed misery. "She did it."

"She's gone mad! Who's in charge on the Mount?"

"My lady," said the priest, "the Secundros is, but I suppose it's the chamberlain you'll want to see."

Distress and elation warred in Mandine's face. "The chamberlain?"

"Majolis Latias, Luminessa," the priest said. "He's still here."

Sleepless again, Theatana paced the Red Chamber. A single lamp burned on her desk, and outside its dim halo the room brooded in somber maroon shadows. It was well before dawn, and she was waiting for Dactulis. He should have been here by now, and she was growing more irritated by the moment.

She yawned and shook herself. Her body needed rest, but sleep fled her so often now; as soon as she closed her eyes her brain burst into feverish, aimless activity. Of late she could calm herself only by thinking of Erkai. She would picture him sitting before his tent, and her breathing would slow as she imagined his eyes meeting hers, and imagined the power that she could share with him. A sweet languor would steal through her, and she would finally drift away. He was in her dreams, she knew, though she didn't remember them; but twice now she had awoken with a shudder and a delicious warmth fading in her belly.

She paced the chamber. She wanted to see him. She wanted to see him *now*. She needed him; she needed an ally. So much was going wrong. The unrest in the city was worse than ever: for instance that riot yesterday evening, over the imprisonment of the high priest and priestess. Theatana's hands clenched, her nails cutting at her palms. Dactulis said the Paladines hadn't liked putting down the rioters, and he'd seemed uneasy about it, too. So, thanks to Temple Mount, she couldn't trust anyone, not the people, not the Guard, not her generals or her ministers. And now, according to Tefraos, the people even murmured that the Two themselves hated her.

Theatana's slippers whispered across the rugs, then across the polished floor that was still a little stained with her father's blood. She didn't fear the Two and never had. The Two didn't exist, anyway; she had long suspected as much, and when they hadn't saved the Perpetua and the Continuator from arrest, her suspicion became certainty. The Two existed only in tales told by the priesthood to frighten the ignorant. She was in no danger from *them*.

She stopped by her desk and touched the roll of crumpled reed paper lying beside the lamp. On the outside was written:

You who value your life, this is for the eye of the Dynastessa alone.

It had been catapult-shot over the outer wall two hours before midnight, and a nervous Guard victurion had brought it to her, unopened and unread. It was the second such message. The first, delivered the same way three nights ago, had said:

> I rule Hetlik now. If the Dynastessa wishes negotiations, let them be with me. There is no reason to prolong this strife. We have much to give each other, the Ascendancy and I.

It was unsigned, but it needed no signature. Dactulis knew about that first missive, unfortunately. He'd been present when it arrived, and she'd felt constrained to show it to him. It wouldn't do for him to suspect her of secret contacts with Erkai; if the treimarch were considering treachery against her, that would be too good an excuse for action. Theatana had made a display of fury at Erkai's insolence, but the words burned in her memory.

Much to give each other.

The crumpled paper now on her desk bore a more enticing message. Theatana unrolled it, and read Erkai's words again.

> My regard for the Dynastessa grows as the days pass. Why should two powers be enemies, who should more fittingly be allies? The Tathars fear and obey me; why should they not also fear and obey the Dynastessa and the Ascendancy?

Theatana fingered the message, then with a quick motion thrust its corner into the lamp flame. The paper flared. She dropped it onto a bronze salver, let it burn to ash, then crumbled the ash to dust.

A soft rap sounded on the door. "Come," she said.

Dactulis entered, his face ugly with disturbed sleep. "Yes, Dynastessa? How may I serve you?"

"I'm going to make an example, Treimarch. Temple Mount's meddling is to blame for the riots we've had, and I want no more such outbreaks. We must wrench this plant of treachery out by the roots. Tossing the Perpetua and the Continuator into the Numera obviously wasn't enough, so it's time for stronger measures." She stared into Dactulis's eyes, and he dropped his gaze. "Send troops up to the Mount, Treimarch. They are to arrest everyone they find there, priests, priestesses, acolytes, servants, *everyone*. Have the prisoners taken to the Numera, and I will deal with them myself in the morning."

Dismay spread over Dactulis's face. "But my lady, with the Perpetua and the Continuator already imprisoned, how much threat can the rest of the Temple Mount staff be? I don't think—"

"Don't think, Treimarch. Do it, and do it now. You will see to it personally. Don't send some subordinate to do your work for you."

Dactulis swallowed, bowed, and said, "Yes, Dynastessa. If I could have Tefraos's Mixtuns—"

"They're busy, looking for people who scribble treason on walls. Take those cataphracts you've been using to seal off the Mount. They're already there, and it's time they did something useful."

"Yes, Dynastessa."

"Go. Report to me when it's done."

"Yes, my lady."

Her eyes slid to the dust in the salver. She felt feverish, and her skin tingled. For a moment the maroon shadows behind Dactulis seemed to take on form, Erkai's form, with his wise and knowing eyes lingering on hers. Her need of him stabbed her deep under her breastbone, deep in her belly. She stood at the brink of greatness; why she still hesitated she did not know. It would take so little to make her leap; a slant look from Dactulis, one more rumor of treason from Tefraos . . .

"On your way out," she said harshly as Dactulis turned to leave, "tell the majordomo to summon my escort. I'm going down to Processional Gate."

✳ 27

"AND THAT'S HOW MATTERS STAND," LATIAS FINISHED. "Arrests by the score since you left—nobles as well as commoners—secret executions, and many empty bellies. Four days ago the refugees rioted for bread in the East Market. The Paladine Guard dispersed them. Some of the soldiers appeared reluctant to obey orders, but they did, and there was bloodshed. And yesterday evening there was another riot, in Bell Square. It was put down, too, but we could hear the shouting up here. The cry was to release the Perpetua and the Continuator. Again, the mob was dispersed."

"I still can't believe Theatana arrested the high priest and priestess," Mandine said wearily. "It's sacrilege. People will believe she's called a curse down on the city."

All four travelers, and Latias, were in the House of the Sacred Marriage, in the small room behind the statues of the Lord and Lady. The hidden door to the stairs was open for quick flight, though according to Latias no soldiers had come up the Mount since the arrests, two nights ago. On the round marble table were fruit, bread, and wine. Several large bowls, where Mandine and the others had washed the soot-blacking off their faces, were scattered on the floor. The water clock showed an hour till first light.

The chamberlain nodded. "What she's done is unheard of.

Theatana has made an extremely serious mistake. The popular outrage over the arrests can only increase." He sighed. "Thank the Allfather and the Lady you're back, Luminessa. And with *it*, no less. You and my lord Brander actually found the Signata. Legends walk in daylight. It beggars the imagination."

"Or it found us," Key said. He tore a rusk of bread in two. "Athanais was right, though. It's not impressive to look at."

"Only a white stone," Latias mused aloud. "Curious, but no more curious than the legends about it. But I don't understand how it's to help us against our entirely-too-numerous enemies."

"We have to take it to the Hill of Remembrance," Mandine said. Without thinking, she put her hand over Key's, and his fingers closed on hers. "Maybe then we'll know. We've come so far, that the knowing must be soon."

Latias didn't answer. His eyebrows had risen, and he was staring at their joined hands. Across the table from Key, Lonn worked hard to suppress a grin. "Truth will out," he said.

"My lord Latias," Key said, as he also tried to keep a straight face, "there's little time to explain, but Mandine and I are husband and wife."

Mandine had never before seen the chamberlain shocked speechless. "We were going to tell you later," she said, as Latias opened his mouth, then closed it. Jaladar was almost his impassive self, but his thin lips twitched.

"I see," Latias managed at last. He tilted his head back and studied them. Then he smiled. "Luminessa, my lord Brander, I am very happy for you. My congratulations are all I can offer at the moment, but they are genuine."

"Thank you, Latias," Mandine said. "But I know you're thinking about the implications."

Latias surveyed them, and Key's first meeting with the chamberlain returned vividly to his mind. The man's power had been intimidating. *But I was only a soldier then,* Key thought, *or I believed I was. Now all has changed. I've changed. The blood of Ilarion Tessaris beats in me, and on our journey west I've felt it stronger in me, day by day.*

The chamberlain inspected a grape, then put it down. "Yes, Luminessa, I'm thinking about them, because it is my duty to do so. I am sure, however, that you and my lord Brander will act in all ways for the best."

"Latias," Key said gently, "I would never presume to know your mind, but is it possible that the word *adventurer* might recently have crossed it?"

The chamberlain hesitated, again thrown off-balance. Key sympathized with his predicament. Latias clearly put his loyalty to Mandine above all else, and now she had chosen as consort, and therefore as Dynast, a back-country, foreign noble who might be a disaster for both her and the Ascendancy, assuming it and they survived.

"Of course not, my lord Brander." Latias set his elbows on the table, put his head in his hands, and clutched at his hair in frustration. Then he said, unhappily, "Very well, since you speak so plainly. If you were in my position, might not the word, or the possibility of it, have crossed your thoughts? Marriage is not as simple for a luminessa as it is for a baker's daughter."

"But is it *really* so simple for a baker's daughter?" Mandine asked, in a voice of total innocence. "I'm sure neither of us would know that, Latias."

"Luminessa, that's not the point," the chamberlain said desperately. His eyes were fixed on a sunsip pit by his elbow.

Key glanced at Mandine. She was trying to keep a straight face, but her eyes said: *Have mercy on the poor man. Tell him.*

"I think I can relieve your concern," Key said. He described briefly the betrothal agreement between Ilarion Tessaris and Critalli Min Banain. Latias lifted his head from his hands and listened carefully. Key paused, and the chamberlain's gaze flicked to Mandine and back. "I think I see," he murmured. "Do I?"

"Yes," Key said. "Critalli was my great-great-grandmother. I am a Tessaris, and as far as I know, the only living male of that line. I wear Ilarion's ring." He placed his left hand flat on the table, so that the emerald glowed in the lamplight. He had put on the ring in the upper catacombs; since he was returning to his ancestral city, the act had seemed fitting.

Latias leaned forward to examine the carved emerald. "Ah, yes. The pandragore was Ilarion's personal emblem, though few now know that. Good. The question of your ranks, then, is nugatory. They are as equal as makes no difference." His face showed enormous relief.

"Just as much to the point," Mandine said, "is that we were united by the Lord and Lady themselves. Key and I love each other, Latias, as the Two love each other."

"Then no power can put you apart," the chamberlain said. He rose and bowed to Key. "My lord Tessaris, I noted a familiarity about you when we first met. I could not place it then, but I can now. I have access to books and papers about our history that others don't, and you bear a strong resemblance to the likenesses of Ilarion I have seen. The resemblance must have nudged me." He looked from one to the other. "I am not the only citizen who will be overjoyed to see Mandine and the House Tessaris in the Fountain Palace together. Welcome back, my lord Dynast and my lady Dynastessa."

"Thank you, Lord Chamberlain." Key grinned. "However, I would be obliged if you would call me, as Mandine does, Key. And please sit down."

Latias resumed his seat. "Key, then, with your permission. I think I am beginning to recover from my delighted astonishment. What now?"

"We go to the Hill of Remembrance," said Mandine.

"With Theatana still in control of the city?" Latias frowned. "That's very dangerous. Also, you can't just walk off the Mount, through her cordon. No one's allowed to pass in or out."

"You said you had a way through the Metradora Cistern," Key said. "Could we use that?"

"I advise against it. Wardsmen almost caught me there two nights ago, and after last night's riot, every thug Tefraos can find will be patrolling the streets. You should proclaim yourself from here, but not until we let the city know that you've come back, and we bring at least some of the Guard over to you."

Mandine leaned toward the chamberlain. "No, Latias, you don't understand. Key and I can't wait. Erkai's far, far too dangerous. We don't know what he's getting ready to do, and he's the real enemy."

The door suddenly resounded with frantic rapping. Jaladar and Lonn leaped to their feet and drew their swords.

"One of ours," Latias said hurriedly, and went to open the door. A young priestess stood in it, her face stricken. She appeared to see only Latias.

"Soldiers, Eminence," she gasped. "On the lower ramp. They're coming up."

"Allfather curse them. How many?"

"I don't know, Eminence. But I counted a score of torches. I think they're those soldiers the usurper put around the foot of the Mount, to keep people away."

"Wait right there," Latias said to the priestess. He turned to Mandine and Key. "Theatana's going even farther," he said. "I'd gamble that last night's riot for the Perpetua and the Continuator precipitated this. I don't know what she's intending, but if she puts men up here—"

"Wait," Key said. "Those Paladines she posted around the Mount. The rank and file can't like this sacrilege. How loyal are they to her?"

"The men on the cordon aren't Paladines. They're cataphracts, from the Fifth Tercia, the men who got away from Essardene with you and the luminessa. There's about a hundred and fifty of them. What are you thinking?"

Key sat up straight. "Who commands them now?"

"Guard officers. Dactulis and Theatana wouldn't trust anyone else."

Key turned to Mandine. "I think it's the only way, beloved. We have to bring the men to us, if you're willing to try."

She took a deep breath, let it out. "Yes, we must."

Latias looked from one to the other. "What? You're going to appeal to the soldiers, *now*?"

"It's our best chance," Mandine said. "We can't run from Captala. I've done it once, and I won't do it again."

"But—"

"I'm with you," Lonn said, and Jaladar grinned ferociously.

Latias's face contorted. "This is . . ." He suddenly laughed, and years fell from him. "Very well. I also am sick of hiding." He turned to the door and the waiting priestess. "Bring torches, and meet us by the high altar. The luminessa must be seen."

"The *luminessa*?" The woman peered past the chamberlain, and her voice rose in surprise and delight. "It is! Sweet Lady, she's really here! She's come back!"

"Yes, she has. But quickly, girl, the torches."

The priestess scurried away. Everyone else walked after her, into the vast, shadowy nave of the temple, where lamps burned between the columns. Hand in hand, Key and Mandine halted before the statues. Hand in hand, smiling their serene and enigmatic smiles, the Allfather and the Lady gazed down on them. The others waited in silence, watching. *Help us*, Mandine prayed. *Give us the strength to do this.*

"If we die," she murmured, "we'll still be together, won't we?"

"Yes," Key said, "but we won't die."

They left the statues and walked through the temple's open doors, into the plaza. Whispering excitedly, a score of priests, acolytes, and priestesses had already gathered by the high altar. The sacred flame burned there, spreading the fragrance of hyacinths and roses. Above the sanctuary hung the star-spattered dark.

The priestess ran up to them, a bundle in her arms. "Three torches, my lord. All I could find."

"It's enough," Key said. "Jaladar, Latias, Lonn, light them."

He and Mandine waited while they kindled the torches at the altar. Then they all crossed the plaza and passed under Pylon Gate. Before them, the long ramp sloped down the flank of Temple Mount, to bend left at the halfway mark. At the bend was a torchlit column of soldiers advancing on foot. In the still-distant glow Mandine could see three men on horseback beside the column, the officers.

They walked on down the ramp. Beyond its marble balustrade, the lights of Captala lay sprinkled across the hills. Mandine looked over her shoulder, into the northeast. Out there rose the Hill of Remembrance, and the Obelisk, and beyond them the walls, and there in the dregs of night crouched Erkai. Though she knew his Craft could not reach her here, she imagined she sensed his hatred: savage, pitiless, implacable. She shuddered and put her arm through Key's.

Ahead of them a voice barked a command, and a Guard peltarch rode to the column's front rank, followed by a victurion. The third officer lingered behind.

"Move up," Key said to Jaladar and the others. "Shine the light on her face."

They now formed a line of their own, a wisp of a line facing the armored, measured tread of the cataphract column. It was twelve men across, stretching the breadth of the ramp. In the middle of the column, torches bobbed above gleaming helmets, and the lead ranks marched with spears advanced. In the flickering red light the blades glinted like the eyes of beasts. Key looked for men he knew, but the faces were too shadowed and too distant for recognition. They would not know him yet, either. He hoped that Melias, his old second-in-command, was in the column somewhere.

The hedge of spears was thirty yards away. Mandine stopped, and Key and the others halted with her. She held up her right hand, palm open toward the advancing men. The spears wavered very slightly, as though a ripple passed through a pool of still water. Key recognized the sign: These men were uneasy.

Uneasiness was not enough to halt them. Their spears had dipped a little, but the relentless tramp of their advance never faltered. Key stepped forward and held up his torch. "*Now*, Mandine."

Her words carried strong and clear through the night. "Soldiers of the Fifth! You who were with me at Essardene!"

A murmur swept the armored ranks. The tread skipped a beat, and the spearpoints wavered uncertainly.

"Soldiers of the Fifth!" Mandine called again. "Soldiers, I have come back. Do you not know your luminessa?"

Now Key saw faces he knew, and Melias in the second rank. But no one was looking at him. All eyes were fixed on Mandine. The spears were a dozen yards away. Mandine did not step back.

"Allfather above," a voice exclaimed, "it's *her*."

"Silence, there!" yelled the peltarch. But the men at the column's head broke step, slowed, and faltered to a halt. Behind them, the following ranks blundered into the backs of their comrades, and in moments the whole column was a muttering, cursing confusion. The Guard victurion bellowed orders at the peltarch, who seemed paralyzed with astonishment. For long moments, Mandine stood perfectly still, waiting. The men gaped at her, Melias wide-eyed among them.

"At the double, *march!*" screamed the victurion, ignoring the peltarch to address the men directly.

The cataphracts did not move.

Mandine took three paces forward and opened her arms. "I am here, " she said. "I am truly your Luminessa Mandine, but if you wish to kill me, I will not run from your spears."

Beside the victurion, the peltarch hunched in his saddle, staring at her. The victurion's mouth worked, and he looked wildly over his shoulder toward the third officer. "Treimarch Dactulis—"

The man rose in his stirrups. "Damn your eyes, victurion, kill them!"

"Up spears!" screamed the victurion. He dragged his sword from its scabbard, raised it. "On my command, volley!"

A dozen spearpoints rose hesitantly. The peltarch also had drawn his blade.

"I am your luminessa," Mandine said, her voice clear and

undaunted. "Soldiers of the Fifth, you saved me at Essardene. Will you kill me now?"

A breathless instant passed.

"No!" Melias yelled into the silence. "Down spears!"

"Down spears!" the peltarch bellowed, and calmly reached out and stabbed the victurion through the wrist. The officer shrieked, and dropped his blade. The peltarch grabbed him by his cloak, dragged him off his horse, and hurled him to the ground. "She's home, lads," he shouted. "The luminessa's home."

A roar went up from the cataphracts. They broke ranks and surged forward, surrounding Mandine and Key, beating spear blades on shields in a thunder of iron on toughened hide. Torchlight glared and danced on steel, shimmered on armor and tossing helmets, and the shouts rose to the sky.

Mandine! Mandine! Dynastessa! Dynastessa!

Someone grabbed Key by the arm. It was Melias. "Kienan Mec Brander, by the Allfather! I thought it was you, but—"

"It's me." Key was ablaze with relief and exultation, but it was too soon, too soon; they had hardly begun. "For pity's sake, we need order here. Where's that Guard peltarch? Get him to help; he seems to be on our side."

It took five minutes to bring the men under control. It helped that Key had once commanded them; they were excited at seeing him, and delighted that he was, for whatever reason, with Mandine. As Melias finished browbeating them into rank, Key sought out the peltarch.

"You've come over to the luminessa, for which I thank you. What will the Paladine rank and file do?"

The peltarch spat. "They'll follow her, my lord. They've no use for that bitch Theatana anymore, not with her executions and her sacrilege. The long-servicers like me will bring the Guard over, and the officers will have to run for it, like the victurion and that breechclout Dactulis just did. The lads'll put Theatana's head in a basket, too, if they can catch the usurping slut."

"I'll have orders for you," Key said. "Wait."

Mandine was leaning on the ramp's balustrade, looking out over the city. Latias paced up and down nearby, obviously thinking. Lonn and Jaladar held the two horses that had belonged to the peltarch and the now-fled victurion.

"They listened to me," Mandine said as Key reached her side. "For a moment I didn't think they would. Now we have soldiers. That's a start, at least."

Latias joined them, and Key passed on the peltarch's estimate of the Guard. Mandine's expression grew worried. "But Dactulis got away. By now he's at the Fountain Palace, warning my sister that I've come back. Latias, you've watched Theatana these three months. If she thought she had nothing to lose, would she do something truly mad?"

Latias said, "Do you mean, would she try to bring the world down with her?"

"That's what worries me most. Would she give the city to the Tathars, or to Erkai, to avenge herself?"

The chamberlain scowled. "She would have to be truly mad to do that. But she's in our grasp, now. She has no time to act on it."

Mandine shivered. "I know my sister. What she wants and can't have, she does her best to destroy. And even if she's mad, she's cunning. She always has been. Key, we have to take the Signata to the Hill of Remembrance. Now."

* 28

A WIND FROM THE SEA SWEPT HISSING AMONG THE
tents, strumming at their guy ropes and making the pennons
flap. Beside Erkai, the cold rush of the gale blew the flames of
a watch fire into long banners of smoky orange. As if in answer, a beacon cresset, whipped by the wind, flared and
gleamed high on the barbican tower of Processional Gate. The
trenches before him were empty, for the Tathar sentries had
slunk out of his presence hours ago. In the east the sky was no
longer quite black, and already the Day Star rode the horizon.

Erkai waited, watching. Theatana Dascaris was ripe, and
he was sure she would submit to his will before the sun rose.

Come to me, woman. Come to me, for what I will give you.

His dark eyes narrowed. Was that movement on the outer
wall, a flash of metal reflecting the glare of the tower beacon?

It was. He saw her now, in the light of the cresset. She
raised something to her face, and he saw the glint again. Cold
amusement glided through him. She was watching him
through a spyglass, as if she could plumb his thoughts by
observing him from afar. And neither her house standard nor
the banner of the Ascendancy flew above the battlements, so
she had come alone. She was ripe indeed.

He bent all the power of his ferocious will toward her and
struggled against the spell that held him at bay. *Let me in. Let
me in, Theatana Dascaris, and find your heart's desire.*

He heard a faint hail from within the wall, and she suddenly vanished. Erkai's nostrils flared, and he bared his teeth. He sought patience, found it, and his lips closed. She knew he was here. She would return.

After a full two minutes, she did. She was looking at him from between the merlons again. Again he fought to reach her, though he was almost sure he did not need to. She had been tainted with the Black Craft when he first laid eyes on her, and he knew how swiftly that power could corrupt.

Let me in. With me you will find the sweetnesses you crave.

He strove to feel her response, and for an instant, and because she had at last reached out to him, he succeeded.

I need you. Come to me, and I will let you in.

She vanished from the parapet. The Day Star was a finger's width above the sea, and the eastern horizon was gray. Erkai stirred, and moved from the watch fire into the dimness. He crossed the trench by a wooden cavalry bridge, a shadow among other shadows in his dark cloak. Then he passed silently and invisibly through the no-man's-land between the siege lines and the walls, heading for the left-hand gate tower. No alarm sounded from the ramparts.

At the tower's base was a sally port, a narrow iron door set deep into the massive stones. As he reached it he heard sounds from within, men's worried voices at first, then hers, harsh and imperious. There was a pause, and iron scraped on iron as the bars slid back.

The door opened. Theatana stood before him, a torch in her hand. Erkai studied her. Her eyes glittered, and her cheeks were flushed. Behind her were two sally port guards and an officer.

"Let him pass," she commanded. Her voice shook with eagerness, and with that eagerness, fear and rage.

Erkai glided into the tunnel that led into the wall's thickness, and the gate clanged shut behind him. The guards must have guessed who he was, for they stood rigid with terror. The officer's mouth twitched, but no sound came out. Theatana thrust the torch at him, and he took it wordlessly.

"Well done," Erkai murmured in his softest voice. She flushed deeper, and he felt her lust; not for a man, but for the feeding of darker, older hungers. Then she put her shoulders back, and he saw the swell of her breasts beneath her cloak.

The little fool, he thought. *She thinks her body will control me. I'll teach her otherwise, when her time comes. But there's more here. She's afraid, very afraid.*

"I come at a time of need?" he asked.

"The city is rising against me," Theatana said. She wet her lips. "We know each other's minds, Lord Erkai. Help me against the mob, and we'll rule together."

Her attempt to bargain was ridiculous, as was her idea that she knew anything at all about him. Did she not suspect what she had let into her city? Could she not see that it was not her city now?

"What of this officer?" he asked, savoring the moment as he gestured at the man. "Can he not help you?"

She almost spat. "Dactulis? He's failed me in everything. Lord Erkai, we have little time. This so-called officer of mine has just now brought word that Mandine my sister is on Temple Mount, and the Guard is going over to her."

Erkai hissed, and the guards cringed and fell back. "Your sister?"

"Yes." She stepped forward, her breasts almost touching him, and he smelled her perfume. "Join me, and we can defeat her. Then we can rule as one."

He barely heard her. "Has she brought sorcery?"

"What? I don't know what you mean. What sorcery? And how should I know? She's still on Temple Mount, or near it." Theatana's voice rose, shrilling along the passage. "Do you accept my offer? *Do you?*"

Erkai thought: *Mandine is here, but she's using soldiers. If she's found the Signata, she's not yet learned to wield it. But I must be quick.*

"I accept," he murmured. Should they accompany him? Yes; Theatana's authority would hold long enough to speed him on his way, and he would use the officer for a spell of protection. "Now we must go to the Hill of Remembrance, all three of us. Do you have horses nearby?"

"I do." She turned to the stricken guards. "Remain here. Call no one. Dactulis, come with us."

Dactulis whirled and hurried along the tunnel. Theatana followed him. Behind her, Erkai's feet whispered across the stones. They passed through the sally port's inner gate, into the chasm between the outer and the second wall. There, three horses were tethered to an empty torch bracket. "I sent my escort away," Theatana said, "but I kept a horse back for you." She gave him a contorted smile, her eyes aglitter, their pupils huge and dark. "Anything I have is yours. What do you need?"

Erkai chuckled. She was half-crazed now with her corruption and her fear. But later, for her attempts to use him, he would deliver her to real madness. "You will know on the Hill of Remembrance," he told her as he mounted. "At the Obelisk."

"Why? What are you going to do there?"

"I am going to break the Ban of Athanais."

"What?" She laughed wildly. "No one can break the Ban."

For that laugh and those words she would flop and squirm and shriek. "I can," Erkai said.

Long reefs of cloud lay pink and silver in the eastern sky. The wind from the sea was blowing the night away, though stars still glimmered in the indigo overhead. The cataphracts tramped along Pallion Street, Mandine and Key riding side by side in the column's center. At their stirrups marched Lonn, Latias, and Jaladar, and behind them in the dawnlight flowed a growing multitude of Captala's citizens. The people had begun to appear as the column rolled from Temple Mount into Optimates' Street, and now the word of Mandine's return was spreading like fire in dry thatch. The crowd's chant rose and fell like breakers combing the shores of the Inner Sea.

Mandine! Mandine is Dynastessa! Down with the usurper! Down with the tyrant!

Despite their acclaim, she felt no exultation. Victory over Theatana was not victory over the real enemy, and she could not cast off the foreboding that had gripped her on the temple ramp.

She turned to Key. "This is taking too long. We have to leave the soldiers and ride on ahead."

He looked uneasy. "It's a risk. Dactulis got away, and by now Theatana must know you're back. She'd only need a handful of Mixtun archers to end it for us."

"Key, we *must* go on. I feel it."

He shot her a worried glance, then leaned from his saddle. "Latias."

The chamberlain looked up. "Trouble?"

"Perhaps. Take over here, with Melias. Mandine and I are going ahead, to the Obelisk. Follow on."

"Is that wise?"

"She thinks so."

"Very well. We'll get there as fast as we can."

Key clapped the chamberlain on the shoulder and straightened. "Let's go, my love," he said to Mandine.

They passed among the marching cataphracts to the column's head, then pushed the horses into a gallop. As the tramp of hobnailed boots faded behind them, Mandine heard Melias shout for double pace.

"The men won't be long," Key called to her. "They'll be at the Hill in half a turn of the glass." Mandine did not answer. The foreboding was now a sick weight in her midriff.

But what must we do? she asked herself again and again, as they raced down Pallion Street. *What will the Signata become, on the Hill of Remembrance? What will it do to us? Sweet Lady, all I want is to live, with Key. Only that. I will give you all else, only grant us that.*

They reached the Hill's foot in less than ten minutes. It was clad in woodland and gardens, with the white stone of Athanais's sepulchre gleaming just below the bare, grassy summit, and at the summit rose the stark black pinnacle of the Obelisk. Without breaking their gallop, they raced through the open lower gate and pounded through the trees toward the hilltop. Clods of earth and tattered flowers flew from the hooves; Mandine bent low over her horse's neck, urging it on as foam spattered from its flaring nostrils. Then they burst from the wood into the open, and there ahead was the granite base of the Obelisk, and above it the colossal stone shaft rearing into the dawn sky.

And at its base, a soldier with a bloody mouth lay on the grass, and a woman and a cloaked man stood near him.

For an instant Mandine thought they were refugees, but then she saw that the soldier was Dactulis, the woman was Theatana, and the cloaked man held in his hands a silver chain. Mandine's horse neighed with alarm and terror, stumbled, and almost threw her. In the corner of her eye she saw Key fighting his terrified mount to a halt, then her own beast stopped, head down, every muscle quivering. She tried to make it move, but it would not.

"He's here," she said with a dry mouth. "Erkai's here."

"Yes," Key said. "Dismount, Mandine."

They dropped to the ground. The wind blew strong from the sea, flattening the grass, moaning around the Obelisk's gigantic shaft. On this very spot, Mandine knew, Athanais had uttered the spell of the Ban; and here, to test its strength, she had tried to break it, and so died.

"Has the Signata changed?" Key asked quietly. Erkai had not moved; though something had terrified the horses, he did not seem aware of Key's or Mandine's presence. Silent, Theatana watched them, her arms folded into her cloak.

With shaking hands, Mandine undid her sabretache and drew out the Signata. She looked at it lying in her palm. It was nothing. It was a small white stone.

"It's the same," she whispered. "And it's all we have. Against *him*."

Key's face was set hard. "It will be enough," he said. "Or steel will be." He drew his sword, and slowly they walked toward the Obelisk and the pair beneath it. Erkai stood motionless as the stone spire itself. His gaze was fixed on the chain, and his lips moved, but no speech came from them. Only Theatana watched them approach. Her cheeks were flushed red, and her eyes gleamed with frenzied exaltation.

"Theatana," Mandine called to her sister, "are you demented? In the name of the Two, what have you *done*?"

Theatana laughed, a wild, cold, brittle laugh. "You're too late, sister," she cried. "Too late. I rule here. I have your death for you, and it will be long and slow." She kicked Dactulis's head. "Not like this one's. He let the soldiers go to you, so when we got here I let Erkai have him. Erkai swallowed him for a spell, so don't bother trying to use steel. It won't work."

"You're mad," Key said. He watched the chain in Erkai's fingers. A silver link slid from right hand to left. Erkai's lips moved.

"Am I? Wait. The spell takes time, Erkai says, but I'm sure he's almost done. Then you'll see who's mad. Are you her lover? I have a sharp little knife for you. You'll love her much less, and she you, when I'm done."

Key strode forward, sword ready, keeping between Mandine and her half sister. Theatana danced aside, grinning. "I'm not going to hurt her now, soldier. But I will."

Key ignored her and swung the blade two-handed at Erkai. The hilt twisted in his grip, a brutal force snatched at his arm, and suddenly the sword's point was buried six inches in the earth at Key's feet.

"I told you," Theatana crowed.

Key wrenched the useless blade from the turf. He watched as another link of the chain slipped between Erkai's fingers. Each link in the right hand was graven with a hieroglyph. The links in his left were unmarked, the symbols vanishing as the chain traveled and the spell wove. Already Key felt iciness gathering in the air around him. He sheathed his sword and backed away to stand beside Mandine.

"His spell won't work against the Ban," he said. "It will kill him. He's as mad as Theatana."

"No madness," Theatana cried. "He knows how to break

the Ban; he said so, and I've let him in so he can do it. I'll share his power."

"What are we going to do?" Mandine said. Her body trembled, but her mind had passed through fear into a cold calm.

Before Key could answer, Erkai threw back his head. The last link of the chain slid through his fingers, and he shouted a single word in no tongue Mandine knew. But the wind did not blow the word away; it echoed, as if from a deep pit, then reechoed, then grew ever louder as it fed upon itself. The hill itself rumbled, and Theatana screamed. A huge flake of stone peeled from the base of the Obelisk, and the pillar swayed as a black swirl of cloud formed above Erkai's head. The air clanged and froze, the grass slid from beneath Mandine's feet, and she fell to her knees.

Erkai opened his eyes and looked at her.

They were not eyes, but drains into an abyss. They sucked at her soul. His form swelled, consuming the cloud above him, and still the abyss stared into her. She put her clenched hands over her eyes and felt Key dragging her to her feet. The hill quivered like a drumhead, and the word resounded in it and above it, as if the wind and the earth roared it into Mandine's ears.

"You can't break the Ban," she screamed into the blast. "You're dying, Erkai."

He laughed at her. The sound pierced her heart and her hope, and she staggered. Her hands fell from her eyes, and she saw before her a roiling shape of harsh light and impenetrable shadow. It twisted her mind and her sight, as if it would draw her with it into a gulf unspeakable.

"The spell kills the living," said a voice from the black pit. "But I am the twice-born. I died, and was raised again. The Ban was flawed. I will live."

"Go back," Key shouted at it. "Go back to the Adversary. Go back to your master."

Again the terrible laugh. "I have no master. But I might spare you yet, if you will serve Me."

"We have the Signata," Mandine called into the wind's howl. "Go, or be sent."

"The Signata does nothing. Throw it down before Me. Serve Me."

"Never!" Mandine screamed. Key's hand clasped hers, and she felt, nestled between their palms, the hard white stone. Together, hands joined, they raised it against the creature from the pit, against the thanaturge. From the clear sky a bolt of lightning speared the tip of the Obelisk. Huge chunks of granite fell from the shaft, into the howling gale. The Signata was a feather's weight against Mandine's palm.

Erkai took form from the whirlwind. He raised his arms, the cloak flying about his shoulders like gray wings. He chanted a curse, and the chain stiffened and rose from his hand. Blue fires crackled about its tip. Mandine clenched her hand tighter around Key's.

Lady, Allfather, aid us now at the hour of our deaths.

Erkai shouted the last syllable of the curse. A plume of darkness, like black oil, shot from the chain's tip, coiled, and launched itself toward them.

The Signata awoke.

The hill was gone, and all with it. Mandine found herself afloat in a sea of light, though it was no light of the world. Nearby she felt Key's mind and thoughts, and the unformed, wordless presence of another. With astonishment, she realized that the other was within her.

Key, I'm with child.

I know. Beloved, Mandine, now what are we to do? How did we come to this? How has he won?

Suddenly, she knew: She saw Erkai flee mortally wounded from battle, saw how he died in fury and pain in his grandmother's arms. She heard the woman call on the blackest spell of the Black Craft, to burn herself away to restore her grandson's life, not for love, but for hatred and vengeance. Because of her hate he was twice-born, and the Ban would not hold him. And Mandine knew, with terrible grief, that the last hope for his defeat lay in nothing less than the surrender of their lives, though even that sacrifice might not be enough.

But she saw also that they could choose to live. If they willed it, the Signata could release them far from the Hill of Remembrance, far from what awaited them there. They could live, and their child with them, but the darkness would win. They had been chosen to resist it, but they could also choose to turn away.

Key, this is what the Signata does. It reveals our true choices. It is not power, but knowledge.

Yes. There is an escape for us, Mandine. But if we do not take it—

Then we will die, Key, and our child with us. But perhaps our world may live.

But will it? Nothing tells me that even our deaths will destroy the evil.

I know. We must decide, without knowing.

She knew he wept, as she did. *Sweet Lady,* she prayed, *let this cup pass from us. Let our child live. We can choose, our child cannot. Sweet Lady, this is too hard a choice.*

She heard no answer. *Key,* she whispered into the silence and the light, *we must accept. We have come so far, and we must accept. Or the darkness wins.*

How? To accept for ourselves is easy. How can we accept it for our child?

We must. You know we must. And we must go willingly.

I know. But are you willing, Mandine?

I will try to be. I love you.

I love you.

Come.

And with that, the Signata touched her again.

—and for a moment that was all moments, Mandine was: each grain of sand on all the shores of the Blue; the living sap within an oak ten thousand years dead; every stone of a temple in a city she had never seen; every leaf of every forest of the world. She was within the Signata, and the Signata was within her. The instant was forever, yet vanished before she could grasp it, and she drifted again in silence and light.

Key, where are you?

Suddenly he was with her, and they stood together at the heart of a love so boundless that it was almost beyond her power to bear. Yet she did bear it, for she knew that she and her husband and child had risen from it, and it was within them. It was the mystery beyond the created and the uncreated, the love that lay beneath the foundations of time, and their strength against Erkai the Chain.

I accept, Key. And you?

Yes.

Without warning, they were on the hill. Around their clasped hands burned a halo of radiance, and into it plunged the black spear of Erkai's curse. Agony blazed through Mandine. She was aflame, she was burning, burning alive. Her sight clouded in a haze of pain. *This is dying,* she thought. *I'm sorry, my child. I'm sorry, Key.*

She heard Key's scream, and her own. Pain seared along every nerve. It flowed through her, into the orb of light around their joined hands, and the radiance swelled. Erkai struck again, and his hate devoured her, melted flesh from her bones, charred her black. Yet the light absorbed the hatred, flared, and bloomed brighter. A third time he lashed out, and now the radiance about the Signata blossomed like a white rose, became a rainbow, swept over Key and Mandine in a jeweled flood. Erkai's chain coiled about his wrist, and exploded in a spasm of blue fire. He shrieked and fell to his knees, a black ruin where his hand had been. The jeweled light was a whirlwind, a torrent.

Out of it came a shadow, and the shadow had a voice. It spoke in Mandine's mind, cold and joyless, and freighted with everlasting despair.

Come to me, servant.

Erkai shrieked again. His good arm flailed dementedly. The shadow hovered above him, implacable in its bitterness and pain.

I have made a place for you, forever. Come.

"Take them!" he screamed. "Them! I give them to you."

They are not yours to give. They have already been taken.

The shadow folded about him, wrenched him howling from the earth, and fled into the light. With a stupendous crack the Obelisk split, and from where Erkai had knelt, a pillar of cold white fire exploded into the sky.

Mandine's hand slipped from Key's, and the Signata tumbled earthward. Dazed, she looked down for it. The white stone was gone. Where it should be, she herself lay on the scorched grass, her eyes open and unseeing. And beside her lay Key, staring as sightless as she at the morning sky, as the Obelisk fell.

From the siege lines Ragula and the king saw the pillar of fire roar heavenward from the hill. Stark terror seized the duke; the wine cup fell from his hand, and his eyes froze in their sockets. All around him the army of the Tathars stumbled from their tents, crawled from their trenches, turned from their siege engines, to gaze in sweating horror at the column of light.

"There are *faces*," Hetlik screamed.

Ragula was unmanned, and his bowels loosened. It was as though his sight were drawn into the pillar itself, and he saw into the Signata, into the faces, and knew all that he had done. He saw the innocent dead, the shades of the multitudes left in the army's reeking trail.

They reached for him. And he knew what awaited him in their grasp: to endure forever every agony he had inflicted, every stake's point and every cut of the skinning knife, the crazed grief of mothers bereft, and of men whose wives and children shrieked and bled before their eyes.

Ragula turned and ran, and the king and the army of the Tathars ran with him. Demented, they slew each other as they fled, sword to sword and spear to spear, and the dust thickened with their blood. Through the tents they howled and fought, past the siege towers and the palisades, past the skinning frames and the stakes, until they came to Chalice Bay.

Still their madness grew, and they killed each other in the shallows, in the breakers, in the deeps beyond, strangling and shrieking until the waters closed over them, and in their tens of thousands they were gone.

And in the gardens of the Hill of Remembrance, Theatana ran howling, and with each step she felt a noose snap tight about her slender neck.

✳ 29

MANDINE OPENED HER EYES. SHE FELT RESTED AND UT-
terly at peace. Above her was a blue morning sky, and as she
gazed into it a warm breeze, rich with the rainy scent of amaranth, brushed her face. She sat up blinking, for the sunlight
was so strong that at first she could hardly see.

Key sat beside her, rubbing his eyes. "Good morning,"
he said.

"Good morning." Memory stirred in her, and she saw
them lying silent together on the burned hill, while the Obelisk
fell about them. But all that seemed very far away, and long
ago, like a grief worn smooth by time.

She looked around. They were in a garden, or a wild that
seemed a garden. Trees laden with amber fruit stood among
fountains of white roses, and drifts of silver amaranth lay like
sea-foam in the grass. A few yards from them, a brook tumbled
over mossy stones.

She looked at him. Like her, he was whole. "Did we die,
Key?"

He shook his head in perplexity. "I don't know. I think
we must have. I saw you there."

"I saw you, too."

"But did Erkai die? I saw something take him."

"I think it was the Adversary," Mandine said, and even in

this gentle place she felt a ripple of dread. "I didn't see what happened after that. We were just . . . here."

"Our clothing has improved," he said, laughing.

Mandine looked down at herself. She wore a green mantle, and embroidered into it was a necklace of grain and flowers. Or it seemed embroidery, but when she moved, the wheat and the blooms appeared utterly real. Key's mantle was blue, and into it was woven the golden wheel of the sun. It glowed as if from a light within.

"Key, what *is* this place? Are we inside the Signata?"

"Everywhere is inside the Signata," said a voice from close behind them.

They turned and got hastily to their feet. By a tree of roses stood a smiling, dark-haired woman in the loveliest prime of life. She wore a white tunic, belted at the waist with gold.

"My Lady?" Mandine whispered.

The woman laughed merrily. "No, I am not she. But the Two have sent me. I am Athanais."

"Athanais?" Key said, wonderstruck.

The woman smiled. "Indeed I am. The Signata marked me in life, as it has you. That is why I am here."

Mandine looked around. "But where *is* here?"

"A garden, among other gardens. A way to other ways, if you like."

There was a silence. Then Key asked, "Are we dead?"

"You are, in the world you have left."

"But did we win?" Mandine said hesitantly.

"Yes. Erkai the Chain is no more, and the killers from the west are dead by their own cruel hands. But my Ban has fallen. What will come of this I cannot tell, though for a time your world is safe."

"But how did we win?" Mandine asked. "What did we do?"

The lovely face turned grave. "You gave yourselves to death that others might live. And far harder than that, you chose death for your child, who was innocent and who would have been yours, if you had taken the other path. There is no greater love than this."

Mandine's peace fled. Sorrow enfolded her, for herself and for Key and for the child she would never know. She was empty, bereft, and she put her face in her hands and wept. She felt Key's arms around her, and his cheek wet with tears against hers.

"But there is a gift for you," Athanais said. "Key, Mandine, look at me."

Mandine raised her gaze to the eyes of the Diviner. "What gift?" she whispered, with an aching throat.

"It is this. Because you so freely gave life away, it freely may be returned to you. If you will, you may return to the world, and know your children."

There was a silence, in which trilled the sound of flowing water. "If we return, will we remember this place, and you?" Key asked.

"As in a dream," Athanais said, "but a dream whose memory never fades. It will, perhaps, sustain you when the way turns dark, as it must do from time to time, for all. Will you return to your world, to laugh and to mourn, to hope and to despair, to live and to die?"

"Yes," they answered.

"Come with me," she said.

They walked to the brook. In Athanais's hands was a cup of common red pottery. She filled it to the brim and held it out to them. Together they accepted it from her.

"This is the water of life," she said. "Take, and drink."

Heartsick, Latias stumbled across the ruins of the Obelisk. He was weeping, a thing he had not done for thirty years. He could not fathom why Mandine and Key had to die in the moment of their victory. It was not just.

The heaps of shattered granite blurred, and he paused to wipe his eyes. Jaladar and Lonn were searching among the piles of broken stone, as were the soldiers. But the search seemed hopeless. The bodies must be crushed and buried, hidden deep under tons of rubble. Yet they must be found. They must have burial and the proper rites.

Lonn and Jaladar scrambled over a wedge of rock to stand near him. They'd been at Latias's side, at the hill's foot, when the ground shook. There had been an incandescence, and a boiling cloud, and Latias had understood that the cloud was of Erkai, and that Theatana had betrayed them all. Then darkness fell, and he was fixed in his place, unable to move or cry out. He had no idea how long he'd been rooted there, but when the darkness lifted the Obelisk was gone, and the crown of the hill burned black.

The crowds that had followed them had promptly run away in terror, and even the cataphracts had been unwilling to climb the hill until Latias harangued them. On the way to the summit they found Theatana, incoherent, mad-eyed, and clawing at her throat, and Latias put her under guard. But at the top there was no sign of Erkai, nor any trace of Key or Mandine, only the fallen Obelisk. Perhaps Orissi or Taras could explain what had happened; Latias had already sent men to the Numera to free them.

"The Tathars are gone!" Lonn exclaimed suddenly, and pointed at the landscape beyond the distant walls. "Look!"

Latias did so. At this hour the Tathar camp should have seethed with the enemy, but all was still. Many dots lay in and around it, and Latias realized suddenly that they were corpses. A tent was burning, and no fire party scuttled to put it out. While the chamberlain watched, a second tent took flame.

"But where did they go?" he said. "What killed them?"

Jaladar's eyes narrowed. "I see things washing along the shore," he said. "Like logs, but I think not. There are too many. Not logs, Tathars. Something unmanned them, and they fought each other, and ran into the sea."

"We're delivered," Latias said, "but at what a cost."

"We have to find them," said Lonn. "They might still be alive. Trapped in a crevice."

"The stones must be moved." Latias squared his shoulders. "We need more men, and ropes. I'll go."

He scrambled onto a huge slab of granite, but as he started across it the rock tilted and began to slide. Lonn yelled a warning, but the slab was already on the move. Latias staggered, fell to his knees, and clung desperately to its edge. With a rumble the stone slid farther, a foot, two feet, three, and Latias saw an oblong cavity slowly reveal itself below him. Dust shot into the air. Coughing, with watering eyes, he peered into the opening.

The stone stopped.

"They're here!" he shouted. "They're here!"

He swung down into the hole. They had been entombed. Key lay there, his eyes closed, his face and armor powdered with dust. Beside him, beneath the shroud of her cloak, lay Mandine. She looked as if she only slept.

"My lady," Latias said brokenly, as he knelt beside her. "Luminessa, come back."

He touched her throat. A pulse beat beneath his fingertips, and her flesh was warm. Latias saw Key's eyelids flicker, and heard him take a deep breath.

Slowly, Mandine opened her eyes and looked up at the chamberlain. She smiled. "Hello, Latias," she murmured. "Are you all right?"

✳ 30

KEY AND MANDINE SAT WITH LATIAS IN THE SOLARIUM of the House Azure. The glass above them was misted with dust from the nearby hillside where, until three months ago, the Dynasteon had stood. Mandine had wanted the gloomy old building, with its dark aura of the time of the Dascarids, torn down, and the work was still going on. Someday, when the Ascendancy prospered again, the residence would be replaced; but for now she and Key lived and held court in the House Azure. Unfortunately, the dust from the demolition got into everything, and Mandine would be glad to see it finished.

"A dispatch from our ambassador in Tatharkar came this morning," Latias said. "I have it here."

"What's in it?" Mandine asked. She pushed a stack of documents to Key for his countersignature. Under their worktable, Ilarion lay on his back and waved his legs in the air. He had just begun to crawl. Both she and Key had worried about his temperament before he was born, and for a little while after. But since his first breath he had behaved like a perfectly normal child, and was apparently unmarked by what he had undergone in the womb. Even so, Mandine puzzled a little over him. He was not twice-born as they were, not exactly, because he had not yet been born when death took them and then gave them up. On the other hand, perhaps he *was* twice-born—his return to life with them on the Hill of Remembrance being his first birth, and his ordinary birth in the Fountain Palace being the second. It was rather confusing.

But she could hardly ask for clarification on the matter. No one else knew of their wakening in the garden, not even Orissi or Taras. Even Latias thought that Key and Mandine had simply been knocked unconscious in the fall of the Obelisk and miraculously saved by the favor of the Two. The population at large believed that it was the Ban that had struck Erkai down, and that Key and Mandine had gone to the Obelisk to kill him before he could weave his great counterspell. Their apparent failure didn't seem to matter; that they had been willing to risk their lives in the attempt was enough to make them beloved. Mandine found in this a complicated irony.

Latias had unrolled the diplomatic dispatch. "The Queen Regent still hasn't put down the rebellion in their northwest, and her son chafes under her authority. There may be civil war between the two of them when the Tathar armies are rebuilt, and he gets his hands on some power. I would prefer if he won. He detests us less than his mother does."

"Will we ever have to fight the Tathars again, I wonder?" Mandine said, leaning back in her chair.

"I rather doubt it. They lost their army by sorcery, remember, and they believe you were the sorcerers."

"Even though we're not," Key said. "Well, we probably shouldn't disabuse them of the notion."

"It would be better not to," Latias agreed. He slid another sheet of reed paper from his leather document case. "Ah, here we are. My lady, I'm pleased to tell you that the farming couple Quill and Ardis have been found, in reasonable health. They have received the highbred cattle and the wherewithal to construct new farm buildings, as you instructed." He smiled. "Apparently they were somewhat overwhelmed to discover whom they had sheltered. Ardis fainted."

Mandine's face lit up. "Well-done, Latias. You helped me keep my promise to them. Were they happy?"

"Overjoyed, is the word my factotum used."

"I'm so glad."

The three adults watched Ilarion as the child crawled backward across the mosaic floor. Eventually his bare pink feet collided with Latias's ankle. "Don't bother the chamberlain, Ilarion," Key said.

Ilarion ignored him. Latias grinned at the child. Ilarion rolled onto his back and studied Latias with his wide gray eyes. "Guh," he said.

"My opinion exactly," the chamberlain answered. His face became serious. "Now, there is one last thing I need trouble you over. Theatana."

Mandine put her pen down. "I haven't changed my mind. I will not have her executed. She's a monster, but she's mad, and I won't have a sister or a madwoman's blood on my hands."

"I didn't mean to suggest execution. Her madness is lifting a little, I think. She's stopped wailing about ropes around her neck. I merely wanted to know if you'd have her put under less restraint."

"If the doctors agree." Mandine picked up the pen and chewed the end of it. "If she does recover, I'm not sure what to do with her. Having her in the Numera is like keeping a nightmare in the next room."

"We could send her into perpetual exile," Key suggested. "To the islands, or across the Great North Wall to the steppes."

"Perhaps." Mandine sighed. "We'll decide, when and if she's sane again."

Latias stood up. "As you wish. May I take any of your decisions up to the Kellion?"

Key handed him a sheaf of papers. The chamberlain slid them into his document case, bowed, and silently left the solarium. Mandine looked through the glass at the top of the sunsip tree she had once clambered down in the dark. "Strange to live now in a world without the Ban. It was always there. A safeness, even though so many things in the world were so dangerous. Thanks in part to my sister, it's gone."

"We're still safe enough," Key pointed out. "Everyone believes that the Ban killed Erkai, except for our few friends and relations who know about the Signata. They've sworn silence, and in this case I trust even Naevis to guard his tongue."

"Do you think perhaps we shouldn't have told them the truth?" Mandine asked pensively. "Perhaps we should have told them the Ban held. It's such dangerous knowledge, that it hasn't."

"I couldn't lie to my father. And if not to him, then not to the others."

Mandine sighed. "Nor I to Orissi or Taras. Then should we have told them about the garden, and coming back?"

"I feel that was different." Key took up a penknife and began cutting a reed's end into a nib. "I feel that was between us and the Two. A private thing. And I think it would make people frightened of us."

"Yes. That's so." Mandine watched slivers of reed curl from the blade's edge. "What still troubles me," she said after a moment, "is that Theatana knows it wasn't the Ban that destroyed Erkai. She saw him finish the spell and become that *thing*."

"But she's mad, and everyone knows it. Even if she does recover, who would believe her? It would sound like the madness coming back."

"Yes. I suppose so."

Key put down the reed and the knife and took her hands. "My love, even if a few people eventually come to believe that Erkai did overthrow the Ban, it will be a long time before anyone is sure enough of it to risk meddling. And a longer time before anyone learns enough of the old knowledge to act on it. If anyone ever does. The knowledge may now be lost forever."

"So you think we're safe from such meddling?"

"I do. Moreover, the world's at peace now, for the first time in a century, and I think, if we're wise and careful, we can give our people another golden age."

They watched Ilarion wriggle as he tried, without much success, to sit up. Key grinned at their son.

"I'm so glad we came back," Mandine said.